COVET NOT

BY

GEORGE V. HENDERSON

To Betty Lou
Best Wishes

August 19, 2003

THE PUBLISHER

First Published 1999 , The Publisher
Second Publication 2001, The Publisher

ISBN 0-9685032-1-7

The Publisher
17-700 McLeod Rd., Suit 272
Niagara Falls, Ontario.
L2G 7K3

This book is dedicated to Ron Lambertus
and Dave D'Orsay they know why.

Printed in Canada by: By the Publisher
Niagara falls ,Ontario. Canada

Chapter One – 9:20 A.m., Near Anse Marcel, St. Martin, Dependency of the French Overseas Department of Guadeloupe

A Feat Of Strength.

Darkness, then pain but warm darkness. My mind did not want to come to the surface. It was to far away and too real. It was calmer here in the dark. There were no decisions to make, no problems to face.

Then, like a bubble breaking the surface of a pond I was there in the light. My first reaction was to close my eyes. The bright Caribbean sun burned into them. Slowly I focused. I could not move. My arms were asleep. I hurt everywhere. The objective had been to destroy a little of me at a time. The me, in question is Michael D'berville McFurson courier to Her Majesty's Secret Service.

I looked out the open door of the shack. It was made of gray weathered planking perhaps 12 by 20 feet in dimension, one room with a wood floor. The eighty-degree heat made the interior stifling and heavy. The air seemed to brood and sit on us like a blanket. An Atlantic wind passed through the open door and blew the heat back a bit but not enough.

The door was open to show me freedom tantalizingly close but eons away. The beach was there, a few small palms, royal blue water.

I was thirsty, my mouth dry and covered with pap. It took me a minute to get some fluid together and free my tongue.

Outside was a picture perfect place of escape and ease. However, this was not for me. The Japanese mind never fails to amaze me with its subtle cruelty and cold bloodedness.

The beauty framed by the door, was not for the girl either, chained naked by her hands to the floor, only a few feet away. She smiled softly as if to give moral support at least. It was a sad knowing smile, too sad and too knowing, for a sixteen-year old.

My mind came on line again, it was up to me. I had to save her and myself. The question was, how much time did we have?

Ray was not in the shack. I looked around. He must be confident, I wouldn't wake up for a long time, given the beating he had handed out. I should be in the hospital. I shook my head hard to clear it. He could be outside but I had to try.

I had a plan constructed last night. Simple, I would turn the chair over. Then drag myself across the floor to her. Yatomi would untie the rope and I'm free.

Brilliant, I notice now the chair is nailed to the floor, for to start. I weigh 210 lbs. So I jam my body against the strength of the chair to the right, nothing. To the left, nothing! Only my breathing comes to me heavy and strained.

At least Ray didn't darken the doorway with his compact 280-lb body. Don't ask me how those two things went together but in Ray they did.

Ray was a Sumo, a warrior of the wood ring, large and predatory. He had been dropped from the sport for some disgrace. The Yakuza (the Japanese Mafia) recruited him immediately, I would figure. I would have. It was possible he owed money or a personal debt, a life debt, to someone higher up the gangster food chain.

No one could mold a machine like this man. At six foot, tall for Japanese, he had hands like toilet seats, a body that was crisp in movement and powerful to the optimum. I would figure, he had taken up the other martial arts after his fall from grace, his body was now more muscle then meat.

It was his responsibility to get Yatomi to St. Martin from Japan. I rescued her by accident, as usual. It is hard to mind your own business when life continues to throw opportunities to stick your nose in. My personal rules dictate that I will not turn down a kid in trouble. It is my blind side.

Ray was not my tormentor's name, it was Ramoki, or something. When the St. Martin French had problems with the pronunciation he became Ray. I don't think it mattered greatly what they called him, he lived in his own world. I had harmed the value of his master's investment, this was not to be tolerated. As a result, I was to die. The girl was to watch this circumstance, to take any thought of escape or negative action from her mind. She had been paid for. She would comply.

I figure they would beat me up and then remove the girl from the shack and tell her my life was in her hands. This would make Yatomi behave. They would then kill me. First, however, I must be broken suitably for the lesson to be learned.

It is impossible to describe the kind of punch that can be launched by a man who is brute force. The pain was intense with out killing me. He did not leave a scar such were his abilities in the art of pain. Slowly all night he had brought me to black out with targeted punches. Then stopped for a while sitting quietly like a stone Buddha on the floor two feet before me watching with his cold, black, intelligent eyes to see the results. Just as I came back enough to get my breath and curse him, he would hit me again and the pain would come to a point where it was unbearable.

I vomited only once. He cleaned it up stoically. Then got really creative. I passed out and stayed there. He must have left us in the morning to report in or get some smokes.

I heaved my body against the bonds that held me with animal fear and unimaginable fury. The chair legs were not made of the best wood and snapped above the hardware metal foot that was attached to the floor.It went with a crack that sounded like a rifle shot. I ended up on my side on the floor. I had hit my head on the way down, so the only part of my body Ray had not gotten around to, now hurt like hell.

I began to move across the floor by sheer will power. Slowly inch by inch using my hand and the foot on one side slightly lifting myself and then forward. My hands being tied tightly to the arms of the chair it wasn't easy. Fortunately, I got one foot loose off the broken chair leg and this helped a great deal. Yatomi said nothing as if her words might bring the demon back.

I reached her. I had a horrible feeling Ray would walk through the door just in time to stop me. His flat emotionless face, lightened by a slight smile, like a fat Japanese Cheshire cat that had the mouse. I suspected he would think in that direction. Removing freedom, just at the moment it was achieved, would be the ultimate torture.

He did not show up so I concentrated on getting loose. I turned my back and Yatomi began to work on the knots with one hand. She spoke in Japanese and under her breath, whether she was praying or cursing, I wasn't sure? Well, there are no curse words in Japanese so I figure she must be asking for divine help. I tried to facilitate her work by tightening my grip then letting my hands go limp. It took time but I could feel the cords loosen. I pulled and the strands loosened more it was the most trying twenty minutes I could remember. The knot was gone the ropes divided with some effort. The blood ran back into my arms. At first the arms were useless flopping about at the elbow but soon I could massage the pain back into them. I didn't mind. I was Free. I removed the remaining foot restraint as my fingers came on line.

Standing was a whole different thing all together. Once up and I almost fell.
For a moment I was free. Exultation! The rope lay at my feet. I breathed as well as I could with the punishment my ribs and chest had received. The wind, as if heaven sent, blew in and cooled my brow.
Yatomi looked up at me from her position on the floor sharing my joy. Her eyes were brighter now.
"You must save yourself." She said in her soft, even, reasonable voice.
"Like hell!" The search began for suitable tools or the key, little chance of finding the latter. The small, gray, metal box hidden in the corner contained exactly what I needed. A small crowbar and a rusted steel hammer. My body was starting to feel a little better as I staggered back to her. The crowbar was jammed under the metal plate that held the right hand chain to the floor and hammered home. This lifted the plate a little. I then jumped on the crowbar with all my weight. The rotting wood was levered out in a chunk with the screws attached. I went to work on the other floor plate and a few moments later she was free or at least not attached to the floor.

Yatomi stood up with grace I think only Japanese women have in the nude. The chains clanked but her smile was radiant.

"Domo!" she said softly as If she might break the spell.

Sixteen years had brought Yatomi to womanhood. Her long black hair surrounded the white oval of her face small single strand bangs lined her forehead. The great almond black eyes shone out in splendor. Below, her small painfully thin nose with its slight rounded base was lost in the expanse of the face. There were no cheekbones or seemed to be none. Long plains of emptiness ran down from the eyes to the wide full mouth and small pointed chin.

A swan's neck gently flowed into cream coloured shoulders. Her breasts were full. Her tummy was flat accented by an hour glass waist that subtly flowed out into squarish hips A slightly raised pelvis, dark and downy. Her legs were well formed and full, as they should be. Yatomi was all of five foot five inches, again tall for the average Japanese. The feet were splayed and rather large but not ugly.

Overall though she was all eyes soft enfolding, Almond eyes.

This of course is why she had been kidnapped from a Tokyo street and put us both here struggling to escape. It must be pointed out here that I am a heterosexual and no pedophile but not to notice Yatomi's supple body would be like ignoring a Rembrandt.

I ran to the bed and found her Fuku the traditional sailors school Japanese uniform laid out neatly. It was the blue sailors uniform of the Tokyo Prefectorate. A white, sailor's shirt with a blue neck cape and red silk kerchief, a blue pleated skirt long white socks and black saddle shoes completed the outfit. There would be a jacket as well but I could not find it. I hurried back.

"Hold the plates in your hands." I helped Yatomi put them in the proper place. I helped with the clothing as much as I could. It took a couple of minutes as the metal caught in the fabric and I wondered how many we had left.

She was just attaching the buttons on her skirt when a car stopped. We both froze like mice in the light of a torch. Then her face seemed to fall like her spirit was being sucked out.

"Come on!" I half dragged her out on the porch. Fortunately the car park was away from the house. We had a couple of minutes.

There was a palm tree next to the path and a stump next to it. The tree would be wide enough to cover my body, from someone coming up the path from the parking area, until he was passed the tree. I had to gamble Ray would be concentrating on the shack. The stump would give me height. You make decisions on the moment in a situation like this.

"Lend me your scarf?' I demanded.

"I am sorry, domo?". She said not understanding the word.

"The red silk." I pointed.

"Oh, Hai!" She gave me the thin strip of cloth.

"Get to the Dutch side of the island find Japanese Consul. Now run!" I pushed her and turned away.

In a moment I was on the stump. I made a knot in the Red silk half way between the ends and tightened it using my knee. Then wrapped my hands around until enough fabric remained to go over a man's head.

Covet Not (11)

I heard him only moments before he came even with the tree. Would he be alone? Yes! Of course, his huge pride, would not allow him to bring help for this task. I heard him step forward lightly. For a man his size he moved like a ghost. He then snapped something off in Japanese. There was a moment's silence. I knew he would look for me when there was no answer. Then Yatomi said "Hai!" in a thin voice that seemed to come from behind the shack.

I heard him grunt softly and start forward, he passed me, not looking to the side. In one movement I dropped the silk garrote over his head and pulled back. Using the garrote as leverage I jumping from the stump placing both my knees in his broad back.

I braced myself at almost a ninety-degree angle from his body and pulled with all my might. He should have fallen on me or at least backward, his neck broken. He should have but he didn't. He braced his feet and took the weight like an acrobat. The neck muscles stood out like tree roots, for a moment he trembled, but by extending his hands out he stood firm. I jerked to the right to snap the his neck, nothing!

The great hands began to reach back for me. They hesitated as I jerked again, to the left this time, putting all my strength into it. The hands continued toward me there was a faint little laugh. The strength of the man was unimaginable he exuded pure power.

I gritted my teeth, closed my eyes and pulled back on the silk with every bit of force I had. The man should die. He did not. The hands simply stopped, then having weathered the storm, slowly came back toward me again.

I heard the whirring noise once, twice. I opened my eyes to see Yatomi swing the intersnaked metal plates at the end of her chains into Ray's face with all her strength. The sixteen year-old eyes were full of determination and hate.

Ray howled like an animal as the steel and wood tore into his cheek just below the eye.

In that instant he laxed slightly and all my strength was flung against the red silk to the right. The snap was audible. Like someone had broken a small branch. Ray's body collapsed on me as if it were made of water. His neck was broken. I didn't let up I continued strangling the corpse with all my might. He might still be alive, he wasn't for real and I wouldn't lose because of a mistake.

Chapter Two – 10:10 A.m. Near Anse Marcel.

Aftermath

"He is dead." Yatomi said matter of faculty as if she had seen it many times before. She seated herself on the ground in front of us.

I slacked off and lay back heavily from my efforts. I drew in great drafts of air and relaxed my over tensed muscles. His corpse smelled of sweat, lavender and cooking oils.

"It is sad." Yatomi said softly, tears starting around her eyes.

"Why, that I won?" That was nasty and uncalled for but I figured she might have said something more positive.

"No! This is a great victory. If you were Sumo they would give you Kanto Sho, The Fighting Spirit Price. You are a true Samurai." She smiled.

"More like a fat Ninja. I took him from behind. A Samurai would face him down, like you did." I put my free foot on his heavy body and pushed.

"A Samurai," She said carefully, 'does not kill in any specific way. While his sword is most important it is not his sole weapon. Miyamoto Musashi, a great Samurai, was required to fight Kojiro a powerful and regimented swordsman. Musashi cut a sword from an oar and struck Kojiro on the head once. The fight was over his enemy was dead. The sword of Kojiro cut his headband and his kimono but Musashi was untouched. A Samurai must defeat his enemy as best he can. What I did was insignificant." She looked very uncomfortable.

"What you did was fearless. The Warriors way. If Musashi had seen you, there would have been a sixth ring. Beware of Samurai in fuku, very fierce." She smiled then put her hands over her mouth by habit. I did the same mimicking her hand movements She laughed even harder and blushed.

"You shame me. You must think I am a fool."

"No, I tease you, because I like you."

"Tease," She said as if trying to capture the meaning for later. 'We have no word for this."

"Sometimes when you are with a boy he will say something foolish to make you smile?"

"Hai" She responded.' But boys have other interests." She said knowingly.

"Do they?" I asked, ' maybe they collect sour cherries. Because without a smile you look like this." I made as wrinkled and sour a look as possible. She laughed again leaning forward and putting her hands over her face. I mimicked her again and she laughed louder.

"You are, I do not know the proper words."

"Crazy?" I suggested.

"No!' she became very serious. 'This is an insult, a person who cannot think for them self, is to be helped and pitied. You are not that."

"We'll see." I pushed harder and Ray's carcass rolled off. I got up and stretched. Then I scratched myself under the arms and made ape like sounds. This brought a gale of laughter and a slow shake of the head, which said in the language of women 'boy what have I got here?' However, her smile was warm and benevolent.

I started to go through Ray's pockets. The car keys were first, a Renault, great a stick. In the other pocket was the small key for Yatomi's handcuffs. I leaned forward and removed them. She rubbed her wrists and smiled. In his inside pocket was a wad of bills. I took the two hundred U.S., I had been carrying and put the rest back. I am no thief. The gun was in the waistband of his pants, a French made Automatic 1950. It was a good gun. The

French started making better handguns after the war before that their weapons were crap. The clip had ten rounds in it.

"Lets go." I said we had wasted far too much time but I didn't think we would be disturbed.

" It is sad," she said staring at the fallen Sumo. She sighed and continued, ' In my country the Sumo is revered. My father loves the sport and we go often. Small children love them. They are heroes. Their power, strength, size, tradition, adherence to the rules of the sport, speaks of who we are. They are at one with the Yamato Damashu, the Japanese Spirit. How could he abandon his people? He might have been a great Sumo." She seemed personally hurt by Ray's actions.

"He make a decision the wrong one." A cop might have said that.

"You are unfeeling." Yatomi seemed to accuse.

"Doing right is right, wrong is wrong. Sorry, I don't forgive my enemies. I try to ignore them but if they threaten to harm me, I punch their ticket."

"Hai!' she agreed but just to agree. 'He has lost his life but not his honour for he has died with purpose, even if it was incorrect. I have lost my honour and live. I must commit skitsu and get back what I have lost." She said firmly.

"What's skitsu."

"Traditional death." She answered.

"Suicide " I corrected.

"Gentle passing." she countered.

"Crap, you can't kill yourself you owe me a life." I said with a flourish.

"I owe you a life." She said surprised and wary.

"Hai,' I said ignoring her as if it was nothing, 'I saved your life twice and you only saved mine once. You owe me a life."

"You tease again, but this is a very important matter." She was really angry now. "Honour for you is not valued the same."

"Alright if I have no honour why did I save you?"

"I did not mean that. I apologize greatly Domo." She bowed. " But you confuse the matter she continued picking her words. 'The things that I have done have taken my honour. My father is shamed. Therefor the honourable thing to do is to end my life and remove the shame. My ancestors demand it."

"You are still a virgin?" I asked.

"Hai." She swallowed very uncomfortable.

"Then you have your honour the rest is bad but it will pass." I said reasonably.
"The appearance cannot be changed. They will display photographs of what I have done on the Internet.' She said the word with difficulty. 'Others will believe what is not true."
"Screw them! Who cares what they think, or if they think? You will know and your father will know when he looks into your eyes."
"In Japan we are joined by the group. The opinion of others is important. Very important." She shook her head.
"Your sixteen you have your life ahead of you." I tried to reason with her.
"Life is a teardrop." She said sadly, 'without honour."
"You still owe me a life. My opinion takes precedence cause I get first call. Anyway I killed the guy who hurt you that should remove the stain."
"I will honour your "Call", for the moment." She gave in grudgedly.
"It is so sad." She said closing Ray's eyes, his ugly flat face was relaxed in death. She began to cry.
"Yes, " I said cry a few tears for him or he'll wander alone for eternity."
"What." She really looked frightened.
" In the Scot's culture, if a man is so evil or

unlucky enough that no woman will cry tears for him at his death, he must wander alone as a spirit for eternity."

"Hai!" She said taking one of the salty tears from her face and placing it on the dead Sumo's cheek. It came then, she cried, her body racked with the pain and the suffering of the passed few days. I lifted her and held her to me. Her tears wet the shoulder of my white cotton shirt. Yatomi's body shook like a leaf. Finally, after sometime, she stopped.

"We have to go."

"I must have my coat.' she said wiping her eyes with my clean hanky 'My father is a policeman and honourable but he gambles on the Sumo. He has always paid his debts. However, there is little to eat sometimes. I have only one fuku and if I lose it, I will have none." What it took for her to admit that I cannot honestly say but it was a lot.

The jacket was by the garbage. In the can I found my high blood pressure pills and took one from the aluminum package. There was some water in a bottle. The remaining water and two apples went outside to Yatomi. She devoured them and drank the water as we moved away from the shack.

With the Automatic in hand we went to the 1996 Renault. There was no one in it and it was unlocked. The engine fired right away and we were gone.

Finally we cut into the road to Cull de Sac. The soft green fields eased up toward Red Rock. I went toward the center of the island then toward Dutch territory. St Martin is the only island in the world jointly owned by two colonial powers.

Finally, I cut off toward the ocean and found some trees. Deep in the grove, the Renault growled to a stop.

I would sleep now. The enemy would not find Ray for a while and going in any of the towns during the day would only get us killed or recaptured. I lay on the front seat and collapsed. Yatomi sat quietly in the back.

"

Chapter three - Monday 7:15 P.m. Marigot, St. Martin, French West Indies.

In the Beginning

The island of St. Martin looks like a demented teapot set between the Caribbean Sea and the Atlantic Ocean. The upper half of the island plus a good portion of the spout is owned by France. The Tricolour floats softly in the Caribbean dusk. Marigot is the capital of the French Empire in this small world onto itself. Only eighteen thousand people inhabit the island. The lower part of the teapot is Dutch. Her Majesty, Juliana, rules there from the Halls of the Governors Mansion in Philipsburg..

It all started with the Salt ponds. Back in the time of buccaneers, in the colonial hay day salt was a much-wanted commodity for curing hides and preserving food over long periods. As a matter of fact, a group of countries fought over St. Martin. The island was named by Columbus for St. Martin of Tours, who seemed to be popular at that time. The original combatants included Spain and Britain. However, the French and Dutch finally got control of it.

The story goes that to settle the size of the

holdings of each power, a race of sorts was run. A Frenchman and a Dutchman started from the same point on the coast and headed out in opposite directions. It was decided that where they met on the other side of the disputed island would create the dividing line for the two colonies. The Dutchman supported by Gin and carrying too many pounds, was slower, hence the French control of the larger part of the island. The Dutch got the largest salt pond so the real winner is hard to define.

The dusk fell soft and fine on the streets of Marigot. The village is created on a slab of land beside its harbour, which is usually packed with expensive yachts.

The white structures that make up this town were left in purple hues as the sun disappeared over the horizon. I was at the far north of the town, beyond the Rue Marseillaise, where the police have their offices and the Hotel De Ville where the city is governed, even beyond the hospital. The Rue St Louie is populated by high walled beach houses and villas of the rich and well placed. These view the ocean and its never ending beauty. My loafers lifted little dust spurts as I strolled along between the white walls topped with broken bottles. It seems solitude had a price. I had dressed casually khaki pants and a white Islands shirt. My Panama Jack pushed back on my head. My dark hair is still fairly plentiful. It sits on a face, which is honest and open with high cheekbones and brown, I hope, intelligent eyes.

At the end of this small road is a medium sized bungalow with the mandatory white eight foot tall stucco wall. The important parts of the house face out over the sea. I stopped for a moment to look at the wall of the villa. It was quiet, a bird sang softly into the early night. Shadows made the building part of a Monet. The soft brush strokes of colour and descending grays begged the addition of a farmer trundling home with his horse and cart, to make the scene complete. For a moment I was completely at peace with myself. The sea softly kissed the beach behind my destination. Today's heat was now bearable. The sky was Navy blue, just slightly tinted with the oncoming night. The melancholy of the moment touched me deeply and I waited a minute to enjoy it but just a very short time, For Henry Say was waiting. It did not do to be late to meet Mr. Say.

Henry Say is not a friend he is an acquaintance. His past is forgotten by anyone who should remember. St. Martin and the other French Islands are his reward for years of unerring service in the field for the Firm. Her Majesty's Secret Service is lucky to have had and to have Henry as a line agent.

Less positive things might be said about me. Mike McFurson courier for the same Firm, from the less exotic and more tedious wilds of Niagara Falls Canada. For fourteen years I have carried about, this and that for the British Government. I will not knowingly take any action, which has negative results for my native country Canada but aside from that the Queen's enemies are mine.

A day before Brit line, a chat sight on the Internet directed me through a coded message, to pick up and drop off a package to Henry.

Today, after getting past the customs at Queen Juliana Airport. I had made for the Prince Eugene, a medium quality hotel, in the low lands of the Dutch side of the Island. St. Martin's lowlands, is a flat piece of land between the foot of Philipsburg and the French part of the spout.

The Prince Eugene is a three, story motel like affair, with large breezeways. As hotels go, its not bad, having a clean white painted face set with bright red doors, large windows and each suite had its mandatory air-conditioner. It is just across the road from the beach but in August I tend to be less of a beach person. The heat is bad, around 98 degrees. So the bar is a better location for the average visitor during the centre of the day.

Forsaking the bar I take the little bus, the hotel offers, downtown where I look around the multicolored shops and a wide variety of products. My daughter had made dad 'do this for me eyes,' and asked for a Spice Girl doll. Philipburg situated between the Caribbean and the Great Salt Pond is pretty and has many interesting things. The Spice Girl doll is not one. I buy her a gold bracelet instead and will have her name engraved when I get home.

I stop off for a good solid steak sandwich at The Road House, for lunch and back to the hotel for a wash and some sleep through the August heat. Finally after a long shower and a drink at the bar. I am off to find my rental car for the trip to Marigot. There are no customs posts at the border on the island. The trip is short; I park the Gray 97 Tercel a short distance away near some shops just off the Rue St. Louie.

. At exactly 8:17 the buzzer at Henry's gate sounds. The black steel gates opened inwardly with electronic precision. Beyond the entrance one passed through an opulent garden populated by a variety of flowers red, yellow, white and rose. A small white-skirted fountain, shot water high in the air, cooling the area around it. The smell of flowers in the twilight is refreshing .

Henry was on the porch glancing at his watch.

"Good Evening?" He said in a flat questioning voice.

"If the humidity remains stable." I answered.

"That could mean rain." He countered. The little word games of the day we play in the Firm have always seemed foolish anywhere else. Here with Henry, forgetting your lines could and would get you killed. You didn't reach fifty-eight in this business without learning and keeping the rules. We shook hands.

Henry led me through a dark, lacerated, oak door, trellised by white roses, into a white sitting room with plush brown leather chairs. A bust of a Roman Emperor looked out regally from a low black table. Solid hard cover editions, face the far wall, surrounding a television.

However, we did not stop and went directly to an alcove, before a great open bay window on the other side of the house. The ocean breeze blew back thin white sheers. The tang of the sea touches it and cools the room. Here a small dinner table was set with Royal Albert and Sterling silver tableware.

Thick linen napkins were set fan-like before each place setting. Once seated Henry filled two fluted wineglasses with white wine. I sat back and enjoyed its flavour. A woman of substantial girth bustled in and placed plates of shrimp in butter sauce before us. These, one eats like grapes. The butter sauce caresses the palette like velvet. In the end one looks for more but the second course is set down. Chicken in wine sauce, fragrant and so well prepared it falls apart at the touch and melts in the mouth. The chicken is accompanied by green beans in a second butter sauce but this one is spliced with spices, tangy and tempting. I am not one for vegetables but the plate clears of them along with the rice mixed with small vegetables.

It is a feast and I enjoy every mouthful. A fruit cocktail follows hand cut and slightly sugared. At the end I realized we had said nothing through the meal. I sit back and look at my host but Henry is enamoured with the view.

"Michael, do you think I have found paradise?" The question was rhetorical

"If not as close as possible." I said enjoying two French women thin but graceful completely unaware of us. They laugh, and wander along the beach dressed only in bikini bottoms, their small pert breasts pointed and proud. Dark hair flows around their joyful faces. We watch them disappear beyond the next Villa toward the town.

"That was a wonderful meal. Thanks Henry." I say honestly. Henry does not look at me.

"You have something for me." He says in a clipped voice.

"I remove the small bar from my pocket. It is eighteen carat gold from its weight, this is placed on the table. He removes it. The second package feels like money but it is unopened. This too is removed. Finally a small box, I have no idea what is in it. He nods and this too disappears like a waiter's tip.

Henry is a cold fish; he has a very frosty outside and no door. No business is allowed at his table unless he instigated it. Then it was very quick and straight to the point. Since I had started coming here we had always had a meal like this just at dusk in this same place. I believe Henry was lonely or perhaps it was the proper way to do business. I was about to break Henry's rule about talking shop and I was wont to do it.

"Henry I know Firm business is forbidden but I have a problem with a case I was involved in back on the Virgins. There was a man involved. I think you might know him. We lost the man and I thought you might help me with finding him?"

"Is it true you spanked that American agent on the bare bum?" Henry asked with a soft smile.

"Henry is there no one in the entire Firm who hasn't hear that crummy story ?" I said doing a slow burn.

"A little puritanical, old thing." Henry was enjoying himself. He seemed to be in a good mood. "Granny said you'd ask." He threw in. So our fearless leader, Director of the North American Section of the Secret Service, Theodore Boothby – Staters was steps ahead of me again. I smiled good old Granny Staters, he would be.

Henry made the picture materialize like a magician.

"Is this the man?" Henry asked. Mohammed Tisani looked back at me from the white tablecloth. The hair was different, his mustache was thinner, he wore what seemed to be, bottle depth, metal rimed eyeglasses but it was the same man.

"Where was this taken?" I demanded.

"Here!" Henry confided. "About two months ago."

"What the hell is he doing here?" I said surprised and a little confused.

"What can you tell me about him? " Henry 's weathered wrinkled face beneath his styled gray hair, set on me. The eyes were cold like five-day-old steel and of the same gray colour. The mouth a short, lipless slash, abutting a straight West Country nose. The room was silent.I leaned forward and studied the picture trying to remember what I could.

"This gentleman is a real treat. He was trained by one of the big shops, Russian or US. He knows the rules of engagement. Tisani isn't a fanatic, religious or otherwise. It's too bad because sometimes it can be an Achilles Heel. Old Mohammed is cold, a good mind, and he thinks things out but he can react on his feet. He's very competent Henry, if you're going up against him watch your back. He will kill without thinking to hard about it and big time. He did carry a Jordanian passport but he isn't that."

"I know he has a Yemeni Passport right now. Henry interrupted.

"Tisani was the center of things. He usually carries out other people's orders. Our friends in the Middle East are getting together. That Nairobi bomb was nuts but it's from the same playbook. The problem is our countries in the west are too open. Freedom has its price. Do the Yanks have an Embassy here?"

"So you figure him for a bomber?"

"I don't know? The last time it had to do with computers. Granny will have filled you in.' It wasn't my place to give out too much.

"The French were in Desert Storm too." Henry considered the possibilities.

" I don't think so. The bombs in Africa were in major cities. This place isn't big enough, who would care?"

"The inhabitants for a start." Said Henry with a chill this was his home, ' However, you may be right"

"What kind of support can I expect on his side?"

" Some very tough and competent people. He will use muscle as he finds it. Old Mohammed likes other Arabs though. Family is always best. He will use dupes for the dirty work where he can find them. Last time it was lots of people but he had backing then. I would figure you're looking at four or five trained personnel anyway." I finished sitting back and sipping from my glass.

"He had two with him last time, like some U.S. thug." Henry informed me.

"Mammoths with the brain of a squirrel?" I asked, Henry nodded.

"They were on the Virgins with him." I confirmed.

"What would he want here?" I asked. 'Can you tell

me who he was with?"

"Vincent Arman Au Clair,' Henry rubbed his chin thoughtfully, 'he is the local organized crime boss. I suspect he makes a living. His people probably help the Cartel in small ways. Prostitution of course! He controls a few legitimate businesses. He launders most of the sheets and towels on the island and probably a lot of money. The hotels pay very well for the service or else! There was another fellow in competition with him. A Chinese called Chin. He disappeared with his whole family, 'boating accident'." Henry looked at me knowingly. 'After that he obtained the two or three remaining small laundry shops and controlled the business."

"Don't the police do anything."

" They need a complaint, if you know what I mean." Henry 's eyes were contemplative "Au Clair is very small change."

"Knowing Mohammed he must be setting up some sort of front for something else. This Au Clair guy could be the chump. He's cold blooded enough, is he ardently French?" I asked.

"Au Clair is ardently Au Clair. Don't underestimate Au Clair though he is no fool but he is very small change. He has no connection with the world.' By that Henry meant the spy game. 'Also he has no power beyond the island."

"It's possible the Caribbean is Mohammed's home turf for the Middle Eastern group. That would answer a lot of questions. Maybe Au Clair has friends elsewhere, or maybe old buddy, you've got a hot potato on your little paradise. If I were you, I'd call up Granny and ask for backup. I'm around till tomorrow if that's a help." It wasn't much of an offer and Henry didn't take it seriously.

He seemed to retreat into himself for a few moments and I drank the Bailey's Irish Cream, which had been served after dinner in a small glass tumbler. The sweet liquid burned down to my belly in a warm, pleasant manner.

Finally Henry moved. He had been studying the sea and his eyes remained on its rolling surface as he spoke.

"Ever think we are the last line of defense for Western Civilization?" he asked offhandedly.

"How so?" I asked a little taken a back.

"The bombs in Africa and the last one in Ireland are getting larger and are only the tip of the iceberg. You can't fight small groups of fanatics with an army or the police. They have enough to handle. No we are the last chance. The doors are open as you said.' Henry continued. ' These animals can get in or are associated to others who will help them.

"I personally do not want to see the glittering towers of the west fall. With them fall history as we know it." Henry said that with such sadness I had to speak.

"Henry lighten up. The Russians are gone and the woods are not full of goblins." Henry smiled.

"The Russians are nothing or if they fall back into Communism they might be part of the problem. The real consequence is that no one can walk the streets of any city without fear that he or his family will not be part of a similar attack. As they become more frequent and more general the power that exists will crack down. They will have to. At that point freedom will be sacrificed on the altar of safety and the west will pass as a place of thought and art to a place of fear. Most people in the United States can't walk the streets at night now.' He looked at me, perhaps to see if I were listening,

'My escape is this place and this area to work in. I believe you are right. No damage will happen here, its too small but Copenhagen and Toronto beware."

"I think you're over reacting Henry. The Americans or for that matter Britain can handle the problem they just have to get the grip on it."

"The Americans are electrified to incompetence. They don't spy anymore they tap phones and look at computer screens. Technology is only as good as its ability to override the competence of determined men.' Henry was livid. 'The people we are up against, the Tisanis and others, are smarter then we give them credit for. They know the rules and are making new ones. The western firms have no way of infiltrating, third world nations. The Americans are hated; the rest of us are tolerated. Local people will not turn, unless they get a substantial amount of money and then they give you very little. You usually find them dead as well. The Americans don't know what Saddam is up too because they can't get anyone to work for them. Everyone knows what the CIA is up to, before it happens. I know I was in the Middle East for years. Even I'm not safe there and I know a lot of people. For god sakes the Israelis are going blind. When Granny offered me this lot, you couldn't see my backside for dust." He stopped to catch his breath.

"You were lucky beyond words in the Virgins. I knew Lacy. He was very good. He died because Tisani was better prepared and faster off the mark. If his people hadn't overacted we would be wiped off the board. Remember that! You did well, spectacularly well. I am pleased to work with you. Things are changing the Americans already know they can't control the world. They might not even be able to influence it. To exert their power they must use it. To flex it, they must use the bomb and remember the bomb is in the hands of the third world. We must make a peace or at least an agreement with the have-nots or go down fighting. The third world has nothing to lose. I am too old, these times will last at least for me, it's your children you have to fear for." He was finished. His praise lifted me but the rest disturbed me deeply. I didn't have an answer so I said nothing.

He smiled and stood. The evening was now officially over. At least I knew Henry was on the trail. If anyone could corner Mohammed it was Mr. Say.

We shook hands at the door and I walked through the garden with its overwhelming floral smell, out the already open gate.

It was getting dark and as a cop you learn basic truths. You walk away from the wall or storefronts and you walk aggressively, like you can kick ass without thinking. Look like a victim and become one. In ten minutes I was back in the area of shops where I had parked the car.

Henry's little dissertation surprised me. I had always had absolute faith in the strength and abilities of the Firm as long as men like Henry Say faced the enemy. I wondered if I should mention the conversation to Granny. However, it was Henry's opinion given freely and without a negative proviso for the Firm. The man had a right to his opinion.

Some conversations bother you. Henry was of course correct about the Middle East. The CIA had been too dependent on technology for a long time. His doom and disaster part of the sonario was possible but farfetched. The world was safe tonight, so putting the whole thing behind me, I made for my car.

A black Citroen drove toward me but pulled into an alley one house up. I passed the alleyway just as two very French men got out of the low black car. These were obviously local thugs. Surely not the upper crust. They were greasy looking dressed in dark pants and loose island shirts. There were guns in their waistbands or I was very much mistaken.

The two girls, that were being hustling into the building, were intriguing. They were Japanese schoolgirls. The sailor fuku's were authentic as hell. I had only been in Japan once and that was ten years ago but the uniforms are so much a part of the passing crowd, you don't forget. If they were prostitutes someone had gone to a lot of trouble. The taller girl's eyes locked with mine; there was terror there. I stopped. stock-still. Perhaps she recognized the cop in me. Maybe she just took a chance.

"Save us!" She screamed in accented English and dragged the younger girl with her in a second. They were both running toward me.

"Stop!" The taller of the two thugs said, in English and moved toward the girls.

"Stay out of this." said the second, to me in French as the girls rounded my body and hid behind me.

"You the kids body guards or something?' I asked in English, to keep it going for a moment, while I got the fountain pen from my pocket.

"No, they kidnap us from Tokyo they bring us here in box." The tall girl said hysterically.

"Listen if things go bad run and scream fire. I'll do what I can." I said back to her.

"Hai" she agreed.

"Get out of here and forget you saw this, eh!" Said the tall thug. He was the power. Both men were white, I would have expected otherwise. They were upset because shooting me might hurt the girls. There was no way for me to talk myself out of this one. To hell with it. I don't think they will start with guns right off. I began to back up and the girls went with me. The boys weren't going for that. They moved forward and split up. Screw this.

"Allez, donnez moi un bon bec." I smiled

"You want a kiss English?" snarled the tall one. Anger is a great ally if you don't lose your own temper. 'I give you a kiss." His hand went under the shirt. I saw the Colt short nose outlined in the cloth as it came out. Whispering a short prayer I pushed the clip on the pen. The chemical package separated before now mixed in the pen's body. The force of the controlled reaction shot the poison tipped pin through the air at about 70 miles an hour. The needle cleared the thin cloth of the tropical shirt and the tall Frenchman's rib into his heart. His body dropped like a sack. His friend looked at him and back to my pen, which I now pointed at him. It was empty but he didn't know that. He raised his hands.

I walked down the alley warily removed the Smith and Wesson .38 long nose from the thug's waistband and hefted it at its owner. It was then that I noticed the hand cuffs on the back seat of the Citroen. My face must have shown my anger, he swallowed and backed off slightly.

"Stay still." I said and he stopped. We left him in the car attached to the seat track with the doors closed. I took the precaution of knocking him out with the thirty-eight.

The girls and I ran to my Toyota and jumped in I shot out to the Rue de Hollande. Twenty minutes later we were across the border, a few minutes later at my hotel.

Chapter four -10:00 PM The Prince Eugene Hotel, Stint Maarten. Lowlands. Netherlands Antilles

Evil In Plane View.

The door was closed. The room dimly lit but safe. I had parked the car away from the hotel. The enemy would not know my name. We had come in from the breezeway and seen noone else. I believed for the moment, we were reasonably safe but on an island this size information seemed to ease through the walls.

Yatomi Katsuda sat on the bed cradling the head of Kaori Mitsubishi. It seemed the younger girl of fourteen was related to the family that had provided fighters to the Japanese Naval Airforce during the Second World War but it was only a far off relationship. She had a sweet, rounded face with apple cheeks and a monkey smile full of mischief. Of course now she was tired beyond caring.

They were hungry so I had purchased hamburgers, fries and Cokes as they requested. When the food came they hid in the bathroom. The waiter seemed not to be looking for anything specific but you really never knew. I took the food tray at the door and signed for it. His exit and the closed door brought my charges creeping out. They fell on the food like tigers. I watched with a smile. After eating Kaori was sleepy and I lent them two of my white dress shirts, for sleep things. Kaori was asleep as soon as her head hit the pillow.

Yatomi looked up at me. Her father was a police detective for the Tokyo Prefecturate.

"She is very tired, Kaori must sleep." Her eyes went to the bed where the younger child slumbered and the place beside her with longing.

"Fine you sleep,' I took the thirty- eight and placed it on the table beside me. 'I will watch. Nothing will harm you tonight. Tomorrow we will go to the police.

Yatomi, can you tell me what happened?"

The great almond eyes seemed to thin as the memories came back in a rush.

Tokyo is my home. The city is 11 million strong. The number of people on the streets is much larger then on this tiny island or perhaps anywhere else. The city is light and dark but mainly gray, built it seems of concrete and neon. This is a faceless world, perhaps to the outsider but we who live there love it's vibrancy, the life under the life. The taste of noodles, the sights and sounds the movement there is always movement.

My high school is not far away from our apartment in the city. One can take the subway but this method is crowded, great numbers of people being compacted into a small place. While it is of little importance, men will attempt to place their hands in or up ones skirt. The crushing proximity allows them to violate your small area. It is most uncomfortable and I do not wish to be touched in such a way. As a result I walk. It would be incorrect and very rude to complain or even to tell the offending person to remove his hand.

Our apartment is an opportunity waiting, which is my father's way of saying he has obtained something by outsmarting another. A Yakuza was shot in the entrance to the apartment. My father was called to the scene. This was in an earlier crime war, there are always wars in the paper, one clan or another is always killing the members of a rival. My father, who is always looking for an opportunity, took the building superintendent aside and asked to see the apartment. As the Yakuza had no more use for it, father wanted it for us. We were then living in a miniscule slum over a rice shop with windows that looked out onto concrete.

The Ueno Pank or 'the promise to view the cherry blossoms', the right of all people in Tokyo to see the sunshine is sacred. However, the guarantee has lost much of its reality in our day of huge skyscrapers and developers with more money then reason as my father says. At any rate the apartment was worth more then we could ever afford. My father said the stain of having crooks in the apartment could be balanced by having a policeman in residence. The Yakuza are often involved with the purchase of real estate and control it; the owner felt a little protection would not hurt. The owner first faked upset but my father also pointed out certain building violations that might be looked into. The owner bowed to the wisdom of my father's observations and a deal was set.

The apartment is a joy to me. Only one small room with the kitchen and living space in one compact area but it has two very special things. One is a real bathroom, which although very small was separate, shared privacy is no joy. Another true wonder is a shower, which I much enjoy. The other most important and very special thing our apartment has is a balcony. This is wonderful because the builders saw to it that our apartment looks out into a court with a small park. Green things are much appreciated in the gray world of buildings and roads. Being on the eighth floor our view looks out over the city and there are always things of interest. While most of what we see is factories, it is a beautiful cool place, for homework, which is so important and dreaming on quiet summer nights.

The sun rises in the face of our building and sets behind it so that there is always shade in the evening. When my father is not on duty he sits with me in our little space and reads his paper. Then after picking his bets he will talk to me about my day. Sometimes he will say I now look like my mother and is sad. The cancer, which killed her, was not well mannered nor kind, she died in great pain. I miss her happy smile.

These must seem like small pleasures but they are very good. I have my friends and the city to explore. I never was afraid in the city.

On that day there were many of us who left school together but some departed for the subway and others met boys. For the last blocks there was only Kaori and I. We laughed discussing boys, singers and our teachers. Girls prattle I suspect but that is part of what it is to be me.

I remember there was a tremor, there are always tremors in Tokyo, the entire city shakes. My father would try to calm my fears when I was young by saying there is a dragon under the city and that when he moves in his sleep the city shakes. I know it is simply rock moving against rock but a friendly Dragon is better, I think?

My capture happened with great speed and accuracy. The car stopped next to us the two men who had been following us placed pads on our faces. There was a thick, moist, medical odor and blackness.

I awoke to find myself naked and chained to the floor. Being naked was a shock. I have been naked many times in the baths and in change rooms but not with men around. I still have my flower, still a virgin. I cried. This was unseemly because it had no value. The men stood around and discussed me like I was a cow for sale. The room was small with dark walls. I remember the cigarette smoke, men leaned forward and touched my breasts. I could do nothing. I looked away. Finally, they left me and I was alone. I wished for my father, I cried once more because there was nothing else to do. The place smelled of floor cleaning liquid reminding me of my school. The walls were featureless, there were no windows. I felt very small. I had no say in what was to occur, I could only think of my father and how frantic he would be.

Finally the door opened and I was unshackled. I

moved down a blank corridor, windowless and cold, still naked in the hands of a Sumo. The man was tall and strong. His face was passionless. I feared him.

We got into a small elevator with a smaller man with a rats face who reached over and grabbed me between my legs. I screamed, it was so quick and I had not expected it. The Sumo turned, with one hand grabbed rat face by the throat and lifted him kicking off the floor.

"She must be undamaged." He grunted and threw Rat Face into the corner like a terrier might handle a mouse. The little man apologized profusely, staying small in the corner to avoid attention.

At the top the door opened and we entered a great office. The windows covered the wall behind the desk and offered a spectacular view.

Behind a large wooded desk in an elaborate chair sat a man who was old but might be ageless. He was busy at some papers and we must wait. My father was always saying I should be observant so I studied the room. It was plain, there were pictures of children with their parents on a small bookcase. If this man was a grandfather, how could he do this. There was an expensive computer and around it in shelves was a small collection of rather expensive tourist keepsakes, which broadcasted in an appropriate manner, that he had traveled far and to many countries, which gave him great importance.

Kaori was brought in from the same elevator. When she saw me she called to me but this was brutally stopped with a side hand from her capture, a tall, thin faced Yakuza, who had a single eye and cigarette hanging from the corner of his mouth. I told her to have strength. What more could one do?

With this the little man behind the desk raised his head. The face was wizened and old. The skin was parchment. He had small hairs growing out of two moles; his cheek bannered an ugly one being almost red in colour and a second in the shape of dot of putty on his neck. He wore designer metal-framed glasses that surrounded evil, brown eyes. A small rim of tired gray hair was all that remained on his small head.

"Yes," he said to himself opening a binder in which there were pictures of Kaori on the street with friends, naked in the shower at our school.
He looked up at her and back to the pictures.

"She will do." He discounted her I felt her shame.

"This one,' he indicated me without looking up. There were more pictures in a second binder. Pictures of me on the toilet at my school. In the showers there, in the change room naked. There were cassettes as well. It was if I was a rock star or a person of importance but I knew I was only a prize.

"He looked up and I met his eyes without flinching. My father had always said look them in the eye. Show them no respect, it will unnerve them.

"This one is fine but she has no respect. She will be contrary, we should kill her and find another but I have no time.' His prune face pursed.' Soften her up but no penetration, we have a contract and it is valuable.

"Yes, Harada San." said the Sumo. The little man winced at his name but said nothing. I would tell no one.

"Bring her to me." The Sumo lifted me from behind just above the elbows and carried me around the desk, feet dangling. Harada's small claw like hand reached out and touched me running over me like a snake. I have never seemed so dirty. The monkey like paw touched me between my legs. I tried to shift away, pain instantly cut into me from the Sumo's grip. My eyes did not leave his I projected my hate.

"This one will cause someone trouble. Take her away." He returned to his papers.

Kaori and I returned to the elevator to hell. I do not say this because it was a return to my place of my original captivity. A floor above that dark holding area an entire world existed of props, bathrooms, change rooms, furnished apartments and cameras of all types. The men moved girls some as young as seven or eight too proper poses and photograph them.

It is all a fake. Only fools and the sick must buy such pictures for the children are terrified and only participate because of outward force. I see things, which are too terrible to tell about. I am forced to urinate on other children, on men. I am photographed in different positions but not showing my face. The positions are obscene but I am not sexually harmed.

It is hell. I tremble like a rush to think of it. I hate Harada all of them with all my being. I have never killed but given the chance I would. Perhaps that makes me no better than them. Where is the justice? Where is the honour our days are based on?

In the end I was nailed into a box perhaps six feet long by four feet high. The inside is covered with soft padding. My mouth is covered with tape; I am chained to the floor of the box. There is a small heater and a miniature chemical toilet that we must sit on.

The box travels through the city I try to bang on the sides but the cloth mutes this.

Finally, we are on the plane. It takes off, I am leaving Japan for the last time. I will never see my father again.

Hours of darkness follow. We land, the Sumo returns, he feeds me. At first I refuse to eat. He threatens and I believe him. I eat what else can I do? I am in Hawaii. I have seen pictures, people pay great amounts of money to see this paradise but I am there in a box, I see nothing.

The plane leaves after a short lay over. More hours of half sleep resting against the box. We stop again, the voices are Latin, Spanish I think. We are off again after my toilet is changed and I am fed again like a dog.

Finally, we stop. I do not know the place. The box is removed. I am placed in a large white room with a toilet, couches and other girls.

One has very blond hair Tammy Butler, of Osage Texas she is cheerleader. I believe her she has great blue eyes and is fine limbed. We talk, memorizing names, perhaps if we escape we can help the others. Kaori cries and will not eat, the others talk to us and try to help. All of us are afraid; all of us have traveled in boxes. The question on every lip is where will we go. There are two Americans, a

British girl, a girl from Iceland she cannot speak English. The French girl seems a little lost in it all, as if she has left this place in her mind. There is a girl from Poland, Anna.

It is strange to see them walk about naked. Their bodies are the same as mine but the colours are different. I have never met Gai-jin before.

The Sumo calls us. I hold Kaori's hand for this last walk together. In a separate room our fuku are set out for us. Kaori and I put these on. They are clean and smell sweet like spring flowers.

Handcuffs again are attached, the Sumo tells us that we are to meet an important man to do as we are told. The two Frenchmen take us to the car, they both smoke and chatter to each other. We pass a policeman but he does not see us. It seems he looks away, perhaps I am mistaken.

I see the Dragon; I could never pronounce McFurson San's name. He will always be the old dinosaur or Dragon to me. We get out of the car. Our manacles are removed as they might be seen. Dragon sees us. I look into his eyes he has my father's look. The slight uncertainty look, the questioning without asking look, the hardness of seeing what others do not, the lonely look of the police officer. I decide to take a bet.

Yatomi sleeps now her arm protectively over the younger girl and I wonder what she is dreaming? God help us. There are times when the mind demands something of God. How can men do such things? For a moment I remind myself it isn't just them, it is the perverted needs of the end-user that are the real evil. Money drives this horror. Men watching computers who want to see this sort of sick fair.

These animals were really well organized. The photo's from the schools, the cassettes, the various poses, it was obvious someone had paid big money to have exactly what they wanted, a Rembrandt. A pervert with more money then brains and a cage in his basement was the trigger that set off these awful crimes. A well off swine who wanted to possess his fantasies a real cheerleader, still a virgin, a Japanese School Girl in her Fuku. The amount must be huge to make sure the victim does not carry AIDS or some other like problem. That would require bribes for medical records or a hacker to obtain them.

Of course she had to be caged, a very nice cage a perfumed and silken cage but in the end a cage. .

I could see them stealing down after diner to look at their prize in its captivity. To enjoy the child, like a stolen painting. To be consumed by the one owner who were in turn owned by their avarice.

A vast sum to have the object of his sexual needs at beck and call, bliss.
What happens though when the girl gets fat or cranky or well, doesn't want to play anymore. Death of course, or sale to some brothel owner who will never let this child see the light ever again. A web of criminals and St. Martin as a central exchange point. For frightened children destined to servitude. Torn from loving parents, family, love ones and a life of growing to maturity to woman hood. Money and lots of it drove this and what did Mohammed have to do with it? Was he purchasing for a client? No, that didn't work. I put it from my mind other things were more important right now.
What to do. Well first the Japanese Consulate. I would have let the girls call home from my room but if the animals are looking and they will be that would include electronic interaction with the limited phone service. They had connections the island was small enough to control. If so the phone call to Japan would bring them right here. The huge investment and the possibility of exposure were to great a gamble. I had to factor in the possibility that the police would be on the pad. If that is so, a nice boat ride to the American Virgins might be in order. At least I have a friend there, if not Breakleaf the Governors security advisor on the British Virgins

will help. The British girl Evelyn Summerset sounds like the Viscounts daughter that had disappeared. If that was true no level of society was safe that also meant that the girls were being kidnapped to specification

'I want a red head, fifteen years old with big tits. Oh by the way, she has to be part of the royal family. That would mean the profits would be astronomical.

I logged on to the Internet with my laptop and soft coded what had happened to London. I included the Summerset Girls name as well as the others, my conversation with Say and the fact that there was one less thug in the world. Granny would take action. I was unaware at the time that all faxes and internet messages on the island had been rerouted for that night and the foreseeable future.

Finally I sat back took my high blood pressure pill and watched the children sleep. I was the 'Catcher In the Rye'. The sea shall not claim these but what about the others.

Chapter five - 9:30 A.m., The Lowlands, Stint Maarten, Netherlands Antilles

Just When You Think...

The morning came with soft colours and a warm wind. Down, below the hotel, the ocean sauntered to the shore on Mullet Beach under a bright and beautiful sun. The sea is the world's beating heart, constant, powerful eternal.

Behind me the girls were getting ready. I had showered earlier. They are checking out the mirror, as my daughter would put it. Meeting the Console was very important. As a functionary of Japan abroad he was due great respect. I wonder if he was bought too. My paranoia was getting to me. No one can own everyone all the time, or so I hoped.

Yatomi came up behind me, staying back from the window, as I had instructed. I sensed her but she made a little cough to obtain my attention.

"Yes." I said not looking back.

"We are ready now, if it is convenient?"

"It is convenient.' I smiled, 'After we see this Yamura guy. I am going to buy you some clothes."

"Our Fuku are incorrect." She said a little hurt.

"They stand out like a light in a dark room."

"So, I understand." She agreed.

"Stay close to me. If I tell you to drop, fall to the ground. If there is a car near by stay beside the engine, it's the heaviest part of the car and will offer the most protection against bullets."

"Hai,' came the answer, then Yatomi translated for the younger girl. There was a small "Hai!" from Kaori.

We got to the car all right. The trip to Philipsburg from Mullet Bay follows the Actvoware Rd. This passes through lush hills and skirts Fort Amsterdam before turning into Front Street at the foot of the town below Fort Hill. You cross a small, festive, lift bridge into the city, on a street comprised mainly of shops. Small bungalows dot the side streets with large, older homes. Drukker extends up from Front St. to the Salt Pond. Finding the address we stopped and went in as quickly as possible.

I had gotten Yamura's name from the hotel. His office was in his jewelry shop. He served as the defacto consul, more of a rented factor for Japanese visitors, then a real government official. A smiling island girl sent us in to a back sitting room where a middle aged Japanese uncomfortable in a dark gray suit waited for us.

He was round faced and nervous obviously he was surprised.

"My, name is Mike McFurson, I am a Canadian

but these girls are Japanese citizens. I introduced the three, there were bows and polite discourse. He could speak English so I plowed in.

"These girls were kidnapped from a Tokyo street three days ago. I was able to help them escape from their captures here on the island. These men seem to be part of an international cartel of slavers. I would like them to call their parents from here. " He swallowed. "I will pay for the calls. You can understand the men who run this slavery ring are well organized and well financed. I was afraid if we called from my hotel we might be listened to and found. You're in touch with Japan all the time that means the call might be missed. " I went on to explain the rest of the situation not mentioning the dead Frenchman. Yamura was in his forties and looked in pretty good health but I thought he would have a heart attack by the time I finished. He sat.

"You are sure these girls are not simply getting away from their pimps?" That was nasty but I guess a fair question. There were a lot of scams around where girls paid their ways to exotic places with their bodies.

"I must apologize' he continued, ' but if I understand this properly they have no papers. Without a passport they could be anyone." He spoke almost American English; the accent was originally from the Midwest United States.

"Yatomi's father is with the Tokyo Police Prefecture, Kaori's is a businessman. One call to each will confirm what I said." The girls looked scared, not guilty. If they were scamming me I had killed in cold blood without a reason. The next moment I looked into Yatomi's eyes and knew they were on the square.

"If you, don't let them call. I know people who know people in your embassy in Washington. Anything happens to these kids and I' ll see you eat it."

"One call.' he agreed as if he wasn't sure. "I don't like being threatened." I got him to dial the code to Japan and the number Kaori gave him. It was correct. I had checked before. So far so good. Kaori spoke into the phone.

"She is asking for her father." said Yatomi in a small voice.

" The next moment Kaori was crying and speaking in rapid fire Japanese. Yamura now took the phone. He confirmed the situation in Japanese. There were many bows as he was hailed as a saviour on the other end of the line. "

"Let me speak to him I said. Yamura gave up the phone with reluctance, perhaps too much.

"Listen. My name is McFurson."
"Thank you so much.' came the broken English, the man was ecstatic. 'My daughter is well?"
"Yes, look how long before you can come and get her? She is in danger every moment she is on this island."
" My brother Tekken,' he hesitated looking for words. 'In Texas, Dallas, on business. He will come today, Hai!"
"He'll have to come through Miami. We will wait for him at the airport for the first reasonable flight time in. I will give you a number to call me at.' I slowly dictated the numbers. 'use it only if there is a change.'
"Hai, I do this. Thank you, I am in your debt."
"Come take her home safe and well, the dept will be paid."
"Kaori spoke again and for a long time.
Yamura came over and asked if I would go to the police. I said I would call them. First, I would get the kids out, then I would call them.
Yatomi was not so lucky. There was no answer at home but she left a message. We left a message with my phone number, which is a cut off, at the Prefecture of Police in Tokyo.
"What will you do now? " Yamura asked.
"I will take care of the girls until the plane comes.

Where the hell did you get your English?"

"Columbus Ohio.' Came the reply. 'This is a sideline. I make a few bucks covering the place for the Japanese on a 'pay as you go' basis."

"I should stay with kids,' he suggested, ' it is now a matter for the Japanese government."

"I agree, fill out all the paper work and tell your superiors in Japan about the situation. I will take care of the girls."

"They are my responsibility now and I want the police brought in."

"You have a gun?" I demanded.

"No! I never needed one."

"With a jewelry store like this, you got to be kidding. "

"This is a Dutch Island the crime rate is very low."

"If these bums turn up it is going to take a lot more then your government position to stop them. You'd end up dead and the girls back in their hands."

"That's why you should contact the police." I knew he would do it anyway as soon as we left. If he was square.

"I think some of the local constabulary might be on the pad. This thing is too big for someone not to be looking the other way. The question is which ones? You do what you have to."

Yamura spoke to the girls. This disturbed me as I didn't understand.

We went two stores down and the girls had a great time trying on and purchasing shorts, tops, rubber sandals, dark glasses, brightly coloured visors and basket island purses. Always look like a tourist and you will blend in. The girls changed in the store, the Fukus were now hidden. I put on a pastel pink open necked shirt and placed the thirty eight in a sports bag, with the positioning line "Stint Maartin the Friendly Island" on the side and an adjustable shoulder strap.

While I wandered along wit the girls, I asked what Yamura wanted. Yatomi told me, he had asked if I had a gun and what our hotel was.

We left the car by itself. I would come back for it later if I could.

A quick cab ride to the Lowlands brought us into an area where motels were plentiful. The lowlands are one of the small plains that dot St. Martin.

After a short meander down the beach and through some shops to see what turned up in the way of opposition, we took a second cab to a place within walking distance of the De Ruyter Motel. This small clean American style accommodation was at the head of the town of Philipsburg. I didn't feel like I had been followed and there was no physical evidence of a tail, so far so good.

I registered as William Phelps, a British Contractor. The girls came into the room through the breezeway. They sat on the bed and looked at me as if more was to be done,

"Watch the television." I suggested. Sitting before the door with the Thirty-eight out I said a small prayer, I would not have to use it. Nothing happened! No cars passed by slowly. Without a car to track, the opposition would have to check out every motel on the island. They wouldn't have time before six when the brother came in from Dallas. It was now 10:50 A.m.. I had to rest or be useless later. Yatomi got responsibility for watching at the window and wake me if anything happened. My charges had breakfast at the old Prince Eugene and I wasn't too upset about them missing lunch. They would survive.

Kaori watched American cartoons on cable as if I had given her an endless stream of chocolate.

I changed into a white terry bathrobe provided by the motel in the bright yellow bathroom, lay down on one of two comfortable mattresses, covered myself and allowed the air-conditioner to lull me to sleep.

5:47 P.m., Queen Juliana International Airport, Simpson Bay, Stint Maarten

The Dutch had built their big runway beside Simpson Bay, facing toward the sea. Beside it the airport terminal isn't spectacular but it does handle as many as 750,000 passengers a year.

There was a steady flow of people in and out. At six we waited in a lounge area away from arrivals. The girls sat reading magazines apart but close enough to get to. I stayed away from them and checked the area out. So far I had picked up only one maybe and he looked police rather than thug but the lines cross sometimes.

This guy was definitely a Netherlander short hard looking with dark hair, a solid plaster like face with colourless lips and a dull stare.

He disappeared but I got the impression I was being watched.

My friends on the other side knew that a confrontation in a place full of people was dead wrong. I would shoot. They knew that and a gun battle was the last thing they wanted with the possibility of the kids getting hurt. That could spoil their investment if Yatomi or Kaori were hit and an international incident wouldn't do. They would wait. I wanted to let both girls to go with the brother if possible. If that wasn't possible for some reason we were going right to the police station from the airport.

The American Airlines flight from Miami was called. The building reverberated as the 737 roared in. It took time for the plane to stop and come around still no problems no potential enemies but there were watchers as sure as God made little green apples.

Passengers started coming in from the plane. Tekken was one of the first, off and the only Japanese. He was a short, solidly built man with a week oblong face. Sweating profusely he searched for us frantically. Kaori saw him right away and ran to her uncle. One of the airline people tried to stop her. I hit him with my shoulder and faced him down. He smiled weakly and apologized. Kaori was in Tekken's arms. He smiled and said little things to her. Tekken came forward and smiled bowing first to Yatomi whom he obviously recognized, then to me. I took my hand out of the sports bag to clasp his wet palm.

"I cannot thank you enough. Ah, re are in your debt. Yes?" He started his memorized speech.

"Listen,' I cut him off. 'There is a flight to Atlanta in ten minutes. Here are tickets."

"I must pay you." He protested.

"Fine, Get on the plane." Don't get off for anyone. It will stop in Atlanta then, on to

Oklahoma. From there you go to Vancouver and Tokyo via Air Canada.

"Take this pen." I handed over the maroon fountain pen.

"I have no gift for you." He said very upset. Friends in Japan especially honoured ones, always exchange small gifts on departure.

"No, if you have trouble, turn the body of the pen, to the right, see?' I showed him, 'and remove the cap. Point the nib at whoever is threatening you and push the plunger." I pointed to where it was. 'They won't bother you again, period." He realized it was a weapon and looked at the planes.

"They won't pick it up at customs, just put it with your change and keys."

"Hai" I cannot thank you enough."

"I could only get two seats' I had waited till the last minute to screw up the opposition. I am sorry Yatomi we will call your father but first we will go to the police. It's the best I could do."

"You have done your best McFurson San." the sixteen year old said holding up to the reality as best she could. We moved over to the departure area in a group.

"My bags." protested Tekken.

"I'll send them back to Tokyo. Better no shirt and

alive."
The plane was already loading. Yatomi and Kaori hugged.
I shook Tekken's hand once more.
"May your road be flat and straight and may the rain fall at your back.' I said
He smiled and nodded
" May you find your way." He answered. Kaori hugged me hard.
We watched as they got onto the plane from the lounge window. The 747 with the American Airlines double A design and eagle rampant clawed its way into the soft blue, island sky out over the ocean. I half thought it might explode. Finally it turned out and north away from this place of fear and danger.
I read somewhere that people watched planes land and depart in the subconscious anticipation of a crash but then with the rest of the world so screwed up I guess its just another symptom.
We walked away in silence. Yatomi seemed kind of down and I put my arm around her. She looked up at me and smiled bravely. I took the arm back and put my hand into my sports bag. There was no one I could twig in the building entrance. We passed out of the air-conditioning into 85-degree

heat. A soft evening breeze made it just about right. Yatomi held my free hand. It was a little girl gesture. She was scared, tired and alone, a long way from home. I was the only thing in this world of normally friendly people to cling to.

The little dark Dutchman was back. He looked out of place with his light sports jacket. I brought the thirty-eight to bear on his chest. Yatomi slid behind my body and I did the policeman's one step. This involves placing your right foot at a 90-degree angle behind your left. The move gives wonderful balance and makes you as small a target as possible. The fact was not lost on Franz Tinker, he moved forward cautiously.

"Mr. McFurson?' he started. A big, light blue Chevy police cruiser came up to the curb. Two tough looking, black cops, in light blue uniforms got out. I saw their hands drop to their holsters.

"Yes. Might I ask who is asking?" I smiled but it wasn't inviting.

"I am Detective Sargent Laar, St. Maarten's detachment, Royal Netherlands Police. He nodded slightly.

"And what can we do for you Detective?" I nodded too, keeping my smile.

"We were called by the Japanese Consulate it seems you have taken captive two young Japanese girls." He said.

"No, McFurson San is our special friend. He saved us from those who took us from Japan." Yatomi came to my defense.

"I see.' said Laar with a slight inclination of the head which brought an answering bow from Yatomi. 'He is perhaps, a policeman also."

"No, he is a Marketing Consultant for Epsylon Computers." I corrected.

"I see' he had a limited vocabulary and a nasty way of looking like he had found Jack the Ripper on his little island. 'Why would he have a gun in his possession then?"

It was a fair question and the answer is, well, to protect the girls. Which was what I told him.

" I am here now. I do not believe the girl is in any immediate danger, perhaps I could have the gun." He put his hand out.

Question: did I trust this guy? Answer: well no, but he looked good and what he was doing was reasonable. Let's get the gun away from the nutball before he does something stupid. Yatomi was a possible hostage situation in the making and he had to do what he was doing. By the way, he was doing it very well. Most American and a few Canadian law enforcement officers would have shot me by now.

I might have mentioned a couple of names in the Netherlands Secret Service but that would be telling and he wouldn't know them. Of course telling him I was part of the Firm was strictly out. I could mention I had an international gun permit but I had good old Phelps papers on me. The license was under McFurson.

"Might I see your badge?" I asked.

"Of course,' he looked relieved. The identification was correct. We were trained in recognizing police identification and if this was fake, it was very good. No, it was real.

I removed the sports bag from my shoulder and handed it over.

"I want the girl placed in protective custody. She is to call her father from the station. He is a Japanese police officer. I will provide suitable identification for myself.

He put his hand in the bag, found that he had been the target of the thirty-eight and gave me a 'You dirty bugger' look. The shorter heavier black cop came a round and placed cuffs on me. I moved but

Laar held up his hand and said.
"It's only precaution."
I let them place the manacles on they pinched but were not too uncomfortable. Cuffs change a human being into an animal. This was my first time under custody and I could feel the fear of loss of freedom that so many of millions of mankind have felt in the same situation over the centuries. The stares of the people passing by were enough to make you look away like you were some kind of felon. The other cop placed cuffs on Yatomi.
"Wait a minute that's not necessary. "
"I will decide what is necessary until we have this matter settled." Said Laar in an even neutral voice. I had pointed a gun at him and would have been pissed too.
"This way please." He led us toward the cruiser, which was behind what looked like a blue unmarked Renault paddy wagon. Just as we were placed behind the wagon its the doors opened. The Sumo sat just inside the maul. His gigantic hands reached out and grasped our clothing the next minute we were in the van. The doors closed. The truck started off its engine covered the girls scream and the heavy thud of my body hitting the floor.

8:10 PM, Marigot, Saint Martin, French West Indies,

The term ‘too stupid to live’ came to mind. I was awake. The chop, the Sumo called Ray had landed had only put me out for a few moments.

I was now shackled to the chair in the center of the room. Laar or what ever his name was and an associate was ignoring me. I had a good idea Laar was a real cop. The tall Frenchman with him was a real cop too. No one stood like that who wasn’t. They were going through fat envelopes full Guilders and Francs respectively.

“That went well.” said the Frenchman through a mouth that seemed to form a constant kiss.

“So you say, I almost got shot.’ said the little Dutchman, ‘I am good though, hun?” He nudged his taller companion who smiled.

Yes I speak French; it’s the family connection. Mind you my Quebecois French didn’t help a great deal with Parisian or European dialects. I get about every third word.

“ No hard feelings, eh Jacob?” the little Dutchman said smiling and they left. Three greasy looking thugs; two black and one white sprawled in chairs smoking while discussing soccer scores over wine to my right. To my immediate left, Ray sat on the floor in the lotus position unmoving and unconcerned. Beyond him Yatomi was chained to the floor naked. She was crying. I felt like an idiot. Her protector couldn't even protect himself.

Technically the pick up was immaculate. Everything was well thought out. I should have seen it coming.

I had to get out of this and save her. Who was I kidding? I was done this time. As a matter of fact I couldn't figure out why I was still breathing. The answer came through the door of the office behind the table where the thugs were entrenched.

"Evening, Mohammed' I said pleasantly to the short wiry Arab. ' How's the golf business." He smiled we were equals in a separate world. I knew now why it had all been so well planned. Good old Mohammed had set it up. Just enough of everything to make it work. Nothing heavy handed you had to respect the little prick he was good.

"I am afraid I am out of that business. As are a great number of my associates." He had lost a lot of friends in our meeting in the Virgins and the Caymans (See Spy Not).

"My heart bleeds." I said casually

"It could." He answered with a razor edge.

"Could I ask what you're up to here?" I asked pleasantly.

" Nothing really.' He responded, 'and yourself?"

"Oh! keeping the world free of scumballs who grab little kids. You're a real hero. I never would have figured you for this you're a professional." I said. Mohammed's face didn't show it but I was sure he was uncomfortable.

"We borrowed your interesting watch and shipped it home unopened this time,' he smiled nastily. I hoped who ever was carrying it, had it in his lap two hours from now when it self-destructed responding to the fact that I hadn't checked in with it's computer. I was in the mood to know I had blown someone's balls off in my last act of defiance.

'and those wonderful pens. At first our native friends thought you had some strength in the area of Voodoo.'

"There are a lot of half baked religious zealots around. Blowing up a couple of hundred people in the street is another really heroic act, of course you're more into gas. Right on the side of the angels this time aren't you?"

"Watch yourself' he said very precisely, 'I could borrow a gun from one of these gentlemen and end this very quickly."

"Unfortunately, my dear fellow, you won't,' said a rich French voice. 'Your shipment wouldn't get where you want it and Jewel would be very upset. Anyway, the last time you had Mr. McFurson at your disposal you were not very successful. Bien! Mr. McFurson has killed one of my men. He will answer to me." Mohammed was not happy but he ate it without comment.

The 'me'! In question had to be Vincent Au Clair a man with a face that other men remembered. It was a satanic visage. Coal black but European to the nth degree. A white man's face painted black but it was natural enough. The fine brows the small compact mouth, Romanesque nose, only the hair was close to the head and crinkled. The eyes were the face, they were almost cobalt blue and seemed to shine out of their portals like lanterns.

"Holly shit." I said. It was involuntary. The man in a metallic, gray, silk suit and standard gold chains smiled down at me fiendishly with clean white teeth. He couldn't help it, his face forced the presentation. The pointy ears didn't help.

"Eh, bien! You are impressed Mr. McFurson?"

"A little surprised. You have an interesting face for a thug." If my little act with the fountain pen was impressive for the local voodoo enthusiasts. This bird must be the hometown Baron Samedi. The two black thugs moved away from him like being in contact would not be good, just for a start.

"Yes, of course I am vile, evil, un enfant terribble." He flicked his fingers like he was removing dirt. 'You're Victorian morals, don't kill, don't steal, covet not. It's ridiculous, money is available, I offer a service. Most of these poor cows live lives they could only dream of because of my intervention. So let us dispense with your disapproval of my business. I need a question answered."

"How long do these poor girls live like queens? Do you come a long when the pervert who pays the money gets tired of their toy and dispose of them like some unwanted cat?"

"Merde, How many children do you kill in a year from abortion. Children are dispensable. Don't preach you've killed and you like it. You're a professional like me." He pointed at his chest. I said to myself I am nothing like you.

"Why you have formed the attachment to this young woman? That is the question. I need an answer."

"My name is Michael McFurson my sin number is..." Was I really like him? Had I enjoyed killing? I knew it was becoming easier. Were we so different? I accepted Mohammed as an equal and he was mass murderer. I really should retire but then I guess I was going to do that anyway?

"I don't think this will involve you giving away secrets.' Au Clair laughed high and clear. 'Did you sleep with this cow? He pointed at Yatomi.

"Get stuffed." I snarled

"I need an answer or I will obtain one." Au Clair's smile was a real tool. It scared the hell out of me.

"What are you going do, have Bonzo the Ape beat the shit out of me." I indicated Ray who turned to look at me.

"The Sumo speaks English." Yatomi shouted to warn me. Ray clipped her with his left hand.

"If that puck touches her again. I will tear his head off and piss down the hole.' I said with crystalline passion. Ray stretched his right hand and hit me in the kidney. A punch in the kidney, just for those who have never had this opportunity, takes all the wind out of you. The pain is so intense that the body seems to stop. I was like a marble bouncing along the edge of a roulette wheel of agony. Finally, I dropped back down and could breath.

"If that puck,' I snarled just over the pain, 'touches her again I'm going..."

"Yes, Yes, I believe you are a bien tough.' said Au Clair in exasperation. 'Did you sleep with the girl?"

“No! I did not. Your doctor would have told you that.” I knew Yatomi had been checked out, it just followed.

“There are other methods of penetration and use. She must be clean.” He finished; the look on my face was answer enough.

“Good! We are finished. Ray take them to Anse Marcel and do what I told you. I want him to suffer a great deal. Take your time; use what ever you need.” Then he spoke to me.

“That was a very nice trick you pulled with the tickets. We hoped the girl’s uncle would stay and we would have both of them. They are a set you see but the problems Harada’s now and my money is tied up. This is not acceptable, so you will pay.” With that Au Clair turned and was gone.

Chapter six - 10:30 A.m. North American Section, Her Majesty's Secret Service, Epsylon Computer, London, England.

Ruminations

The oak tree that centered Ganny's quiet court was heavy with leaves. At its feet the yellow and red flowers that surrounded its roots, blossomed in the August heat. Sunshine lit the entire court from a clear blue English sky. The heat was increasing, up another two degrees in the last day or so, touching ninety. Tourists and Londoners alike were basking in or cursing the weather relative to their needs.

In Granny's aerie above the court the air-conditioning had started automatically. It was all computer controlled of course. A steady seventy neutral, nothing like neutrality. Granny wished he could be neutral.

Beyond the court, Embassies were going to blazes in massive explosions in Africa. Hundreds of people were perishing. Victims who had nothing to do with the combatants or the fight. They just happened to be downtown that day; arriving at a meeting just in time to be buried.

Granny ran a hand along the wheat blond hair on the side of his head, he had just had a hair cut more of a styling, I suppose. The movement was automatic felling the difference in density from only a few hours before. Prior to this afternoon he hadn't had a hair cut in two months, couldn't get away. The Foreign Service was screaming for some kind of support. A warning of any kind to take some action to save themselves. Granny could do very little, almost nothing, his people were doing their best.

The problem, of course, is that the enemy was buried in the Arab world where the actual in depth service coverage was almost nil. Granny would not risk top people, hidden people, to find out what some mad man in Afghanistan was up to. Tactically Her Majesty's Government had not yet been targeted. The Americans were putting pressure on everyone from the Prime Minister on down for help. Bubba was in deep trouble at home and this allowed him to look presidential. Of course Granny was being obtuse, people were dying and the Americans were at least hitting back.

He wouldn't be the head of the Asian Section that was primarily Middle East, after the Red Chinese took over Hong Kong, for any amount of money. Of course the spill over was effecting his people, they were being drawn off to work in Africa. West Indians going home, God what a horrible thought.

He wasn't getting anything done. The Embassy people were as edgy as long tailed cats in a room full of rocking chairs. Every little thing was reported and had to be followed up on. With whom he might ask?

He lay back so that he was almost horizontal in his chair. He found he thought better that way. Personnel was going mad. The world was under threat of war and of course McFurson that bugger colonial was off saving maidens in distress. The fact that the Sommerset Girl was involved made it pursuant to British interest. However, Granny didn't need this on his plate right now.

Brilliant, Mohammed Tisani was at large and in St. Martin. To bloody bad Dr. M couldn't come up with that git instead of some Japanese schoolgirls.

A truly horrible thought passed his mind, With McFurson's proclivity for having sex with twenty-year-old American Naval Intelligence Ensigns he wouldn't? Granny's Oxford Don, blond good looks, darkened for a moment. No! Not McFurson he was out playing Sir Gallahad.

Henry Say was livid. Granny couldn't blame him. With McFurson's disappearance, Henry had to waste valuable time looking into his demise, if that was what it was. In doing so he was endangering his cover, one that had been developed over a long time for a very specific reason. When Mike hadn't signed in, as he must each evening, Granny had moved immediately. He had called Japan to check up and see if the girls were missing, sure enough they were.

McFurson had left his room without his luggage. He had just disappeared. Well, bloody McFurson would have to rely on his vaunted luck this time. God help him.

Granny sat up, leaned forward across the desk and asked that his appointment be sent in.

Peter Gravelly was Chief Constable for the Special Investigations Branch of the International Crimes Division of Scotland Yard. Peter was medium height, with a head of moonlight silver hair above a hard, bland, reddish face. He was in a gray worsted suit but looked like he should be in uniform. His walk was crisp and forceful as he came over to the desk. Granny stood to shake hands, the clasp was dry and crisp.

Peter sat in one of the two comfortable cloth chairs before Ganny's desk. His hands at rest, folded in his lap, the ramrod posture was exact and voiced total attention to the matter at hand.

"Nice of you to come over Peter." Granny opened

"Always nice to see you Granny." Peter replied

Granny leaning back in his chair and looking off at

the wall while he chose the words he would use to pass on the information he had.
Gravelly sat quietly waiting he knew Granny his time would not be wasted.
"I'm sorry Peter. I'd love to talk about the children and Mary but I don't have the time to turn around with this bombing thing in place. So this is going to be short and very to the point.
One of my people feels he has found the Sommerset Girl on St. Martin.
"Are you sure. We knew she had run off before but this last time she disappeared completely. St Martin, that's French territory isn't it?"
"She was kidnapped by a gang that grabs girls to specification." Granny said the anger in his voice was solid.
"Good God. Have you spoken to Gilbert Sommerset?
"No, She might well be dead. My man saved two Japanese girls but he has no idea where the others are. The positive point of reference is that there is a great deal of money tied into these acquisitions. Harming them is the last desperate act, I would think. Dead, they are less then worthless. The result is that the girls will be moved out soon. We placed a watch on the airports. That is how the Japanese girls were brought in. I would think by some sort of

commercial transport plane certainly not Air France or KLM. So far nothing has moved.

My problem, as you can understand, is that I have no interaction with the police on the island and can't really. However, you do have connections in both France and Holland."

"This is my bailey wick certainly. What do you think I might do?" asked Peter.

"I believe if we show up in force, they will kill the girls, there about seven on the island right now, thereby cutting their losses. What ever has to be done must be done very slowly and with great tact. On the other hand we just can't let it go.

"Full steam ahead, stop. Eh!' said Peter, 'They could take them off on a pleasure boat any time they liked." He continued rubbing his mouth with his left hand. It was something he did when he was thinking. 'Have you done anything so far?"

"I spoke to the Dutch Secret Service and they got on to their Coast Guard. They have fast patrol ships out there that they use against drug people. They have been very successful this year. Thirty-two arrests they were telling me. There will be a watch for boats leaving the island. As a matter of fact they have already stopped some."

"So, in effect, you seem to have bottled them up."

"This lot isn't going be put off by that sort of thing." Said Granny

"Has your man made any progress?

"He has disappeared."

"I see bad show.

"Peter, please get on to the people in France and the Netherlands see if they can move on this. If my man surfaces he might have more for us. The local man is very good and he is looking into it but I have a high ranking terrorist out there too and I'm afraid he takes precedence."

"I see, right I'll do that right away. We're all tied up with this pedophile thing. You helped out with some of the international stuff. We're just about ready to prag the bastards and their computer porn all over the world. We'll get the North American and European pervs but the Japs and others well you know how difficult that is." Peter opened his hands to show the futility

"Yes, depends on how high they are up and what grease they have. Peter do this favour, tell your people we may have some police and others in this thing on the island."

"Are you sure." Peter would just love to tell the Gauls their people were crooks just before asking their help without proof.

"My man has a nasty way of being right and it was

his opinion that this was too big for someone not to know. He suspects the island was chosen because it could be controlled. So make sure the outside people from France and Holland go on stocking feet so to speak".

"Quite, Lets have lunch in a day or so to catch up. At my club if that's acceptable."

"Jolly wonderful after this lot, but call in first will you?" Peter nodded to Ganny's request.

"To bad we can't see each other under better circumstances." Said Peter and they shook hands as he left.

The door closed and Granny lay back in his chair once more. All of this would probably have been less of a priority. Not mind you that McFurson or the Sommerset girl weren't important. It was just that Silvia his wife of ten years had quietly along with a list of other little things he took care of had mentioned, he was to be a father. It was so off handed he almost didn't pick it up. Then he had hugged her and told her how happy he was. It was only after he got to the office that the news really hit home and he faced the reality of being something to someone.

Marriage was, well, it was good but it was really non-confining. If you wanted to go out you did. Now they would have new responsibilities. Not that Granny minded a wit but given the world as it was and with his knowledge of its workings, did he want to bring children in to it?

Of course he did a sweet little boy or girl to hug and love. Dad or Papa perhaps father when the problems of communication arose.

The other part of the equation was there too. Never seeing the poor child because some git was holding the world ransom with a toupee bomb or something. What would he do if on their thirteenth birthday they disappeared? He would probably be a rotten father away all the time forgetting birthdays. He understood poor old McFurson better now as well although he didn't like to admit it.

Dr. M was coming along fine or had been, his deliveries were on time and he was showing his old self again at least with the new callous visible. The

Caymans thing had taken a lot out of him.

Granny should have let him retire now he might be dead. However, Granny could not believe that. Something told him that somewhere out there Mike McFurson was dragging himself out of one disaster and getting ready to dump the next in Ganny's lap.

Chapter seven - Wed.1: 00 PM, Near Lucas Beach, St. Martin, French West Indies.

A Day At The Beach.

The heat in the Renault was just bearable with the shade and a cooling wind coming through open doors. Old leather filled my nostrils combined with the musty smell of dirty floor mats. I was awake and hurt in a hundred places but the sleep had helped. I dragged myself to a better position; there was none. In the process, I softly shook the car.

"Are you well McFurson San?" Yatomi said from the back seat where she too had dropped off.

"Yes, go to sleep."

"Hai!" she said softly and I heard her cuddle to the seat.

What do we do now? I considered the situation calmly or as calmly as possible. One, I was betting Au Clair did not know Ray was dead. The local mob boss had given him a job. He would not disturb Ray until the responsibility was completed.

Two, Ray had checked in this morning. That would mean they should believe things were going as planned. Three, our showing up near a major town would be suicide. As soon as we were sighted the chase would be on. Four, even if we got to a police station it would be our word against Laar and the tall Frenchman. Who would they believe? Not that we would get a chance to tell our story, strange things happen in jails to people who can do harm to the local police. Especially when the closest authority is in Guadeloupe or Holland. Five, there were seven other girls out there.

Want to hear the options? I asked myself, sure let's hear them.

We could take a boat over to the British Virgins planes were certainly out. That meant being at sea after stealing a boat, renting one would give us away. Hours at sea with the uncertainty of the season, this was hurricane time and a small storm could put us out of action. We would be on the open ocean with no help. If they found us my Automatic would be useless. Once on the British Virgins, of course, Breakleaf would help us. Could we make it?

Then of course there was going to a phone and calling Granny on an open line. That would be a brilliant idea. I had to figure that could also mean Au Clair would know two minutes after I put down the receiver. No! This time it had to be me. I got into this spot, time to get out.

Henry Say was the answer. If he didn't kill us and bid us farewell in the basement, while shoveling us under. I didn't think old Henry was all there but then who was? It would mean driving back into Marigot after dark and making the house. Once we were with Henry at least we would have a chance. Either he would get us off the island or whatever Granny suggested. The information I had was only of value if I got it to the authorities without the local people knowing.

Mohammed was a completely different situation. Granny had to know the relationship between Au Claire and this very dangerous agent. Also there was the question of who, Jewel was? Specific things had to be done; all of this had to be co-ordinated. I even had the beginning of an idea of how to get the girls back. That was tonight, however, we couldn't spend the day here.

We would go to the beach. That would be the last place they would look for us.

I sat up; right away Yatomi was full awake. Her deep brown eyes looked at me pleading for something to cling to.

"Listen Yatomi, up there by the road is a general store. I'm going up to the store and get you some clothes. We need some food and other things then we are going to the beach for the afternoon. After that we are going to see a friend of mine."

"I cannot go?" She swallowed deep. "Please do not leave me."

"I will not leave you, but in your Fuku you'll be noticed someone will talk. It is so different and out of place. Right now they don't know where we are. I want to keep it that way. If we go to the police you know what will happen. This is the only way.

"Hai!" she said and dropped her head tears trickled down.

" I must do this." I said" Here take the gun."

"No, come back quickly."

"Ok, get out of the car and hide but not too far away. If someone comes run to the store."

I got out of the Renault, straiten myself up and finger combed my hair. A quick glance in the mirror showed a tired old man, who looked half dead. I decided to go around the trees so it would look like I came into the store from the back or beach side. There were no cars parked out front of the magazine. A small, black dog looked up and barked half-heartedly, I smiled.

I didn't move fast, not wanting to draw attention. Yatomi was hidden in the trees and watching me as I came up on the two story wood building. Looking at the sights like a meandering tourist. I stopped to read the sign, which offered Gaulois in rusted blue and white. At the front there were five weathered stairs leading up to a wooden and glass front door with the inevitable Coca-Cola sign in French. The mildew smell of wood came from the building, old and stale. Inside was the smell of French cigarettes like a putrid perfume. It permeated everything. The store was a display of ancient wood showcases with an ageless, black woman, razor thin with a green cloth wrapped about her hair, behind the counter. Her shapeless body was draped in an ancient blue dress, which sported small designs. Her eyes were sharp, probing evaluating me. The Automatic was hidden in my sock under the leg of my pants.

"Bon Jour." I faked an American accent. Slowly a small pile of items accumulated beside the cash register. I chose an old Seattle ball cap, two tourist T shirts size large, one with a Razta on it and the phrase "The Friendly Island" in French. The other one was resplendent with the Colonial possessions of Caribe Francaise on white cotton. Added to these were an orange mans bathing suit size small, rubber sandals also small. Butter, salt, aluminum foil matches, Jujubes candies, some cupcakes, a loaf of French bread as well as cheese and a six pack of Coca-Cola in cans. There was a great old fishing rod perhaps seven feet long with a reel and hook. This fisherman's tool I took too, although it looked old as hell and used.

I paid in Yankee dollars and haggled a little over the exchange to Francs speaking English with a slow Texican accent. The woman smiled politely but it was a front. She was just passably amiable to the stupid tourist, she wasn't suspicious just French.

I left returning to the car the same way I had come. When I called out, Yatomi rushed over and hugged me so hard she nearly knocked me over.

"You have no trust." I scolded shaking a finger." You thought I would not come back." I shook my head as if very upset. Poor Yatomi just about freaked.

"I waited as you said." She was frantic to think she had offended

I leaned over and kissed her forehead.

"You tease?" She accused in a hiss, really mad but when I smiled she smiled too. "Perhaps I was a little uncertain."

"To be honest I would have been too." I handed her the shirts, trunks and ball cap. "Your choice of shirt." She took the Razta with the French phrase. Dressed like that with her hair up in the cap she looked sexless and very Japanese, well. you couldn't have it all.

Our Renault passed the store at speed with Yatomi crouched in the back seat.

The turn off to Lucas beach is through the poorer

quarter of St. Martin. Rubbish lines the road and the shanties. The residents watch the gray car with little or no interest it is a simple diversion from the normal. The Norm is little food, empty hands and no work. Past this area you over look a forest of trees created by a mangrove swamp and beyond that the beach in golden glory. We followed the track, it wasn't a road, down to the beach then drove along a little way and hid the car in a dry patch of trees on reasonably solid sand.

I changed my shirt; blue water outlined the islands of the French West Indies across my chest. I spread out the old, reddish brown, car a blanket from the trunk for Yatomi. The beach was deserted, it being a Wednesday and this area not well known by the tourists under usual circumstances.

The sea came in sultry waves slow and relaxing like the island.

Unwrapping the cheese and I tore off a piece of bread from the loaf. We ate slowly relishing each bite. It was quiet and safe here or so it seemed. Visions came of some button man showing up with the sumo's lunch and finding him bloating in the sun. I jettisoned image from my mind. I was too hungry, and we both needed to rest.

A man has to trust to fate a little. I didn't have any other choice.

The coke was cold and rich to the taste. We sat in the shade and watched the panorama of the beach with its almost pure white sand.

The Mangrove swamp smell reminded me of South Carolina and Georgia. Small hotels or motels just off the I–95, early mornings, stashing belongings in the car before the next leg of the family vacation, checking the room for what might have been left. In the background the soft smell of the swamp not far away. Another world wrapped in memory.

"My father took me to the beach once, no twice.' Yatomi began 'I was smaller then. One year with my mother. The sand was not so fine as here and it was full of people. Sometimes I am frightened that there are so few people here so much empty space. It must be lonely.

"You haven't been north of Barrie on the Trans Canada. There's nothing up there, just nothing. Canada is all space with no people in it. About 90% of the population live within 200 miles from the American border. The rest, well, you can go for days without seeing anyone, if you don't want to. We have more food, more space, more of everything and the second best standard of living in the world. We live in paradise and bitch all the time."

"Bitch?" I am sorry?" Yatomi questioned.

"Complain about things. I have to watch my language." .I admonished myself.

"We have no words for swearing in Japanese, although words which are impolite are used more frequently. It seems we are becoming like you."

"Is that bad?"

"Yes, the Americans all have guns. They are not disciplined.

"Americans are free spirits. They like to quest, to go out and do things. Americans will take a chance. Canadians want a guarantee before they do anything.

"That is intelligent, there is strength in a group each having different things of importance to add until the correct decision is made."

" Sometimes but it can mean a lot of wasted time and things not getting done."

"Not quickly but perhaps with more base strength.' Yatomi said with great certainty, 'Of course you are correct. I do not understand such things well." Yatomi apologized in Japanese.

"When equals meet then their thoughts must be given equal weight." I said and bowed to the sand from a sitting position, which made Yatomi laugh and put her hands before her mouth. I immediately did the same. This made her laugh harder. Then she looked contrite still smiling and placed her hands under her legs so she wouldn't get caught again.

I now got on my knees, no easy trick, and bowed to the sand.

"Au! Samurai, corrector of wrongs, wise in judgement, possessor of teeth."

"She laughed again bringing her right hand up but stopping half way and continued to laugh uncontrollably. I joined her, it was refreshing and the best part of a bad day.

"You tease" she scolded, once she got her breath back.

"I tease." I agreed.

" Thank you for making me laugh. You would make a good clown or comedian on television. Hai."

"So, I am a fool " I looked very offended.

"No, do not tease about that. Her face became quite solemn 'I would never insult you and it is hard when you say I have. I believe it. I only have good thoughts for you." I had been properly chastised and would remember.

"All right." You were talking about the beach.

"It is of little importance."

"All things matter."

"Do they?' she seemed to look faraway and think for a moment. 'I gathered shells at the beach and gave them to all my relatives as gifts. My family is not rich. The shells are kept to honour my father but it is nice to know that they remain there to remind others of me." Her sadness was tangible.

"Don't look down, let's look up its almost over now." I hope.

"Dragon!" I did not understand the word but I figured it was her special name for me and I knew she wasn't cursing me. Anyway I'll come to just about any name after so many years of not being myself.

"Yes" I had a feeling it was going to get heavy now, I didn't know if I was ready for it.

"I have seen a pillow book. One of the girls from my class borrowed her mothers and we all looked.

"And Giggled." I added in.

"Hai,' Yatomi smiled sadly, 'what I saw there was very normal though.' Her head was tilted down and away. I listened, this was very important. Always listen to kids, don't interrupt, sometimes they just need to talk it out without your endless advice.

"What I saw was beautiful, in some ways, it made me feel excited. Some of the pictures were very real. The pictures showed people enjoying each other. There was nothing bad in that.

Dragon, what is beautiful about making water on other people? What is beautiful about seeing a man place his fist in a small girl's sex? The pictures they took were only of the sex not of the pain on the child's face, the fear.' Her face contorted with the memory. 'Am I wrong? Is this normal? Do all people do this? Who would look at such a thing?"

"The sick look at things like that.' I answered, 'I think the reason in some cases it is because they had bad experience when they were young. Their first sexual experience twists their mind for the rest of their lives. Others look because they are jaded, au, they have seen everything, they crave something new. Others are born with their sickness.

In the U.S., children have lost their value. There parents in many cases divorce. They are alone, the single person wants companionship. They are never home. Many hate their children because they hinder their lives. This devalues children, makes it easier to harm them. The terrible things that Harada does don't shock anymore.

I think we become hardened to it because children are not taught to respect older people, have no supervision or morals. They become the enemy in our minds. We accept them as equals, as small grown-ups, but they are just trying to find boundaries. Without controls they do as they will and the cycle becomes degenerative.

Your father is a good man he takes care of you. He is there for you. That makes the crime of taking you away, even worse.

I am not very smart, Yatomi. All the advice I give my own kids never seems to help them. However, I know this. You didn't look for this thing to happen to you. You were a victim of this situation. It is hard but you must not believe you are evil or bad because of what these sick people did. If you do these evil ones will do it again and again to you because you will make decisions that will hurt you. You will have less personal worth, in your own mind and let bad things happen because you think you deserve it. You don't deserve any of it.

You are a Samurai. The road you follow is harder because you have been given more strength to face it. You will forget, you are good and in the end you will have a normal life. Look to your ancestors for help. I pray to my God. He helps me.

"What is your god like." She asked

" Well to me he is kind of a presence. You know he's there,' I was uncomfortable. I did feel him.

That much was true. 'Believing gives one, closeness to something."

"It must be nice to have a presence to be close to. Ancestors have other problems and must look for themselves. It is my responsibility not to dishonour them as this would disrupt their peace."

"You read Ann of Green Gables right? She had her problems right?"

"Yes of course. Ann of the Red Hair." Yatomi's eyes were bright. The Japanese are nuts about the little Red headed girl from Prince Edward Island. "She overcame her problems, right, so should you."

"You have been to her house?" She was interested now and looked right at me.

"No, I was down to Charlottetown once but that was for a hockey tournament.

"Hockey, hai. At the Olympics they had hockey we watched it on television." I got the feeling I was going to be asked if I knew Wayne Gretzsky.

"We weren't as good as that, I played College Hockey we got beat out by York University." I was embarrassed telling about old battles." I'm going to try to catch us dinner." I took up the pole and started to put Jube Jube candies on the hook.

"Fish will come for that?" Yatomi was incredulous.

"Sure it's the colours, if not I'll try the cheese."

"I feel dirty I wish I could wash." She said softly.
"Here, ' I passed her a small bar of soap I had picked up at the shack. I wanted to wash my hands after killing Ray. I had not had the chance.

" I got up and went down to oceans edge to cast out. I wore the ball cap, as Yatomi didn't need it in the shade. She have should slept but in a short time she was hunting for shells cradling them in her shirt. My offering of candies didn't have much interest for the fish.

Finally, Yatomi was back. This caused a double take on my part. She came down to the water naked. Her black hair pushed slightly back from her face by the wind. Her cream coloured skin moved softly glovelike as she walked into the water. She looked over her shoulder knowing that my gaze was on her. She knew the effect she had on men. In a moment the only thing I could see was her squarish bum disappear into the water. She swam like a dolphin, then stopped some distance away, so as not to interrupt my fishing and began to lather her body. I went back to my fishing leaving her to her bath.

The Tarpon must have liked my cheese because he hit the hook like a truck. I felt the strength of the fish and was happy I had inherited the heavy test line on this pole. I could derrick up a freighter with this rig. The tarpon pulled and dived but I just kept reeling, against him. He fought hard and turned twice over on me. But soon I could see his flat silver body coming in. My main worry was that a shark would get him. One of the reasons there had been so many shark attacks off Florida was that they had fished the waters clean and the sharks had to chase their prey in farther. When you're hungry you don't give up. On the other hand if you're hungry splashing legs and hands look very interesting. Today the sharks must have been elsewhere. Yatomi was beside me and ran out to get the fish when it came in close enough. He had to be a good 15 pounds. She came back smiling with the fish at arms, length. Her body swaying to it's own natural rhythm under a Caribbean sun.

I pole ended the fish to make sure he was dead, then took him up to the trees to gut him in a hole I had made. The white flesh was divided into portions. Yatomi now clothed in a shirt, grabbed a portion and with a smile began to eat the raw fish.

"Barbarian" I said. She giggled in between mouthfuls.

The two remaining portions are placed in aluminum foil well coated with butter and salt. I then got a small fire going and cooked the fish with a reconstructed coat hanger, found in the car. Soon the smell of roasting fish filled the air.

I opened the metal packages and we ate the buttery fish with bread and the little cheese that was left. Yatomi wasn't sure at first but it tasted good and she polished the food off in short order. The Hostess cup cakes with the squiggles are a favorite she said she had never had anything like them. It was around six in the afternoon the day had gone quickly.

Yatomi dried herself with my old pink shirt, dressed and then lay on the blanket. I sat with my back to a near by tree and looked up at the sky. It was empty but for a single pelican. I considered the pelican pillowing my head with my hands.

"Everything is perfect,' she said. 'Why must it end? I have noticed that good things pass quickly while the bad last for a great time."

"You can't have good times without bad ones I guess." It was lame but I was full and not into philosophy.

"If you wished to pillow with me it would be agreeable." She said hesitantly.

"No I said ' This is a gift, which is far too far above my sight. If I looked so high, my eyes would be burned from my head. This is the gift for Emperors, princes, perhaps, a very special person. You want someone young and strong, brave beyond words, that will love you forever."

"It would be romantic but I wonder if such a one exists? In Japan marriage is difficult. Men work long hours. Women have children. there is love but the time for each other is small. It is said a man is married to the corporation before his wife. In many cases the man will be transferred to another city and the wife must remain at home. When the children grow up wives become prostitutes so that they will not be so alone. The cash men, executives die at their desks.

You in the west have such strange ideas about us."

"Like what."

"Little things, we are not always polite. We fight with each other. We do not bathe together. Hum, a father may take his girl child into the mens side of the baths, Sento, to do his parental duties and bath her. Only in very private clubs do people bath together then it is to pillow." On firm ground Yatomi's knowledge of her homeland made her more outgoing.

"I see. I always kind of thought those Kimono you wear were very beautiful." I said to fill the pause.

"They are difficult to put on though. When I was seven I had to wear one for The Child Honour day. My mother took me to the Meiji Shrine for photographs. At one time so many children died in

Japan, November 15 was chosen to honour those children, who lived until five, seven and twelve years of age. Now very few die because of modern medicine but the tradition is still maintained. It took twenty minutes to put the silk Kimono on. I was in Yellow, my mother in blue. My father joined us. later in his uniform. It was one of the best days of my life.

"Sleep now,' I said 'we have to go in and hour or so and you will need your rest."

"I am not ugly, am I?" she asked is a small voice.

"No you are beautiful beyond words."

"Hai!" She said and slept.

Chapter eight - 7:10 P.m., Lucas Beach, St. Martin, French West Indies.

Say, If You Can.

The aluminum foil made a poor bucket but it was the only thing we had. Yatomi and I had some fun throwing mud on the Renault and each other. We covered the license plates at least. The mud was wet and sticky from a pond only a few feet away. I drove the car out on to the beach to let it dry. We washed the remainder of the muck off of ourselves in the sea. No one had come to the beach all day. I hoped that didn't mean we would meet a welcoming committee at the top of the slope. It was getting late, time to see if the 'Frog would dance.'

Yatomi crouched in the back seat and I slipped the little car into first. The top of the hill held nothing to fear. The same blank stares followed our progress toward the main road from the tired homes along the track. I went back the way we had come and then across the island up toward Grand Case north of Marigot. Small farms and green hills surrounded us. There were no police checkpoints. The decision to go north was simple. To come across the waist of the island on the Rue de la Concord would take us right by the Gendarmerie at the Rue de Hollande.

I dumped the car in a grove of trees north of Marigot and we began to walk down the beach toward the Rue St Louis and Say's bungalow. Yatomi took my hand and we walked hand in hand. She carried her sandals, I carried her island bag with the pink shirt serving as cover draped over the Automatic in my right hand.

The sea smelled wonderful. Yatomi smelled slightly of Dove soap. We didn't say a word each step, however, was an eternity. I watched the shore and we stayed close to the dunes where possible. August to November is the rainy season on St. Martin. The clouds started to pile up in the sky, black and foreboding. Finally, as we came near La Rue St Louis the first lightning shot down to the sea behind us. The flat explosion of thunder found both of us crouched on the sand.

"I've had enough of this. Lets run, the storm will give us a reason." I directed

"Hai!" was all she said. You don't know how old you are until you run flat out on sand after a full day. The pain was starting in my chest my body was sending the same old signal. It was not amused. The dunes covered our approach until we were very close to the first house. Large heavy drops formed a sheet so thick that it was hard to see. It was this downpour that saved us. As the black Citroen stationed across the street started its engine to turn on the windshield wipers, I dragged Yatomi behind the first house. The watchers didn't see us. We circled the house. Then using it as cover crossed the sand to Say's place

There was a small door on the seaside. I banged on the formidable wooden entrance through heavy steel bars. It seemed paradise had its drawbacks. Two frosty blue eyes stared down on us from a small window above the door, set there for just that purpose.

Yatomi saw him first. She touched my arm, I looked up and he recognized me with something like disgust.

There was a wait, a long one, at first I thought he wouldn't come. At that point, I was going to take the gun, kill whoever was in the Citroen and drive it through Say's front garden. I had, in the vernacular, lost my sense of humour.

The door opened Say looked out around us as if expecting more company.

"Quick let us in." I said exhausted.

"What?" he said and the Beretta he was holding, was leveled on us. It was Wednesday,
What was the phrase of the day? The rain, yes of course.

"It could be a lovely evening?" I said very distinctly

"If it weren't the rainy season," Say answered. The bastard had almost shot me.

"Then we might have a cloud burst." I finished dripping with rain.

"Come in." he said reluctantly.

"We entered a vestibule. It was small and dark. Say closed and bolted the door. It would take an elephant to move that portal.

"Come up the stairs and we'll have a cup of." Say said with a hard edge.

"Have we offended this gentleman?" Even Yatomi could feel the danger. If Say got cute I had my gun. Trust was a very valuable thing, at this point and I would not give it easily.

"No he 's always like this. It's the weather." I said offhandedly. Say turned his face was braced. I thought of watching hoarfrost move.

"Bill, this is Yatomi." The introduction was simple and incorrect on purpose.

"You have nothing to worry about my dear." He smiled like the evil witch of the east. Yatomi bowed and thanked him Dozo.

At the top of the stairs the big, black woman, who always served us our exquisite dinners, stood solidly with a leveled sawed off 12 boar.

"Dey be still across the street. Dey no see dem come." She said.

"Good." Say said. "They aren't watching the house. They were covering the beach." It seems they found the body of a certain Japanese out by the beach. The local police have been scooting about like bees. Started about an hour ago.

"Saraphina get something for the young lady to wear, dry their clothes won't you. Give her something to eat if it's not to much trouble."

"We've already eaten." I said. Yatomi nodded.

"Good then lets get you changed. He threw me a towel. I changed in the bedroom, which was sterile and Spartan with only a cross on the wall over the double bed. I wondered if Say and Saraphina shared the white covered expanse. The shirt and pants were baggy but comfortable. Say was shorter and less heavy then me that meant he had expected us. I came into the living room. Yatomi was settled in front of the television in her Fuku, she gestured helplessly and I had to smile. The RAI news was on. Bubba's latest scandal was unraveling in Parisian French. I noted the drapes were closed tightly.

Say, motioned to me indicating the dining room. After we entered he closed the door and sat across from me. The weathered face was uncompromising and as cold as death.

I held the Automatic in my pocket on his stomach. Yes, I know, but there had been too much going on that day for anything else.

"Now, you silly ass, what is this all about." his tone was just above contempt.

"I saved two little girls. One of them I got off the island. The other needs your help.

"Oh does she? Do you have any concept how long it took me to develop this cover? We have spent thousands of pounds to create something here that you have no concept of. This operation is more important then you, the girl, Saraphina or me. Your being here puts all that in jeopardy. " He was building to something and I thought I knew what.

"Look I have information that Granny has to have."

"Granny knows about Au Clair and his white slave trade, everyone does. He is unimportant." There was madness behind those eyes, I had to calm it.

"Mohammed is on the island. I saw him last night."

"I know that he was with Au Clair."

"Then you know he has a some kind of shipment being delivered by Au Clair and somebody named Jewel." Chew on that you prick my mind snarled in frustration.

The single word worked on Say like a hypo. His face looked uncertain for a long moment.

"What do you know about Jewel?" he asked.

"Just that he was mentioned while I was waiting to get killed."

"You are bloody stupid. They took you like a novice."

"I am a novice. Who is Jewel?" Say almost smiled.

"Au! There you have a real question." Henry seemed to drift back to a prior time and place. He looked at me thoughtfully, for a moment and made a decision .I knew then that we were pretty close to safe.

"Jewel is still a force to be reckoned with. in the world of crime." He started like a man ready to eat a full meal. Outside the storm broke with a crash. Rain beat on the window. Beyond the heavy curtains the sea was being whipped into frenzy. Here inside we were safe and dry. I had the same feeling of intense enjoyment that my grandfather provided when he told an important story about the family, long ago, at night before bed.

Henry relaxed totally sitting back in his chair looking out at other things.

“Jewel is Emil La tour Dubois, he was a member of the firm at one point. A brilliant mind. Oxford! When he first started with us his successes were legendary. I knew him and admired him immensely. He was sent out here to be a liaison when Cuba began to be a problem. Dubois became the central figure for the entire intelligence network in the Caribbean. Open knowledge of our people of course, French, Dutch he knew the whole system including the Americans.

Something happened around the time of the Bay Of Pigs, I don’t know what. He turned.’ Henry shook his head, ‘ We lost everyone, I was almost killed. The French weren’t hit as badly but the Dutch, God they had bodies popping up all over the place. The Russians did it from Cuba used the Cubans. It was terrible.

Of course not one Yank was touched and Jewel disappeared into the dark places of New Orleans. Granny would dearly like to get that one. If he is behind Au Clair, London and I will help you put him out of business.

"If we know where Jewel is why don't we get him? Hell, the Americans should help out."

"I agree completely,' said Henry in a snap, 'its been tried. He is still there, well protected by the local people. The Americans must have gotten something out of it but I truly don't know what.

Dubois is from the Louisiana originally. His mother was British and brought him home when his father, an American, died in an auto accident. He has a whole tribe up the Mississippi. Relatives thick as flies on a carcass and all just as evil." Henry seemed to know and I wasn't going to push it but he continued.

"He's gotten very wealthy and strong over the years. He owns very high priced prostitutes and brothels. Unique men and women who are specific to the needs of the jaded and wealthy. His personal preference runs to boys. However, this white slave fiddle is just his sort of thing, the man is completely ruthless. He makes your Mohammed look like an escapee from the "Boy's own Annual'

"Look I found this on Ray the Sumo, who died this morning," Henry looked impressed

"You've have had a busy day." He commented. Short powerful tanned hands opened the note. It read. 'To Sapphire, Two gifts of small value for your approval.' signed Jade.

"I figure Jade is Harada. He's the perv that grabbed Yatomi and her friend off the street in Tokyo. Sapphire has to be Au Clair. The reason the note wasn't delivered was that the girls never got to Sapphire, big loss of face."

"Yes and what's this about a shipment."

"Au Clair told Mohammed if he wasn't good Jewel wouldn't like it and his shipment wouldn't get delivered. Mohammed ate it and shut up. Henry that shipment is a real problem. A lot of people could die.

I was amazed Mohammed didn't plant Au Clair. He could have killed me but didn't for the same reason. Whatever this thing is it's important.
I want to call Granny. I know you have a clear line."

"It stays clear because I don't often use it.' Say got testy 'However, in this case yes." Then his eyes got very cold.

"What does the girl know about this?

"She was there but nothing. Her father is a Tokyo cop. She goes home unharmed. She doesn't know my connection to the firm.

"Humh! She knows me. My cover is blown."

"Crap, she leaves the island, that's it. She doesn't even know your name. You're not killing that brave honest kid to cover your ass."

"Watch yourself." Henry didn't warn much, he acted. I had come close again." No harm will come to her."

"Fine."

The phone was a satellite bouncer, with a cut off. I was through to Granny in London, on a clean line, in moments.

" So your still alive, you have more luck then any sane man I have ever met." I could see the China blue eyes as they focussed on the ceiling.

I imparted the information all of it.

"Gad,' Granny said when I finished. " What am I to do with this mess? " The question was rhetorical. 'Listen carefully and don't bugger this up." The threat was blatantly obvious.

"One, Both the Netherlands and French Governments will co-operate but if you foul up relations with either of them, you'd better find a place no one has ever heard of.

Say has laid on a meeting with a Joe of his tomorrow and the man is local the information should help you.

The mess you found will be cleaned up. People will be coming in from outside tomorrow to do that job. You will contact Chief Inspector Maurice St. Amard at the police station in Marigot tomorrow after one. Don't just walk in. Say has connections at the airport and will confirm his arrival. I will fax a picture so you know who you're talking to.

Your plan has merit but the final decision will be made at a meeting with other individuals from both Holland and France. Their island, their decision, you just help out, if you can, stay to your marketing cover if asked.

Now put Say on and get some sleep this isn't over yet."

"About the girl."

"What about the bloody girl." Granny was angry now.

"She needs to get home."

"Fine, send her home, but that is an end to it." Granny couldn't be pushed further so I gave the phone to Say.

Henry had fought it but Yatomi had cried and Say had crumpled after Saraphina had given him a look like hell on water.

We didn't call Yatomi's home or the Prefecture. I had a feeling neither was safe. There was a bar near their apartment, her father frequented with an officer called 'Fat One'. That, of course is a rough translation. The correct pronunciation was far more acceptable from the standpoint of polite conversation.

The barman answered. He was an ex-cop who had been hurt in a traffic accident and was on pension. Yatomi asked for her father. Detective Shojiro Katsuda a little less for drink wandered over to the phone. No one was nearby.

"Hai." Shojiro said in a defeated voice, fortified with booze and desperation.

"Listen my name is Mike McFurson I am here with your daughter. For the rest of the room look like this is a usual call. Here's Yatomi." I hoped his English was as good as Yatomi said.

"Father," she started.

"Butterfly, are you well?" he said. Joy flooding though him.

"Yes, I am well did you not get my message at home or at the Prefecture."

"No, there was no message. Where are you."

"I am on St. Martin, in the French West Indies, in the Caribbean Sea. Harada a Yakuza and his men kidnapped me from the street. McFurson San saved me from them. I am safe. It is exultation to hear your voice, dear father.

"Were you harmed, touched." The pain in his voice was terrible.

"No, I was to be sold and I had to be pure. I

apologize greatly for your discomfort in this matter." Yatomi's eyes filled with tears.

"Oh! Butterfly what can I do. It is so far. How can I come? I will borrow from Fat One and all our relatives. I will come for you."

"Father, listen to McFurson San he has a plan."

" Shojiro?"

"Hai!"

"Look, did Kaori Mitsubishi or her uncle call you?."

"No. She and her family were killed outside Tokyo Airport yesterday. Their vehicle was in collision with a large van, um, truck Hai! Truck. I knew she was with my daughter so went to the crime scene"

It took a moment to settle in monkey face Kaori , the little angel with the dimples who Yatomi had cradled was dead. This baby was dead, a martyr to someone's sexual perversion. I had killed her. I should have known Harada would be waiting. Christ! what a mess. There was only blind anger. I liked her uncle Tekken he was a nice man. These bastards were going to pay.

"Listen, I got Kaori and her uncle onto that plane I saved her but Harada was waiting. If you take Yatomi back you'll die too. There is too much money involved in this. How much grease has this Harada got?

"Please?" Yatomi's father was confused.

" Power, connections how high up is he, can he be arrested?"

"I see," the light dawned on Shojiro " Harada has great face. In his world and in mine."

"I can take Yatomi to Canada. You can come there too and start over. I have some influence with the government."

"No, McFurson San, I am Japanese, my daughter is Japanese, I will deal with this situation. If something should happen to me protect my daughter.' The request was a plea.

"I would be honoured to protect a samurai who is in turn the steel blade of a strong arm." I said. It sounded empty but it was sincere.

" Thank You, Domo!" he said a little embarrassed by such a strong compliment.

"Here's Yatomi talk as long as you want."

I knew one thing Shojiro Katsuda was not paying for his trip to this island. That much I could do.

Chapter nine - 5:00 Pm, Shokaku Bar, Jimbo-Cho District, Tokyo, Japan

Vigorous Action

Shojiro stumbled back to the table. The Tokyo policeman was a blunt block of flesh. Like the Sumo he loved so much, he had no neck. He had a sumo's square face and heavy brows as well. Yatomi's nose was from his face, but the rest of the girl was a duplication of her mother. His daughter was beautiful not a square shouldered sturdy peasant like himself, more of a porcelain doll. The tired almost gentle eyes were tormented. Cheeks, reddened by too much alcohol, dropped like solid rock faces to a square chin. The face was forceful but lacked something. A strength, a power, perhaps determination seemed to be missing. Something was lost, if Fat One Nagumo had not been so drunk, he would have seen the change. The hardness of the slash mouth boded poorly for someone. Shojiro gave small indications of anger. Yatomi knew them and stayed away. If she had seen her father at that moment she would have taken refuge on the balcony, until he was his more reasonable self?

"Prostitutes!' slurred Shojiro drunkenly and shook

his head as if trying to clear it. 'That one had a small fish. I have better things to do." He said this loudly enough that the cop from the Kabuki-Cho district sitting two tables away relaxed thinking that an informant wanted to give Yatomi's father a small-time criminal. The detective could see Shojiro was still hurting. He was a purchased man from the Harada area of Tokyo. He had given his honour away, for the rich white powder, so he watched his fellow policemen. There didn't seem to be any ripple in the water. The girl had not contacted her father.

"There is no respect for you, my friend." Fat One said shaking his head. Fat One rode a desk at the main office. He had never been on the street. Nagumo pushed paper but he was Katsuda's true and loyal friend. He would drink with the big man until Shojiro wanted to go home, then he would help him there. His frog face showed real concern for his friend. The small felt hat Nagumo wore was pushed back on his head, he still had his overcoat on and he was soused to the gills. His fat belly lay in an untidy pile at his midsection.

"Lets go I have to check my answering service." Katsuda commanded and tried to rise. He stumbled and sat down again. A second try got him up. Fat

One rose too and called for the bill. The thin faced bar owner shook his head to the negative. The saki was free, he was an ex- policeman.

The two men staggered out into the daylight and started down the street. This was an unseemly display. The detective from the Kabuki-Cho paid quickly and followed.

Block after block of gray concrete and neon passed as the two men walked raggedly along bumping into each other, saying little. Finally, Shojiro stumbled over to an alley way and leaned with one arm against the wall as if he were going to vomit. Fat One wandered over to be of what ever assistance he could render and to partially screen his friend from onlookers on the street.

"Fat One,' Shojiro started, 'Listen very well." Fat One's face became sharp. The cool afternoon air had settled him a little. He realized Katsuda was completely sober.

"I thought you were drunk."

"So did the watcher from Kabuki- Cho. He should be at the end of the alley. He's a thin noodle, with a ferret face and a black coat. Look back, but off handedly.Fat One turned sloppily but he was now very clear. The detective was there for a moment and gone.

"Yes he is there."

"Good he can't hear us and I need to talk.".

"I am listening."

"Good, they found Yatomi."

"Banzi," said fat one in mid voice but he would have gone louder if a big fist hadn't grabbed his jacket.

"Quiet!" said Kadsuda.

"Hai" his fat friend agreed.

" Two Growths Harada had Yatomi kidnapped from the street, to sell like livestock. She is on an island in the Caribbean Sea, on St. Martin. I don't even know where that is. I will have to look it up but she is safe for the moment. Remember the Mitsubishi girl who appeared at the airport then was killed in the accident. Harada set that up. He murdered the whole family.

"Evil is!' This was Fat Ones favorite saying. His face became hard. 'They will kill Yatomi if she returns."

"Hai, I think it is time for some vigorous action." Said Katsuda

"What?"

"I need you and your gun. Talk to Nagata and his brother. They owe me a favour and the young cop

Suzuki. I need at least eight but no talk and perfect trust.

"For what." Fat One was slow on the uptake.

"To correct the wrong." Katsuda's face was a mask; Nagumo had to make a decision, it was not a hard one. He loved Shojiro, not in an incorrect manner, but as men will who are friends and owe each other much.

"Hai!" Said the Fat One.

"We will meet outside Harada's building in Kabuki – Cho. I want everyone there at 10:30 tomorrow morning exactly. There is a side door at the back." Talk to the accountant Myoko, he will open the door at ten thirty. I let him off on an embezzlement thing. He had put back the money so I let him off the line but his office is in that building. He can get past the cameras at the front entrance. Now take me home for a while, I have to sleep."

While Fat One made the contacts slowly and carefully. Shojiro slept for a while then planned a little. When the plan was clear he went to work on the details.

He then went into the Prefectorate. He methodically checked if there had been any news of his daughter. There was none. Eyes were averted. Other police did not want to cause embarassment.

This was an uncomfortable matter.
Kadsuda next went to his desk and shuffled papers for a while. Then he was off to different parts of the building. There was no comment. Everyone knew his problem.
Finally, Katsuda reached traffic records and play acted looking up information. In the end, he removed a single parking infraction from the file and palmed it.

It had taken time for Shojiro to lose his tail. The tall thin detective was a determined pursuer and wise to the ways of those who tried to escape him. By means of a rouse the detective was now on a bullet train to Nagoya.
Katsuda was first at the door. Slowly the others came up, one at time, in-groups of two and three. All of his team were new, none but himself had ever fired their guns in anger. However, as he looked into the features of Frog face Nagumo and fresh faced Suzuki he would have no others.
This was a unique situation each man was here on his own. There were no orders for this action. Without question all of these police officers would go through the door for their friend.

Police work in Japan is not like American or even Europe. There were definite rules for the Police and the 2,500 Yakuza Clans with their 110,000 members. Shojiro was about to break all of them. Crime in Japan with the exception of standard murders are fairly simple .A man places a false overnight deposit box on a bank. Over the normal slot he places an out of order sign. The next day, before the bank opens but not before the deposits from twenty to thirty stores are dropped into his private cash, the thief returns to collect the money and remove the sign. Simple but well conceived and effective. There were other less attractive circumstances. In one case all the staff from a bank are asked into the courtyard to take medicine to remove the possibility of a malady. The staff dutifully lines up and drinks the clear liquid as a group. They all promptly die of cyanide poisoning. The robbers clear out the bank.

The group is everything in Japan. If there were not eight men here then the action would not occur. A single man even hate filled would never attempt such a thing. They are uncomfortable and check their Taisho automatics.

At exactly 10:30 Am. Myoko 's worried face

appears in the open door.The men swarm in and up the service stairs. Myoko will come with them at least to the eighth floor to give them cover if the Yakuza spy them.

Fat One is heaving by the third floor but continues against his better judgement. A heart attack here would destroy the plan but to be left behind is impossible.

"If Fat One makes the eight floors we cannot fail with that much audacity how could we?' Says Katsuda with a smile. The others smile too. Frog Face is to winded to reply.

They reach the correct floor. Myoko's pass key will get them through the door. Bathrooms are all on the stairwells and are used periodically. However, the keys and locks are all the same on each floor. Myoko found this fact when he slipped down for a soft drink during working hours by way of the stairs. The wedge he had placed on the ground floor door to insure his safe return, had been removed. His key opened the door thereby excusing the accountant of his sins and insuring the team's entrance.

The stairs smell of dust and moisture. The hallway smells of wood polish and new carpet. Shojiro reflected that two years of his honest salary would not pay for this carpet.

Kadsuda starts toward the large entrance door his badge out the others follow opening overcoats to show their uniforms.

Shojiro rounds the corner. The receptionist, taken by surprise, stands then bends forward to push the alarm. Suzuki places his Taisho automatic in her face and tells her to step back. She sees he will kill her and does so. Fat One runs around and pushes the button that opens the large, lacquer wood doors behind the desk. Shojiro is through them. They move through about one hundred office workers in a large room. The senior man rises to confront the policeman. Nagumo shoves him into his seat. One of the Nagata brother's places him under arrest.

The door beyond enters into the foyer of the bigman's office. Two Yakuza are on guard here, both armed.

Shojiro shows his badge. He shoots the left hand thug when he goes for the gun on his hip. The Taisho makes a sharp hard bang in the air-conditioned room. The bullet hits the rounded-faced man, with the ponytail, in the chest. He falls backward and fires his own gun. The bullet slams into the floor. The other Yakuza, a fat bald animal, almost gets his Mac automatic out. Frog face and Suzuki fire almost simultaneously and the fat crook folds up with a surprised look on his face.

Katsuda kicks the large wood door open to Harada's office.

The little man is standing behind the desk. He screams that his rights are violated. He screams get out.

It would be easy for Shojiro to just shoot him but he now is caught with conscience. He is not a killer. Pony Tail had drawn and died. The little gang leader had done nothing more then scream. Could he kill Harada and become like him? Should he kill this tatooed scum and lose his honour as a policeman? He must kill for his child or all the Kaiori's and Yatomi's in the world were not safe.

Harada must have looked into Shojiro's eyes. He read the hatred there and made a stupid mistake. His hand went into the drawer in front of him for the hidden Ruggar pistol. Shojiro had no more thinking to do. He aimed the Taisho and fired the frail body stumbled back. The automatic spock again the body slammed against the large window. Kadsuda's fore finger became separate from his body, the gun sounded again and again until the number of holes in the glass undermined its strength and Two Growths Harada, jerked out of the window with thousands of shards of glass, to the street below.

It was done. Katsuda was lost for a moment as if the venting of the hate had vented the very strength that brought him here.

"This is terrific' said Takarabe, the local television reporter, Shojiro called just after he had freed himself of his tail. He and his camaraman had been stationed outside to follow after a few minutes.

"Take lots of pictures and come with me. I'll give you something to really talk about."

Katsuda, Frog Face and Suzuki piled into the small elevator with the camera man with his hand held and Takarabe with his wireless mike. Outside police cars were coming to the scene from all over the city.

The elevator went down two floors and opened onto the film set. Children stood naked men had camera's now frozen in their hands.

Rat Face came forward with a Taisho of his own. Shojiro, who had changed clips, blew his face away. The rest of the Yakuza and their helpers surrendered.

The elevator returned with the rest of the team and the regional commander. The TV camera was on him from the first moment he stepped out. The senior police officer, was about to put a stop to the filming when Katsuda grabbed him and dragged him back to the elevator. Down one more floor there was a dark set of rooms. The Yakuza's on this floor had already flew the coop, as the Americans say.

Here Katsuda took the Regional Commander from room to room. He showed him little girls and boys, in some cases, chained to the floor in desolation and crazed fear. All the time Shojiro said softly under his breath into the Inspectors ear.

"My child was here squatting in her own dirt. Do you see? Do you see?" The muzzle of his automatic was in the Commanders ribs. The Inspector agreed, he saw very well.

Chapter ten - 10:00 Am., Marigot, St. Martin, French West Indies.

A Few Truthful Words.

A gentle cough brought me to the surface. I awoke after a deep restful sleep. Soft morning light from the window splashed across the floor from a crack in the draperies and touched my face. I turned from the window to find Yatomi standing near the door. She was back in her shorts and a "T" shirt again, smiling brightly. She had the small bedroom at the end of the hall last night and seemed to be more rested.

"Bill San " says you should get your lazy behind out of bed, but I think he teases."

"What" of course Bill San, Henry Say. I had slept the night through and felt better.

"Did Bill San mention if there would be breakfast so that one would have a reason to get ones lazy behind out of bed."

"Saraphina has made a great deal of food. It seems your lazy behind has a reason for venturing out." She giggled and left with a scream of laughter as I tossed a pillow at her.

My clothing was in the room from the Prince

Eugene. A minor miracle. I had a feeling the rats had started to leave the now sinking ship. As a result, there was less possibility for attack. They had to figure I had contacted the external authorities. If so, the local cops and perhaps, Au Clair would all be leaving the island. I hoped the girls were still alive.

I went into the bathroom and removed two days of stubble. Showered and clean I ventured to the dinning room. Breakfast comprised of bacon and sunny side up eggs perfectly made with good cold milk to wash it down. There was toast, kept warm in cloth-covered basket, marmalade and jams in small dishes. Yatomi sat watching me eat and we exchanged small talk. Finally, Henry came in from an early constitutional.

"We need to talk old thing," he said.

"Fine." I made to get up but Yatomi was up had bowed to Henry and disappeared into the kitchen to talk to Saraphina.

"She is a real sweat heart." I said looking after her.

"Yes very pleasant, their Secret Service is a different kettle of fish." Henry pursed his lips as if debating an issue. 'You realize she has a mountainous crush on you."

"Henry I 've been keeping her alive for the last three days what do you expect. When her dad gets here she won't even notice me.' I shrugged it off.

"In the vernacular, horse manure, you'd better put her in place right away. It will only hurt more later. Talk about your wife, that should do it."

"Advice for the lovelorn from Henry Say,' I went into a fruity public school accent. 'Well, I never.'

"I have set a meeting with a friend'. Henry ignored me. 'He is waiting outside. You can trust him. I will take care of Yatomi. You'll be back for your meeting with the Inspector."

Trust is a precious thing at times but I figured I could give a little. Henry was reading my mind he smiled and said only that the man I wanted was in a red Mercedes outside.

I put on my Panama Jack and place the Automatic in the pocket of my baggy trousers. I wore my leather deck shoes and a sea blue golf shirt.

The sunglasses went on as I ventured out into the dazzling sunlight. Outside the gate was an older, four-door statement of German over padding. It was maroon and the chrome shone in the morning sun, twinkling in the clear air after the rain. I looked into the window, the driver was black and mid thirties. He had a golden tooth pick in his mouth and a fine straw hat on his head. A persona that was lean and very French. A broad smile came from a face that you wouldn't normally trust. I got in, if this was the end then so be it, but I didn't think so

"Bonjour,' he said in a mellow voice. 'I be Ti Buddy. "

"I am Michael McFurson." The car immediately began to move. He headed north on the Rue Hollande to Grand Case. The white stone houses passed by, then shanties. He was a good but not a serious driver.

"You don't need the gun." He said matter of factly

"Why?" I asked.

"Bien, The enemy of my enemy, is my friend.' He stopped the car on the beach and sat back to look at me. 'I hear you can kill a man by pointing your finger at him. . Au Clair thought you had the juju.' He laughed 'It is a very special trick but not Voodoo, N'est pas?"

"Oh! Ya, I'm the old rolling scull in disguise."

"Don't say the name, sometime it comes when it's called." He was serious and made a finger sign to ward off evil. The rolling scull is the unearthly messanger of certain Voodoo cults.

"Also you killed the Jap. That was an even better trick. Au Clair was coming apart after they found him laid out on the beach. Which is good for Ti Buddy."

"Why is that?"

"If he were to die, then all of this be mine. I be the boss compri?"

"Yes, I understand." I said in French.

"No, man, speak English. I don't understand you. The second most used language in the world is French but we two Frenchmen must speak English Merde c'est grave. Quebecois qui?"

"Canadian! My mother is French. In Ontario I was a frog in Quebec a God damned English. In every family there are insults between brothers but I am Canadian to the outside world.

"Bien." Ti Buddy was long in body and moved with a reptilian slowness as if every action had to have a specific reason and the energy was already allocated for it.

His chocolate form was clothed in a red Island shirt and light gray pants. The air-conditioning was on full and he had some kind of perfumed car air freshener that made me ill, with its strong scent.

A face void of emotions looked out at me. Under the hat. The visage was round with a large spread nose and black intelligent eyes. The smile was wide and white but the eyes gave the warning of other things behind Ti Buddy's clean features.

"So if Au Clair leaves the island you inherit the family business."

"Pha, don't insult me man. I'm not related to that pig. Also his dieing would be much better." There was real anger here deep hatred.

"Why?"

"Dead men don't come back later." Ti Buddy smiled evily.

"So you going to hit him?" I don't like mob parlance but when in Rome.

"I thought you might take care of that little thing while you was here? Maybe point your finger again," He smiled again more conspiratorially.

"No, not my style. I kill when I am in danger."

"The Jap was strangled from behind but then I don't worry about the direction of danger either." Ti Buddy seemed to have a clear if twisted take on life.

"Old Ray would have killed me straight on.' .I said honestly. 'He got sloppy and bought the farm."

"Oh! Don't worry I don't judge you." He looked out to sea.

"We can get rid of Au Clair though. Those girls he is holding, if we can get them out alive will put him away for a very long time, back in La Belle France or maybe in a jungle gang in Guinea."

"Your problem is you don't understand the enemy, my friend. Au Clair will not go to jail. He has very big friends."

"Yeah! I know Jewel." Henry said Au Clair had no power off the island he was wrong.

"Then you know he will never go in the box. The flick will be paid or he will be allowed to escape. Later he will come back. I want him dead. If you can not help me then, that is that, as you say."

"Get me the girls and I will see to it you're not disturbed here."

The hard reptilian eyes came up. Ti Buddy scrutinized me for a moment.

"You will kill him then."

"No, I don't murder. But there are those who want this, Jewel, who will see to it he doesn't come back." The lifeless eyes were pensive for a moment.

"I don't know where they are but I got a guess you want to see?"

"Sure."

The hill went straight up. The brush or cover was nonexistent. Through the binoculars the pillbox looked like a fortress.

The "V" shaped entrance to the compound was carved around a wedgeshaped pillbox a fifty-caliber machinegun made its appearance. I couldn't make out what kind with the old Victory binoculars Ti Buddy provided, but French no doubt. The grade had to be at least fourty-five degrees. You'd have to shell a position like that then take it foot by foot. You could lose half a command just getting up the hill.

"What the hell is that?" I asked innocuously.

"During the Second World War the local military built three or four boxes up there with an underground corridors to link them as strong points. It was to be a last strong hold against les Bosh. The Germans didn't make the party. I am sure they were very sorry. After the war, someone figured out helicopters could take it out in ten minutes. The government put it up for sale. Au Clair invested in it about five years ago to develop a hotel; you can appreciate the extent of the construction.

The Machinegun is operated by one of Au Clair's, PINPIN,. Ganja smocking Voodoo believers. There are five or ten stationed there. They will die for him. The ability to have people die for you, at will, is of value. No! They believe he is the Dark Baron. He is the Black Hand. If the girls are up there,' he indicated the low hill. 'I would not want the job of getting them out but then the military you will meet today will tell you just what can be done if anything, n'est pas

"Why hasn't he killed them?" I asked

"Simple, mon cher, alive they are hostages, dead they are a problem of disposal. Alive they are money to collect; dead they are just meat. Alive they guarantee his life. He is afraid to move them out of the country for fear you catch him, no.

"Who is Au Clair?" I asked after a moment of evaluation.

"Finally you begin to ask questions that make me think I have not made a mistake. Au Clair est l' enfant de bijou. A child of the Jewel."

"In New Orleans, Jewel has a house. It is unique. The prostitutes are held there by slavery from childhood. He purchases the most interesting. It seems parents will sell anything.

The most outrageous fare can be tasted there. Your choice of women, men, boys, girls, children, anything, available for a price. The price is money and yet it is also entrapment for those who are addicted to their passions.

The price to maintain this perverse series of events is bending to Jewel's will. The reason he had not been taken out and shot, is that he owns to many people.

Owns them, M. McFurson, like a puppeteer owns a puppet. Dubois is able to maintain the illusion of sexual passion with fear. Not performing for his caged wonders is a death sentence.

Those who survive, who graduate to become part of Jewel's empire, his children, his things. Their are many in the Caribbean in control of small places like this but like a chain of many links it creates a strength, an empire. Like Au Clair these things are intelligent and evil. They poison the people on my island." The gold toothpick was removed and Ti Buddy's face became grave.

"I am evil ' It was a simple admission like a man admitting he smoked. 'But evil in a man's way. I want money, women, food and valuable things. I am a voleur, a thief and so be it.

Au Clair wishes to own those who he is in contact with. It is if he wants souls not riches. His power extends like a cancer, until nothing is correct, until all the powers of good are destroyed. Even I know there must be a balance. You cannot control a criminal regime in anarchy. At that point it becomes a matter of force only.

A frivolous thing, a failing, gambling, a woman can

be a thing of joy. However, when Au Clair has touched these things they are tainted with a blackness. There is no joy when the people you must deal with are afraid all the time. Also it is a trap, the user becomes trapped as in a spiders web. Jewel is without a soul. He will kill without warning.

"Au Clair doesn't have horns or cloven hooves," I said. He might look like the devil but he's a man and I didn't figure you for a philosopher.

"Philosophy is something I know little about. I simply state the truth. We, in the islands, can live with hurricanes, sickness, and little or no money. We have our music and our lives, which are rich in friendship. This man would steal that simple pleasure from us.

"He wanted you dead, you are honest. He knew you could not be corrupted". I thought back to Cindy Connors.

"He was wrong, I too, am a man."

"Spoken well and bravely. However, you do not let your passions control you. You war against them they do not own you. Your price would be high, too high for Au Clair".

I considered my price for a moment and thought it would be low because I didn't want anything maybe that was the point.

"You said Au Clair did not have horns. You are right but he is a reminder. There was a Jew. In Germany before the war, he had acquired papers to leave Germany with his family. At the moment they were to leave Eichmann walked in and personally removed his papers and shipped him and his family to Auschwitz. The Jews family died there, he survived. In the end they captured Eichmann in Argentina and put him on trial. The Jew was to be a witness against that scum.

The Jew sat in the courtroom and looked at this animal that had condemned his family to die and was stricken. He had to be helped from the room. It was not because of hatred or loss. No, mon ami, it was something far more terrible. He realized that Eichmann was a man. The Jew realized he was also a man and was capable of the same monstrosity as the Nazi. He had the same evil in him.

These are my islands Mr. McFurson. We have many evils here but our laughter and joy of life keep them at bay. Au Clair reminds us we are as evil as we maybe. He destroys our illusion and without that how can we be what we are? How can we enjoy life? No! I want him dead." The anger was righteous.

I hate true believers but I understood the enemy

now. Au Clair wouldn't run. Thinking he was safe even if his henchmen fell from a great height. He would put all his efforts to removing the girls making his sales because failing Jewel would be terminal. Our jails and courts were nothing compared to that kind penalty.

"How would he normally move the girls from the island?"

"He would normally use the cargo planes at Grand Case but the Legion took over there last night. It happened very fast. There are little whispers that Captain Pernoit, the senior police official on the island, was arrested.

"Is he a tall creep with black mustache and a mouth that looks like he's puckering to kiss someone's ass?"

"Yes!" Ti Buddy laughed high and loud

"Good!"

"No one has seen a local police officer for the entire night.' Ti Buddy continued 'The legion is keeping an eye on things. Crime has come to a standstill. The island people would rather cut their throats and swim with sharks then run across the Foreign Legion."

"So, this is bad for business."

"Oh! Yes."

"How else does he move things? I have two reasons. The girls and a special shipment that I have to track down."

"Something of real value?" The reptilian eyes brightened with avarice.

"Not on a money level but on a human level, something very unpleasant. This one's way out of your league."

"There is a ship the Parrot she is a small island steamer. One thousand tons perhaps. He has been known to move things in and out on that. However she would usually birth in Philipsburg

I considered the fortress on the hill. There were a million places a small boat could take the girls off. Sedated, they would be a little heavier to carry that was all. Of course the coast guard would be looking and they were very effective. Whatever had to be done must be completed quickly. Ti Buddy was way off base. Real evil and I had seen it was never as all powerful as he seemed to think. The old Voodoo darkness and fire thinking, tended to develop these evil pictures of the future. I also knew no one was going to break the back of the Island people. They were far too strong for that. As long as he was willing to help out though, I would take his help.

One thing was sure Wally the Wombat with a pee

shooter could hold that hill against the entire Third Regiment of the French Foreign Legion until hell froze over. Unless the military wanted to use an electroset missile, helicopters, flame throwers or concentrated artillery fire, which would make crispy critters out of the hostages. I didn't see much hope. No a little subtlety was need here, I hoped, I or someone else had some?

"Ti Buddy what do you know about Mohammed Tisani." The French gang boss paused for a moment.

"There is a man who hates. He tries to cover it but he hates deep. Watch yourself Cher with this one. He hates Americans but British or Canadians will do. I do not know why.

Tisani or Hassaraara, came to the island three months ago. He purchased a company, Ignace AC. This small plant in Grand Case makes aluminum cans for the Caribbean. If you feed your cat or open soup its probably coming out of one of Tisani's cans. He makes money on this matter, not much, but some. I have a cousin working there. About a month ago he hired a second shift and started to make special cylinders. An inch thick and rounded at the ends like a pill. They have an opening in the middle. One night only selected people came in. My cousin is very industrious. The finished cylinders had some kind of a clock in the middle of them. They were filled at the factory. That, Mon Ami, has never happened before."

"Where are these cylinders and how many are we talking about?"

"They have disappeared, off the island I don't know where. There were perhaps eight hundred."

Well, I knew what the shipment was. Where it was to be used and what was in it were other questions.

Chapter eleven - 3:00 P.m, Central Police Prefectorate, Tokyo, Japan.

A Falling Cherry Blossom

"A parking offence?' Assistant Superintendent of Police Tono, who was astounded and livid, paced the paneled conference room. This was unheard of; no one had ever seen a senior personage walk a floor before, it was contrary to everything Japanese. However, Tono's agitation was so deep he could not sit.

Shojiro Katsuda sat at the end of the table around, which were ranged the senior commanders, from each Cho or district. The looks ranged from discomfort and anger to fear. These men understood the rules, they lived by them, as did their officers. Independent action was not simply frowned on, it was impossible. An intricate web of deals and little agreements were the bridge on which the war of crime was fought in Tokyo and across Japan.

The problem, however, was two fold. The independent action of Katsuda had destroyed a kidnapping ring and saved a large number of children. The TV news had it on almost every moment. His Superintendent, at this very moment was taking credit for the action and the victory over Harada. If they simply arrested Katsuda, there would be a lynched in the press. The population, appalled by the very fact that this sort of pornography was going on or at least afraid of their own children being victimized, were pleased with this victory over evil. No one wanted to imagine the reaction to removing Katsuda for doing his job. Nasty questions about money might be raised in the press. The people would not trust the police and then there would be real trouble. The Japanese, for all their subservience had a point beyond which they would not go. The representatives from Kabuki Cho were sweating profusely and there was no sympathy for them. However, sticking a gun in the ribs of a senior police official was inexcusable.

The fact that a policeman's child had been involuntarily snatched for sale to some pervert was on a higher plane of unacceptable. In fact Shojiro's action had probably saved all of them because if that fool from Kabuki Cho had tried to save the moment and shut the camera's down. The press could never have been controlled The entire Prefectorate would hanging from the city wall by their thumbs. This disaster have lead to a departmental shakedown that would make a typhoon look calm.

On the other hand, if every officer went off on their own, the symmetry of Japanese life would be destroyed. Order would be destroyed and anarchy would reign.

The financial problems facing the country didn't help and high unemployment was a real problem. What to do? Tono stopped

"By what authority did you commit this action." Tono demanded

"A fathers love." Katsuda looked him directly in the eye. Tono looked away.

"It would be hard for anyone to find that on a code of law. If every wounded parent shot the man who touched their daughters in an impure way on the subway, the streets would run red."

"Our banks are dying, without them our economy is dead, our politics, business and the Yakuza are sleeping in the same bed.' Shojiro had no misgivings about what was to happen but given he could not escape his actions, he at least would speak his mind. 'Everyone pats everyone else on the back, all are friends but the small man, like myself, he has no friend. It stinks like a rotting corpse. What is the next level of enlightened direction, to sell each other to the highest bidder?" Shojiro's face was hard and the words came like bricks.

Tono looked into the sad tired eyes of a man who questioned every part of what he was and what every man at the table was, without caring. That was the danger without rule of law they were all lost.

The question was of course valid. Would Tono have acted, used his power, his position, developed from the interactions with many others, in concert, over many years in one sword stroke to save his child and others. He looked at the Kabuki Cho senior men and despised them like nothing he had ever hated before. They were the mirror to his sins. Tono knew what they had been doing. He knew who and what they had turn a blind eye to. Tono felt something he had not felt for a long time, shame.

In this moment and having discussed the matter before hand with the others. He bowed low to the junior detective

"I apologize for my grave error." He then straightened and the others knew he was not being sarcastic.

"The Netherlands and French Ambassadors have requested that we send you to St. Martin as they feel only you are capable of handling a circumstance concerning a Japanese national.

The Emperors servant has made inquires into who planned and completed this important raid."

"It is our decision and that of the government, that

you will go' Yes, go as far as possible and don't come back, Tono thought, but you will return won't you, then we will see. 'It is further decided, that you will be made a Sergeant.' There was dead silence.

Katsuda was stunned he expected arrest, perhaps assassination, by Harada's people but never promotion. St. Martin it sounded like a golden land, paradise Yatomi would be there and poor old Fat One, would not have to lease his soul to help Shojiro get to her.

The Emperor was interested. This was high praise indeed but he did not deserve it. What he had done was purely selfish. Had he fallen over Harada's horror show without Yatomi being in danger, he would have filed a report and stepped out of the way to allow others to deal with it. However, this was not all, it could not be. Tono and the others would not sit quietly and allow this to pass. He would pay. The simple question was how large the payment would be and would he survive it?

"On your return you will be placed at a desk. The light around you will fade…." Tono left the sentence unfinished. "You will be provided with a gold card from the Prefecturate. Use it well.

"What you have done is fundamentally wrong. There is a hierarchy for a reason. If this situation was passed up to me I would have taken appropriate action. Our nation is the whole. The individual is less important so that the whole can move forward. There is a very small place for cowboy behavior, even if it is warranted."

"If your child was abducted, you would pick up a phone and correct it with the source of the evil. I have no such magic phone and my daughter must be safe on her return. Or perhaps I will request the name of the Emperors servant."

"You threaten me?" Tono's mild square face was red with anger.

"You rebuke me for saving small lives. Which of us is more evil?" Tono bowed woodenly.

"The matter will be resolved." This took great strength on the senior officers part. Tono's eyes were blank and cold. However, Shojiro had simply voiced the multiple fears of those assembled for their own loved ones and children. The clans had crossed a line, they had no right to pass. This must be corrected.

"You are dismissed." Tono turned from the room. He entered his own office and sat behind the desk. Instead of buzzing his secretary, his fine fingers dialed a number. When the receiver was lifted he said one word, a name and was passed immediately to a middle aged man with a moon face and a look that said he had seen all things twice. Nemoura was the head of all the clans. The Emperor of crime. His slightest breath could be death for someone.

Fortunately, he was a reasonable man, if that can be said of a man of Nemoura's importance in the intricacies of crime. At least a thinking man.

"Hai." He said in a level voice.

"Harada is dead. He kidnapped a policeman's child to sell. Harada is dead because of this inexcusable thing, The issue is settled.' Nomura knew that he had just been warned not to grab another police child. Namoura was also upset about the TV coverage. It was too much light on a thing that enjoyed the solitude and opportunities offered by the dark.

"Who do you think your discussing this with?" his voice was now dragon bain.

"You, Tono said simply, 'Katsuda and his child will return to Japan. If either of them catch a cold you will catch pneumonia. Every agreement will be void and the circumstances will not be negotiable." Tono 's voice did not flinch he had done what he could. He had the power to make a dramatic amount of trouble. Namoura was impressed. Also he was forced to accept the reponcibility for Harada's actions. This was required of him even though it was difficult.

Harada made money. In his own way he paid his dues and took care of his business with precision. On the other hand, he was involved with a dirty and cowardly profession. Further, he had made deals outside the circle. Selling Japanese children to foreigners was unacceptable. It struck at Namoura's very soul, this desecration of his race. Harada had also had dealings with certain religious groups which could have damaged the entire Clan system, had they been known. No, Harada would be buried with his sins.

"I apologize most deeply for this dilemma.' Namoura said, 'this will become my personal responsibility. Your suggestion will be implemented." He said into the phone. It hurt a great deal but the life of a cop and his cow daughter meant little in the overview.

Namoura hung up and dialed Harada's successor. One Eye Kono, was impressed by the call. Namoura congratulated him on his rise. Kono made appropriate noises in his gravelly voice. Quickly, Namoura came to the point.

"I suggest that your organization stay away from your normal pursuits. We need time for a cooling breeze."

“Harada made the decision. However, I am honored to be of assistance. Of course this will mean substantial financial loss.” Namoura was pleased with Kono. He placed the blame where it was due, he was reasonable and he had demanded compensation which he ignored but would see too.

“.One last insignificant thing. Katsuda and his daughter will return. Nothing is to happen to them. This I will hold you responsible for.

“If they have an accident?” Kono asked.

“They will lived charmed lives. There will be no more accidents. I don’t like television cameras they are bad for business.

“Hai , It will be as you dictate.” Namoura smiled the problem was solved and he would be on time for golf.

Chapter twelve - 9:10 A.m. Grand Case Airport, St. Martin, French West Indies

Are we Belgians?

Chief Inspector Maurice St Armand stepped off the two engine passenger plane provided courtesy of the French Airforce.

The inspector was a tall man, with a long forceful Gaulic face and a substantial amount of silver hair covered by a navy blue kepi. The forehead was square and unwrinkled. Large clear brown eyes looked out on Grand Case Airport with little interest. The rest of the face was lean, angular, centered by a prominent nose and terminating in a small rounded chin.

The Chief Inspector was responsible for the overall police operations for the Guard National and the local Gendarmes of the Prefecture of Guadeloupe.

At the moment he wore the local service uniform, an open neck, short sleeved white shirt and highly creased navy blue pants. The black, service shoes were polished to perfection. At sixty years of age St.Armand looked forty. His long bare arms tanned and muscular.

A man is his stance. Maurice carried his body taught but completely unperturbed. 'Le Monde' was folded under his left arm and his black briefcase shone in the sun.

At the moment the senior policeman was happy with the situation. He had Pernoit and Sergeant Denault in custody and would shortly deal with these cretans who had marred the glory of the Republic. St. Armand had no time for fools or criminals, he had personally put too many away. The insult of being duped by these idiots was far worse than a slap in the face. This had to be rectified, after all he had others to answer to, senior people who would also look foolish or might, if this matter was not handled properly.

A black Citroen, followed by a small camouflaged Renault halfton crowded with battle dress Legionaries, came to a stop before the plane. The driver of the car got out to open the door for him.

Lieutenant Recco alighted from the Renault's cab and saluted. The new, gold wire Granade on his beret glittered in the sunlight. St Armand handed his briefcase to the driver and returned the salute with an old soldier's correctness. The Citroen's back door closed. Maurice began to evaluate the international situation as defined by his newspaper. The little convoy shot through the colorful, single story buildings of Grand Case and made its way quickly to the Gendarmerie at Marigot.

St Armand's people from Guadeloupe were already in place having come in on an earlier flight to clean up the mess and take over from the army. The legion was still around, having taken command of the situation the night before, when no one could be trusted. They sat about with bored stares but leapt to attention as Maurice entered. Lieutenant Recco followed, removing his beret and buttoning it under his shoulder tab.

The Chief Inspector entered Pernoit's office and sat behind the desk. He removed the kepi and smoothed back his hair. The desk's gray metal surface had been cleared of everything but the case file of the Au Clair investigation as he had requested. Recco, the swarthy Corsican with a lean fox's face, stuck his head around the partially open door.

"Bring him in." St. Armand ordered without looking up.

"Qui, Mon Commandant." Recco said in a soft Corsican accident.

A few moments later the ex-Captain was dragged in by two powerful policemen and dumped into the wood chair before the Inspector. Pernoit was guilty until proven innocent, under French Law and rather more so as a police official.

"Sir, I am pleased to see you, now we can get to the bottom of this terrible mistake." Said Pernoit smiling weakly, he was sweating profusely.

"I have already gotten to the bottom of this matter.' St. Armand said cruelly, 'That is why you are in handcuffs." He went on ignoring any response on the Captain's part.

"Perhaps we of the Territorial Prefectorates are expected to be corrupt. After the movie Casablanca it's almost a cliché. I am not completely stupid or blind. A few Francs here or there, the odd prostitute. Little things given with the hope of favours or leniency. Perhaps, the body of your wife's lover found in a ditch, there is precedence. At least it's understandable."

"However, steeling children from the street. French citizens, to order for some alien pervert. My God! Do you think we are Belgians?" St.Armand was painfully aware of the kind of perversion that had been all over the news in France's neighbour and the blind eye provided by the police in Belgium. Little girls found in dungeons under houses and worse murdered. His anger went cold and this was when Maurice was most dangerous.

"It will be my privilege' St Armand said in his rich Norman voice, 'to have you put a on plane for Guadeloupe and there placed on trial to remove this stain to French arms and the Republic. I will personally request that the maximum sentence possible be imposed and that you serve out your term clearing swamp in Guinea." Pernoit was a twenty-year police officer and tough. However, this threat made his face blanche and fall. He knew Maurice St. Armand had not just made a threat but a promise, one he would carry out. Maurice gave him a moment to absorb his position then he dropped the bomb.

"If you want any kind of clemency and that will be little at best. I want the name of everyone involved in this sacrilegious insult to all of us. If I find anyone not on the list after the fact, God help you."

"Of course Commandant I can give them immediately."

"Quiet.' He dismissed the prisoner with disgust. 'Take him to another room and give him paper and a pen. Have him write it all down and sign it. He can see a lawyer but he knows we have him. Get him out of my sight." A lawyer would of course subvert his little coup but it was the best he could do for the moment.

Yatomi was dressed in her fuku again. It was spotless and fussed over by Saraphina, who had adopted her.

"Dey ask you improper questions. You tell me and I go down see dem. Dey have respect den, n'est pass?" Said Saraphia with her huge hands on her ample hips. Les flick had better watch out.

Yatomi came over and smiled a little shakily. The last time we had any interaction with the police was very bad. Say's home was a place of safety.

"Well Samurai are you ready? I asked.

"I am not a samurai, you tease."

"No, Sailor Moon San?" This made her blush and laugh.

"You know Sailor Moon?" She asked incredulously surprised that I would know about the cartoon character that also wears a Sailor Fuku.

"My kids watch it, or did I don't know if its on television anymore." The story of the blond Moon Princess who fought evil but was just an average teenager at other times, was well known in many parts of the world.

"Then I should summon my magic powers.' She ran her fingers across her face like the cartoon character, finally bringing her pointed finger to rest on me in the crook of her arm. She laughed again with embarrassment.

"I wish I had magic powers. I would take you home with me, you could meet my father. He would like you. We could spend time looking at my city.

"Would you keep me in a little box and feed me every day?"

"No." she seemed confused.

"I have a wife, Hai."

"Hai.' Her face fell with pain and shame. "I understand."

"Do you? What you feel for me is gratitude. Soon your father will come here to get you. It will change then.

"Hai!" The smile, the relief, the joy, were so visible. Whoever said these people had no emotions was full of it."

"When will he come?" It was almost a plea.

"Later today."

"This is wonderful news." Tears slid down her thin cheek.

"Then you won't need me anymore but remember you still owe me a life."

"Hai,' she nodded. 'How can I thank you, I have no gift. You do not want to pillow with me and I do not have great wealth to give you."

"Do the people your father helps pillow with him?"

"No!" She shook her head and her raven hair moved softly as if a spring wind had touched it.

"I am like him. I need no reward. If I were younger and free I would appreciate your offer more. You are beautiful and have a body that would make a brass Buddha awaken." She went crimson now and laughed uncertainly. 'I am old and I am married. Where I come from being faithful is important, Hai?"

"Hai, In our country men sleep with other women, with pleasure girls and this is acceptable. It is expected." She said frankly

"Where I come from some people do this too. I do not break my word to my wife. When we marry we give our word to be only with one." I am a lying son of a bitch aren't I? But well, this conversation was required. Don't hurt her just let her down easy. This seemed to take care of it.

We left the house and walked to a predetermined location where a Peugeot and a second Renault truck, crammed with legionaries waited. We were whisked across town to the Gendarmerie. Yatomi took my hand and we entered the large, white building.

The conference room was small but adequate; three windows shed light into the air-conditioned room, which smelt of furniture wax.

Five men were seated around the table. On Yatomi's entrance there was a fair rumble of chairs as the group rose to greet her. I recognized Peter Zeeland immediately. We had bumped into each other a few times. He would represent the Dutch Secret Service in this matter and I was pleased. His small round face brimming with a smile, he reached across the table to take my hand with obvious good will.

"You still stealing cars?" I kidded

"Only the ones I can catch." He returned," It's good to see you Michael."

"May I introduce our host, Chief Inspector Maurice St. Armand?

"Bonjour." I slipped in to French.

"It is my pleasure.' He took my hand, 'But if you will forgive me, I have always had preference for beautiful young women." Maurice smiled at Yatomi, who bowed automatically.

"May I have the honour to introduce Miss Yatomi Katsuda?" I indicated Yatomi who blushed to tips of her toes, overwhelmed with the attention.

"Enchante Mademoiselle" Maurice reached forward and kissed her hand with an old world elegance that made me envious. Yatomi was speechless for the moment, then she bowed and mumbled something.

Maurice now took over

"May I present Superintendent Van Klem of the Royal Netherlands Police." Klem also kiss Yatomi's hand. He was less elegant but he knew this attention was terrifying and exciting her in equal measures. Klem enjoyed prolonging the moment with Dutch good humour. The Superintendent was solidly built and so black that his face looked blue in the morning light. He was a resident of the Islands and had risen on his own initiative. A self made man, he was blunt and hard His smile showing immaculate white teeth from a rough oval face. He eyeballed me with the standard distaste reserved for interdepartmental gits. Spies and their ilk, were not appreciated. One up from swamp gas on the food chain. He sat as far from Peter as possible and would be no end of fun to deal with.

Maurice went on introducing Mr. Ary Derputten the Governors representative, who would speak for the Dutch government. He was early fifties with a balding head a small goatee, quick slippery eyes and a nervous habit of wring his hands. He smiled softly and touched Yatomi's outstretched hand for only a moment.

The third man introduced from the Dutch side was Commander Yan Trump of Her Majesty's Royal Netherlands Coast Guard. Six foot two inches and two hundred and ten pounds of solid muscle. The clear blue eyes met Yatomi's with frank interest, which she returned, then quickly looked away, her heart beating like a tom tom. Yan's cliché rugged good looks seemed to be enhanced by a broken nose and square powerful chin. Just a touch of arrogance there; surprise, surprise. He, too, shook her hand holding it just a little longer then necessary.

"You are an exceptional young woman for sixteen years of age. "Chimed in Maurice to rectify any misconception. Yan's face fell and he physically took a step back. My cherry blossom obviously looked older than her age.

"Gentlemen' Maurice continued while I shook hands with the three men.' Gentlemen, Lieutenant Edward Recco of the Foreign Legion.

The introductions completed Maurice moved along quickly.

"Mademoiselle Katsuda, I wish to apologize on behalf of the Republic of France for your poor treatment on St. Martin. I can assure you that this not the way we normally treat our guests. Be assured that you are now perfectly safe. Nothing will harm to you as of this point, you have my word.' When Maurice St. Armand gave his word, it was kept. 'I will need a statement of the circumstances leading up to this matter and so forth. If you dictate the information in English to Sergeant Le Bon Lyon, he will translate it into French and I request that you read and sign the document in both languages. I will impose on you to be my guest along with Mr. McFurson for lunch after our meeting. However, our present conversations will include subjects that have no interest for you. I am sure we would bore you to distraction in a few moments. I will, therefor ask that you complete your statement in the next room and we will be with you in as little time as possible."

Yatomi left with a bow a little dizzy from the attention and a smile of support for me.

Maurice sat down the smile was gone. He looked at me grimly.

"Well Monsieur you place us in a very unpleasant position. It is not your fault and I suspect we should thank you for shedding light on this odious matter but I can tell you this has been difficult to the point of discomfort. We have arrested Pernoit and his associates. At this point we are ready to move on our friend Au Clair."

"We picked up Sergeant Laar at Curacao Airport. It seems it was the only and earliest flight out. He had turned over the names of the scum that were using their badges to work this sick game." Van Klem was pleased with the outcome and it showed. Police, for the most part, have great leniency with their own kind but child molesters were something rather different.

Maurice took over once more. He thanked Superintendent and directed the next question at me. "Please explain the situation as you know it and we will ask questions as you go along. Please be brief."

"There are seven more young women being held on the island. Like Miss Katsuda they were kidnapped based on the specifications of very wealthy perverts. I had contact with an individual who has suggested they are being held at the old National Defense bunker in the center of the island.

"Merde." Snarled Maurice, under his breath, the fact that the British had found out about this matter was one thing. For them to be this far in the lead, was insufferable. The Dutch contingent shifted uneasily and gave sour looks. 'Get us a map of the bunker Recco." Morris snapped.

"I took the liberty to go to the land office this morning.' I said and lay a small diagram of the sight on the table.'

"Good, efficiency, the investigation starts well." Said Maurice with qualified good grace

"Good God!" Van Kem said in Dutch and rubbed his face.

"I don't know much about ground warfare but that place looks like a death trap." Yan suggested

"You're absolutely correct. A frontal assault would be suicide. However, the location is susceptible to artillery and helicopter attack, that's why it was sold." Said Maurice motioning Recco to the table.

"During my short stay with the opposition stinger missiles were mentioned." I said off handedly.

"What! How many?" Maurice's face was a picture of surprise and upset.

"At least two, probably more. I don't think a helicopter would be an option. The artillery or a rocket attack would kill everyone. Also the men holding the bunkers are Au Clair's Pin Pin,. These men are religiously faithful to him because of a voodoo cult he has created and will die without question if necessary.

"The problem is simply solved ' Recco' s soft Corsican voice commanded the room. I will take ten men up the outside of the hill and drop sleeping gas down the air vents."

"Yes good, but that presumes they have no mines or booby traps on the blind sides of the hill. Also, if I remember correctly, the bunker had an air safety system when it was built. This would vent anything you threw in. That is if it works. I know the bunker was stripped of anything valuable before it was sold. If they even think you're trying something, they will kill the girls." Maurice finished and Recco looked a little less sure.

"Perhaps we can do something else' Derputten broke in ' Why not promise free passage to this Au Clair in return for the girl's lives. We can then put out a warrant for him through Interpole and Carib. The man shouldn't be that hard to catch."

"Well yes of course.' said Maurice putting on his diplomat's hat. 'However, letting this thug work an agreement would be odious to the Republic. Our orders are not to negotiate with hostage holders. Unfortunately, at present, the young women are on French soil." There was no way in God's green earth Maurice was going to look the fool when this deal came up in the papers. They might try and fail but he would not be dictated to by this crook again.

"Gentlemen,' I started obviously attempting to be

of help in a small way. 'I am only a Marketing Executive and ,of course, this situation is strictly under your control. I only hope to help a little but lets see how this works.

Trying to take the bunkers we all agree is unacceptable unless it's a last chance situation. Further, we know that Au Clair is probably more afraid of Jewel than ourselves. He will go to any lengths to get the young lades to their buyers in order to recoupe his losses and to make his master happy, so to speak.

So we can believe with some assurance that he wi not hurt the girls unless it's a last desperate act. Even then, perhaps not. The point may be to offer him a way out that makes sense and let him walk into our trap.

I have it on good authority that there is a ship called the Parot, a small coastal freighter presently in Antigua waiting to come in and pick up the girls.

"You have very good sources for a Marketing Exec." Yan threw in nastily

"Sergeant Katsuda of the Tokyo Prefectorate, will come in this evening, to Grand Case Airport to mee his daughter. Lets say we leak this information to the local press. We move all our Legionaries to the airport to cover the arrival as if we were afraid an attempt might be made on Yatomi, her father and me as the primary witnesses. The story itself can be related to a smuggling scheme, which is true, and that there have been deaths involved, which is also true. As a further precaution we move some Netherlands police from Philipsburg where the Parot will dock to support the Legionaires at the airport. This would be a show of island solidarity.

Also as Sergeant Kadsuda's party will be the guests of the Governor for his stay, he will have to be transported to the other end of the island. Your people can draw straws to see who rides in the cars. Yatomi and her Father stay at the Airport."

"There are a number of problems with your thinking.' Maurice broke in. 'We will be putting yourself and the Katsuda's in terrible danger."

"No,' I shook my head. 'Au Clair knows you have Pernoit and Laars probably. One of them has to have cracked. He will realize we are really of no value."

"Then why the charade?" Van Klem demanded watching me closely.

"Au Clair has boundless arrogance. I can hear him laughing from here, all this pomp and circumstance for nothing. Also it would take him time to set up a hit. I've seen his people they couldn't do it if they had wings. It would have to be someone off island. There is no time.

He will also realize that it will be dark when the plane arrives and that he will have clear run at Philipsburg. "

"So you expect him to take the girls to the ship and be gone before we react. " Said Van Klem ' "It's an obvious trap. Why would he move? Also, the Parot would have to clear the Harbour Master's Office.

"He will move because by then he will be very uncomfortable. We will put every other available officer we have into hitting his main locations of operation and hauling in his people wholesale.

"We know where he is." said Yan

"Yes, but he doesn't know that. However, he will realize we will figure that one out real quick. Remember that fortress of his is also a trap. Unless he has a new back way out that we don't know about, he can figure on a frontal assault will develop with limited delay.

If we attack the place then he has to play the only card he has, negotiation, which will end in him surrendering. Au Clair will spend the Pin Pin's Lives but he won't kill himself.

If we don't trade and Maurice can't, he has to kill the girls. At which point he will wish he let us flatten the place with him in it. He will have to move.

"Of course it doesn't matter where, the moment he does we have him.' said Maurice, 'yes, very good."

"If I were him I would booby trap the girls and use their lives as a trading point. Remember he will be in Dutch territory in a few miles." Suggested Recco staring out the window at the green fields beyond.

"Yes, I agree,' Peter threw in, ' Imagine what a nice big hole he could make with some C4. He has that too you know.

"Tisani?" I asked, Peter nodded.

"That nice big hole could be Philipsburg." said Derputten ringing his hands a mile a minute and about to put the kibosh to my little plan.

"Peter are you bringing people."

"Yes, we have Royal Marines coming in from Curacao

"Bring them in by KLM as passengers. Make sure there are lots of sharp shooters among them."

"Yes with telescopic night sights. ' Peter said grimly

"Kill them all, no warning." This ran against Maurice's sense of fair play.

"I have four snipers in my squad.' Said Recco 'with myself that's five."

"Don't get too carried away we have innocent civilians to think of." Said Derputten.

"Listen Gentlemen here is where we are.' It was time for my speech.

"One; we let this puck dictate to us and every half-wit with explosives will line up.

Two; we have to get him out of there. We can't rush the place and if we can't take it fast enough we'll never find the bodies. If the Parot doesn't set sail we have lost nothing. He may decide to try something else, a small boat maybe. At that point Yan's clipper and the French Corvette can go to work.

Three; if Parot does sail Yan and his people will block the harbor once it's in. Then attack on the ocean side with scuba tanks. Sneak on board and clean house. It will have to be quiet because you can bet they will be in radio contact. When the truck shows up we let them take the boxes on board. Then we ask them nicely to surrender. If they don't we punch their ticket."

"What!" asked Derputten.

"Terminate them with extreme prejudice." I said.

"I don't understand." He asked again

"Kill them" St.Armand's voice cut like a cleaver.

'Are you sure you're not with the CIA?" Maurice snapped at me.

"Oh." said Derputten crestfallen.

"They might try to escape by helicopter." Yan said covering all the potential problems.

"We have that covered there are two attack helicopters at Grand Case. If they show up, they will never get to the hill. If they do they won't get out. We have also sent the word around. We could man the helicopter ourselves if they come to our undercover branch and fail to realize it is us they are dealing with." said Maurice with a wink.

"Great, as long as we win." I said.

" Well at least we have a plan,' said Maurice 'I think you agree the raids occur under any circumstance.' he said to the Dutch Contingent. Van Klem nodded and Derputten held his final judgement.

"We might even catch Au Clair' Maurice continued. 'A few minutes with two or three Legionaries and we'd have the girls back safe, very quickly.

If the Parot moves, well, then we must decide. As you say McFurson we lose little by putting security on the airport. Au Clair will know before the message gets to him by radio but we will try that too. We have nothing to lose" Maurice finished with his hands spread in a very Gaulic manner.

Chapter thirteen - 11:15 AM, Marigot, St. Martin, French West Indies

Ideology

The Rue De St James has a small café. In the manner of all French café's, the coffee is strong, the wine is as good as your money can buy and asking for a Coke is an insult to the Republic. The presence of the Chief Inspector was the only thing that saved me from the waiter's wrath.

Maurice sat in the shade of a bright blue and white-striped awning and allowed the soft morning wind to attack his perfectly coiffed silver hair. The wind sped by refreshingly cool, a forrunner of rain, which was building for an attack off the coast. The dark towers of angry black cloud would soon remove the sun and drench the streets of the Colonial Capital.

Yatomi was busy giving the details of the situation to Sergeant Bon Lyon, a mustached Parisian. The majority of the island police at least those of the national force are brought to the colonial possessions from major cities in France for short periods. This was an opportunity and, of course, one the average French police officer appreciated. Bon Lyon had a hardy laugh to match his broad honest face. Yatomi felt safe with him so more talkative.

When the meeting with the Dutch contingent finished the Chief Inspector and I, had strolled to the café for a few moments discussion. I had no misunderstanding that this conversation was going to be pretty heavy.

Maurice sipped Chablis and considered the brewing storm, which was whipping the white caps to frenzy.

"Your plan won't work you know?" He said finally.

"Well if it fails you can blame it all on me."

" I do not blame people. I get things done then there is no blame." I nodded and he continued. ' You killed two men on French Territory. In each case, so the girl says, you were only defending yourself. Pernoit seems to agree in his statements but, of course, his lawyer will have no end of fun taking that apart."

"I don't think we will have a hearing. Unless of course, I get further information to the contrary. The Japanese was killed from behind. ' He finished as if this wasn't very sporting.

"Maurice, if I had taken him on face to face after a full night of having the crap beaten out of me, he would have quartered me with no need for horses. I didn't have any choice."

"The girl must be very special for you to kill two men for her. You wouldn't be making love to her."

"That's not a gentlemen's question." I said a little ticked off.

"No, it is a policeman's question." Maurice was flexing his mussels.

"I have not made love to the young woman but as to doing my best to save her ,yes." I said with melancholy, as I wouldn't be seeing her much more.

"My problem with you, is that given your occupation you would choose to expose yourself like that?"

"Would you have walked by in my case." I asked honestly.

"Yes, I have done undercover work before. Exposure is the last thing one wants." Granny had fed the French the line that I was on semi-service with the International Division of Scotland Yard with respect to the huge Internet pornography project that was in the works at that moment.

"I am just a marketing guy on a little business who walked into a mess and did his best."

"That of course brings us to your business. "Said Maurice looking at me hard.

"I sell computers. Well, I market them really." I was here to see Ignace the can manufacturer. I wanted to speak to our mutual friend, Tisani.

"We know him by another name but he is a terrorist, isn't he?" Said Morris considering light through the wine in his glass. The Zouk music of St. Martin played by the local radio station provided a background for our conversation .I enjoyed the sultry Caribbean melody of the French possessions and listened contentedly as Maurice considered his next question.

"If you are a computer salesman, I am Joan Of Arc. Your here after Tisani, Au Clair was involved with him. This could be a vendetta between you and the crooks. The girl is just a wedge to get our support."

"Maurice lets cut to the chase shall we? Tisani or whatever he is called here had eight hundred aluminum cylinders made up. They have time controls on them. They were filled with something and shipped off the island. Tisani was getting Au Clair to move it somewhere with the assistance of Jewel's organization. The question is, where is he sending them? Who gets to be the target?" Maurice made a sour face.

"We know Jewel has moved these children all over the world. He has an organization that controls customs and other powers that be. Tisani is smart no question, he will use the network Jewel has developed to get this stuff in to whatever country is selected. He will get away with it because the customs et elle will not question the shipment because they already think they know what it is. They've been paid enough not to check that its not more then some terrified child." Maurice was now listening to me intently.

"Whatever is in those little presents has got to be lethal. Probably explosives or some much nastier stuff." I finished.

"You mean biological?" The Inspector asked looking old for the first time that day.

"Probably." I have to have Au Clair to find out where this stuff is going, so I don't want him dead. You can prag the rest of these idiots but I want him. God knows how many lives are at stake."

"You've been honest with me I will be honest with you." Maurice's eye's bore into me.

"If you disappeared at this very moment I would be immensely pleased. The seven girls might not exist."

"Give me a break Maurice, why the hell am I going to tell you a story like that? Under normal circumstances I would have made others aware and someone else would have come in and cleaned up the mess, more than probably your internal affairs division, at the least the spy system.' The Chief Inspector gave a pained look. 'How could you not pick up this mess?"

"You must understand, each of these islands are controlled by the local chief of police.' Maurice said slowly. 'I do inspection trips periodically but Guadeloupe is a much larger island then this. I control the central problem solving seat for the entire Prefectorate.

I believe that Pernoit was honest. He seemed a good man, perhaps I am getting old.

This island and the others are my nest. A place where I can live with a little dignity and great beauty until I pass on to whatever hell is reserved for ex-inspectors of Police." Maurice breathed out heavily.

"Why did I not pick on this matter? I am honest for a start. No one would aproach me, knowing I would throw this cretin, Au Clair in a cell far enough from the light that he would emerge with mushrooms growing on him. They knew I could not be bought. I am sure they made calculated inquires into each of my islands. It could have been the senior man on St. Barts or one of the others. Pernoit it seems was the easiest to corrupt. I believe he is a deviant and this hunger was feed. Finally they had enough on him that he had no other alternative but to participate.' The old man made a throwaway jesture, 'He isn't a victim. Pernoit could have gotten out at the beginning simply by coming to me. I would have corrected the matter and given him space to move.

I'm not a monster. No he made the decision, took the money and must pay the price.

It makes me look incompetent. I don't like looking incompetent. You can understand that.

I don't want to be some pensioner on the beach. I enjoy my position and its perks. I must get back those girls and that animal. I need a trophy. I can throw Pernoit to the wolves, but if I don't get anything else, you go too.

"Why because young girls were foolish enough to get ripe and be targets of these men or because I've embarrassed the French and Dutch police who should have been doing their job? On an island this small who didn't know?"

"Voodoo, my dear McFurson, is something rather different than the normal. People die in strange and mysterious ways. The black population is frightened of Au Clair, with that face and his reputation well they stay quiet.

The white population never saw anything or anything that was out of place. You must understand that children the age of your little friend pay their way to this island paradise by means of their pre offered favours. Little girls who think they know everything are brought down here by pimps and sold to cover the price of the return trip. Little girls who lose their money and can't get home sell their bodies and there are always predators

It goes on and on. If we can stop the trade, if they will testify, well and good. We arrest the pimp and he has a very nasty time. If there are warrants, or even a missing person report out on them in the U.S., Canada or Europe, we hold them and hope someone will come to get them or will pay to ship them home. Most of the time they will say nothing believing they are in love. So you can understand someone must scream rape, before we think rape.

The local people don't want to get involved. Then ,of course, we have you. The knight looking for a dragon. Well, you've found one." By the look of it his name was Maurice St Armand.

"Maurice you're not throwing me to the wolves. For one we have witnesses to the pick up at the airport. Real not fake. Two, the powers that be won't like it. I'm a Canadian citizen. Everybody likes Canadians. Hell! The Americans keep telling everyone they're Canadians just to get by in most parts of the world. Thirdly, you know I'm right about Tisani. Remember those little cylinders might be going to la belle France.

"I am overwhelmed by your logic but let me bring

you up to date. The Japanese Consul, such as he is, wants you arrested for a large number of reasons some are very persuasive,"

"I think he's in on it.' I interjected, 'He was the only one who knew we would be at the airport. Did you know that our friend Au Clair helped kill the other girl I rescued and got out of here." Maurice's face said he didn't. ' Kaori and her whole family went under the wheels of transport truck. , to keep your little secret."

"Fine, then it seems I can't throw you to the wolves but you will go out with Recco and take care of this problem in person." Maurice went cold but I didn't want any part of the combat aspect of the arrest.

"Listen, I'm a non-combatant, I saw combat once that was enough for a lifetime. Anyway, all I do is sell computers."

"You want Tisani don't you? Good!' He answered his own question, 'If you want him alive I advise you go along." Maurice finished

"Do I get a bullet in the back for my trouble."

"If I was going to have you killed I'd have done it by now.' St. Armand glowered. 'Your not dealing with Chief Inspector Dreyfus. You came up with this little plan now you will see to its completion."

"I've had more then enough killing. ' I shook my head no, ' I won't lead any charge.

Maurice, I believe that when you kill you lose a little of your soul. A year or so ago I had never knowingly harmed a human being. I don't even hunt. Then circumstances caused that to change. I killed to save the girls in self-defense but it's getting far to easy."

"That's not the best confession to make to an Inspector of Police." Said Maurice coldly.

"Perhaps made to a friend."

"I'm not your friend."

"An equal then." I said with equivalent metal.

"I am not your father confessor. I cannot give you absolution. Even if I could would it matter?' Then with a little more conciliatory tone. 'I had the opportunity to be at Dien Bien Fu. I was in one of the last drops before the fall. I understand killing. Perhaps you are right and you lose a small part of yourself. The question, of course, is justification. Every action in your life is governed by what you believe. We are weighted to right and wrong. A part of the general population is not, it is evil, if there were no one to stop them, what is the end result?"

"You're talking about arrest not death."

"Semantics, death when there is no other way.' Maurice became very intense. 'What is the value of what you defend. A child's welfare, a nations way of life, what is it worth in blood. That is the question. The answer must come from you. You have taken the job, at that point right, is what your ordered to do. However, it is only correct if you believe totally in it and are willing to take the end results of your actions and not hide behind the orders. The answer is never so cut and dry; beware of underestimating your enemies or misunderstanding them. We did in Vietnam and an army died." Maurice looked out to sea and I considered his words.

"Your plan seems to have at least had some effect.' Maurice said finally as the rain began to fall, 'The Parot sailed this morning."

Chapter fourteen - 10:30 P.m, Philipsburg, St. Maartin, Netherlands Antilles.

An Improved View

With a full throated blast of farewell came from the Carnival Liner, stationed at end the long, gray pier, as she took in her lines and slowly set out. Her great white body crossed the harbour mouth to be silhouetted against the island of Saba in the misty, evening light.

Soft waves of sunset washed a living seascape making the liner's sides the colour of rich, fresh cream. Sunset also lined the seemingly constant cloud halo that topped Saba's single great peak with mauve and pink. One might have been looking at a 1930's poster promoting far off travel.

Insignificant, in the magnificence of this portrait of paradise, the stubby, shabby Parot chugged slowly into Philipsburg Harbour. A trawler-like hull that might have once been blue was now a tired rust colour. Her stern castle, which also housed her helm, was a weathered block of grayish teak. A single, thin straight funnel pointed to the sky belching black smoke. A few crewmembers hung out on deck enjoying the evening cool. With long practiced movements the little ship moved into its usual birth about half way down the pier, her bow pointed toward Philipsburg, the impact of berthing softened by truck tires attached to the pier.

Two local dockworkers took lines in and tied them off. Jokes and news were passed back and forth as the dockers and the crew enjoyed the very human by play of the islands. Slowly as must be, work moved at its own pace here, drums of heavy oil were removed from the old hull and placed on the wharf by a small rail derrick. These were followed by small containers of groceries, which were placed directly on flat bed trucks for shipment to a central source to be redistributed to shops, hotels and restaurants as required.

Finally, the work was finished. Conversations and laughter continued under the over hanging lamps in the soft, sticky darkness. Time has no sway here but after a while the locals headed for town and cold beer. On foot, or by car, at a leisurely pace, their laughing voices becoming whispers on the summer wind.

Parot settled into silence as her skipper, a Jamaican pirate named Langandly, slouched off to the Harbour Masters Office as tradition and law prescribed.

This later day Blackbeard was short with a small sharp face that was both cold and bloody minded at a glance.

Langandly's conversation with the nervous clerk, we had the port official wired, provided little real information. The Parot had to restow cargo and a shipment from Ignace S.A. to Puerto Rico was late so he would have to wait till after twelve before Parot could get off to its next destination.

The clerk asked if customs had been informed, loud enough so we couldn't miss it. Someone wanted to be on the side of the angels. Langandly's rich, rummy voice insured the clerk 'It bin taken care of mon.' We, of course, knew that much. We were sweating the customs official at that very moment.

If the crew moved any cargo it was the stuff of dreams. Guards were armed with AK 47's and posted in the shadows on Parot's stern. .

The Ignace Manufacturing truck left the factory about 11:30 P.m.. Our radio kept us informed, as it roared by small fields of cactus, which cover the flat center of St. Marrten. A climate, which paralleled that of Mexico, allows for the cactus. The Mercedes five ton, high geared passed the fortress like Defense Command Sight on its hill. It did not stop.

It became obvious that Tisani had taken one look at the potential death trap and told Au Clair to move out. Ti Buddy had been wrong or his information dated, or he lied through his teeth, nothing stands still. The possibility that the girls were not in the truck was not lost on either the French or Dutch and units were sent to all potential locations where the girls might be held or that Au Clair might be hiding.

Each police unit was told not to move unless there was clear evidence that the kidnap victims were in peril or being moved. These orders would be in effect until our little drama on the Parot was played out.

Zeelander was a 60-foot sailboat with a Verting inboard engine. Her great, white sails were furled for home. A mixed company of four sat in the stern cockpit drinking wine and talking as the boat was steered toward the yacht anchorage off the town of Philipsburg. While her royal blue hull was lost in the night, running lights and bright deck tube fixtures around the revelers were the statement of her passing.

On the seaside of the Zeelander, three ropes properly spaced and supported dragged groups of four men. Dressed in a variety of rubber scuba suits hastily requisitioned by the Dutch government. These worthies held on to Hague Undersea Torpedo's. The Hague units were really made to pull a single man but Netherlands technology was always built for a challenge, I hoped. Yes I was one of the twelve-man team of Royal Netherlands Marines and Coast Guards led by Yan Trump.

The force was armed with submachine guns of the standard, M 16 NATO type in underwater cases. The group was tough and determined. I, personally, held on to the Hague for dear life. Having only been diving once on a family vacation to the Bahamas, my expertise was pushed to its limit. At least I seemed to have the breathing part down and hadn't embarrassed myself yet.

As the Zeelander came even with the docked Parot, a small red light flashed on the first Hague. Hague one, disengaged its towrope and we sank down as the light towmotor tried to get the upper hand on the extra weight it had been allotted.

In the dark water behind us the others followed. Each group had two Van Doolen 540 Lanze spear guns accurate to fifty yards.

Unfortunately, the anchored yachts were in some cases, less than politically correct with the disposal of their garbage and sleek sharks accompanied by other scavengers were always interested in a free meal. Sharks are predominantly night predators, lucky us! I saw a gray shape materialize out of the darkness but the throbbing, overworked engine seemed to make us less interesting as a prospective meal and the sea hunter shored off with a final evaluating look from a cold, mindless eye.

Zeelander with her police crew, glided majestically onward as the three teams dropped down under her keel and made for the stationary merchantman. Fish swam up curiously to the hooded light on the nose of the torpedo. I saw Parrot Fish, a small Grouper and some large Angels their colours reflected in the muffled light beam. These scattered as the object of their curiosity moved aggressively toward them.

A bronze bullet flashed by very close to my head. Barracuda, five feet long, are no ones joy. It hit a fish on the periphery of our group but the fish was a mouthful and there was little blood. My heart rate must have jumped to unheard of heights. The soft buzzing in my ears warned of my high blood pressure. The shark would return at deaths' scent. A battle with these marauders would make us late and could be disastrous. However, the distance was short and a light breeze came up to blot out our bubbles as they rose tell tail to the surface.

I broke the surface behind Yan and another young Marine named Zeke. We left our tanks and fins with the Hague at the bottom of the harbour. As we clung to the rusted hide of the Parot, I unlashed the Eypsilon Murcury Two, L11, which looked somewhat like a cross between a blunderbuss and a pregnant air rifle.

This equipment I had signaled for, was grudgingly provided by special equipment section. My message was met with down right bloody-mindedness at first until Granny stepped in. It seemed only trained line agents need apply. A small Lear arrived from Bermuda only minutes before we were to leave with the equipment on board.

An ex-guardsman, named Walters, explained the operation of the short-term loan equipment like a rent a car agent might suggest the directions for driving new Neon to an orangutan. Nothing like the support of your colleagues, to get you off to the right start.

The Murcury was aimed upward but not fired immediately. A sniper on Point Blanch directly behind the Parot, was targeted on the guard lurking on the main deck on the oceanside of the stern castle, immediately above us.

The concept of killing without provocation was odious because if we were wrong about this little deal, the amount of explanation for the unfortunate dead would fill books. Nothing like your good old fashion international incident.

The Parot might fly a flag of convenience, which, meant of course that the flag was convenient to lower the insurance requirements. Ships flying that flag would never be boarded by an inspector to evaluate the capability of the ship to sail without killing the crew, even if Parot happened to show up in that country. Those nations, were still nations and killing alien nationals without some provocation was not cricket really.

It was then we had our first bit of luck; the guard on the stern entered the galley for a moment. Jan signaled and I got ready to fire. Murcury had a height based computer sight. The hull which seemed to rise into the heavens from our lowly view point was estimated. The proper distance the line had to rise was calculated in seconds, I hoped. I triggered the magnet tipped bipods, which extended from the gun and felt the weapon attach securely to the hull. I then pulled the trigger. There was a slight cough and hiss as the line silently shot upward. At precisely the correct height it stopped and fell on the rail led by its weighted claw grip. Padded for silence the claws of the Murcury clamped over ther rail and tightened rod straight.

I then pulled the trigger a second time and the titanium-molded steps snapped down from the line. In a second Yan was on his way up. He climbed like scaling hulls was his Olympic specialty. The guard immerged at the sametime, Yan peered over the scuttle relying on his camouflage face paint to remove any flash. Guards are inquisitive by nature or should be. Our immediate adversary was no different. On exiting the galley with a darkish cup of coffee he immediately moved to the rail as the wire from the Murcury was visible against the lights of the town. As he looked over the side Yan's great paw grabbed the front of his shirt, as the Dutchman fired the hypo dart into the guard's chest. The crewman collapsed over the rail, his AK fell into Yan who held the dead weight of the man and gun on his shoulders while bracing against the rail. The coffee cup was out of reach, it plummeted to the water, hurdling down at us almost indiscernible from the darkness around it. The splash might bring a second member of the Parot's crew to the side and then we would have to move immediately with only one man aboard. My hand reached out but Zeke was faster. Youth is a great equalizer. With no trouble at all he picked the cup out of the air and handed it to me. I smiled at his triumphant low laugh and made a mental note to call the Blue Jays when I got home. I believed I had solved their center field problems.

It was now my turn to climb. A hull is a straight up and down affair. The ladder was steady and I was fresh or relatively so. Ascending with the versatility of a cement mixer, I heaved my carcass up hand over hand and regretted every pound I had put on since the Caymans, when I had really gotten into shape. I reached the top heaving and sat down by the stern castle bulkhead. The ship, like all ships, smelled of old food and grease. While Yan got the men up and to their positions. I took one of my high blood pressure pills from its blistex pack and swallowed it with a small drink of water from the flask hidden in my dive suit. Yan motioned me to the edge of the well deck. Here we hid in the shadow of the superstructure where we could watch developments on the pier.

The white Mercedes five-ton rumbled down the road from Front Street, passed the two large marinas that flanked the pier between the Parot and Philpsburg. The road paralleled the eight-foot frost wire fence, which enclosed the pier. The five-ton sung through the gate without slowing. It turned 180 degrees so it faced the gate and stopped only a few feet from Parot's gangplank. The ship's crew emerged from the various parts of the ship but mainly from the starboard side, which allowed the marines to dart the two crewmen who, chose our side of the ship.

The men grouped by the gangway and moved across. There was little talk just the fall of heavy work boots. Two men descended from the truck cab the engine of which was still ticking over. The Pin Pin leader was a heavily muscled man, with a blunt almost emotionless face. The name Pin Pin was derived from the drugs taken by the followers of the grand Au Clair making their pupils degrade to pin pricks.

The man was energetic at this point though. He wore a military type shirt and pants with beret, but was no soldier. Stomping up and down the pier cradling a Danish made Madsen Lar submachine gun on a neck strap like a martinet from a movie the man evaluated the situation. Finally he motioned arrogantly to his partner, a thin obviously frightened man who also had a Lar, to the back of the truck. The thin man wearing an island shirt and Bermuda's his eyes bulging moved to the back door of the truck and opened it with a metallic rumble. Boxes were removed quickly by the crew while the Pin Pin and guards searched the surroundings for trouble.

Crouched by the well deck I carefully removed the Flash Light from its case. This gun like product that looked vaguely like a torch with a pistol grip was attached to a small 4 inch TV. The Flash Light had been originally developed to see through walls by a US University so that police could detect potential threats. This one had been revamped by the

Equipment Section to see through concrete. As to the technique I am not terribly scientific I do know it had something to do with sound waves, infra red rays and ultraviolet. Like the movie cameras that were called back because their infrared technology allowed the owner to see through clothing.

The Flash Light is just another means of removing what little privacy we had left. I can see a time where nudism will be accepted because clothing will have no value in covering your body. Everyone will be able to see you nude, clothed or not. As for me, I don't look at myself any more than I have to and the sight of some people of my acquaintance in the nude is too frightening to contemplate.

To be honest the boxes weren't a big problem. The girls were there all right. The question was, were they the right ones? Best of all there seemed to be no wires or potential booby trap problems. Well, we would see.

The last box hit the deck and I held up seven fingers to Yan. He nodded and brought a small but powerful megaphone to his mouth.

"This is the Netherlands Military, you are surrounded throw down your weapons you are under arrest."

The Pin Pin leader didn't let Yan finish before he

turned the Lar on the boxes. A single shot rang out and the big negro's body jumped then fell like a sack of sand. A bullet hole appeared on the right side of his head with an exit wound the size of a baseball on the left.

The Parot's crew and the thin Pin Pin immediately dropped their guns knowing that the sniper or snipers above, had them hands down. The truck seemed to tilt to its left. Recco, it seemed, had taken the precausion of putting a hole in the front tire. There was a commotion behind and above us as Yan's men cleaned out the stern Castle. There were no shots.

Yan was up and moving I followed stumbling over deck gear. The crew was placed on their stomachs on the deck to be cuffed by the assault team. Zeke slammed his crowbar into the top of the first box smashing the outside lock and prying the front off. Yan's torch spot lighted the interior of the box to show great blue eyes surrounded by a mass of blond hair and a honey brown body that would make playboy center fold weep with despair.

"Oh, ma God, Oh ma God who are youall.' She screamed on the verge of hysteria

The girl was chained to the floor of the box as Yatomi had been to the floor of the shack. She was stark naked the whiteness of her bikini lines defining her sexual areas like a painters brush.

"You're fine this is Lieutenant Yan Trump of the Royal Netherlands Coast Guard. You're going home. Yatomi sent us."

"Oh, Oh thank God. I prayed and prayed. Can I talk to my daddy?" She pleaded.

"Sure, we'll get you out of there first, OK."

"Zeke get some cutters and a blanket." I snarled taking off my wet shirt top and placed as best I could to cover the girl's body.

"It's OK' she said sadly 'Everyone in the world has seem my butt up till now."

"It's not OK. It's your butt and you should have a say in who sees it.If anybody" I sat down next to her and tried to make conversation. The night air was sweet and cool against my naked upper body. A squadron of police cars streamed on to the pier blue flashers spun turning the night into a carnival of lights.

"A female officer rushed over and placed a blanket over Betty Joe.McCalum, Texas cheerleader and ex-captive. Zeke was back with a huge pair of power shears and made short work of the chains.

I took my leave to see if I could find the Sommerset girl. I had just turned when it hit me like lightning; I turned in time to see Yan helping the Betty Joe from her mini-toilet. I got off one word "No!"

Jan at that point saved all our lives by pushing Betty back down. She struggled but I returned and got down next to her.

"Listen,' I said soothingly. 'There might be something in the toilet."

"A bomb, Oh God! Oh God!" Yan was going to hit her but I stopped him.

"Listen, you are in no danger but you might be if you take your tush off that seat. We will just check it out and if there's nothing then you're fine. If there is then we'll remove it."

"What my tush."

"No whatever it is inside.' I laughed she did too but it was tentative and almost hysterical.

"You can't give me straight lines like that, I might take advantage next time." She smiled wanly. I held her hands and smiled at her.

"Yan, listen, there have to be keys to these handcuffs. See if our illustrious skipper can be induced to provide them.

"No problem." said Yan and barked some further orders. He had already ordered the rest of the girls to stay in place.

"Now, I want you to stay still and I'm going to look

around the back of you to see what we have, OK!".

"OK" she agreed. Great tears flowed down a pure American heartland face.

" I turned on the Flash Light and trained it on the toilet.

"Damn," I said it was involuntary. There was a timer I could see the digital numbers displayed clearly through the plastic.

Betty breathed in loudly and passed out. The policewoman caught her and held her on the seat. Propping her against the back of the box.

"What?" said Yan returning with the key's he had found on the dead Pin Pin.

"It's a pressure plate I think. That's C4 pressed into the bottom of the toilet around the base. The toilet was an oval affair and about five inches thick. If it was C4 I could see, then there was enough in this one alone to have chunks of us rain all over Anquila if it went off. If all seven of them went off, it would create a disaster on a level I could not imagine. Of course I wouldn't be there to imagine anything.

For a second! No more then that, I contemplated just leaving Yan with the problem. Just taking a walk over to one of the police cars and going to the other side of the island. I didn't want to die. I thought that my own daughter back home would not have me to comfort her anymore. One look at Betty's defenseless form sprawled against the back of the box and I knew that I could not just leave her.

This of course was my plan. I had set the trap and closed it but the prey was not there, only defenseless children left in death to cover his trail. Au Clair had to know I would be here.

Not Au Clair, of course, Tisani he would be the mastermind. Au Clair didn't have the people to set up this sort of thing. He would never let valuable cargo be transferred all over the world wired like this. Some girl getting off the toilet for a moment just to remove the stress would cause planes to be blown to bits for no reason. No these little presents were specially made and set for this situation. The chains would be measured to insure girls couldn't move.

"Yan do you have a bomb expert? " I asked.

"Yeah, I requested one." The Coast Guard Captain nodded.

Samuel Brokker was short his face was intelligent and he had been a police officer for 12 years. Bomb disposal was part of his training. He had graduated from the Interpole school in Paris with top marks but with the exception of two pipe bombs he had never faced a real explosive device outside of the confines of a school. He looked at the Flash Lights television with real amazement.

"This is fantastic." he said in a soft Island voice. As this was pretty new stuff I wasn't surprised.

" I thinks it's a pressure plate, weight based. " I said.

He looked at me for a moment. As if weighting what I had said. Then Samuel shook his head. His fine features above the heavy lips contracted.

"Also heat based." He said with unshakable calm. 'This seat splits its set on four small piston like supports. See there is a separation where the girl's weight is lifting the edge." Samuel took out a pencil thin torch and looked into the toilet.

I had the policewoman move Betty so her weight shifted as far back as possible to increase the opening.

"So!" the Dutch policeman said exhaling.

"What" Yan looked scared for the first time this happy night.

"It's C4, there is a single detonator, the bomb looks simple but it has at least six wires from the computer control and the detonator. The digital reading is intermittent weight and heat. If the girl comes off, boom! If we place equal weight on it but no heat, boom!

"I bet we could find 100 lbs. of sand, a plastic bag and a heating pad to slip on." I said.

"If the exchange is off just a little, boom!" Samuel was definite.

"Christ on a crutch," I snarled in frustration.

" What should we do?" Asked Yan of Samuel, he was the expert, it was up to him.

"I could cut the wires.' He suggested.

"From what I remember from bomb making 101, two wires and a lead maybe, electricity goes in one out the other?" I asked Samuel nodded he knew where I was going and rubbed his face.

"You say you got six wires. That means a back up detonator."

"Worse,' said the little St. Maartener, 'Its timed. When she took the pressure off, the timer started, ten minutes less now. Also, I think the back up is mercury"

"Well a short life and a merry one, I said to the sky. It was a beautiful night to die on but I had no great want of it. At least the girl would feel nothing.

The hard step of boots brought us up. Peter Zeeland's round face smiled at me.

"Evening, this is Horst Luffe." Horst Luffe was huge, a man of perhaps six foot three inches, he topped Yan which wasn't easy. Horst was in Dutch military uniform without a hat or identification.

"What do you think?" he said to Samuel in a low metallic voice, ignoring the rest of us.

Samuel reiterated the situation."

"You comfortable with this?" Luffe spoke rough English for my benefit.

"I've never done one of these before.' The islander answered honestly. Horst grunted as he got down on his haunches and looked into the separation at the bomb.

"You have long nosed cutters?" he asked.

"Yes." said Samuel.

"Good, look see the red wire?"

"Yes,"

"Cut it." I for one felt my heart enter my mouth.There was an audible snap. We were still here. So far so good.

"Now cut the other one. No the green one.' A second snap followed. 'Take her off. Its all right." Luffe swung up and away to take on the other six bombs.

"Nice fellow,' said Peter, 'part German. Doesn't say much but he's effective.' The little Dutchman smiled wickedly.

"You little fink. I almost crapped myself." I growled.

"You have to have faith."

"In St. Peter of Zeeland we trust."

"You're still breathing, stop complaining." He ended off with a laugh as he followed Luffe.

"Well, fellas we did great,' I said to the others. 'Old Yan here the superhero scaling ships with a single bound with his golden locks blowing in the breeze,' Yan smiled under his blond crewcut.

"Zeke, the next Willie Mays,' The red head smiled a kind of 'aw shucks'. 'Samuel who turned out to be a hell of a plumber." Samuel laughed out loud. 'And Luffe that magnificent bastard who saved all our asses." Nods all around to this one.

"I think you get top price for getting over the railing without us using the crane." Threw in Yan. I laughed and it felt good.

I thanked the boys and walked down the deck to find the Sommerset girl once more. Her bomb was being removed when I stopped. Her long silver blond hair was tangled and her slender face had a trail of tears on it. She stood up unsteadily, once Luffe was finished and hugged her blanket. I lent her my cell phone and showed her how to use it.

She thanked me profusely and called home. The voice on the other end was not used to expressions of passion but it unbent mightily this night.

I left them talking on the phone and made for the gang plank. The clean cut face of Harry Breakleaf evaluated me from the other side. I made no indication I knew my old friend who was assistant to the Governor of the British Virgin Islands. He in turn said nothing. A quick “I’m sorry’, as we passed on the thin wood gang plank was all. Harry made for Audrey Sommerset I knew she would be in good hands.

I exhaled to release tension; fatigue washed over me but it was a good tiredness, one of a job well done and victory. I stretched my shoulder to loosen a knot, my body was telling me my age. I was a little sad our friend Au Clair was not here. In all it had worked out well. I would do my ruminating later now I headed into town for cold beer and some Jump as only the islands and their music can provide.

Chapter fifteen - 8:00 Am, The Beach Between Marigot and Grand Case, St. Martin, French West Indies.

Touching Base

The soft light of morning crept along the surface of the incoming waves. Its gossamer strands warming the air and raising my expectations once more.

Pelicans had been sliding out over the quiet sea, in their squadrons, for an hour or more. One landed to bob on the waves only a few feet away as the sun came full up.

I sat quietly against a tree half sunken in the sand. Its surface weathered grain, the ocean having stripped its bark covering, before pitching it back on the beach.

The tranquility of this moment was a perfect venue in which to thank God, that I was still around, to thank him.

Harry and the Sommerville girl were on their way back to London via Bermuda where the Baronet and his wife would meet them. I knew this, because in a quick turn over at the airport, Harry had taken my lose only on pain of death equipment, back for the government placing it on the special BOAC flight that would carry him home.

Audrey looked fine but wasn't. The little nervous responses, craning her lovely neck to make sure that armed police flooded the area until embarkation, reflected her fear. None of the girls would be right for a long time. Some would never be. The French girl was unable to answer simple questions. Her mind, a seeming blank, was simply repressing a reality she could not control with a complete retreat from it. God help her.

The Republic had moved swiftly flying in a psychiatrist from Martinique who immediately began the slow steps to recovery.

Lothing, Au Clair was simple. There was no space for anything else with the blue eyed hobgoblin. Killing him out of hand would be an equally simple solution. No one would grieve his passing. Many would applaud the act. I caught myself in half thought. Had killing become so simple? Was it balanced on a matter of percentages? On one side, no one cared, for the target, on the other hand, he is a real criminal evil so dispose of the target and solve the problem. No! correction, not target, Person! Breathing individual, real human being with the same small flickering spark you share. A human being that might see the beauty of this morning, as you did, were he here. A man who was loved, perhaps not by a wife or girl friend but in a different way but equally well by another human being. Someone would miss his presence, his smell. My own mother had gotten rid of my father's clothing when the old man died. Not because she did not love him but his smell on these objects made the remembering too painful.

When was a human being throw away? The movies seemed to believe at will. They had used the dead wife and dead partner justification for massive retaliation until it was a cliché. The death of twenty or thirty individuals was equal to the life of a single loved one. Was it? How many people would I kill for my own daughter? As many as need be so the question was mute but then I am a killer. The common man may not be, some people who are trained for this never can kill. In the end they become victims. Faced with death they do not fight back. Like the Jews who were ordered to strip naked and then to stand in line beside a ditch while they were shot one by one. I speak for the victims but does that make me God? Does killing the bad guys because they need it make it right? No! How many of us would die if the negative feelings of our work place associates, acquaintances or wronged wives, were allowed to make us dead. Of course that was different, isn't it always?

McFurson looked into his soul and knew he would never be a victim, never allow himself to just be killed. He would tear at his persecutors with his bare fingers if he could. 'If death is all there is, then it maters how you go.' It was this fact that had made, Yatomi, as frightened as she was, still make the final gamble to come to him. It was this that tied the dragon and the lady samurai's spirits at vortex. Made them one, not sexually, but in raw courage.

At any rate Au Clair was gone. With him went the possible termination of how many people's quiet everyday lives. His mind kept saying this was not his problem anymore but his gut was repulsed by the inability to finish the matter. He would have to take the marbles he had won home and call it even.

The couple materilized out of the corner of his eye. They were mid twenties, the girl was a looker. Light, brightly coloured nylon shell windbreakers hid their bathing suits. The girl had strong athlete's legs, which tended to the white with only a light dusting of a tan which indicated they were new to the island. The man, or boy, had furry hands and legs and a dark Mediterranean look. You would think that the

78-degree heat would make the jackets redundant.

The man went to the water placed his feet in and yelled back, ‘it was great’, in English. They were Americans probably from somewhere in Wisconsin. The girl who had been laying out towels stood at his call. McFurson was hidden from their view by the low dune that had built up around the big piece of wood. From his blind he watched with growing interest.

The girl removed her light blue jacket throwing it away with an unconscious grace. Breathtaking! The shocking pink bikini just covered her perfect body. A ‘C’ cup was awash with soft full flesh. Her face offered delicate features and shoulder length blond hair pulled back from a curved textured neck by the morning wind.

Elegant in profile, subtle cheekbones supported a short turned up nose. The mouth was generous set in a slight frown as if she were concentrating on the boy’s words. Blondie’s head tilted slightly toward the speaker as if there might be some hearing trouble.

Idle hands restlessly tugged at waistband of her bikini bottoms, as if there were some immediate fear of losing them. The bum incased in the bathing suit was small but solid. A lot of hours had been spent at the gym to acquire that kind of balance but at twenty-something it could just be a given. The tummy was flat as a pancake, fronting a waist you could encircle with two hands. Her feet, on the other hand were large with protruding up pointed toes but then something had to support her five foot seven frame.

The boy was back, he kissed her and she responded with equal passion. Lord! Was I ever that young? As they finished he looked up and down the beach with that truant, 'what if', look men get when they want something their not supposed to have.

The boy said something that made her scan the beach minutely. Her face seemed to become two huge blue eyes and reflected real fear. I almost ducked but thought better of it. After all if she saw me that would put an end to something I really shouldn't see but if she didn't, well at least I wasn't hiding. Why did the words 'horse manure' scream to mind?

His blue jacket crumpled beside hers. In one slick movement he removed his royal blue Speedo, and raced for the water yelling ,'Come on,' over his gorilla like shoulder. Blondie's mouth fell open then she laughed like tinkling bells.

"You idiot!" she yelled after him still laughing.

Her hand covered her mouth for a moment and the skin on her cheeks went a beautiful shade of rose. It was kind of nice to find that there was still some modesty left in this Old World.

She looked up and down the beach once more then made a finite decision. Her body seemed to shiver with the fact, even though it had to be close to eighty. Her long fingers reached back and the bra slid away. My mind considered an expletive but rejected it. The word hasn't been forged that covers that kind of wanton magnificence. Pink nipples pointed upward in a savage joy at release as if in reverence to some pagan deity. Committed now she slid the panties off her small hips to her feet. In a moment she was running down the beach.

I could hear the girl talk now in my mind's ear, from back home in Wisconsin. Blondie giggling and then saying to a friend or cousin.

"We went skinny dipping on the beach in St Martin, butt naked in front of God and everyone." Her little memory a special one. A moment's freedom had been stolen from an antique Victorian puritanism. Little does she know, that most areas of the island beaches are clothing optional but that didn't matter. Good for you kid. Be young, it finishes too soon and every moment you lose is unforgiving in its pain. For a moment she stopped at the waters edge to test its temperature with an outstretched toe. In that moment she became part of nature. Framed against the ocean and a blue Caribbean sky, as real and part of it all as the pelicans or the waves themselves.

Many years ago at Woodstock, my generation had made their defining statement. My wife was there but I was not. I remember the film though. The one segment that impressed me was the sight of a group of the revelers wandered down to the pond to bathe. They moved together completely unperturbed by their nudity; men, women and children. I was reminded, while watching the film of a herd of deer or antelope. The truth is we are all part of that moment. Our bodies are no different, nature and our place in it was only a thin manufactured shell away.

Blondie's arrival at the water caused the lovemaking, which the two young Americans were now creating waist deep in the ocean. The girl's legs wrapped around the boy's hips.

'Don't drink the water fish frolick in it.' The sixth grade joke came back to me.

Right or wrong, tainted with the possibility of disease or heartbreak the purity of the act of love is what we are. The need to reproduce ourselves, only one up from survival itself drives us makes us kill, search, spend our treasure, seek and find; made the Au Clair and Jewels of this world rich and powerful. The beauty of the act and its promise had been turned into the oldest profession. What could you do? When the right to choose was removed it became a different sin and one I would not put up with. A prostitute knew and agreed. It might not be morally correct but it was acceptable. Those over eighteen lived it daily. A child could not agree.

I looked away at the sky not wanting to watch. The two kids deserved their privacy. If I got up and walked away it would spoil their moment and I wouldn't do that. So with nothing else to do I lay back against the wood and went back to the Parot.

From the dock I had gone back to the Prince Eugene showered and slept fitfully. This morning after a breakfast comprised of a lemon Danish, half a grapefruit and rich tea, I had called in to the Firm on the Brit line.

The message came back that the mission was finished, I was to go home. I got a congratulation from Granny and above. The French had offered a small medal. Of course we in the Firm are not allowed to accept any kind of decoration. The fact that we don't exist plays a factor . It would be nice to get a medal, oh well.

I was however, to meet Maurice at nine at the Cafe Du James for coffee.

I pictured my wife naked taking a shower. I would watch her sometimes until she caught me. Then depending on her mood, I was either chased away or offered to join her. My equipment was in good order; of course I knew that while watching Blondie who was now lying out a towel next door making love again no doubt by the noises she was making.

I personally subscribe to the philosophy that you should never watch a man eat a big meal if you have no money and are hungry.

So I put the wife away for a moment and returned to the assault on Parot. Au Clair was tipped. There was no way he would let the girls out of his sight otherwise. The fact that he had left the island at the same time we were making the big raid told me it was planned. The hobgoblin didn't want to be here when those little presents he had left went off. He had written the girls lives off along with mine, the assault team, the crew and about a third of the islands population. Someone had made a deal, someone we missed or someone who did not want a messy trial that might bring out a lot of nasty secrets.

The girls had been taken to the hospital in

Philipsburg from the ship and after a complete work up were allowed as much time on the phone as they liked. Happy voices crowded the lines. Parents made arrangements to come and get or receive there lost children.

Happy endings are a poor man's dream. However, this time it had worked out. Good! We could all use that kind of luck.

I had to move soon, my appointment was coming up, I looked at my Epsylon to check the time, then back at the beach. Blondie was back; her sleek body moving with a slow sensual rhythm. Few women project pure sexuality in a walk. It is generated in the hips, the bottom undulating as if to silent music. Blondie's pink nipples moved softly to that internal melody.

My body ached for my wife or perhaps more for the girl. Sexual need distorts the reality. I need to get home and make love on my own bed in the mid-day sprawled in a thrashing heap with a cascade of peroxide blond hair encompassing my lust. I needed the wife to love me. For a moment I thought of Cindy, the sailor, and hated myself. My fall from grace still weighted heavily on me. A deep depression washed out the enjoyment of watching the girl while she nudged something on the sand with her big toe.

The Buddhists say that those who love the flesh are doomed to nothingness as the body dies and rots. Those who love the soul, on the other hand, enjoy the purity of that love forever. Perhaps the memory of this glorious young woman, in this perfect moment, unaware of my gaze, was part of loving the purity of the soul, even if you were not aquainted with the real person. I hoped so because even she would soon begin to fade like a rose in winter but her memory would always live in my heart.

Blondie crouched down to look at the something wagging her full behind at me exposing much more of her then I might have expected. She then looked over her shoulder right at me.

I was caught fair and square. The great blue eyes showed only pity and an arrogant dislike, no surprise. She had known I was there all the time. An audience, had that made the sex more intense. Nothing is pure, I guess. I always hope so but life seems to bluntly correct me each time. I rose and headed for the car, she looked away to the sea, stood and wandered along the shore.

Chapter sixteen – 9:00 A.m., Marigot, St. Martin, French West Indies.

Maurice looked as if he had remained in suspended animation since the day before. The Chief Inspector sat reading, 'La Monde' at the same table, in the same chair. His Kepi had not moved from its place on the white linen surface. A white coffee cup stood at the ready. The blue and white canopy still guarded him from the ever present sun.

St Armand caught sight of me through steel rimed bifocals, as I sauntering up the road toward him. His face soured as he regarded the island "T" shirt and beige shorts. My Panama Jack pulled low, over swept back mirror faced sunglasses. A little too touristy for my mentor perhaps. I smiled.

Brown hands folded the newspaper precisely as if it were a magic trick. Maurice removed his glasses and slipped them into his shirt pocket as if they had committed some offense. Then having checked his watch, he smiled at me and motioned to the waiter who brought a steaming cup of coffee, which arrived as I sat down.

"Well, my dear McFurson it seems we have much to be grateful for. "

"I wasn't blown to bits, I guess that's something to be grateful for?" I said nastily

"Merde, you see tne evil in everything. What if? What if? You're alive be grateful.' He dismissed my complaint with a wave of his hand. 'I on the other hand,' he continued' 'have been commended for the destruction of an odious slaving ring. St. Martin as a loyal territory of the Republic, has been a small part of a worldwide attack on pedophilia on the Internet. I received a commendation directly from the Minister himself for helping remove this stain from the integrity of France.

Add to that the fact, we have removed what little organized crime that existed on the island. I should think we have much to be grateful for?" He smiled at me like a Cheshire cat.

"We have also removed Diamond, one, Rene St Denis, a pimp of Bordeaux of all places, as the head Jewels ring in France. Your people have an excellent idea who the patron in Britain is and our friend Langandly has given us other links." Maurice was exuberant. I was less so.

"Someone tipped Au Clair, Maurice."

"I am sure you wouldn't accuse me?" The Chief Inspector's voice became brittle with anger.

"Oh! Of course not. The fact that his trial might bring some nasty realities to light had never crossed my mind." I ended with cold precision while removing my hat and shades.

"Really! Good!' Maurice said with equal candor. 'I can assure you, the tip, as you call it, did not come for me."

"The Dutch then?"

"Who knows? " Maurice gave a Gaulic shrug that spoke volumes.

"Crap, you got together with the Netherlanders and made Au Clair a deal.'

"Why would I do that? My men were at that ship too if you remember."

"I don't think you figured on the little presents he left but, yes, the words 'double cross' gallop to mind." I didn't give ground and he was furious.

"What does it matter, we won, is that completely lost on you?"

"No! And if Au Clair were just a simple crook I'd say fine. But he will find a place where he can hold up until other things take our attention away and then he'll be in business again."

" I can only deal with what is in my jurisdiction." Maurice said evenly without remorse "Au Clair isn't here. You must remember you filled my plate with a great deal of trouble. I have brought the situation to a suitable and successful conclusion. I will not be accused of wrongdoing. Remember there is still the matter of the Japanese. ' He added testily.

"Mon Dieu, I even suggested you receive a decoration.' Maurice seemed frustrated to no end and I became a little more conciliatory. After all he had made the decision that caused the least negative fall out. Granny would have done the same. I, as always, am a pawn in greater things. In this case it had turned out well.

'Thanks, I heard about the medal." I said honestly.

"You did not accept it, were you that insulted?" The old policeman asked with real pain that his gift had been so meanly pushed away.

"My agreement with the British does not allow me to accept." I looked at my hands.

"Ah! Of course." Maurice seemed to accept this explanation.

"Its Tisani and his little canisters that are driving me nuts." I sipped the hot coffee, found it bitter and set it down again.

"On that issue I have had some luck." Maurice brightened immensely being able to address the real problem "It seems the manager of Ignace has a habit of keeping samples of everything they make. He didn't feel a canister more or less would matter."

Maurice took what looked like an exaggerated aluminum horse pill from the seat next to him and placed it on the tablecloth. The metal tube was fourteen inches long and perhaps four inches across. The ends were rounded, the skin smooth. The only variance was a box like protrusion on one side with what looked like a space for a digital watch face. At the moment the opening yawned empty. On the other side were two magnets, large ones, three inches by three inches were inset into the aluminum of the body. Half way down a thin line in the metal indicated a point where the tube could be unscrewed.

"Anything in it?" I asked Maurice, who was watching with interest, shook his head to the negative. I unscrewed the pill and looked at the insides. The interior surface was darker than the skin and on touching it, I knew it had been coated with a polymer or resin.

Putting the halves together I placed it back on the table.

"That's really interesting Maurice. Very good work on your part." The Chief Inspector smiled benevolently.

" What's your opinion Maurice, off the record of course."

"Hmm,' Maurice handled the object as if looking at

it closer might give him a better reading. 'Explosives perhaps."

"C4, will adhere to anything why cover it? " I asked.

"Aluminum does not deteriorate my friend. You could make a surprise a long time from now." He said sagely 'Whatever is placed in the cylinder won't lose its strength." He added.

"Why the coating?"

"Something nastier.' He paused " I'm sorry, I am just an old policeman, the world leaves me farther behind every day."

"You're a cagey old fox.' I said with a slight smile. 'We have to get Au Clair and if not him then Tisani because this stinks." I considered the possibility of every type of death dealing chemical and explosive out there the potential was endless and frightening.

"I have informed every Western nation, Interpol, CIA and the UN. We can do little more." Maurice commiserated

"My people would like to take a look at this thing." I said finally.

"We will send you a complete evaluation after it's been studied in Paris." Maurice agreed.

"Maurice don't sit on this. It's really important.' I hesitated, 'You said that when someone killed for a cause, it was based on the fact, that they believe it was right without reservation, Tisani believes. I've been up against that kind of belief before. Death becomes immaterial. Tisani is not some simple fanatic. He is a competent player.

"I will make sure those involved understand this.' Agreed Maurice, then with fatherly honesty, 'You, on the other hand have nothing to do. Enjoy the time with your Japanese friends. Everything is as the Americans say is 'on the house.'"

10:24 A.m., Prince Eugene Hotel, St. Marrten Netherlands West Indies.

It was silent in the room. I stripped off my cloths and lay naked on the bed. Pain stalked my tired body. There still was blood in my urine from the punch in the kidneys Ray had landed two days ago, although the Dutch doctor said it would pass. The ugly deep purple bruise was a visible and tender reminder of the experience. I lay out and tried to get comfortable. Strained muscles waled their pained story to my brain like a Delhi beggar in search of baksheesh. The wreck of the Titanic must have looked like a game land ride next to me.

I should call home soon. I wanted to see Shojiro

Katsuda and Yatomi before they left but sleep wafted over me like a soft, kindly friend. In the end fatigue won out and I drifted into a golden mist.

About an hour later I awoke gently to some outside noise. Adrenaline shot through me and I grabbed the 50 Automatic from the table beside the bed removing the safety. No! Everything was as it had been. The door was locked from the inside, the chain in place and the travelers friend a small metal door jam inserted into the bolt hole next to the door knob, had not been disturbed, or perhaps had withheld against the force of an intruder.

I got up and went to the door, opened it and looked out. There was no one on the balcony. Nothing !Interesting! Remembering my nakedness I closed the door. My scent for trouble was very sensitive, it has to be. Normally I know when I am being watched. There was no little twinge now. Perhaps it was nothing but a good dose of paranoia will keep you alive.

During a long steamy shower, the hot water drained the pain and most of my nerves away Afterwards, dressed in a white island shirt and blue-bathing boxers I went out to the little gray Renault.

In the interim I had raised the Brit. COM site of the

week and checked in. Nothing more had come up. I was clear to leave the next day.

Next, I called home through the Cleveland cut off. The wife was waiting for me. We discussed mundane things like bills and so on. I suggested we have sex when I got back and received a half-positive feminine reply. The kids available burbled down the line about their baseball games and swimming lessons, the little things that made life worth living, at least for me. I said goodbye until the morrow.

At the car the game started. I zapped the car with my watch for bugs and found nothing. There was no tail, back or front. I drove about from place to place, no sign of the opposition, if there was any. Sure, I had done all that was possible, I ended up at the beach to see if anyone showed up. I had scanned my clothing for a tag before leaving the room. If they were there they weren't coming to play. No helicopter. Of course if they were big league they could spot me from a satellite but if that were true they would have finished this at the hotel.

The St. Martin Royal is a group of three bedroom single story villas perched over a magnificent view of the Caribbean. Red tile roofs and luxurious extended balconies pampered the guests by offering an option of steps or an elevator to the beach. In the center of the almost pure white sand, sheltered beneath the overhanging accommodations, was a large bar surrounded by bright muli-coloured umbrellas. Here I found Shojiro Katsuda ensconced behind a glass-topped table with a cold Heineken at hand and a large ham sandwich with all the trimmings, which he was about to enjoy.

My arrival was met with a cold-eyed police officers evaluation. I bowed to Shojiro who stood and responded with a bow that brought him up with his head just a little lower then mine.

" Katsuda San?' I asked.

"McFurson San." He returned with a smile. ' Am I so easy to identify?"

"You are the only Japanese here."

"Hai,' he smiled sheepishly. Then in Japanese 'I apologize profusely."

"How did you recognize me." I said in return.

"The hat." My turn to look foolish. ' We are now even.' I said with a laugh and shook his preoffered hand. It was strong and dry.

"Please sit" He was having problems with the words. ' A drink, yes?'

"A Coke is fine." The waiter came over and I

ordered another ham sandwich with fries.

A quick scan of the surf and there was Yatomi coming out of the water her raven hair, wet and stringy. She waved and smiled but stayed by the shore wanting her father to get to meet me as men will. The silver Budweiser one piece bathing suit, kind of surprised me. It seemed a little skimpy but that was none of my business.

"We owe you much, McFurson San." Shojiro started hesitantly as if he had a speech memorized for the occasion.

"Call me Mike and you owe me nothing." I said.

"Please call me Shojiro, Mike San. You have killed two men for my daughter.' He said 'You must pardon me if I disagree but this is a great matter."

"I did what was necessary' I replied with finality and changed the subject. 'I hear congratulations are in order. You are a Sergeant now."

"Yes!' he said embarrassed.' If I deserve such a high office, is the question, as you say." Concerned eyes looked out to sea. Deep in an uncomplicated man was great complication. The war that raged was about killing and if it was necessary. I decided to let him talk about it if he wanted to.

"Removing a major crime figure provides opportunity for promotion." I suggested.

Shojiro laughed bitterly.

"It seems that hard work and honesty is not required to achieve promotion Mike San, only the ability to kill. We seem to place too much emphasis on killing. The hero's of books and movies now are assassins. People seem not to understand it is murder with a coat of paint, they are applauding. ' Shojiro considered the next sentence for a moment as if it were the most important thing of all. 'You must know McFurson San, that at the end when I had the opportunity to kill because it was right and not legal. Harada tried to shoot me. I fired at him within the law. At least my conscience is quiet in that matter."

"He needed killing if that is any conciliation Shojiro San."

"No! He was a man who should have the right to trial. In my country a man is innocent until proven guilty. It is the difference, Mike San, between he and ourselves."

"Who speaks for the Yatomis and the Kaoris of our world Shojiro San? I would kill again for them. Kaori was a child and he crushed her. She died without reason and I am as guilty because of my incompetence." I finished bitterly.

"You confuse the best possible action with the impossible. Kaori would feel her death was important if it had reason. The reason she died was to destroy the evil that harmed her and many others. Her death and that of her family, will bring them great face before their ancestors. All of us must die, McFurson San, without reason it is just death. With reason it is more, it has meaning."

"Life is a raindrop." I said

"Yes, unless it freshens `the ground so that greater things can grow."

"Then Harada should have great face because he died so that innocent children could live free." I finished bitterly.

I meandered down the beach to where the silver samurai sat on the base of a palm, which had bent almost parallel with the sand. Yatomi dried her hair and tried to comb through it. The pain of doing so contorted her face.

"So Samurai another enemy to fące." I made a poor attempt at a karate position. She smiled.

"It is difficult to pull the comb through. " She admitted.

"Here give it to me I've got a daughter of my own and it's the only thing I do well for her." I removed the comb and slowly drew the plastic teeth through her thick black hair. At the bottom I adjusted the angle to pull through the knots.

"You did well I felt nothing."

"You try, it is all in the wrist."

"You seem to know everything." She teased.
"We dinosaurs usually do." She laughed again but louder and more freely.
"So you're going home tomorrow.' I said witlessly
"Yes! It will be hard after all this excitement but I will find a way." The sadness was back.
"You're going to be fine, your dad is a great guy and he won't let anything happen to you."
"There has been an agreement that we will be left alone. "
"That's nice." I said with a certain sarcastic snap.
"You do not understand. What was done to me has lost face for the local criminals. They have interrupted the 'Wi" of our country."
"I don't understand." I said honestly.
"Hai!' Yatomi admitted and thought a little. ' Wi, is what we are in Japan. It is the ability of the whole to interact with the individual. It is the politeness, the acceptance of incorrect action, which may not be yours. The blame must fall correctly. Wi is what binds my people. It defines what we should do or might do and what cannot be done. Those who ignore Wi are in peril and can be removed from the group. When the Yakuza took me they damaged Wi, as I am the child of a policeman. No matter how evil or good my father, they stipulated that no

Policeman's child or family is safe. There are many concessions that are made on both sides so that Wi will remain in place and that the flow, which Wi is, will not be interrupted. The senior Yakuza accepted this mistake as his own and has corrected it. It will give him much face; the police will gain much face for demanding he do so. I, a single girl, have no real value but I have my life and my father his. Wi is supported and assured. Life then can continue without ripples in the pond.

"On behalf of all us goldfish at the bottom we are pleased." I Bowed.

"You tease." She smiled. "Also I am only a girl not a samurai. It is incorrect to call me this it is an important title and should not be joked about."

"You have the heart of the samurai, although you do not see it.' I said 'the everyday is sometimes more powerful then the momentous. When you were called on to face the enemy you did so better then many men would."

"Did I ever tell you the story of the girl who was made a samurai because she killed a dragon?" I asked straight faced, as I watched a single gull glide out on the afternoon air.

"No! She said I would like to hear the story." Yatomi was all polite interest.

"There was a village on the edge of a hill near Mount Fuji. A dragon lived on the top of the hill, in a cave. Sometimes the dragon would spit fire on the village and parts of it would burn. Crops would be lost the people killed. The land was good and the villagers didn't want to move so they stayed.

A girl lived in the village. She was very intelligent and beautiful. She had long black hair and a silver bathing suit."

"You tease" Yatomi giggled.

"It is very incorrect to interrupt." I said.

"I apologize very much." She said unable to hide her smile.

"Hai!' I said modified, and continued. 'Anyway the girl realized she must do something or the villagers would starve or burned so she went to the top of the hill.

When she got there she said to the Dragon 'What'sa matter for you?' She came from the Italian part of the village." Yatomi laughed uncontrollably.

"I thought there were a lot of Italian Japanese?" I said very intensely.

"No!' She shook her head and laughed covering her mouth, which I aped, which in turn made her laugh even more.' I think your story is in the wrong place."

"Hai! I was confused' I said. 'You are right, she didn't say that. She bowed deeply and asked the dragon politely why he was breathing fire on the village?"

"Hai!" Yatomi agreed to the correction.

"And he had her for lunch."

"Oh! Your story has a sad ending." She said very concerned

"And they had sushi and vegetables.' Caught out by the joke she laughed again and shook her head to say I was crazy.

"It happened the dragon had a bad cold. Every time he sneezed he set fire to the village. He apologized but he had to sleep because he wasn't feeling very well. While he was asleep the girl considered what must be done to save the village. Quickly she took two large corks and stuck them up the dragon's nose.' Now Yatomi really was laughing.

'When the dragon woke up he sneezed and blew himself up." Yatomi was shaking with laughter. Shojiro had come down while I had been speaking to listen and he also laughed and shook his head. I was a little embarrassed to get caught out.

'Anyway the village was saved, the villagers ate roast dragon until they all became vegetarians and the girl was made a samurai for being smart enough to defeat her enemy by making two corks out of an oar." Yatomi thanked me for my story and wiped her eyes.

I watched the two of them Shojiro nonchalantly touched his daughter shoulder. The love in his eyes was so intense I felt like a total stranger, which of course I was. The story was to make Yatomi laugh, she needed to laugh a great deal, there was so much to forget. Both of these very special people needed to escape for a while and so I decided to take them to Never, Never Land for the afternoon.

The drive across the island brought us to Cul du Sac. A white-faced casino like house, sits just before the small pier and the bumboat that took us to Penl Island.

The surface of the lagoon is dotted with moored yachts. The island is the home of one of the most beautiful coral reefs on St. Martin.

Kit the Australian instructor told us how to snorkel. The Katsuda's were a rapped audience. I had been there before. Finally, we were in the water. Fortunately, there was no cruise ship in that day and we had the place to ourselves. I watched from the surface as Yatomi swam down to play with the Angel fish and a small ray, which shot away from her. Kit showed her how to feed the fish. She floated there surrounded as the local inhabitants who darted in for a free meal. Shojiro took pictures of Yatomi with an underwater camera I had bought and had me take pictures of the two of them. Yatomi's hair fanned out around her head like a mermaid's. She was very beautiful there in her undersea world.

After a while I went up to the beach and had a beer with Lance, another of the instructors. After an hour Kip and the Katsudas joined us. Yatomi took some shells from the beach your not allowed to take anything from the reef itself so that others can enjoy it. After a drink and some talk we went back to the hotel.

Shojiro now took his turn. He and Yatomi offered to take me to dinner. I suggested the Turtle in Grand Case, which has some of the best seafood in the Indies. Dress is casual and the service is very good. Louie who owns the place, is originally a Bulgar but the chef is a Cordon Blue.

The atmosphere is tropical and a little over done but then the tourists demand that sort of thing. Marlin steaks are served with a white sauce that is delicate and kisses the meat with a taste you have to experience to understand. Shojiro who likes seafood as most Japanese do enjoyed the meal, which was blessed with very good white Chablis.

The desert tray is another experience. Chocolate Mousse is an adventure not the ending to a good meal. Yatomi ate well but was full of questions about the island and the people so she could tell her friends back home.

It was now dark. Shojiro thanked me and said they should return to the hotel for a quiet night before the grueling trip in the morning. I disagreed and we piled into the car for one more stop.

Juan's house is a white block on the hillside. The heavy walls surround the garden as if the house had been removed from a Roman street and placed on the island intact. Juan is a short solidly built man with a large soccer ball head and a steady smile. We had known each other in Mexico long before. I should perhaps have come here when we were in danger but Juan has a big family and I would not place them in the line of fire. I owe him too much.

"Hey man, how come you didn't call me when you were in the hole?" Juan smiled and hugged me.

"Cause you don't move so good now you put on two hundred pounds." I kidded.

"This is muscle hombre.' Juan patted his ample paunch.

"A lot of something is something." I agreed.

"Hey, be nice or you go home." He said in mock anger.

Juan greeted the Katsudas with the open heart that is common to his people.In the garden we were seated and offered more food. I taught Shojiro how to drink Tequila. The Japanese policeman agreed he had met his match. This was stronger than saki and probably caustic. However, after salt, lemon and two more drinks he was feeling good, his taste buds had taken a permanent vacation.

I love salsa music and Juan's son and brother in law were part of a quartet that spun out a Latin rhythm in the far corner of the courtyard. The crowd was dancing and the beat was calling. I was up and on the floor.

Juan and his friends were kind to an old fat gringo. Quela, a girl so black she seemed part of the night and I began to move to the music. It was fun but I am not what I was. Hell, I was never, what I was. Watching her body move to the tempo was a joy, to intertwine with her slipping in and out of each other's grasp in the grip of the music's force was pure pleasure. Finally, the music stopped and I bowed pouring sweat and truly grateful.

The night was cool thankfully. The band started a plaintive Spanish melody slow enough to waltz to. With a cavalier strut I came over to the table and asked Yatomi to dance with a great flourish and courtiers bow. This brought sarcastic applause from Juan and his wife.

"Bravo, Bravo, encore, encore." Juan kidded and I smiled back with equal sarcasm

Yatomi looked at her father who nodded and she stood. Shojiro had packed quickly the dress Yatomi wore was plain blue but cute and set off by a small white jade on a chain about her neck. As young women are, she was exquisite. Hesitantly, at first but with a flow as she began to have confidence in my abilities, we danced around the red paved court. Her smile was so genuine. This was her first real escape from the regimentation of Japanese life and she was enjoying everything wholesale. The waltz ended and the salsa was back, with one deft movement I grabbed Juan's grandson of approximately the same age as my samurai and stood back. Yatomi's terror was quickly replaced with a shy smile as the tall, good looking boy swept her away with the music. The beat takes you and Yatomi was no different. Her hips started to flex to its hypnotic control. I returned to the table with Anna an old friend of Juan's and a widow. I received a nod of approval from Rene, Juan's wife. I got Shojiro up before he could really refuse. Karaoke is one thing, the Lambada is something different all together. The tequila and his debt to me, overcame his fears.

He bowed and slid out on to the floor with Anna. Soon both Katsudas were having the time of their lives or at least I hoped so. I sat drinking with Juan, exchanging insults and jokes reminiscing about the old times.

By early in the morning when we left Shojiro had definitely bonded. He hugged Juan, the huge sombrero he had admired for its silver work, perched solidly on his head, a gift from tubby Mexicano. The Japanese policeman gave Juan his jade ring he had nothing else to give and the exchange of gifts was important between friends. Shojiro wasn't very drunk but genuinely happy.

At the hotel Shojiro went into the room after wishing me good night. I pitied him the hangover he could expect with the morning light but then.,we all pay for the things we do somewhere down the line. Yatomi hugged herself and swayed a little from side to side as if the night had been to short.

"So Samurai this is good bye." I smiled.

"You are a special friend, Dragon. You come out of the night and save me and disappear into the night after giving me so much."

"Better none of this happened you would have had a nice quiet life and never been teased.

"This has been a bad time. I was very lucky, others were not. I have thought about this much and awake in fear at night thinking I am still in that box. It will take time to have the memories go away. It is too soon and too deep now but you have helped. Tonight has helped. This was a day to remember. I will never forget you Dragon but I fear we will never meet again."

"Oh! You never know. We dragons get around. I might come and visit my cousin under your gray city." Yatomi smiled.

"If you dance like tonight with your cousin my poor gray city will be no more." She smiled at her own joke.

"I am sure he is far too well mannered for that." I joined in but it was time.

"Farewell samurai." I said finally.

"Farewell dragon." She said and kissed me on the cheek. I turned away and made for the car not being able to see her tears.

Chapter seventeen - 2:30 A.m, The Prince Eugene Hotel, The Lowlands St. Maarten, the Netherlands West Indies.

Ti Buddy and Home.

The airport was still lit up but there was very little action. Flights wouldn't start leaving until later this morning. I was tired and I had drunk way too much. My blood pressure, which had been taking a beating over the last, two or three days, would be telling so me soon. I had napped earlier but that didn't count. I would sleep for whatever time was left tonight and then again on the plane tomorrow. Of course my route would not be directly home. The route would be a round about journey with lots of cutoffs. Cutoffs in the jargon ment side trips or visits to preset locations where escapes from the followers could be organized. This meant I would have lots of time to rest before running into my local marketing clients on Monday.

The night was cool and soft around me. I meandering around the pool, which fronted the hotel, looking out to sea. Only the waves were visible slowly lapping up to the shore. Their white toes seemed to dig into the sand, then vanish reluctantly, back to there sourse. I have always loved the sound of the ocean, I would miss it.

I took out my key and mounted the steps. At the top I froze. The lamp infront of my room was out and a body was silhouetted, against the light of the breezeway, seated in one of the two plastic courtesy chairs provided to each guest. I put my hand on the reassuring steel grip of the 50 Automatic and moved forward staying close to the wall.

I heard the laugh and knew it was Ti Buddy before he spoke.

"Have no fear ami, I will not harm you but I have enemies and the lights are very good for visibility." He said amiably.

I got closer and found he was slouched down with his legs stretched out before him.

I was clearly visible. I moved closer to him ,so that the darkness about, the broken bulb gave me some protection. If he had someone hidden it would be out toward the beach and if they had an infrared sight I was toast anyway.

"You did not keep your part of the bargain, ami, Au Clair be alive and gone away."

"Maybe if you gave me some real information. I might have done better." I suggested.

"The information I gave you was as new as possible." He shrugged.

"Your information was old when it was new. Those girls were never at the defense fortress. Just a couple of Pin Pin left there to divert the authorities. I presume that allowed our friend Tisani to create those little packages under the girls. Who the hell are you anyway? You're sure as hell tied into Au Clair somewhere. Are you one of the lost boys too?"

" No! I am what I am, why lie?"

"I think old Jewel is a pretty slick operator. I think he sees things in the sense of backup. Au Clair is a screw up. He made a lot of mistakes in a short while. I think Jewel just likes to have someone to watch over his children. Big brother maybe?"

"Your wrong." He said but that was the third time he had put his thumbs together when he lied.

"Crap, was that you who came to the door this afternoon?"

"Yes that was me." He smiled. At least a little truth no thumbs this time.

"You fancy me or was it just a social call?" the conversation was about to change to the negative. Calculations as to what would occur were already running through my head.

"I wanted to talk to you. You didn't come to the door so I left. Then your friends in the Jetta followed me. So I drove around until they lost interest." No lie on that one either. Who was in the

Jetta? Ti Buddy thought I had set him up using Dutch tails or perhaps my own people. It wasn't Say he knew Ti Buddy. The Dutch would also know him and know where he would go, unless they were using off Island people.

"What colour Jetta?" Something was nagging me but I couldn't place it.

"Black." Ti's eyes met mine in the half darkness. The colour was a bad one for the islands it held heat and let off cool. A white car was better, it reversed the process. Only tourists or those with limited sense would drive one. I had seen a black Jetta, where?

Christ there was one on the beach this morning. It was the only car there next to mine. That meant Blondie and her friend was following Ti because he had tried to make contact with me.

Jewel would want to know about me. Blondie and her lover partner were keeping an eye on me. The cutoffs home would have to be extended. This of course answered a lot of questions.

I must have heard Ti's visit but because of the deep sleep, I had missed him. That was why there was no one to follow me when I went to the Katsudas, they were off elsewhere.

"You see them tonight?" I asked.

"No! But they're yours you should know."

"They aren't mine and their not island police. They could be CIA, those gits are into everything. However, if you picked them up they would have to be real amateurs, you wouldn't have twigged to the Yanks."

" Jewel?" he said shaken

"A girl with blond hair and a swarthy man early twenties?" I asked.

"Yes!"

"Who told you about the fortress?"

"One of Au Clair's people." More truth, it seems that our Au Clair had started his own false trail.

"You think they want to kill you?" Ti Buddy asked off handedly

"I don't think so."

"If they've seen you Ti, they will figure out who you are and where I get my information, poor as it might be. Were, I you, I would arm myself because they might be lightweight but they also could be deadly. I didn't pick them up this morning and I should have." I turned on Ti Buddy, there was a lot I needed to know before this was over and he had lied to me.

"You were telling me how you were tied into Jewel." It came out in a crewel snap. Ti Buddy sat up quickly. I aimed the Automatic at his chest always make sure you do the job.

"Don't!' I demanded. Ti froze with his hand under his shirt, he had not expected the gun. Or he had expected a different outcome.

'You fire and I'll take you with me at this distance I can't miss." I threatened.

"A standoff, ah.' he said ' I don't want to kill you."

"Good, I don't want to die. Tell me about Jewel."

"I know him from before. The racket Au Clair was running be mine. I set it up, not so big but very profitable. White runaways they come down here with their pimps. I pick them up for a sou and sell them for big money. I sold some to Jewel. Then they came in and took it." Ti Buddy was angry and it made his speech quick and slurred.

"You didn't try to take it back."

"Jewel is in with the Colombians. I don't play with those fools. They kill your whole family back to your dead relatives. Them they dig up and shoot just for luck.' Ti literally shook with the thought. Then continued. 'So I waited for my time. I worked for him on the side. They think I am a punk but I live and plan. Then you come. Mon Dieu, where did you leave your white horse. You believe it's wrong, high and mighty. You're with the British you're neutral, so I used you." He finished with a shrug

"Now they know you were in with me. You've got one way to get yourself out of this. I want to know where Au Clair and or Tisani are. You tell me and I'll make sure they get taken care of." I had the upper hand but I wasn't sure that was enough.

"I give you that for what. You did nothing last time."

"You didn't help me. You gave me bad information and you're mad because I didn't do a miracle for you? Christ the Gall.' I changed direction, 'What do you lose by telling me, if Jewel is in with the cartel you need friends." Jewel might have intimated he was in with the cartel but I didn't think he had any input there. The Colombians were drug dealers not pimps. The money in this little scam was peanuts next to their main source of wealth. They were too busy making sure that worked to get involved here. Of course Ti Buddy was small time he would not have the overview. While he had a lucrative idea, his own limited vision and fears had been his downfall. Jewel had screwed him royally.

Ti looked at me and made his decision, it would be purely tactical.

I wondered if Blondie and Co had caught Ti. If so he might have come here to kill me or make a deal I would find out which real quick.

"I won't leave my island. This be my place." Ti Buddy had come to me for the simplest of reasons help and for the bassest of emotions the need for survival. When our friends latched on to him, he ran scared.

"I don't know where Tisani is but Au Clair went home, back to New Orleans and his dada." He almost spit the words out.

"How much trouble will he be in?" I asked trying to figure out what could be done.

"A son fass.' Said Ti Buddy with a certain glee. 'He made the deal with the Flick and he was the one behind the bombs that didn't work. He lost the merchandise and ran like a liked a wipped dog. I don't think he will get a hug." Ti laughed but it was flat and tired.

"Anything else that might help me? "I asked.

" I don't know much about Jewel. Nothing about New Orleans."

"Tisani's shipment?" I grabbed for straws.

"It left by plane but no one knew where. It will move around a little before it be in the place." I don't know the place. Truth again, damn it!

"Fine, you want to call it even?"

"What will you do now."

"I have to check in, you know the drill someone

else will make the decision.' I hesitated then ' Did they catch you today?"

"No!" he also ducked his head when he lied.

What did that tell me? Someone wanted me to know Au Clair was in New Orleans." It was time to close it down.

"So we call it even right?" I said with an edge.

"Sure!' Came his reply. He rose and backed away then stopped. "Would you help me. If they come?" The fear was tangible. Question, did I owe him anything, no? I wanted it over so I improvised.

"Go to the governor's house on the British Virgins and give them your name. They will take care of you." This thin hope seemed to pick him up right away. He immediately moved away from me backward along the terrace and disappeared. I would see Breakleaf placed him in the first prison cell available and brought charges against him for slavery and prostitution of a minor. Ti would plead no contest to it if he was smart before the French required his extradition. He was useless to Say or anyone else but his death would also serve no purpose.

I left everything in the room no telling what interesting surprises were in there. In minutes I was shifting the stick in the Renault and was away.

12:35 Home

A Quiet Place

The smell of sex permeated the quiet room. I was still floating in the golden balance of internally manufactured drugs that created the nirvana, which is the product of full-unfettered intercourse. I was still sweating. I could feel her sweat in the hair on the back of my head.

My pillow was her full buttock. I reached down to caress her leg with my right hand moving the rumpled used up floral sheets. She made a little feminine noise deep in her throat.

I turned my head and the smell of her skin struck me sweet and powerful. The simple scent of her always turned me on. My equipment was being reinforced for immediate action stations. I began to kiss the small of her back. Little nerve ends hide here in a fan based on the top of her bum and moving upward to the mid back. I sucked the skin, not to harshly, just enough to activate the pleasure points. I heard the cats purr of her enjoyment.

"Don't you ever sleep." She grumped.

" Neither snow, nor wind, nor dark of night will deter this messenger from his appointed rounds." I spoke verbatim the promise of the Persian mail service from a century before Christ. I had always loved the words and the simple brave promise in them.

"You ready for a delivery." I bit her a little on the buttock.

"You God damned postmen are all crazy as hell."

Two smiling blue eyes looked imp like from under a curtain of blond hair.

I began to kiss and lick my way up to her face. The wife turned then moving her full body to me. Hips locking, her mouth on mine, bringing our two bodies together in a soft glove of flesh. Then as I took off hammering her body she responded in kind. Her strong full form with its powerful thighs meeting me again and again into oblivion.

For a moment we lay exactly still allowing each other a moment to relax. The kids would be home soon and the football game would be starting soon. The Steelers were taking on the Seahawks in the NFL and the Argonauts faced Calgary in the CFL. I would have to choose.

We rearranged our bodies so the wife lay on top of me between my open legs her blond head on my chest. I ran my fingers up and down her back softly and tenderly. The soft little gold hairs split as my fingers covered every part of her. She pressed her full breasts on my chest. Moving her body softly against me with the sensations I created in her back.

"Your going away again." she queried

"Yes!' I answered, 'in two days'. The trip home had been torturous. The watchers had been there but they had been taken care of. No one knew where I was. I would have to go to New Orleans. I knew why too. I had a lot of work to do to make ready but today I would do nothing.

Vacant thoughts slid by. The middle ones marks were down I would have to speak to him. I would go to mass at five.

A couch and a quiet afternoon at home are a wonder if you haven't had them for a while.

"Was it bad this time." She asked.

"Yes! But I got a lot done and helped some people who would have been toast if I hadn't stepped in."

Her fingers touched my bruise and I jumped with the pain she had a little girl look she showed sometimes, she gave me that now and then the' you poor creature' look then she kissed me hard.

"Are you coming back from this one? Don't go."

"I have to. Sometimes there aren't any choices.' I said as honestly as possible. 'Don't worry everything is worked out and all I'm doing is delivering a message. Then I'll come right home for another delivery." I knew it was a trap, Jewel wanted me on home ground, and Granny had placed me there. I was the goat for Jewels lion but victory or death the family would be covered.

The wife sobbed on my shoulder for a long time. We said no more about it. She knew she could not stop the flow of my life. I had decided on its direction and must follow the stream to its end.

Chapter eighteen - 9:30 A.m., Monday, New Orleans, Louisiana, USA

The Father of Waters

Old Man River is brown. The silt he carries to the Gulf of Mexico colours his surface. The Mississippi is cleaner now. At one time it was so polluted that areas of it would spontaneously combust covering parts of the river with flames.

I have traveled its path in times past. Up from the Gulf past the refineries and the ships parked in lines awaiting entrance to the Big Easy. Up past mothballed aircraft carriers and cruise ships waiting to be recalled to service or the nackers yard. I see the pathos in the waiting, others do not, perhaps it is age.

The Big Easy, New Orleans itself, is a truly great city, surrounding an ancient Spanish-French heart. The Delta Airlines 737 swings into the New Orleans International Airport dropping down gracefully kissing the tarmac, settling with little trouble into the sweltering September heat. I walk the required miles to obtain a shuttle to the Empirium New Orleans Airport, a fifteen story white tower that neighbours the largest landing field in Louisiana.

If I am seen there is no tail but I have the twinge and know I am already behind in the game.

An Olympic size swimming pool, huge lounges, and a large Parisian style sidewalk restaurant center the huge atrium central lobby of the Empirium. America has become rainless streetscape; a movie set reality, football and opulence for the minority. The middle class still exists but the pendulum is swinging. The three richest Americans hold wealth equal to the poorest 100,000,000 of its citizens. The difference in this country is that anyone can still rise as high up the ladder, as they want or can.

Bubba's inability to curb his sexual needs is splashed across every newspaper front page. Meanwhile, his popularity ratings rise exponentially, to my amazement and amusement. I purchase a Picayune to thumb through later.

A credit card is required to quell the fear, on the part of the innkeeper, that I might bolt in the night. The bellboy smiles a great deal, resplendent in black and gold, he talks about the city. I listen and don't. The room is large white and sterile. I can see Lake Pontchartrain as a cusp in the distance. My tip to the talkative little Frenchman is more than required. I once worked on a furniture truck during a summer in between years at university. I understand the value of a gratuity, many that have never worked with their hands, don't. He thanks me and suggests that if I need anything I should just ask. I don't have to; I don't need a lady of the evening or any artificial stimulant.

I sit in the wine-coloured wing chair by the bed and remove my shoes. The room smells neutral. I think of the smell of my wife and an article I had read. The gist of what it said was, we meet eight people in our lives, that we could be happy with for the duration. As one of the few who lucked out, I am grateful. It is my opinion that scent has a great deal to do with it. Being in close proximity to my lady can make me horny. The perfume of her body, not the three days without a shower and no underarm variety but the day to day odor at the back of her neck still drives me nuts.

For the moment the room is a fortress. It is the same as all other rooms in all other cities. American sameness tends to dominate our world. A nice double bed, the obligatory television, this one encased in cherry wood . Chairs and lamps that were purchased en mass for savings. Bright prints make the room a little warmer. They depict large Southern homes with wide gardens in full bloom. Gracious ladies of the 1862 vintage, stroll the ancestral home.

I love the south, it never changes and is one of the few places left in America were the persona of the people is still strong. There are still characters here, unique people, who live uniquely and are different. I love New Orleans because of this sense of difference that is being bulldozed, by a balanced sterile PC society, in most other places but cannot happen here. Perhaps it is the influence of the French culture, which is part of my life. I carry the genes of generations of Norman blood myself.

I love the wonderful faces, the carriages, the masks of pre Lenten wantonness, the beat of the city's heart, which is sensual and free.

The link for a computer, a nail hole in the wall, brought me back violently to reality. It is the primary statement of the new world and the mandatory requirement for the ultra modern hotel room. As mandatory as a refrigerator bar, the bottles carefully counted. I was getting way too cynical but then I had lots to be cynical about.

In a few minutes I would link with Brit. COM and check in. Then a meeting with my contact, our local man, Taffy Sanders. He was a Liverpuddlyin, short, tough and confidant. I had not met him but was told he was all of this and more. He had better be.

That wasn't fair either as he would only be a conduit. No damage should come to his cover

unless

absolutely necessary. All I had to do was deliver my message and leave. That was it. Oh! Right! and I'm just going to dance in bow, tell my story like some laced messenger of old and take my leave. Over whose dead body I wonder? Knowing the answer was bad for my blood pressure.

The Brit. COM line is clear, no real information beyond what I already possess. I do the standard tap check to make sure I'm not sending my message into a closed system or to some enthusiastic hacker. No, the connection is true.

I strip to my briefs and lay down on the soft comfortable bed for a couple of hours sleep. The trip from Canada had been round about, the final leg started from Denver. Endless but important hours in the air take their toll even if you sleep them through. I will need all my energy for the next day and a half so rest is a good investment.

The room is completely dark but for a couple of small bright spots trailing down one side of the curtains where they don't quit meet the wall. At first I am disorganized. Place, lost in years of new places but it comes to me. I am in New Orleans getting ready to balance life and death. My body shivers with fear like a horse whose privates have been touched. I swing into action.

Floating down the tube of one of the great cluster of glass fronted elevators that rise like a clasp of Kryptonic crystals against one wall of the atrium I perceive the god complex some people of wealth might get.

Pop-Ups is the smallest restaurant on the floor and the darkest. It has an antique oak bar. Small, round, highly polished wood enclosures for various group sizes fill its small floor space. Standard antique signs for old, now long dead products, line the walls. It is a pleasant place with the smell of Cajun cooking wafting out to the patrons. There seem to be no tables left but the wait didn't look too long, so I ask to be seated and would wait at the bar. A beautiful, dark haired girl, with a little too much make up and a heavy Alabamian twang, agrees to get me as soon as possible. The smile is returned but with little interest, my mind is elsewhere. At the bar, throwing caution to the winds, I order a rye and coke. Screw my blood pressure. The Coke is Pepsi; the Black Velvet is rich and full. I settle back and scan the place. It's second nature just to see who's looking or not. I see him coming and know it is me he is coming to.

The white Stetson looks like something Hopalong Cassidy would wear. It has a green snake skin band.

The man underneath it, is dressed in a very light beige suit, which seems out of character. Too small for his great round body certainly. The face and head look like a pile of mashed potatoes someone had sculpted. With a thick nose and whitish almost non-existent brows, the head bells into a large slash mouth. His chipmunk cheeks, seemingly stuffed full of cotton, are pure ugly. His intense eyes were something else again, watery blue and flat, a convict's stare, regarded me as a possible mark no doubt. Some people have definitely been in prison. This was one. The over all expression conveyed the fact that here was a man who could do you grievous bodily harm without too much fuss. I had seen it on football players and others of their ilk who face physical interaction on a day to day basis and have no fear of it. When he smiled, which he did while nodding to me as he sauntered up, no teeth showed at all. It was as if a jack-o-lantern mouth had been carved out for a moment then filled in as quickly. Physically, he was powerful in the upper part of his body but the lower part had gone to seed without so much as a by your leave showing a paunch that stretched the buttons on his white western shirt. He wore no jewelry on his hands but his shoes were black Nun and Bush fashion boots. Instead of the string tie that should have been around his neck, was an Indian turquoise beaded neck piece, probably Apache in origin.

I had never seen the man in my life but he knew me or what I looked like at any rate.

"Howdy." He said in a drawl that was more Alabama then Texican.

"Hello.' I said off handedly. As if I was not interested in making his acquaintance. I was, however, intrigued by who he was and what he wanted.

"Mr. McFurson I believe?" He said and smiled again like a big happy hound hoping for a pat.

"Why yes.' I played along, 'Mike McFurson of Epsylon Computers." The little Twenty-two, key chain derringer, provided by special equipment section. Had been fashioned like a cigarette lighter. It was now in my coat pocket pointed at his head. He was way too big to stop with a bullet in the gut. If he meant to harm me he was going to get a big surprise.

There was a soft rumble deep down, which passed for a laugh as he leaned forward on the bar placing his powerful stubby fingered paws flat to show he meant no harm.

"If I wanted you dead you'd be there.' He said matter of factly and I knew he was capable of it. 'Them little things are a caution ain't they?' He nodded at my pocket. 'Ain't worth shit unless you an inch or so way though. Mess up your suit and you'd miss anyway."

"Maybe." Never lie when caught out it makes you weak.

"You got balls." He said this to himself more then me and nodded.

"I'm afraid you have the better of me sir, as I don't seem to recall your name?" Good manors are always important in the south.

"I apologize, you are right, sir.' He responded in kind, 'I am Sayleen Lieless. My mama wasn't sure who my daddy was, so she gave me a good honest name, figured it might hold true in life. Never worked but she had good in her heart, God rest her.' He nodded to himself and continued, 'We have a mutual friend who requested I look you up and help you out much as I could." He nodded again. This seemed to be a constant at the end of a truthful sentence. Body language for a spy is important. Any edge you can get on the opposition could be the difference.

Sayleen Lieless, ex-Klansman and entrepreneur who had put together package tours for various American hate groups to True Love, Tu Tu Bay, The US Virgin Islands. Flying them down for a little sun and visceral examination by one Mr. Lionel

Adams of Chicago. Less then a year ago I had run into Adams before having to fight World War Three with a group of terrorists lead by Mr.Tisani, my present target. My joy at being in Lieless's presence was boundless.

"The last time I met your friend I almost got killed and a lot of people who mattered to me weren't so lucky. You can understand my total lack of interest in your help." It came out hard and Lieless turned slowly. The big man didn't like the tone or the message. His face didn't change personality but his forehead went pure white. Some animals give physical warning before they strike. I had just been warned and braced myself. Sayleen breathed out long and then thoughtful the colour came back to his forehead. Sayleen made a grunting noise like my uncle did when he was considering things.

"He didn't say it would be easy.' The nod again 'But you got to understand two things. I got me a hair trigger, real fractional, so you should think on it before you try to get a rise out of me. Second, I won't hurt you nun unless you cause me trouble. I am here to help you cause my friends best interests are the same as yours. Also he has respect for you" He nodded again and I decided to take a chance or at least see where this was going. I have to say I was a little flattered that Lionel Adams, the black computer millionaire and part time super villain even remembered, let alone had respect for me.

The Alabama Smile was back saying she had a table for "Youall gentlemen." Lieless immediately went into huggy bear mode. His ugly face softened to show his appreciation and Linda , from her name tag, showed limited coquettish interest. She led us to our table and left huge picture based menus for us to peruse.

"Nice little filly." Sayleen Nodded again to Linda's retreating behind.

"Yes, on that we agree." I said

"Good, this is goin to be alright." He said good naturally but no nod.

"How can you help me? Just to cut to the chase." I opened.

"Good question?' He nodded. ' Well seems to me you lookin for Tisani. My friend and him ain't partners no more. Them Ar-abs can get meaner then some fool who buy's his self a woman and finds out he done made a mistake and got a shemale instead. Tisani intends some harm to my friend. Seeing you want him and my friend wants him gone cause he know just how crazy this here greasy carpet merchants is, he asked me to support you best I can.' And a nod, So the enemy of my enemy is my friend interesting.

"I need to get a message to a Mr. Emil La Tour Dubois."

Sayleen who had been studying the menu froze. His eyes came up with something like fear. The magnitude of the enemy I was up against seemed to be heightened.

"What the hell do you want with Jewel Dubois?" Lieless demanded.

"I have to give him a message." I said unperturbed.

"Boy, you must have balls the size of melons.' He paused

"You've done work for him?"

"Hell, I ain't no pimp." Sayleen said more amiably ' Do you know who you are about to disturb?"

"Tell me." I said blandly.

"Well, Jewel, he runs some very high priced cat houses. Fillies, mares, colts, stallions, foals, name your poison, he has it at a price. Had me a woman at one of his houses oncet costed me One Thousand Dollars. That ain't no lie neither.' he nodded ' Best piece of ass I ever did have. You've got to see the elephant there and again, if you know what I mean. Do yourself good, have the best. But oncet boy, only oncet that's danged expensive."

"What about AIDS and things like that?" I asked just for reference.

"Guaranteed clean, tested and all. You got to wear a cover too, of course." He nodded.

"So he's a pimp. So what?" I said off handedly.

"You are wronger then pissing into a hurricane. Old Jewel is into everything you want. Smuggling art, jewelry, kids anything that's high end and makes a profit. Hell the local mob won't go near him. The po-lice take no interest. He has power over people so high they shit turds bigger than us.' he paused for a moment to allow me to absorb this revelation. 'There have been people, big people heed, disappeared just for looking sideways at Jewel. He has stuff on everyone who ever walked into any of his houses. Course in my case don't make no nevermind cause I ain't anything important. I wouldn't be surprised ifin he had pictures of President humpin a duck and given the present occupant of the White House, that ain't hard to believe."

I smiled and he laughed the same rumble.

"I'll take your message to him myself if that's what all it takes." He nodded and I knew he would go down trying. Adams had a real ball breaker of an edge on this man, I wondered what? Lieless wasn't stupid. He knew death was an option of the action he so simply suggested.

"No! Better from someone he trusts' I said. 'You don't know where our friend Tisani is do you?"

"Hell no! If I did I'd be there discussin the weather and whatnot with good old boy."

"A short discussion no doubt?" I suggested

"Sure enough." Lieless agreed and from the look, while he would take no pleasure in it, it would get done.

Alabama was back. Lieless requested a full order of back ribs with the works and a Bud, while giving her his patented puppy dog face which Linda rewarded with a down home smile. I started out to order the tuna salad but went for a cheeseburger, fries and rings instead, with a large coke, no ice. The amount of ice they put in a glass is directly proportional to the amount of soft drink you pay for and don't get. I hate being taken, on just about every level and will respond if aware of it.

"Why Dubois?" He asked watching Linda leave.

"Nothing to do with your friend for sure." I said honestly.

The grunt again

"I know this, you go up against old Jewel your goin to need me boy and a divison or so of marines.' He paused. 'So you don't know where Tisani is either? Dubois, he know?" Lieless asked rubbing his chin while offering about as much subtlety he could muster.

"No, another matter. I've got other fish to fry as well.' I lied. The grunt this time said 'That dog won't hunt,' he knew I was lying but it didn't seem to matter. It was Lieless who had caused the twitch he was following me or maybe Dubois's people. Now he would be for sure. I, on the other hand would know he was, this gave me the edge. If Jewel didn't help good old Sayleen with Tisani's whereabouts, should I lead the hulky ex-klaner to him, I definitely didn't want to be Dubois.

. I had thrown out the message as bait to get Sayleen's reaction. If he were tied to Dubois he would have gone for the opportunity in a very different way.

We discussed the President and his sexual habits waiting for the food. It was Sayleen's honest opinion that a man of the President's stature ought to be sexually serviced on demand just to take the pressure off. He pointed out the President got his naturals done during a phone call to some foreign head of state, probably just to balance his temperament, so Bubba could make the right decision. At this point the twenty-one year old intern in question had been brought to the level of a combination secret weapon and working patriot in Lieless's mind. I didn't laugh. Sayleen meant it and I wanted to keep my teeth.

The food arrived on two huge pewder trays that passed for plates. A burger is a treat if it's juicy and well done. This one was huge and good but there was too much for me. Sayleen on the other hand ate with a slow patient enjoyment of the greasy fare, which allowed him to clear his plate. At this point he ordered keylime pie for both of us. Best this side of Florida he assured me. The first mouth full offered tartness that was just this side of electric enrapturing the taste buds. Sayleen knew his pie and we both had a second portion. I knew I would need a derrick to get out of the chair.

We discussed the Falcons and their chances this year. They were Sayleen's team although he lived in Dallas. Then quarterbacks, he liked Marino who is flashy and little over his prime. I personally liked Farb. He is workman-like and could be magnificent on demand. Sayleen thought he hadn't peaked yet and I disagreed.

The meal came to an end and I picked up the check, which he appreciated without letting on.

"Well I'll be around,' He said as if to reassure me, 'here is a number you can get me at. Just ask for

Sayleen." He passed over a matchbook from Continental Airlines with the number scrawled almost legible inside.

He meandered off to talk with Linda and I went for a taxi ride downtown to see who followed.

Chapter nineteen – 2:00 P.m, The French Quarter, New Orleans, Louisiana, USA

Footprints

The cab brought me to the French Quarter, the very heart of the boozy, jazz capital of the world. I was still in my lightweight, gray Brooks Brothers suit; the tie was a dead mistake in the humid heat of the delta. Eighty degrees here, was 106 otherwise causing streams of sweat.

We literally flew down Highway 61, the driver making light conversation as we passed the Louisiana Superdome. I exited on Decatur St. near Jackson Square.

The opposition in an old reddish brown Chevy Nova, following us as unobtrusively as possible. The car contained two black men, both with shades, both bangers by the look. I meandered into the great park, past the horse drawn carriages lined up and ready to show the old town. Multi colored square faced buildings set in thin balconied streets marked with the Spanish coat of arms, the personality of France and the unique mixture of the south. For a moment I stopped to admire the statue of Andrew Jackson the savior of New Orleans and once

President of these United States. I found Jackson's Horse look bored. While ruminating on that discovery, I noticed one of the two Chevy men had followed me into the park. Looking nondescript in a red basketball jersey and shorts he walked right across the park and stood by the Cathedral entrance. He then split his time watching me while keeping an eye on the various mimes, magicians and jugglers who entertained the tourists in the plaza before the seat of Roman Catholicism in Louisiana.

My memory worked like mad as I tried to figure out where I had seen the other man in the car. I had only a glimpse but he looked familiar. Nothing came to mind now, maybe later it would click in. These two belonged to Sayleen. They were not professional but they were trying hard.

A little boy, perhaps twelve, eating an ice-cream cone walked over to look at the statue. He looked up with great blue eyes and smiled. As a matter of fact he was one of the handsomest young men I had ever seen. The type of child you'd like to put on display. Not that mine aren't good looking but this kid could have done the cover of American Child or whatever. I smiled back pleasantly and made my next move over to the Cathedral and the Louisiana

State Museum, which I always find interesting when I have a few minutes to waste. At this point I didn't. My entering the great church seemed to cause some confusion on the part of my pursuers. In the warm interior I genuflected and knelt to pray for a few moments. Chevy One, came in and watched then went back outside. That meant that Chevy Two would be watching the side entrance.

I rose, went to front of the church past the sacristy, through a small hallway and out on to St Anne St. I then took the first cab available and was whisked away from Bourbon St. to the Rivertown area.

Rule one, know the ground, have ten or twelve dead end escape routes ready in any city you've already visited. On most trips you have sometime for yourself. Wandering around in tourist mode not only screws up the opposition but also makes you better prepared the next time. I took a second cab and then a third, I used public transit twice and finally a fourth cab, at the end I walked. A small restaurant bathroom offered an opportunity to zap myself for electronic tails, there were none in my clothes. No real tail showed up, it was time for my meeting.

The old warehouse was standard fare, lots of metal in the walls to stop listening devices, open spaces to see who is coming and a metal roof to screw up satellite overview. The interior of the hundred-year-old brick derelict near General Meyer Ave was hot and dry as tinder. Overlooking the river, it sits empty and ready for demolition. I look for the steel staircase and find it exactly where it's supposed to be. An empty, white plastic bag is in place on the third step. Taffey is here. I walk across wood floor making the dust jump. There are no other foot prints but mine. Taffey is watching from above or somewhere close. He has entered elsewhere, this gives him a chance to see what's coming. I go in blind but it is his meet so his rules. Meet locations are usually unpleasant, inaccessible or overcrowded and in many cases down right dangerous. This one isn't bad, as they go, with the exception of the heat.

I consider my lunch with Sayleen as I walk toward the stairs. Lieless is here to find Tisani and kill him. Adams, as most rich men, is self centered and watching out for himself. Whatever the breakup is between his nibs and Tisani's people, who were his allies, must be a dilly. Tisani is too professional to kill without reason. Unless it is very personal he would not do it himself. A simple contract could be just as successful as a direct assault. It would not only distance himself from Adam's demise but also keep his masters out of the spotlight.

Adams is scared out of his mind for a reason. Why? Maybe we should start with him. Money or no money, the Yanks have little patience for anyone tied into terrorists, even ex-associates of terrorists. Knowing why Adams was afraid might be important.

A second thought comes to mind. While I was able to get rid of Sayleen's people, I know without knowing why; my venerable self was the attention of a second party or parties. As they were not pros I can only figure that these were Jewel's children, as he likes to call them. If so, he knows I am here and that really scares me.

Taffey Sanders sits in a small windowless room. Light from the large windows on the river side of the building shines in. His five-six frame is draped on an old wooden chair, feet in Nike walkers, elevated on a rickety table. He has a dark sinister look even in a green polo shirt and gray shorts. Brittle brown eyes scan me like an x-ray machine. He sums me up and smiles to himself. I wonder what the evaluation is? The eyes look out from under dark Irish brows. Like his hair, which is jet and combed back from the face into a non-existent ducktail, the little Englishman looks as healthy as all get out. As a matter of fact everything about his well-muscled compact body speaks of a footballer or soccer player. Taffey was an individual who worked out by playing, not by lifting, although that would probably be part of the regimen. His hatchet face with its down turned mouth spoke of someone who could hold his piece. A hard man, as the Scots are want to say. A good friend and bad enemy.

" Magic! You're late then." He started.

"MG used to make a good car." I said in keeping with the first meeting and spread my hands like I had come in one.

"Stone me, are we on about that lot? ' Taffey said with impatience. ' Magic!"

"If they had the right engine." He completed the second sentence of the identification process.

"And the wheels." I finished it.

"Right, so you're who you are and I'm who I bloody am." He said

"Magic." I said and he smiled reluctantly.

"Sorry mate. I always hate this bit, if I could just call home daily and put a few quid in my pocket it'd be all right but this lot." Taffey waved his hand to indicate the situation, 'they can sod this for a start."

'Too right." I agreed nothing like putting your life on line to make you jumpy. 'So lets get started."

"You followed." He asked off handly.

"Yes, by someone interesting."

"You didn't bring them here did you?" He tensed his feet fell from the table.

"No!' I continued in a businesslike manner. 'When you get on to the firm, please tell them I was contacted by Sayleen Lieless." I told him about the meeting and the results finishing off by asking him to have the authorities in Chicago lean on our Lionel.

"And the other lot?" Sanders asked, interested.

"Not important now.' I waved it off. ' I need to get a message to a Jewel Dubois."

"Stone me blind, nice mates you have. So what's my part in this litle drama.'

"I need a contact who knows the man."

"Well if it's something simple then." The sarcasm oozed all over the place. Taffey looked away. We didn't have much time. If I had expected this change of venue before the meeting we could have cancelled and would be talking by Internet right now. Also if I missed the tail we would be in trouble deep.

"Right,' he said finally.' Well there are a couple of villains who know him but they're drug based, bad area to move in. I know some of the small time family people but I'm just on the edge of it, if you know what I mean. Anyroad they won't have anything to do with him.' He seemed to consider the situation a little more. 'Word is, there's one copper who is bent and in Jewel's pocket. I think he knows Dubois real well. He might be all right if the message is the right sort of thing, if not it will have to be drug or smuggling people. If I go to them they're going to twig, I'm with you and my cover will explode mate." He looked at me reproachfully.

"There is a girl called Dearing, Emily Dearing, she was grabbed by slavers. We caught up with the gang. One of the victims we saved told us the Dearing girl was with them for a while. The parents, who are in construction up in Boston, want her back. Jewel knows her whereabouts and they will pay two million, anywhere in the world, on her safe return. You get one half percent, the contact, say your cop, gets a full percent. That covers you, you're just into it for the money. I have to meet with the contact."

"At that point the message changes?" Taffey said.

"Yes, I'm working for the family or at least that is what you're told."

"The cop and just about anyone else will think you're looking to find Jewel for a hit or something. Dubois hears, I'm dead."

"No mate!" I said, " my story will make sense. You'll just look like a friend I know."

"Why not see the contact yourself? Just show up and give him the message." Taffey asked snidely

"Well for one, they don't know me. Right away they want to know how I found out about them. It has to look like I'm someone fronting for the family and offering big money, who through a chain of leads has come to the right person. The message that gets to Jewel is written. I don't think anyone will steam it open."

"Right!, I'd personally like to be standing there when someone sends old Jewel a 'sod you' note and I've delivered it." I laughed. He didn't." I think it stinks."

"Look, there are a lot of lives involved. Lots and lots of lives. I have to get to a villain and Jewel knows where the bastard is. The window of opportunity, is say, two to three days. Then it will be too late. We have to try. Granny came up with this one. I think we're going to give Jewel something he wants, for something we need, just business."

"So it's got nothing to do with the Dearing Girl?"

"In a way it has a lot to do with thousands of children like Emily. You took the lady's tin, now you have to go to the wall." I went into my lieutenant from Sandhurst act.

"Balls to the tin and the Government. I was a smalltimer with a sweet fiddle in the midlands. Lots of loot no problems till the bill got me. The deal I got was work for us overseas or Dartmoure.

Surprise, I'm here. So sod the British Empire and you in the bargain.' He went morose on me and I figured I was on my own but then he came around. 'Jewel won't give you the time of day."

"He has to do business with some people, how does he make his deals?" I probed

"Very carefully mate, very carefully.' Taffey stopped for a moment. ' You the one who caned the Yank somewhere in the islands?"

"Oh! For Christ sake!" Lord was I tired of that story.

"It's a good story that's all. Also, I hear tell you cost our friend Jewel a packet when you did over his gang down there. He'll have you with truffles mate."

"We have got to try." It sounded empty in the room. It sounded stupid even to me.

Taffey looked at me as if I was already dead.

"Magic, I'll talk to the cop today after five." Taffey agreed

5:23:P.m., Tommy's Bar, New Orleans Louisiana

Tommy's is a blue bar. Cops only, other patrons came in but didn't stay. They aren't wanted because the New Orleans police department relaxes here and doesn't want to be disturbed.

Taffey felt the eyes on him and knew what his presence signaled. Lieutenant Rene Obain sat at his usual table, at the end of the line of booths at the bottom of the room. Here he did business on certain days and with certain people. The off duty officers secured his interaction with others because he had a room full of witnesses who would back him up. This put the other guy at a distinct disadvantage, which of course was the point.

"Evening Lieutenant." Taffey said loud enough for the heavyset policeman to hear him.

"Sit down Cher." As most Frenchmen, Rene talked with his hands. He had removed his suit jacket and his fourty-five was clearly visible on his left hip. Obain was a big man. He carried extra pounds but his cream suit, which was tailor made, to fit him like a glove. His underarms and back showed sweat even in the air-conditioning of the bar.

The Police Lieutenant had a face like a punch, hard, square and straight on. Metallic brown eyes summed up Taffey as a small time crook and left it at that, for the moment he was nothing more.

If Taffey was stupid enough to wear a wire, the zapper provided to Rene didn't see it. He was clean, one of the lieutenant's minions had frisked him in the bathroom before he sat down.

"So Cher, what is the matter with you, huh?' The Cher meant nothing. Taffey knew the policeman could beat him to death in the next moment and fifty men would tell the world Taffey had attacked him. This was the Big Easy and things were different here no matter how often they changed Chiefs of Police. Taffey went in straight and honest.

"This mate of mine he came down from Canada. He represents the Dearing family up in Boston. Their daughter disappeared. Anyroad, they think Jewel Dubois might be able to help find her. Of course they want his help and would be willing to pay a great deal for his time and consideration."

"That's missing persons Cher, another window." Rene made a face; he was forty something and was starting to look it. Little wrinkles showed around the eyes.

"Well this marketing chap came to me but I don't know Jewel. Mr. Dubois is very busy like and doesn't see just anyone. Now some said you might know him like. The Dearings want to offer him two million.' Taffey stopped for a moment to let that one settle. 'I get a half point finders fee. If say you know someone who might give the message to the gent in question, that person would get a full point."Rene whistled softly.

"That's a lot for a message. What is the catch Cher? Don't screw with me now." Rene was interested but it was all wrong.

"Look, if I get this money I'm made. Jewel wouldn't waste the time spitting on me mate and you know it. Also, the two mill is based on the Dearing's getting their kid back all in one piece. What the chances are of that I have no idea but we fulfill the deal, we get paid no matter what."

"No one pays two hundred thousand dollars for nothing, Cher." Obain came down like a hatchet.

"Well I had to try anyway. Sorry I bothered you Lieutenant," said Taffey looking as crest fallen as he got up.

"Wait a minute Cher, tell me about this fellow who you talked to. He a cop, FBI, something like that? Rene was hooked. The story was too weird not to look into. Years of police work demanded it. Also, it might be true.

"This McFurson bloke." Taffey started.

"What you say his name is, Cher. " Obain interrupted and his face changed.

"McFurson, he spells it funny with a "ur." You know him?"

"No! How do you know him, Cher?" The big policeman leaned forward.

"He used to live on the same street as me up in Mississauga. Its part of Toronto now.' Taffey stopped. 'Listen I didn't give him your name mate. If he's some kind of grass, then I walk and you can have him. He's at the Emperium Airport room 872. He ain't no cop. I know cops." Obain smiled and Taffey realized his mistake and smiled too.

"Did he say he wanted to meet with this Jewel."

"No! See that's why I thought it was straight like. Said all he had to do was give you the message then he expected an answer. He said he didn't need to see the man."

"Why not put him with someone else and get the money without the problem."

"This here Jewel is a Cajun Brit. The accent would be somethin to reproduce, anyway he ain't stupid. He knows the ins and outs. Jewel would have a lot of people around. You know what I mean. The scam is too expensive to run. Too many people to pay and so on."

"People get killed for wanting to see Jewel you know. He likes his privacy." Threatened Obain.

"Look you think he's a rat, I'm finished with it." Taffey said as intensely as possible.

"No! Cher tell him I'll see him for breakfast tomorrow at his hotel in the Rue Picadilly under the atrium." Obain smiled, Taffey shivered and he was no coward.

Chapter twenty - 8:45 A.m., The Empirium Airport, New Orleans, Louisiana.

Old gods and Little Fishes

The night had been quiet. An expected visit from the opposition, had not occurred, but then they didn't know it all yet. It might be a trap my precious, McFurson, McFurson. With this gloomy thought in mind I descended to the atrium and my visit with Lieutenant Obain.

Obain was hunched over a large plate of sausage and eggs. Black coffee sent out an aroma that made me salivate. The morning sun brightened the floor of the atrium but the air-conditioning, which is probably why the room rates were astronomical, made the setting a pleasant seventy degrees. The Lieutenant had chosen a table behind one of the four huge pillars that held the glass cover up and was thereby shaded from the rays.

I made my way over through a large breakfast crowd but realized the tables around the heavy policeman were empty. All the better to hear you out, Cher.

He saw me coming but didn't show any interest. I arrived as he placed a large mouthful of sausage under his heavy black mustache. He smiled and gestured to the chair across from him.

"Sit down, Cher." He said swallowing his mouthful and using his napkin at the same time.

"Thank you." I said rather formally and offered my hand.

"Michael McFurson." Obain smiled for a moment looked at my hand then made the effort to half stand and took it in a vise grip. I have very few attributes from my father but strength in the wrist and fingers is one. I simply increased the pressure and the two of us stood there for a moment looking each other in the eye and strengthening our hold.

"Ha!' Obain.' He said as if he had found out what he wanted to know and we disengaged at the same time. 'Only Canuks and Brits shake hands, we're more casual in the Big Easy."

The girl came over and I asked for a small stack of pancakes to be preceded by a tall glass of orange juice.

"So you have a message to send?" he said moving quickly forward. Was he wired? Not that it mattered.

"I would like to hire you as a consultant. The amount of your commission was discussed before. The objective is to have a message delivered to an individual of your acquaintance."

"So, I bin told." He said non-committaly

"The message has nothing to do with the Dearing girl that was for Taffey. Nice fellow but not terribly bright, also not terribly trustworthy.' Rene nodded as if to agree. There seemed to be no surprise.

'The individuals who I represent want the whereabouts of a man named Tisani. He has a lot of aliases but the gentleman will know him by that name. Also there was a package, which was to be sent by your acquaintance to a specific location before Tisani arrived. We want the package too or it's location."

"Drugs.' Said Obain brightening up considerably.

"I wish." I said with real ardor. 'No! something much more lethal."

"What? " The big hands opened and the face became bemused.

"I don't know exactly, explosives or some kind of poison, maybe something else even nastier."

"This stuff destined for America?' He demanded.

"We don't know. If it were just coming here we'd call in the NSA and let them go nuts on our friend. However, if we can't prove what's in the package or where it's going then no one's going to do anything." I finished with a knowing glance.

"No one is above the law." Obain said with high dungeon.

"You'll pardon me? Horse shit." I said. Obain didn't like it but he knew I was right.

"So you are what, a spook for the Canadians?" Obain smiled broadly as if the two items formed an oxymoron.

"No! Just a marketing consultant that someone knows and asked a favour from. Just a messenger" I dropped into French. " The matter is of the utmost importance my friend. If you do not assist me I will find another."

"Watch your self Cher, I am a police officer and you just tried to bribe me."

"Crap, I offered to hire you as a consultant. To do something which is completely legal and in reality is part of your job."

"Are you on the job, Cher?" He asked, the face lost all sense of a smile.

"No! Just a messenger." If I were on the job I would try to make you fall into a mistake.'

"God damn, your French is horrible." He said.

"Sorry, I learned it after English and I think in the first and speak in the second. Also it contains a lot of Quebecois jeual yours contains Acadi but many times removed.

"Yes, the British were kind enough to ship us here with very little luxury after the fall of the Port Royal. We had no possessions or money. The only place to go was the bayou. " he finished indicating a good knowledge of the history of New France two centuries before, if nothing else.

"So you want this man Tisani and you're willing to pay two million dollars for the information."

"Yes, in any currency your acquaintance wants, to any numbered account he requests. When we have the information and it is verified. If we miss Tisani through our own stupidity he still gets paid. He knows us. He knows the offer is valid." Obain was thoughtful.

"What if he won't give you the information?" It was obvious he was thinking of his own well being.

"Then you and Taffey get your money. However, I want an answer from him. On tape whatever, something verifiable." I finished.

"Do you wish to meet him?"

"No! I have no desire. If he needs to meet me, then at an agreed upon location by both parties." I considered the possibility of that happening about as feasible as a snow ball in hell, but you never knew.

"He know you're here, Cher.' I must have shown my surprise at his candor. He smiled 'no wire Cher. The tables huh. His big hands waved about 'I'm a prince of the city. Le Roi du Poopoo.' He kidded 'If I want privacy it happens.' He considered the matter for a moment.

"You know when I decided to become a Captain of police?' it was a rhetorical question and I didn't bother to respond knowing the answer was coming. 'When I was little I saw Casablanca. The moment I heard Louis Renault speak, I was sure. He was class, Cher.

He spoke like me but better. He had power but he knew how to control situations without losing his respect. Beautiful women wanted him. I decided to be a police captain. I'm almost there.' Rene leaned across the table. 'But Cher I learned one important thing from Louis Renault. He couldn't arrest the German Colonel. He was the real criminal but he was above the law because he made it. Understand what it's about?"

" Renault may have bent but he didn't fold in the end. He goes to free France and fights for what is right. I have always thought his character far more real then Bogart's role. He had flaws and knew it but he never let himself be destroyed by them."

"He was on the pad, Cher. He closes the casino but takes his winnings." Obain offered.

"Yes, he was corrupt in a corrupt world." I didn't say more there was no more to say. Obain had warned me. This was a major concession. However, he was wrong, Dubois had to be pulled out of his cave and made to pay for his crimes. It spoke volumes that no one had done it yet. It was easy to do nothing, in a world where a truly guilty US President, who had stained his office and its place in history, would probably be allowed to walk away scot-free. How could you damn Obain for putting his finger in the pie? Simple! It was wrong. Right was right and evil was evil. If no one drew the line then there was nothing left. I will always draw the line. I am no more perfect than Obain but you keep trying. If you fall down, the answer isn't to stay in the gutter.

"Lieutenant when I was small my mother said I had a little voice in the back of my mind. That voice tells me right from wrong. It has never lead me astray." I finished and looked Obain in the eye but he would not meet my gaze. How can you spew this crap? You're as bad as him! No! I corrected myself, living by a code may not make me better but it allowed me to sleep at night.

I removed the letter from my inside pocket containing the message for Dubois. Rene moved away from it as if it might be poisoned.

"Don't you worry Cher. I will remember your message." The big man left about the same time my pancakes arrived. . I should be glad it was over. The message was in Obain's hands. All I had to do was wait. I ate slowly and enjoyed the food, which was hot and filling. When I offered to pay, I found out my money was no good, so I left a twenty-dollar tip.

I returned to my room for my hat. I would then go down to Bourbon Street and listen to the music, have a long drink and enjoy the scene. I headed for an empty elevator. The two young men who followed actually came in from opposite directions across the lobby and got to the door just after I entered. The Army fourty-five was in my back. The weight of the man was against me, slamming me into the metal back of the lift. While I shook off the pain in my face from being rammed into the steel, an agile hand slipped into my pocket and removed the gold coloured, derringer key chain. The elevator moved into the floor headed for the underground garage three floors below.

"I will kill you but slow. I have time now no one will come to your assistance." A whispery voice floated in my ear. Of course I tried to turn and my assailant hit me in the kidney. The pain, as usual, was unique and I almost vomited. The one very small concession was that it wasn't the one Ray chose to hammer back in the islands, which was still recuperating.

"If we are going to see Jewel that's fine with me. I won't cause any trouble. I need to see him." The weight was removed.

"He wants to see you too. If it was me, I'd fight for my life, fool." The voice was young. He moved away and I was able to turn around. The chromed muscle of the fourty-five nosed out from under the gray silk overcoat my assailant had covered his hand and arm with.

The man was one of the handsomest I had ever set eyes on. Unless you're homosexual you don't look at other men much, perhaps the clothing sometimes if it is unique or well worn but Pretty Boy was model material.

His close cropped hair was in small ringlets but for some reason this was not feminine at all. The face was black or at least a cream colour and unblemished. The contours were fine but well formed. A mouth that was soft and sensual a solid if pointed chin made theface easy to look at. The features were well balanced. Eyes I do believe are the windows of the soul. This man had none. A shark's black orbs had more humanity then Pretty Boy. He would kill easily and without much reason. The man was a six footer with an athlete's body in a hand made silk suit that looked Hong Kong and fit like a glove. Everything the man wore was dove gray with the exception of the white shirt, which was crisp and new. The mouth got off a lazy smile.

"We are going to the garage. You will get into the car that's waiting or I will kill you and we will dump you in the trunk." The soft voice whispered.

I had no interest in the trunk to start with and I wasn't going to get killed just yet. I had a mission to finish.

"Give me your watch and your pens." I passed them over and he handed then to his associate. Surprise! Surprise! It was Furball from the beach in St. Martin. He and Blondie had put on a private show for me. I had missed them completely. The acting had been great. I realized that I was moving into a sexual substructure of life, where everything had erotic substance and direction, completely separate from the everyday. The Furry one grinned sadistically like a big child. His features were attractive too, if you liked Mediterranean characteristics.

"I say we kick his balls in or cut them off. Give Loft someone to play with." Furry said with childish glee.

I simply did the policeman's two step and waited. Pretty Boy noted the change and told his partner to close it down.

"You got anything else on you?" he demanded.

"I have a message for your fearless leader. Nothing else."

"Lets strip-him and find out." I simply held eye contact with Furball who seemed to get the drift. I wasn't going to be frightened by him. I knew, as he did, that if I did get killed between now and when Jewel had had a chance to pass judgement on me, there would really be trouble. There was a lot of unprofessional talk that led me to believe these two although totally lethal, were less than in control.

The elevator opened disturbing my ruminations concerning the two twerps. Framed in the door was a big man, strong I was sure but more body mass then muscle.

"Is this him?" The falsetto voice seemed ludicrous coming from the shaved football head, which seemed to have all its features compacted into about an inch of the center of his face. Two small pig-like eyes, a bump like nose and a feminine prissy mouth. This guy, dressed in his ill fitting black suit, didn't scare me, just to show you how stupid I could be.

"I hope the car is half decent after this fowl up." I growled pushing past the surprised villains into the back seat of the Lincoln Stretch Limo. I sat comfortably, smelling the leather interior, waiting for the idiot brothers to catch up. Furball got in next to me. Pretty Boy sat across, the gun now naked, pointed at my heart. Loft took the wheel.

I watched the scenery without a blindfold. This might come later but it was a good indicator that I wasn't going to tell anyone what I was about to see. That meant I would not be coming back. I knew this was sure to happen but I felt that I could discuss the situation with Jewel and like reasonable people come to a suitable conclusion. My mistake was the reasonable part. So far my chances were slim to none of living but at least I wasn't in the trunk.

The pick up was excellent but I would have not expected any less from an ex-firm member. The fact that they had pinched me from the hotel lobby was a statement. It is difficult to do and was carried out with precision. What bothered me is how I was able to sidebar the fay three so easily. With that much competence my attempt to buffalo these guys should have put me in traction. It was as if they were so used to taking orders, they responded poorly to giving them, unless the victim was very subservient or perhaps overwhelmed by Jewel's reputation. I didn't think they would do very well with Sayleen, should, they cross his path.There was no talk as we traveled back toward the French Quarter. I expected to end up on Bourbon Street.

I am always amazed that most Americans don't know that Bourbon is the name of the last French King and that their Bourbon Whiskey is actually named for that ancient European Monarchy. The harsh Burbon of American pronunciation as opposed to the fine Bourbon of the French. Canadians would know the difference but we tend to be detail people.

Slightly north of Rampart there is a small apartment building with underground parking. It was into this attractive twenty-year-old building that we disappeared.

I was hustled out and through an underground walkway then through a door, which became a tunnel under a street, which brought us out into a second parking garage with bright yellow walls. We descended to the ground level and up to a maintenance room door.

This opened and I was shoved into the darkness. The door closed and it really got to be stygian. There was a rustling noise, soft giggles as if a third grade classroom was trying to be on its best behavior. I remained still, braced myself and waited.

The lights were blinding. A moment of so later I was able to focus. In fourty-nine years you see a lot more then you need. Nothing I had been involved with could possibly make me ready for this.

Sitting in an ornate oak armed chair, rising to an intricately carved crown, with a crimson cloth seat and back, was a small white haired man. He looked at me with a slightly sarcastic smile. He had fine sharp features like a ferret. His skin was marble white like someone who had not been in the sun for a very long time. With the exception of the odd age spot only time had changed the man from the picture on his file. He was dressed in an emerald smoking jacket and gray-striped pants that ended in brilliantly shined brown Oxfords. A frilly maroon cravat covered his thin neck and folded in to his open necked white shirt. The chair was elevated on steps covered by a rich red carpet with levels of cushions and pillows.

On the pillows were ten children, the youngest perhaps eight or nine to Blondie from St. Martin at the bottom of the small pyramid. All of them were completely naked. That much flesh presented so quickly and dynamically was not only disturbing but gut wrenching. If the objective was to gain the upper hand in negotiation Jewel had won.

The faces that looked back at me, small or large, were beautiful; more like portraits with all the imperfections removed. Soft eyes, half-opened mouths mincing looks from under the eyebrow, attention getters, the smell of sex, which is pleasant when I am in my own bedroom, was overwhelming and revolting. I realized that of the ten children, all but Blondie, was male.

Question what does one do? One, you come to terms with the situation. Where was my escort? Pretty Boy stood to my right and Furball to my left. Just far enough away to enjoy the action but close enough to step in if I charged.

Two, evaluate the why. My immediate thought was for these poor children. What might have been a pedophile's dream only revolted me. It looked like a change room scene after a swim at the YMCA in my youth when nudity was expected, or in the much feared shower room after gym.

I breathed out deeply and started.

"I have a message for you from the firm."

"Yes, I know, ' the accent was some where between the French Quarter and a good British public school, 'I am very disappointed in you, Mr. McFurson.' He continued in a fatherly manner. 'I offer you delicacies and you show no interest. My babies feel they have let me down. Why are you not interested in my offerings, I wonder?" For a moment

I was taken aback. What offerings? Then it hit me, the children. The demented old bastard offered me kids to see my reaction like a gerbil in maze. I understood now, the little boy with the blue eyes by Jackson's Statue was one such offering. I knew this because my eyes fell on him in the group. Without clothing it was hard to separate the faces. He met my eyes and smiled a come hither message. He stood and the others all seemed to make a soft 'ah' sound.

I could feel myself shake my head then I riveted my eyes on Dubois. The little boy's head fell forward in failure.

"It's alright, little one come to me." Jewel said in a soft consoling voice. The little boy ran to him and sat in the old pedophile's lap. He hugged the old sod like his grandfather while Dubois ran his hand down the boy's thigh.

Pure anger is a unique thing there is a white edge to it then the mind is lost in the need to destroy the creator of that horrible feeling. I took a step forward. Pretty Boy grabbed one arm and placed the muzzle of the fourty-five against my spine so that the bone would be severed but the bullet, which would continue on, would end up harmlessly in the concrete ceiling. There were squeals from the younger children and Jewel's face hardened. He obviously didn't want me killed in front of them. It might make them less valuable. With a tremendous strength of will, more then I thought I had at my disposal. I dragged myself back. This had to be business but someday as there is a God, I would kill this man.

"You are jealous my dear." The same sugary, fatherly voice reached out to me. I almost lost it again but caught myself. The implication that I was a pedophile cut me to the quick. Where would he have gotten that idea? It didn't matter.

"The message is this we want Tisani you get two million dollars in whatever currency, where ever you want it delivered. Also your providing us with this information and the location of the package you delivered for him, will go a long way to removing other past mistakes." Why be coy? They will forgive you for killing all those agents in the West Indies and for this too. To save helpless unaware people, the loss of the few was outweighed by the loss of the many. I had delivered the message. If the answer was negative then straight for his throat.

"You'd never make it dear boy.' Jewel seemed to

read my mind. 'The babes would throw themselves at you until Gaiten could kill you. You see they love me." Dubois's thin hands spread to encompass the children before him. I looked into the eyes of his babes and knew he was right. However, whether it would be for self-preservation or love was another question.

"If you don't give me the information and Americans die then I don't care if you have pictures of the house and Senate in full orgy. NSA will come down here and drag you out by your heels." I finished playing my hold card. He ignored it completely

"The question is, why don't you approve of my gifts? I perhaps have forgotten the oldest rule of all, listen to the customer.' Dubois nodded as if apologizing for his mistake. 'but it did seem clear my dear. You had no interest in the beautiful Shirl and you did not take advantage of the Asian Lilly, what was I to think?" Oh, I see, it's my fault.

"The lives of thousands of people are at stake. We have to find that package or at least the man. Maybe you didn't know it but those tubes are full of Saran, or some other kind of poison. It could be coming here."

"You are a frightful bore, my dear. Are you more interested in men or perhaps a dom? Shirl would be glad to help." Shirl, alias Blondie, smiled and looked away.

"I have a wife, you ignorant, self-indulgent old pansy." To hell with it. If I was going down then so be it. I had nothing to lose. He did not like that I heard the boy take aim to my right.

"Good God! how foolish of me. You're just a common man. An incorruptible, common man. How interesting." His expression intimated I was about as interesting as dog manure on his shoe.

"You want the location of this man Tisani, he has the lives of many people in his hands. I really don't need two million Dollars. At any rate, you cost me five million with your little circus in St. Martin."

"Don't blame me for your mistakes. I notice your blue eyed Hobgoblin isn't around. Did you have him put down?"

"By George you are something. You have no idea what I am capable of."

"Oh, I have a pretty good Idea." I snapped.

"Are you disgusted with me? Oh! I am sorry. You insignificant little piss ant. Granny and the Knight-errant will forgive me my sins will they? For what? I didn't sell out those agents. Oh! I'll take responsibility for my evil, which as you know is deep and horrible. However, someone else accounted for the deaths of those men, not me. The Americans know it or I wouldn't last here one minute." I will admit Jewel's little admission stopped me. Why would he lie unless he was going to let me live to cause trouble at the firm? Have us looking for a mole that didn't exist. Why, on the other hand should he lie?

"You aren't happy with my lifestyle are you?" he continued with cold sarcasm. 'How unfortunate. So you're the last uncorrupted man are you?" He leaned forward his eyes blazing. 'We shall see." He pointed a finger as if ready to level me.

"You an uncorruptable man, someone who looks down on the corruption of others, who is above that sort of thing. You are a fraud. You smuggle and call it necessary. You murder and call it righteous. I will give you the information you want if you will have sex for me right here on the floor. You may pick your partner. Entertain me and I will allow you to save the world. Well, my incorruptible, friend?' He sat back very satisfied with himself.

"You're going to kill me anyway, the point is mute." I said knowing it was true.

"The question is, will I? If you put on a good enough show perhaps I will let you go with your precious information. Which is more important; your self-righteous pride or all those lives? The pit or the pendulum?

Sex for the queen, humping in the line of duty. The actual opportunity to make love, not war, to save millions. The orgasm that saved the world. It was laughable. I really didn't mind making love to Shirl in front of this sick man if it did the job but I knew he wouldn't fulfill the bargain or would he? That of course was the rub.

"Here let me help you dear boy. The sugary voice came again. A simple wave of his hand and Blondie and her male counterpart, from the other side of the small pyramid, a boy of perhaps nineteen with a well muscled body stood and came toward me. The boy was erect in moments, a neat trick. I looked at the girl. Blondie's nipples stuck out like nails she licked her lips and running her hands over her thighs, stalked toward me like some vamp.

I wasn't going to do this but I was going to make a point. I stepped toward the girl. Jewel nodded his approval from his little throne. I reached out and took the girl's face in my hand. Then with a twist of my wrist I made her face the appalling, old pervert, half lifting her off the floor.

"Do you see sexual erotica and wanton need in this face? All I see is fear and self loathing. I let the girl go. She began to cry and fell in a heap. Jewel went whiter, if possible and said two words.

"Kill him." They were his last. The explosion of concrete sent splinters into the crowd of children and deafened us all. The 222 Gloshun bullet penetrated four feet of concrete from the outer wall, like paper. Under normal circumstances the outer casing of the shell would have stopped at the wall and the interior 7.2 NATO round would have been propelled into the individual directly in front of the penetration. The bullet, unfortunately, was manufactured for ten feet and better of solid concrete. The entire shell broke through and emptied Jewel's body cavity. The little pedophile simply deflated and rolled down on the screaming children.

Pretty Boy, who had been transfixed by the death of Dubois, turned almost mechanically to fire at me.

The second explosion ripped through the wall and threw the black beauty across the room, where he came to rest like a ruined puppet.

I turned to my left and Furball opened his mouth to scream, he ran for the wall. There was no door the third shot splattered him there like a bug.

I looked at the half-foot hole in the wall behind where Dubois had been sitting. Just for a moment I saw the cold, hard, blue eye of Henry Say checking his work and knew there was a God.

Chapter twenty-one -10:15 A.m., The French Quarter – New Orleans Louisiana, USA.

The Aftermath

Particles of concrete dust clogged the nose and blinded the eye. Explosions deafen the ear and the mind, in hours, or perhaps years, the faint sounds come back. Small children cried, sobbed from fright and minor wounds. The soft movements of small feet and hands in the rubble. For a moment it was just enough to know I was still alive and standing. Then survival set in. In short but sure steps I reached the body of Gaitien and picked up the chrome plated army 45. On the edge of my vision, I saw the blue eyed twelve-year-old from the park go toward the body of the other guard.

"Hold it." I croaked and turned with the fourty-five pointed in his general direction. He stopped, but a fierce look of pure do or die touched his face as he attempted to stare me down. Meandering over I took the thirty-eight snub-nosed revolver from the pant waist band of the second bloody corpse.

"Please help usall?' Shirl's voice was a little thin and very Georgian. 'I'll do anything you want don't hurt us. Please." She made to move toward me but my backward step stopped her. I still didn't trust her; a moment before she would have watched my death. Of course, in fairness, no action Shirl could have taken would have changed the end result.

"Please don't kill us." The boy who had offered himself a moment before had great tears rolling down his face leaving grimy tracks. One of the nine-year-olds came over to Shirl. One thin arm circled her thigh, his thumb firmly in his mouth. The other little ones moved behind her and peered at me from round her hips. She was the only woman and they looked to her for protection. I felt ashamed and small.

"No one's going to kill you. I'll help you as much as I can. Listen son.'This to the crying twenty year old. ' Don't cry the others will need you calm for strength, right?" I felt funny talking to a grown man like a school child but battle affects people in different ways and he seemed affected to start with.

"You got to forgive Billy. He's real brave normal but he's only fourteen and….' She stopped, probably because my mouth dropped open. I looked at the boy and realized she was telling the truth. The horror of what was done by Dubois was magnified. I wasn't completely ignorant. I had seen young boys selling themselves on the city streets of most cities but this was like entering some lower substrata of inhumanity. I looked back at Shirl. One hand massaged the head of the little nine-year-old, her perfect body relaxed on one hip, but the look told me she was ready to take action. It was obvious she would go down fighting for them. It hit me she wasn't anywhere near twenty.

"How old are you?" I asked.

"Fifteen,' she said proudly standing at her full height. 'What you said, I do hate what I bin doin but I couldn't not do it. You understand? You seem to be real nice and decent.

"Please help us." If it was a come-on it was the best I had heard in years. However, in fairness, acting was the basis of her survival.

I looked around me and things started to percolate in my brain.

I had been the target, the bait. Say had figured out where the meeting would be. He had driven close to the outside wall of the service, storage room, which had been turned into Jewel's kingdom for a day. The line agent had placed the Flashlight viewer, which allowed him to see shadows through the concrete, on the Goshin rifle and fired.

The small penetration area of the bullet and the fact that the chair along with Dubois's body had taken most of the projectile's impact along with the accompanying shards of rock, had saved the children. By the time the second shot had been fired most of them were on the ground. The blood on their bodies was Jewel's. There were a few superficial wounds; these were brought by sobbing victims to Shirl for aid. She, in turn, gravitated undecided between helping them and watching me.

It had been the coldest, bloodiest kind of killing. I shuddered at the terrible effect it would have on the kids but then what other horrors had they already suffered.

I looked at the frightened faces, the courageous faces, the suffering faces and felt the evil of my race and my kind. I was supposed to walk away now. That would be the right thing to do in the manual. Screw the right thing to do.

"Look, I will help you."

"Sweet, so how are you going to do that, Cher?" said Blue Eyes 'the cops will be here any minute." His face was as cold as ice.

"You're wrong son they won't come within miles of the place. At least for a while."

"I ain't your son and how do you know." The kid was tough as nails and as New Orleans as Poor Boy sandwiches.

"Because he was Jewel." I indicated the pulped corpse, that stopped him. 'Listen, all of you have been with and slept with people, important people. These important people are embarrassed by what they have done. It's motivation to cause them to do just about anything or have just about anything done to remove evidence of that. If the police get you then I don't know what will happen. Most of them are honest but there are some who are not and it's not just them, there are others higher up. Listen, you will have to trust me on this." The faces looked back a little more fearful, even Blue Eyes looked scared now, 'First, Billy, right," I said to the tow headed boy with the man's body.

"Yes Sir.' He said instantly, his wide guileless face intent on my message

"I want you to get the kids who are cut or hurt taken care of.' Some might be in shock but for the most part they seemed all right. 'Get some water and clean their wounds."

"Yes, Sir' Given something to do the fear was gone. Billy got the boys in a line and looked them over to make sure they were all right. I took Shirl aside."

"We have to get them dressed and …"

"We don't got no clothes." She interrupted

" What!" I demanded.

"Don't get mad, it was easier for them if we were butt naked." Shirl explained.

"I'm not mad but how did you get here?"

"In the rent-a-truck its special made and looks just like all the others but its got seats and seat belts but no clothes." I had seen the closed cube van outside.

"Put on the coat." I picked up the gray silk designer piece from where it fell when Gaitien had thrown it.

"K,' she said ' poor Gaitien.' she looked down at the bloodied broken puppet 'he was a mean one sure but he was only nineteen and Buddy over there' she indicated the other sprawled figure, 'was going to be sixteen next week." She began to cry a little but then stopped.

"Christ!" was all I could say.' I'm going to put you all in the truck. We'll go to a store; you come in with me. I'll buy everyone clothing, then I'll take you all to safety or as safe as I can make it. I need your help too. Did you sleep with a man named Tisani? He is an Arab, short, thin body, small nose, small face. He'd have a foreign accent." I guessed for that matter that I had a foreign accent.

"I don't think so.' She said self-consciously

" Have you ever heard Jewel say the name or anything about him?" I pressed

"I don't think so. You all hear of this man, Tisani?" she asked the others only silence came back.

"I bet anything, what you want to know, is in the big safe behind his john in the Little Bird House." Shirl brightened.

"What safe?"

"He lived in a house on Little Bird Lane, you know, Ti Wasoo." She mimicked Jewel.

"I was there for special parties sometimes. I was in his bedroom and this fat guy... anyway I saw him go in and pull the chain next to the throne and the wall moved back and there was this big safe." She stopped.

"Ok we'll talk about that later. There will be a medical kit out in the limo"

"Wait, Loft will be out there near the car." she warned. Her face reflected real fear.

"I got a feeling Shirl, Loft isn't in any condition to do anything." For Say, to pull this one off, the opposition would have had to be terminated.

"Well that one I don't care about, he was a man. I don't know how old. He was a unique like he didn't have no balls or things."

"You mean a eunuch" I corrected

"K, well, Jewel he used them to punish us and well, anyone who did't do what their told. If they got fat, or pregnant or sassy or sick, well, Loft or one of the others just made them disappear. Some, I think, they sold but most they was dumped in the swamp up by Blood bayou. It's got a French name but we called it that. There's real big gators up there." She seemed overwhelmed with the reality.

I got them all against the wall and opened the door inward. I swung out and targeted the Lincoln, which was close. Nothing moved. I swung the fourty-five around to the truck, which was parked a few yards away. Loft sat slumped in the seat. He looked dead and I didn't think he was faking. However, you don't take that kind of chance. I circled the truck to find the driver's door open and a small round bullet hole in the base of the bald eunuch's skull.

The corpse fell out of the truck with a sickening thud. Keys for the van and the limo were in the black suit. I ran to the limousine, no cops yet but someone was liable to turn up. A quick search of the interior provided nothing. The medical kit was in the trunk with a second occupant compacted on the floor. Lieutenant Rene Obain of the New Orleans Police department would never call anyone Cher again. A garrote is a dreadful thing in strong hands; Loft was barely competent but certainly proficient. It had been quick, I would say that. Rene's head was half off so it had been brutal. I threw the kit to Shirl, closed the trunk saying a short prayer for the Cajun with the Acadi accent while wiping the edge of the trunk and opened the truck.

Shirl's joy at being free was almost worth it all. She sat in the cab of the truck partially hidden in her coat, watching the traffic and smelling the free air. The boys were in the back. She turned to me and gave an angelic smile.

The store was called Duds and was in a black part of the town. The patrons watched the two of us come in with real interest. Shirl started to shop but caught my glance and grabbed a pair of shorts, a tank top, bra, panties and ducked into a change room.

I quickly selected nine pairs of Levi's, the same number of belts and various T-shirts, three packages of white socks and running shoes, cheap ones. Shirl was back with the tags from her clothes in her hand, wearing new sneakers. She looked pretty and very average without the make up, there was even a pimple or two to remind me she wasn't full grown.

The storeowner, a fourty-five year old black man with a wide gut, looked at me with hard eyes as he took over from the salesgirl. He wasn't sure what was going on but he wasn't happy about it.

"How much?" I asked.

"How you goin to pay for it?"

" Cash."

"That made him blink. Six hundred dollar bills passed over the counter plus some change. The man smiled and checked the money through a little viewer. He seemed surprised it was good."

We dragged all the clothes out to the truck after, Shirl remembered underwear for the boys. I had to stand for an eternity behind a heavy set black woman who seemed to want to talk until the second coming. The owner was kind enough to save me. Shirl outside pushing clothing under the back door of the van.

Bordering Tulane Ave. on the eighth floor of a generic office building is the temporary location of the British Consulate. This vestige of Empire included three offices and a reception area. Here a Consul General, his assistant and a marine guard, for security, are arrayed to increase trade, answer questions, save lost or disadvantaged British citizens and so forth. A local secretary answers the phones and shields the others.

It was before this quiet edifice that our van came to rest. I put the flashers on and prayed everyone was ready, then I opened the door.

The nine came out on queue with only a little whining about clothing that was too big and so on. Blue Eyes made a crack about the cheapness of runners. Being a father gives you a special look that usually quells my ravaging horde. It seemed to work on Blue Eyes who shut up.

Annabelle Wallis had been employed as the secretary of the consulate for fifteen years. A Southern belle, in her mid fourties, plain but well presented with blond hair out of a box. The school group looked a little odd but they were all such beautiful children that she immediately got up to make a fuss. The kids all smiled nicely; they were good at it. You get that way when your life is on the line.

"My name is McFurson, I want to see the consul."

"I'm afraid he's out and Miss Falhout, his assistant, is at a the convention center for a trade show. I'm afraid you just got little old me. What darlin children." She waved at the group.

"Yes, they're lovely. You should have a Royal Marine here?"

"Well, yes. Just a moment.' She seemed confused as if no one had ever asked for the guard before 'Mr. Morgan will you come out.?" Annabelle called.

Sergeant Morgan took God's good time getting out of his chair. He had little to do on this lark and he liked it that way. His six foot four body, in its blue, dress uniform, filled the doorframe. The gang physically stepped back.

"What can I do for you?" His boxer's face and beefy hands made him impressive.

"Sergeant listen,' I said in a whisper having no time, ' 844567391 sigma sigma seven." I recited the memorized number of the day. For a moment he stood stock still as if his brain couldn't react then his years of training kicked in.

"Yes Sir, one moment.' In seconds he was back with a small book. 'Would you repeat yourself?"

he asked. I stated the number one more time. He hesitated.

"The colour of the day is turquoise." I said

"What can we do for you, sir?" Was all he said.

"Fine, everyone into the office." I herded the troops inside, picking up the little nine-year-old who had hugged Shirl's leg named Donnie. The wound in his leg was dripping crimson through the poorly placed bandage and he had passed out.

"Get on the phone. Call a doctor, one that can keep his mouth shut." I said to Annabelle as I placed the fragile little boy on the consul's brown leather couch.

"I have a name." said Morgan helpfully. He gave it to the secretary before moving in to give battlefield medical attention to Donnie who had come around by then. Tears rolled down the round face.

"I want ta call my mumma. She lives in Chattanooga, I know the number." his pain ridden little face pleaded.

"My mumma and daddy live in Blains, Texas", said Billy. At that point most of the rest chimed in. Home, parents and safety, small things in normal life; certainly huge things in the horrible world of Jewel Dubois.

"Look I need fourty-five minutes, then all of you can call home. The sergeant will help you if you have problems. You've got to wait." I said.

"Why, Cher?" The ever-feisty Blue Eyes wanted to know. His chin jutted out defiantly.

"I know it's hard but what if they come after you?' They all looked a little shaken. 'I need an hour then it will be safe or as safe as it is going to get. Shirl, I need to talk to you." I took her into the reception area.

"Listen, do you have a home that you can go to?" Sometimes the place these kids came from was worse then the one they were in. Sexual violation and physical beatings were the most pertinent reasons for running away.

"My mumma and daddy live in Macon. I ran away cause I was stupid. Now I don't know if I can go home but I know they would take me back." She seemed a little lost now, confronted with the fact, that she would have to make a decision about her future when she had had none a few minutes before.

"You're going to be fine, your parents will understand. They will just be happy to get you back."

"After what I done. I don't know.' She looked at me as if I was a bug under a magnifying glass ' would you be?" A few more tears now.

"Yes! I would. If you were one of mine, it wouldn't matter how you came home, as long as you were all in one piece." This seemed to make her smile a bit.

"Listen I'll drive you back myself or at least make sure you get there. Make sure you go to high school, get an education, go out with boys your own age, enjoy your life. Most kids don't get to appreciate what a home and family is about, you do now. Use it."

"K, is that all?"

"No! How well will Billy stand up under pressure?" I asked bluntly.

"He isn't real brave.' She shook her head ' he's a real little kid inside. Kevin is toughest of all."

"Which one's Kevin."

"The one who sasses you all the time. We're heart mates. We do what we can for the others." She said with a little whimsy.

"It won't work. He's too young. I won't put him in danger.' It was my turn to shake my head.

"What is it you want to do?"

"Well,' I blew wind through my teeth, 'In that safe

you talked about will be your picture and where you come from. If I take you home they can find you, all of you. I think I can get you all to England and you can live there. You'd be safe and later you can come back."

"We're Americans. My mumma lives in Macon, I want to go home. Listen you saved us, you don't know from what. I never seen anyone talk to Jewel like that. I knew you didn't understand. That old boy would have made you fall apart if he had the time. He would have had you doin' just what he wanted. You woulda wanted to die but he wouldn't let you. You freed us, like they freed the slaves, guess it's the same. I'll do whatever you want. If you promise to take care of Kev and the others if I don't get back."

"I can't ask you to do this."

"Why, cause I'm a girl?"

"No, because the people at the Little Bird house won't open the door. They will know you would run if you got the chance. I think they will smell a rat. They might think Billy would go back, he's the type."

"You're wrong I coulda run in St. Martin so could Steve. We called him Lance. We all was watched by this big black French asshole called Ti Buddy. But we coulda." I figured Ti Buddy had tried to sample the merchandise or took it there was a lot of hate there.

"Why wouldn't you?"

"Go to the police? What happened when you tried?" She smiled knowingly. 'Yeah, no money, lots of clothes, remember." The smile got lecherous. 'I knowed you was lookin."

"So they figure you would come back." I said changing the subject.

"Yeah, what do you want me to do?" she got real intense.

"It's not much of a plan. How many people would be there now?" I asked

" Just Bitzi, he's the meanest of the eunuchs and the biggest. They ain't dumb and they know how to use a gun. They're like dogs to Jewel, do anything for him."

"You think he'd open the door for you."

"I sure think so. He'd want to know what happened right away. The house is on a court. There is a camera over the door, but no one is stupid enough to go after Jewel so they get kind of lazy. Also, Little Bird is connected by a tunnel to the big house two streets over where we all work and live. There are more of his people at the

Domicile." I had visions of hell opening up to let out Jewel's people to shamble up the tunnel.

"So, what's the plan?" She insisted.

I was kind of embarrassed to tell her.

"The plan, I guess, is that one of my friends and I hide beside the door. You show up in Gaitien's coat. You'd have to be nude underneath for them to buy it. If you have clothes on they'll figure it's a scam. The time should be just about right for you to have walked back. The eunuch opens the door. He's toast. We destroy the information, you and the kids are clear. I will call the police and they can do what they can for the kids at the Domicile, that's the best I can do."

"Of course you're goin' to get a lot of information and stuff to help the people who pay you. Will you get a promotion or somethin?"

"No, but the information could be real important. I'm hoping it will be valuable enough to make up for taking care of you. It's sort of a trade.' I looked at her knowing eyes, no space for soft soap when the truth was required. 'I will get something out of this, no games." I said it cleanly; I was going to anyway.

"At least you're honest, K".

"Listen, if they already know about Jewel you could be shot out of hand." I said.

"No! No one will check up on Jewel. They wouldn't dare."

Chapter twenty-two - 11:45 P.m., Little Bird Lane, New Orleans, Louisiana.

The Raid

We walked back two hundred years in time. Beneath the gray, stone, vine covered archway into a quiet, well-lit, backwater paralleled by gray, six-foot high stone walls, which contained two portals. Each opening was barred with a metal gate, however, neither was locked. It seemed Shirl was right, Jewel's minions had grown slack, begun to believe in their own invulnerability. All the better for us.

For a moment we hovered in the quiet as if we might shatter its fragile reality. Taffey looked over at me and smirked. I had contacted him on his cell phone and he wasn't pleased. He was on his way out of town at the time. It took considerable persuasion to have him pick us up with his tow truck.

As all outposts of the Firm, this one had a cover, which made a profit. It was this innovation that had allowed the Service to survive the budget cuts that occurred at the end of the Cold War. In New Orleans it was Tatters Junkyard. The buying and selling of parts, some with uncertain origin kept

Taffey in contact with the local bad guys and an end stop for information that was essential to the Firm. Taffey also made contact with other ex Brits at pubs and so on, which allowed him to gather information at the industrial level. The tow truck was a simple cover; the broken down Ford sedan attached made it more effective. It would, however, create a poor get away.

"Right!' said the small, cold eyed man. ' The plan is we jump the wall while the bird goes through the gate and distracts them."

"That's it." I smiled at Shirl, who looked very fragile, naked in the gray raincoat. The fifteen-year-old smiled back uncertainly.

"What if things go bad?" Taffey wanted to know.

"Well, some men howl and some men run. I'm a howling sprinter." It wasn't much of a joke.

"Magic, I'll make a note in my diary." The compact ex-villain was not amused.

"Alright Shirl go to the gate and wait until we're over the wall."

"K!" she said and was off.

I offered Taffey a foot up but he was already starting to climb the wall. At the top he stopped and helped my bloated person crest the rough iron arrows that protected the surface. We dropped down, I almost breaking both legs and made it through a garden of brightly blooming flowers to the old square faced gray stone house and crouched beneath the camera on either side of the sedate, black, wood front door.

For a moment I sat and caught my breath. I had looked the house over as closely as possible for cameras. There was nothing obvious but then technology was so good now the camera lens might only be an inch across. There was no helping it, we were here and, perhaps, about to get a nasty surprise.

Shirl came through the gate tentatively and walked toward the house on her bare feet as if it were a dragon and she was the village sacrifice. She could really act but that was preservation. She stood in front of the camera, looked around like she thought someone might be out there, as if she was scared to be caught and then called out.

"Bitzi, please let me in, I came back like master told me." There was a slight sob in the voice, a nice touch.

I could hear the motor direct the camera lens above us toward the girl. Taffey and I crouched hard against the wall.

“What happened?” A thin, hard, cold voice demanded. This had to be Bitzi the eunuch.

“Let me in Bitzi, quick.” Shirl wined.

“Where’d you get Gaitiens coat? What happened?” he said with growing anger.

“Damn it Bitzi, Gaitian is dead, .I grabbed the coat and ran.” With this she flashed the camera with her golden body. I heard Taffey inhale from my place and cursed him mentally.

Then there was a thunder as if a storm was rolling across the delta as the big man descended the stairs like a diesel engine. The next sound was Bitzi dragging at the lock to open the heavy wooden door. Fear for his master or the need for quick action, had overcome his caution. Perhaps caution wasn’t necessary. Who would disturb Jewel Dubois and live to tell?

He came through the entrance with the words,

“You stupid cunt.” Dressed only in a blue silk gown, a red and gold Chinese dragon stretched down over his huge breast. He was fat bloated in fact. Bitzi's ability to move as fast as he did seemed nothing short of amazing, given his size. He had a melon like, bald head with a mindless animal’s face. Here was someone who could take pleasure in other peoples pain. He centered on Shirl who cowered away. Taffey took one step out of hiding and swung his Walther into the fat, red face. The upper cut came right off the deck and extended Sanders compact muscular body with the precision of a prize fighter and the grace of a ballarino. The impact threw the eunuch backwards. The sound of his bald head hitting the concrete had a satisfactory crunch. The dazed, fat man tried to rise but Taffey hit him again, this time with a vicious downswing to the temple. Bitzi lay still.

It took the two of us to haul him over the doorstep. He had to weigh in at three hundred pounds. If Shirl hadn't taken his feet it never would have happened. He was too much dead weight. I closed the door and we turned our guns on the large, empty hall with its dark mahogany steps surfaced in red carpet. The house smelled of some flowery floor wax. Fine, wood paneling stretched away to the back of the first floor.

Nothing moved. Taffey slapped handcuffs on Bitzi with my help. Then while Taffey gagged him, Shirl kicked Bitzi in his fat gut for all she was worth. Once, then twice, then with growing force and abandon until we pulled her off.

"He hurt me, that rotten bastard, he hurt little ones." Shirl was really angry.

"That's enough, alright!" I demanded.

"K!" she agreed but ruefully

I left Taffey to tie up the tub while I and Shirl mounted the stairs. At the top there were three doors. I checked each bedroom; they yawned empty. Large windows allowed the sunlight to explore bright pleasantly coloured floor space. Mirrors covered the ceiling of each room. In the second room was a sort of study. A fabulous collection of hard cover editions masked the wall. The smell of leather impregnated the room. On a table was a computer and monitoring system with a video hook up for the camera outside. The entrance lay static in the television screen. I backed up the tape and sure enough, there we were. I removed the tape and placed it my bag.

The master bedroom, which had been Jewel's, was huge. The bed was oak and magnificently carved. Eighty-ounce burgundy carpet cushioned our feet. The room smelled of familiar cologne but I couldn't place the name. It was a neutral place. Books by the side of the bed, the newspaper neatly folded on the cover. A tidy man, our Jewel. There were pictures of the children on his night table. I found that sick as hell. He had turned his slaves into a perverted extended family or perhaps it was a scam to cover the children's presence if the authorities ever turned on him. The room was private but not Satan's sitting room. Ti Buddy's words came back to me now about the Jew at the nazi's trial. I realized that Dubois was not cloven hoofed and I could be him, but immediately removed the thought from my mind. No one could be Jewel Dubois and live with themselves, outside of that sick man.

Behind the bed was the door to the bathroom. It too was empty. The toilet looked old. It was a throne, lifted two steps off the floor with a chain to flush it from an overhead tank. Behind it was a wall of white marble veined with jade green.

"You pull the chain twice, then stop, then two more times." said Shirl.

"Put your clothes on." I handed her the backpack I was carrying and moved to the chain. I pulled the handle twice and nothing happened, it didn't even flush. I waited a moment.

"Now pull it agin. " said Shirl from the doorway where she was pulling on her pants.

The chain came down twice more, nothing happened for a moment then, with a soft whir the wall behind the john slid back and to the right showing an old antique safe. The legend read in a rich golden scroll against the jet-black surface, 'Albert Walker and Sons, Chicago Illinois, 1892'. The door was at least half a foot thick.

"I think me Gran had one like that.' said Taffey coming over to the safe and touching it with loving hands. There were three hinges on the door and he quickly placed and wired charges on all of them. We then adjourned to the bedroom. The loud bang that followed was muffled by the mattress. Still small metal pieces flew through the open door to imbed themselves in the chest of drawers opposite. The door hung open at one side. It took only a slight push to bring it crashing to the floor. We entered only after Taffey checked for trip wires or any other surprises. The soft hum of a central air conditioner was the only sound. We stepped onto the steel plate and into Aladdin's treasure cave. The safe was a huge room, perhaps twenty feet by thirty feet with cream coloured metal walls, steel shelves reaching to the ceiling in what seemed to be never ending rows. Each was piled with VCR films, photos and sound tapes. All this neatly placed information was clearly labeled by country and person. All of this was pure sexual material, pure pornography. I recognized Senators, Congressmen and other high officials in the US government in sexual situations that surprised me and I was no child.

This, of course was Jewel's power. The fear he held over this State and whole countries.

In separate steel filing cabinets were the children. Photographs so gruesome that only someone with no sanity at all could enjoy them. The small, frightened faces, set in smiles of forced acceptance, being sexually abused, being physically abused. Stacks of them. Pictures, home addresses for reference, who had purchased them, if they escaped, all of it.

Without a word Taffey and I started to place material into the backpacks. We had three large ones and they were quickly filled to capacity.

Senior British members of Parliament, some of our best people indicated as moles and spies for other powers, specific units related to France and other countries including China. Only the choice pieces went with us, the time was limited and the information was priceless.

The question now was what to do with the rest of the hoard. The police could be here any second, not to mention CIA, NSA and God knew what else. We couldn't take it with us. I Turned to Taffey and said two words.

"Burn it."

Taff removed small packets from his pockets and began spreading the petroleum smelling substance on the shelves. I removed a small magnet from the bedroom, while Shirl placed the backpacks in that room. Small, but powerful, the magnet would scramble the tapes.

While Taffey worked, I went into the other bedrooms to find anything I could on Tisani. Behind the bed, two great, gray eyes looked up at me for a moment then disappeared with a little shriek behind the bed. I rounded the huge bedstead forty-five leveled to find a naked eight-year-old boy in a ball on the carpet. He was trembling and had peed himself. The horror filled eyes looked up from a lattice of fingers and cleaved into my very soul. So this is what Bitzi had been involved with, which had distracted him and given us at least a chance. I realized, after the fact, that there were more cameras focused on the wall and the walkway. I had demagnetized the film. Had the eunuch concentrated on business he could have had us cold.

"Please don't kill me, I can be nice to you." It was a half cry, the child held his little hands up in front of him to ward off whatever thing I wished to do to him. He had no protection and no hope of stopping me. I could have cried at that point. The anger welled in me like black bile.

I was about to tell him he had nothing to fear when Shirl and Taffey showed up.

"Allen!" Shirl cried and picked up his small body. He clung to her like a frightened monkey, bawling now in bitter shaking sobs.

"Bitzi was playing with me." He mumbled. There was blood on the floor where he had been sitting and a plastic dildo partially hidden under the bed. My God where did it end? Taffey's face was concrete.

"You finish up I'm going down for one last look about." he said in a soft even voice.

"OK,' I mumbled. Then to Shirl 'Is there any clothing for him?"

"Yes, I'll dress him and carry him." She seemed frightened we might leave the little boy.

I went back to the master bedroom and checked the vault. All was ready. Taffey returned and busied himself with destroying the maximum of the accumulated filth as possible. I never felt so dirty or vile..

Taffey was ready. I got out just as he lit the gelatin there was an instant roar, intense heat and smoke started to billow out. Too bad we had no timer. Shirl and Allen met us in the hallway.

"But these are dress up clothes, Bitzi will be mad." His little voice quivered with fear.

"Don't you worry about Bitzi he ain' hurtin' you no more, you're goin' home."

We ran down the stairs before the smoke. At the bottom Bitzi lay where we left him. A pool of blood still extended from the small hole in the back of his head. Taffey didn't meet my eyes. Shirl made to say something but then ran past the corpse as if it didn't exist, the wide-eyed child in her arms. I followed across the garden, after Taffey shot the camera from beneath with his silenced automatic. We wandered out to the narrow street, like tourists, to the tow truck. The backpacks went in behind the seat and we piled in. Sirens screamed from all directions. Fire in the old city is taken very seriously. As the black smoke rose above the roof top and we faded away down the slender streets to the embassy.

Chapter twenty-three – 6:30 A.m., The Highway to Macon Georgia

A Long Nights Journey Into Dawn

The rain drove itself onto the windshield with the force of small darts, trailing off into rivers created by large powerful wiper blades. Atlanta had come and gone. We were now on I 16 moving toward Macon and home.

Shirl was curled up in the passenger's seat of the 98 Chrysler Concord the Consulate had rented for us back in New Orleans. I watched her in peaceful secure sleep. The tall Georgia girl was safe for the first time in a long while. It was exhilarating to know I had provided that safety and security.

If I have done nothing more on this job, at least one little girl was going home to someone who loved her. Shirl would return to a new life, with lots of trials certainly but at least one of normality. I noted the small trickle of drool that seeped down from the edge of the mouth onto her hand. She was a baby. How could any man sexually abuse a child like that? Of course, I should moralize, on the beach in St Martin it was me who was watching. Well that was then and I did not know. Rationalization is always the better part of stupidity.

Driving becomes a part of you after a while. The night is tranquil. The rain slowly lessens in intensity. You are lulled by country and western music playing very low on the radio. Wilber Tuttle or something decries the loss of his woman. I have never liked country and western music. Some songs like Country Roads, I do enjoy. However, to listen to the stuff for long periods of time drives me nuts. Shirl likes it and is not allowed to listen to it in the house, as it is music for seeds, straw chewers and such, so for now, it is on.

My mind goes on autopilet as we move through the Georgia night to Macon.

Dubois must have gone mad. Only a madman would put himself in such danger. He must have known they would follow me or know enough to find him. The set up was obviously a trap; it amazed me that anyone would go for it. Of course the man in the underground car park could have been a double. The acting would have to be too good. The evil that radiated from the man was real enough. I felt it. He certainly looked like Dubois. Shirl confirmed he was. All of it worked on different levels.

Jewel with his many years of other world experience, knew the Firm well. Perhaps too well. He probably had never heard of the Flashlight and its ability to see through concrete, of course, that was his downfall.

In a perverse way, I rather hoped the reason for his fall could have been a loss of faith. By that I mean, all this time Jewel had remained untouchable because of the dirty secrets he held. Governors and others had run to his call because of what these secrets could do if fed to the general population and their potential for retribution. With the emergence of good old Bubba, all that changed. If the President of the United States could have interactions under his desk without retribution, then what real value did Dubois's dirty pictures have? How could you infuriate a population that had no shame? One that felt sexuality was as normal as grass. What power would Jewel have then? How soon would those he had dictated to be at his door demanding retribution of their own? Give the information to the press. If the morality is no longer there, then it does not matter?

I knew I have been in the business too long when the next thought dropped into place. Who said the poles weren't rigged? Who was to say that Bubba didn't get the press to tell the big lie? Saying again and again the public don't want to know, until it was so, then wouldn't there have been a roar of anger from the people? The problem was if the media wanted the present leader, who would broadcast the truth? The Rush people might tell it but were there enough listeners to hear? Perhaps the truth was, as one religious leader said, 'We have lost the moral battle for America.'"

Perhaps, like globalization, that cruelly balanced blade, the truth simply made Jewel redundant as it had the rotten financial practices of the ultra rich in Korea, Indonesia and even Japan. Without a solid honest financial base to work from, the all powerful money movers could destroy a society and had. Investing huge amounts of money then withdrawing it when they got a wind up. The eastern tigers would have to lick their wounds and change their dishonest ways. At Jewel's age, change would be impossible.

Of course it was all piffle, as Granny was want to say. Jewel had begun to believe his own press. Believed, he was, in fact invulnerable: had developed his king complex to the outer limits of sanity. The naked children, the throne, the imperial mannerisms blared that. He died because he got careless. It did not matter why, he was gone, that was enough.

The thing that had been eating at me all night, was the fact that, he had not taken responsibility for the men who died so long ago in the Caribbean. Why tell me he had not been responsible when I was a dead man or as close to it as possible without a coffin. Was it possible that he had not done it? That would explain the CIA protecting him here. It would also leave a huge loose end in our operation. The Firm had had moles a plenty in its day. It was for this reason that the mundane Sir Mortimer had stepped in. At least he was from the outside and clean, certainly nonpolitical. There were those less kind that said he was indifferent to the whole bloody thing. McFurson felt he was an amateur doing the best he could. It would be better if the great powers within the Secret Service remembered that it had been from their number the traitors had come. It was this reality that in effect created Sir Mortimer.

McFurson would send in the report, after that it would be up to the leader of the Firm to decide where to go with it. That was all he could do. He owed both Granny and Mortimer a great deal but this was different. In the end it must come from them.

He had watched Shirl and Kevin touch at the door of the van that was to take her paramour and two others to the Royal Airforce Hercules. The plane would fly them and the two accountants' briefcases full of secrets, to Bermuda.

Sergeant Morgan was placed in charge of the hoard of information. Specific material of top priority quality had been sent directly to Granny via special fax, along with the information went Kevin and two other children who had no known parents or who had been sold to Dubois. Yes, Toto we are not in Kansas anymore, sold to Dubois without a second thought. They were off to jolly old England for their own protection.

Ceril Long, the Consulate General, was a good head in anyone's estimation. The lank thin faced Oxford don would go along and make sure the information arrived in London sending Taffey along with two other agents from Washington. The boys would be placed in good homes and educated that would be part of the price for the information. At least they would have a chance and that was something.

Parents were making their way to New Orleans from six states to pick up their children from the consulate office. More joyous parents were being contacted with the list Shirl had provided. Their children would be at the Domicile.

New Orlean's finest showed up at that historic pile, ten minutes after they found Obain in the limo trunk. It seemed the good Lieutenant had been involved with a year long investigation into the trafficking of children for sex and was murdered by Dubois and other suspects. We were informed by the evening news.

We watched on television just before we left New Orleans as the pimply faced Toad, the last of the Eunuchs, was hustled into a paddy wagon with other less attractive individuals, if that was possible.

Ceril and most of the diplomatic corps, Holland and France being in the forefront, turned up at the Domicile to insure that none of their nationals were involved. Stone-faced American government types looked embarrassed and uncomfortable. The row got on television as someone had had the foresight to call the local affiliate stations. To avoid an international incident the names of the children were given and the diplomats were allowed to meet them. The parents began to show up just about that time. The various Consulate Generals took their time with the interviews, taking shifts to insure all the children were safe, until their parents showed up and took them back. This caused great consternation around the various U.S. internal security branches, until London called to say that the material they were worried about was destroyed. The heat of the explosion on the phone from Washington could be felt in New Orleans but that of course was Mortiner's and the Prime Minister's problem.

Kevin and Shirl had kissed softly with adult passion. The little rebel then turned to me and with a look of cold fury, reminded me to look after her. I offered my hand. He took it and gave me a man's clasp. As he turned away great tears slid down his cheeks.

Kevin was a little boy with an uncertain future dependent on people he did not know. It is questionable that an adult could have faced it. He walked away ramrod stiff holding hands with the two younger ones, not turning around to save Shirl his pain. I had known men with less guts. He would be all right, I promised to his slender back. It would be my responsibility to make sure he came back home later after things quieted down.

Just beyond the darkness the dawn was lurking like some predatory animal. Soon the claw cuts of its existence would be visible as it raked the night. Soon to my left toward the Atlantic it would conquer the darkness over the Carolinas.

Shirl moved in her sleep, making a small mewing sound as if her dreams were beginning to get too real. I wondered what her dreams would be like, then decided my need to know was not that great.

At the big truck stop just outside the Louisiana border in the dusk of the night before, she sat down and just plain devoured the place with her eyes. Like a prisoner that had seen too much of the same walls she wallowed in the sounds and movements. Finally, when the waitress came, she looked at me with certain nervousness.

"Can I have whatever I want? Is there enough money?" she requested as quietly as possible to save me from embarrassment. I smiled softly and told the waitress who was perhaps a year older then Shirl, to bring her whatever she wanted.

"I'm goin to be wicked." She smiled in a foxy way then ordered a huge steak with fries and vegetables. I have seen some people eat but this was something else. For a girl her size she polished off the food without even breathing. Then, with equal aplomb, she knocked off two pieces of apple pie with whipped cream.

"At the house you only got to eat what they wanted you to. I promise I won't get fat but gee golly howdy that was good." I shared her pleasure.

I would have let her sleep but the dawn was coming up and I couldn't let her miss it. I thought she needed to see it after missing the performance for so long.

Running her free hand over her mouth she caged a look at me to see if I was disgusted, when I didn't react she sat back and watched the cresting sun.

"I'm sorry I woke you."

"That's fine I recognize the buildings. It's awesome to know you're home. Don't matter how good it is, where you go, its always better to sleep in your own bed." She sniffed and I thought she might cry but that didn't happen.

"My Mumma and Daddy took us all to Florida one year down at Daytona. It was real nice. They had double beds and it was right on the beach. We even got to go to dinner at this restaurant called Sinbads. It's real well known and the food is real good. Not like Denny's. I mean I like Denny's and all but you feel a little richer at Sinbads. I enjoyed the vacation, it was the best we ever had. When it was over though, I was happy to be home and sleeping in my own bed."

"Mind if I ask why you left?"

"There was this boy. God it sounds so stupid now. Well, there was lots of boys. Arly, was that particular boy's name. My Mumma and Daddy did not like him one whit. Oh no, they did not. But he had this Firebird car. It was painted black.' she sighed ' It was a fine car. Arly said he loved me. God I am stupid. I had this real big fight with my parents and Arly said we should go to New Orleans and live there, get married and all. He had cousins in the French Quarter. Well, we went. We slept together and everthin'. You get a lot of dreams, you know? They was all smoke. Arly got into drugs big time. I told him not to. He got mean and I got scared and said I call my folks. Guess he thought they might charge him for stealin' a minor or somethin'.

He made friends with Gaitien. Gaitien, he had lots of drugs. Arly and him were real tight. Finally Gaitien asked us to this here party. I walked into the Domicile, lord was I stupid. Arly left with a lot of money and I was just settin' there so I started to leave and go home, but I couldn't go home, someone owned me.' Her voice fell to a soft tremble, ' Well I told them what I thought uh that and they beat the hell out of me. Not so it would show mind and raped me. After that, I did what I was told. I was scared and no one was goin to help me. I didn't want to die.

It was real sick at the house. All these men doin' stuff they would kill people for if it were their kid . I ain't trailer trash neither,' this seemed important and I nodded. 'My father works at the dairy and my Mumma she's a nurse, we got a house and all. Why do men do that? They got to know we hate them?" Shirl stopped and waited for my answer.

"I truly do not know, Shirl." I said honestly, 'I never had a prostitute."

"Oh,' the voice became smaller.

"Listen you aren't a prostitute. You had no say in it."

"I could have killed myself, I thought of it a lot.'

She wiped her eyes, 'maybe that is the best way out."

"You can't, you owe me a life." I figured if it worked once, why not?

"What?" she almost screamed.

"I saved your life. You owe me a life, so I give it back but you can't take it. That's the deal."

"I don't owe you nothin,' the voice trembled with anger, ' Who helped you at Ti Wasoo?"

"I didn't mean it that way.' I stopped to think for a moment, 'I like you. I don't want you to kill yourself. Why do you think I'm driving you home?"

"I thought that was your job you're some kind a law aren't you?" She seemed confused.

"Some kind of law, yes I guess that's what I am." How little she knew.

"Ain't this your chore?" she asked.

"No, I could have got someone else. Look you've got more guts and brains than most people. If you got lost in the shuffle, I couldn't live with myself. You're going to be something important someday and I can say I knew Shirl way back when. I got to help her get started before she was a world famous model." I finished half believing it.

"Gosh, nobody talked like that to me since my Daddy.' She sniffed, 'Thanks lots."

For a moment Shirl got real thoughtful.

"You think I could be a model?" The question came from real deep inside, someone was coming way out from her defenses.

"Sure, I don't see why not. You're beautiful, tall and you have grace. A lot of people started out with a lot less and made it."

"I'll remember you when I get rich and all.' She teased, 'I'll take you to eat at some real nice place like Sinbads maybe?" She smiled happily.

"OK, It's a date."

"K!" the silence set in again. 'It's seven o'clock, my brothers be watchin' Deputy Dog. I really like old DD. He's kind of like us. Sounds down home. My name ain't Shirl that's what they called me. I am Pamela Ann Huggins."

"A name to go home with."

"K, ' she seemed to make peace with a lot of things in that moment, ' you take a right here and take the first cut off." We left the highway and meandered through various parts of Macon. Finally the Concord slid to a halt outside a small ranch-like bungalow with a long driveway.

"This is goin to sound real foolish and everything but I'm real scared." She looked with terror on the very place where she would be safest.

"No one followed us." I started.

"It ain't that, what if they don't want me?"

"Oh, well then I'll adopt you and you can fight it out with my pack." She laughed then.

"Guess I ought to go." This more to herself then to me, 'will you walk me to the door?"

"Sure!" We got out of the car, she not waiting for me to open the door for her. I stood beside her. I felt her hand in mine then tensed fingers tightened with a terrific grip. I will always remember that walk, the soft smell of flowers, the sound of crickets, cars leaving down the street for work. It was placid and middle America. I felt the solid middle class values that had made it this way like a pleasant wash of normalcy after Dubois and his horror show. Perhaps, I envied Pam her ability to walk away from it all, knowing that I would have to go back and face it once more.

At the screen door her hand slipped away. The aluminum was worn but solid. Soft, green siding that incased the little home was old and tired. There was the smell of fresh baked biscuits that wafted out and made my mouth water.

A timid hand rang the bell. The short, blond woman turned the corner into the long hall that lead from the kitchen to the outside. You could plainly see where Pam got her looks. For a moment the tired face seemed to search the girl's then the reality hit her.

"Pamie ,Dwight Pamie is home." With that her mother charged to the door, tore it open and hugged the now crying girl. As I turned away there was a thunder of feet as two little boys roared down the hallway and joined the hug. The tall blond man who followed the boys set his bloodless face and looked at me suspiciously as I walked back to the car.

"Who's he?" the youngest Huggins wanted to know.

"He's a friend, he's some kind of law daddy,' Pam explained to her father. 'He brought me home."

"We should have him in and thank him proper." Dwight Huggins voice was thin and nasal.

"No daddy he has things to do."

"Alright puddin, if you think it's best that way."

The room at the Hampton was large and well appointed. I stripped and took a long, soothing shower. With Pam back home a great weight was removed from my shoulders. I walked across to the bed and settled my naked body on its inviting surface. The mattress felt so good after so many problems I closed my eyes and went to sleep for two hours. When I came around I dragged myself to the board of the laptop and started to send my message to Brit. line. It went in small segments every few minutes to put off watchers.

I had one more card to play but would they let me? I had to try. Tisani was still out there and something inside me wouldn't let it go.

I had made the request, all I could do now was wait. I decided to do that sleeping.

Chapter twenty-four – 9:00 A.m., Her Majesty's Secret Service, London England.

A Meeting of Minds.

"That stuff is appalling." Sir Mortimer Brae looked out his window, pointedly ignoring the figures on the twenty-eight inch television that proved perversion could be fun for some demented souls.

"Yes! I know, I've watched it twice." Granny Stater's cool unruffled voice cut across the soundproof office. The chiseled features, under their golden brows, were looking at the screen. However, anyone observing Staters would have recognized the revulsion in his face.

"I find little humour in this matter." The Knight snapped. His right hand rubbed his almost bare pate. Gorilla-like body hair flushed out from under his silk shirtsleeve. Brae's small bright eyes were clouded with troubles.

"If you look at this sort of thing enough you tend to put on a thicker skin." There was steel in Granny's voice.

"I see." Mortimer played with his watch chain fob a clear indication he was perturbed. His lack of experience handicapped him, made him vulnerable to that kind of dig about his semi permanence.

Perhaps, he thought, I am not suited to this disaster. It all started very civily. A chum had noted he was at loose ends at the club and thought there might be an opportunity with the government. Good show, he had thought, a nice office job with the Department of Ablutions and so forth. A directorship of course, nice secretary and home for four to enjoy high tea.

This was what? An opportunity all right. However, at the point it was offered how could one turn down leadership of the Secret Service? The opportunity to match wits with wily sinister leaders of the KGB and the lesser Communist substates. The power to secure the nation's interests, the ability to change things. The quiet words of awe from the other members of the club as he passed. " That's Brae, head of one of the security departments you know."

Good Lord what had he been thinking? It had become a terror-filled roller coaster ride to hell.

The Russians were gone, the moles were too. One hoped, but one wasn't sure, was one? Four directorates, headed by the finest men in the organization, giving grudging fealty to an inexperience-stubbing peer with only his limited knowledge of business affairs to help him.

He had quickly found out the enemy was more probably the French or the Americans, than some bunch of Middle Eastern terrorists. Oh! They existed, the Virgins thing was a good example. Now Tisani was loose. Where was the bugger? What did he have in those damned capsules? The French had been their normal dark selves with speculations that made one wish one had never heard of the Secret Service and had emigrated to Australia years ago.

'Bugger them all,' he thought vindictively, Mortimer was getting to like the job now that he had some inkling of what it was he was doing. Yes, it had to be admitted, he was slowly getting to enjoy himself.

Certainly not the deaths he had sanctioned. His upbringing and conscience stood in the way. Brae consoled himself with the fact as enemies of the free world their deaths were inevitable. They were the enemies of his Queen whom he has pledged on death to defend. As his predecessors of old, it was he, metaphorically, who held her glove as simile of her trust in him to secure her person.

Therefor, until her trust was removed, he would take up arms against her foes. So be it.

"I am amazed at McFurson. This is real coup. The Canadian went in a target and came out with all this.' The Brae motioned at the pile of tapes, photographs and cassettes on his desk. 'Oh! By the by, we shall have to give most of the American stuff back.' He took a second for dramatic emphasis, 'After we copy it of course." He laughed at his own cleverness, then stopped as he noted Granny's icy smile and suspected the arrogant so and so had already done just that.

"McFurson is a good man." Granny conceded.

"He gets results." The Peer came down hard and let the challenge float in the air conditioning.

"He helped the children and one lead him to the prize. I vetted the little angels he sent along to us. The eldest would find himself at home in any of our better street gangs."

"Wasn't that against rules and regs." Brae probed.

"McFurson, Sir Mortimer, still believes in daring do, the right and helping the downtrodden. Children are his weak point. He wants to be Sir Galahad. Unfortunately we aren't in the King Arthur theatre of operations." Mortimer evaluated Granny's input for an insult found none and plowed on.

"The Japanese girl was the result of that weak point as you put it?" Mortimer asked wandering around the office.

"Yes, funny how things lead one to another. No kidnapped Japanese, no Jewel and of course no information. What do you want to do with the three identified moles in the report?"

"For the moment, nothing, keep them under watch. We will have a Directors meeting and make some final arrangements." Mortimer became thoughtful.

"Why does he do it, I wonder?" the Knight said almost to himself.

"Who, McFurson?" The blond head tilted, Granny was never napping.

"Yes! He isn't Church of England, is he? I mean why work for us?"

"Queen and Country I'm afraid.' Granny leaned back as he did when he was thoughtful, 'The queen is still the head of the Canadian government. It's surprising how deep the old monarchist roots go."

"I see, loyalty, not money?"

"No! Not in McFurson's case. He gets a stipend of course and he can use it. Interesting chap, believed in the cause when he joined up, the need to get rid of Communism. When the Soviets folded he stayed on. I truly think he enjoys the adrenaline but he is getting old. Wanted to retire last year but I wouldn't let him. We needed him, short staffed as always."

“Of course.” Granny’s superior agreed. ‘Perhaps we should put him on full line status?”

“I don’t think so. He has the devil’s luck or perhaps God watches over him. At best he’s just a competent amateur. However, he’s an excellent courier and very important in that capacity.”

“I leave that to you as always.’ said Brae. Granny got off a sarcastic smile ‘He wants to follow up on this Tisani thing,’ the peer continued, ‘seems to think there is a chance to find this Au Clair fellow from St. Martin. Feels Au Clair, in turn, will lead him to Tisani.”

“I have no one to help him. It’s a long shot and Louisiana is very unhealthy for our Mike right now. I’d hate to think what the Dubois clan would do if they got their hands on our courier.. He isn’t set up for it. I’ll send someone else to look into it. FBI can help, it’s in their best interest now that Jewel isn’t with us. Also it’s in their territory and after New Orleans it might go along way to covering over the cracks.”

“Will the Americans help do you think, after this lot?” Mortimer motioned to encompass the table full of papers.

“Oh! Of course they have nothing but love for us.” Granny offered a small compromise smile.

"True! I forget how close we are.' Brae laughed again. 'What will you do with McFurson?"

"Send him home to his family in Niagara Falls."

"I was amazed he went in to Jewel's clutches, he must trust you a great deal."

"It's mutual,' Said Granny. A high compliment indeed, thought Brae. 'Also, he was worried about his family. The perverted old swine wasn't above taking action against wife and children. McFurson wanted the matter taken care of."

"Interesting that Dubois didn't take credit for the Caribbean disaster?"

"Yes! I wasn't out there. It might have been someone else who did the killing. The DNA shows it was Dubois who died in the garage, no doubt there."

"There is always doubt." corrected Mortimer and Granny seemed to agree. There was no arrogant smile.

"Look over the situation, see if there are any other calculations to find the correct answer, will you? I want to know as soon as." The Knight became a schoolmaster when he knew his ground, which rubbed Granny the wrong way. This time however, he was right.

"Yes, Sir Mortimer."

"Fine then,' Brae looked at the screen ' we aren't much up from apes are we."

" No! That Darwin Johnny was spot on." Brae didn't catch Granny's quick sarcastic look at Mortimer's own furry paws.

8:30 P.m. The Imperial Restaurant, Lent, Louisiana

If Lent were any smaller it wouldn't exit. The crossroads are in shouting distance of the swampy bayous that extend from the river. A musty, antique way of life is reflected. A musty, antique smell permeates everything. I will never get used to that flat decaying miasma.

There is an old building on each corner of the thoroughfare. The minimart, with its gas pumps, is the newest and even its pealing exterior is at least twenty years in stagnation.

God is represented in the person of the Late Eventist; Sons of the Earth, Baptist Church. A tired one-story beige building, which crouches on a second corner. Across from this is the Au Just Bait Shop, incased in a dilapidated house that was new when Napoleon One was Emperor of France.

The Imperial, on the other hand is the one really interesting edifice in the flyspeck. A true fifties pierce of nostalgia. A man with vision built it with love. At one time its regal face had sported great wide fifties windows. Sadly these had been bricked in when the place became a bar in one of its many incarnations. The tall steel sign, with its space rocket structure stretched to a sculpted point at least fifteen feet overhead. It still held the original oval of crimson neon with the large scripted 'Imperial' in blazing white. Many of the bulbs had long ago died but enough survived or had been replaced over the years so that it still shone brightly into the southern night.

Two young white boys watched me with interest as I moved toward the large glass doors that still survived. Dressed in bib overalls, shouldering poles layered with a variety of fish, they stood drinking Doctor Pepper in bare feet before the Minimart.

I should have created little interest in my white shirt and khaki pants. Perhaps everything was of interest here where so little happened.

Inside it was like the fifties were frozen in time. Big, battered, red padded vinyl bench seats paralleled arborite single leg tables, which were anchored to the wall. On each table, cozied to the wall or the center section of the booths, was a two for a quarter chrome music selector. Each had the mandatory red lined list of tunes followed by their identifying numbers and letters. The big, brightly-lit jukebox held the center of the main aisle where it belted out "Peggy Sue". Its highly polished chrome exterior reflected the images of the six people who inhabited the bar on this weekday night. Two men, obviously fishermen, stole glances at the rotund bartender and made a hurried departure. This left the room to the five of us.

Cuttie pivoted in his old much-abused wicker-bottomed chair and faced me. The icy shark eyes were the same as I remembered in the Caymans. Behind him and slightly to the right was Long his passionless, pear shaped face blank and empty. They were both wearing flowered shirts that would have been more at home in Hawaii with the mandatory hardware hidden beneath. I realized now why the man in the red basketball shirt had looked so familiar at Jackson Square. It had been the same dead eyed thug who had accompanied Lionel Adams.

"I should have busted a cap in your white ass." Cuttie stated, looking up under his brows at me, his long arms akimbo over his knees.

"You never would have got it done, sunshine." I smiled.

"You want me Muthafuka?" Cuttie stood, the hand went under his shirt.

"Hey, Cuttie now you play nice with our guest." The voice of Sayleen Lieless carried from his place at the bar. It was reasonable but definite. Cuttie sat with a snort, which is about what I figured would happen. I was wary of Cuttie but I wasn't going to let him know that. Meandering over to the long vinyl covered bar, I took a tall, red topped stool perched on a single steel pole and looked at my hands.

"You know, Sayleen, life is shit." I said in a tired voice.

"Amen, brother, Amen." Sayleen agreed with a definite nod. His mashed potato face was emotionless while he eyeballed me with a raised brow. " Course it's all we'ins got." He platitified.

"Amen, brother, Amen." I concurred, 'What you drinking?"

" Mexically Piss.' Sayleen swirled the Tequila in the small glass. A plate of cut lemons and salt shaker were close at hand. 'Now you wouldn't want to take advantage of me in my inebriated state would you champ?" Asked Sayleen.

"Abso-damn-lutly." I replied

"Good,' Quote Lieless, 'I like a man who's low down. Makes it all nice and even."

"Amen brother, Amen to that." I chimed in. 'Give me a Bushmills.' I said to the barkeep, who had a passing resemblance to a football with a beard.

"What's thet?" He requested

"Irish Whiskey, Gus." Sayleen offered.

"Sure enough." Said Gus and went to the back.

"I need your help, Sayleen." I said.

"You got to know that is what we are here to do but a lot of people near you get killed.' He said with his standard nod. 'Now you take that Jewel fella we was talkin' about. I hear he passed away real sudden like."

"Yeah, I was real broken up about that." My voice must have reflected the anger I still carried.

"We all went out back for a prayer meetin ourselves when we heard." Sayleen played along.

"I didn't kill him if that helps." I said.

"Word is they found this other fella all hog-tied and shot in the back of the head." Sayleen slid into that one. He must have contacts in the police force.

"Word is he was buggering eight year olds." The Tex-Alibaman grunted and it wasn't a pretty sound.

"Sounds like it needed doin." He added.

"I didn't kill him either just for the record." I said to cover my conscience. Bitzi's demise bothered me.

"For a non killer, your ass gets its fair share of bodies." Cuttie said taking the seat next to me on my left. Gus was pouring me a Bushmills at that point. I indicated Cuttie as well and he took out another glass. Shark eyes didn't say no.

"Long, you want another beer?" I said over my shoulder.

"No, I'm fine." Was the response.

"Sayleen?" I looked at the big man but he shook his head.

"You was askin about help. ' Lieless prompted. ' You know where Tisani is Mike?"

"No,' I replied and emptied half a glass of the Irish mist into my mouth let it explore my taste buds for a moment then I swallowed. The liquor burned down the center of my chest. 'This guy Au Clair does though. Word is he 's up on Blood Bayou, in an old mansion."

"That be the Been place." Long chimed in.

"Yes!" I confirmed.

" Why, you don't go up there and ask him polite like your own damn self?" Cuttie challenged.

"Now that is a right good question Mike. Word is you got lots of friends to help you." Sayleen said thoughtfully.

"Well your source doesn't know everything. I don't have the resources on the ground right now and a lot of Jewel's kin folk are up there keeping this Au Clair company." My motto is always telling the truth. It completely screws up the thought patterns. 'They're just waiting for me to try to come up and get him."

"We ain't getting our asses blowed off for you, fool,' said Cuttie sipping his whisky.' This real smooth stuff,' he said grudgingly. He indicated Gus could fill his glass again. This was done reluctantly; serving blacks was not something Gus did often. Cuttie either ignored or missed it. The bearded football filled my glass again.

"Fine I was just doing you a good turn Sayleen, I'll go back home in the morning and the boys down at the FBI will probably take over." I sounded as disinterested as possible. Lieless made his grunting noise again and I checked his forehead to see if he was mad. No, I guess he was just thinking.

"Old Long, he from these parts," Sayleen informed. 'What you figure our chances are up there son?"

Long contemplated the problem for a minute.

"They be at the end of a lane. You can't see the house from de road. It got a stone wall all around, maybe five foot high. Real mean ass place to take in a frontal." Old Long was a past soldier or at least knew his business. 'Dey know we be comin' they jap down behind dat wall and dey got a nice clean field of fire.' That sounded as much like suicide as I could take.'And them old boys can shoot." Link finished with authority.

"What about the river?" asked Cuttie.

"You could get up there in the dark, I figure. They ain't no wall at the back and the terrace drops down gentle like. Lots of cover we get in fine. I got a boat. Sayleen you got to plug up the front though." Sayleen nodded in agreement.

"Me and Gus go up there and keep them occupied while youall come in the back." Lieless said with his standard nod.

"Cuttie you go with Long, I'm too fat for boats and so is Gus.' Cuttie did not like it but didn't refuse. 'That leaves you Mike where you figure to be?"

"With Cuttie and Link. I'm the only one who knows Au Clair. I don't want the brother here to pop him by mistake." Cuttie half smiled at this.

"Well boys it's dark enough.' Sayleen said and lowered himself from his perch.

Chapter Twenty-five – 8:55 P.m., D'une Bayou, Louisiana, U.S.A..

What Am I Doing Here?

Back from a gravel road, beneath large magnolia trees, lived Unc Joe. The small home, not much more then a shack, was freshly painted in clean white. A compact stone patio overlooked the D'une Bayou, which was found at the base of a declining slope, shielded by well cut grass.

As the car stopped, Unc Joe walked down to greet us smiling broadly at Long, to whom he was related.

"Welcome Cher, " his small, round face split into a bright smile and he took my hand with gravity. I thanked him, in my poor Quebecois French and he laughed with delight. His body was lean and compact. A patch of white hair topped his small head and silver glasses reflected the dying light.

"You have come a long way from home, Cher. It's too bad others couldn't learn to speak French as well."

"I understand enough to know when I'm getting hell, Unc Joe." said Long in English with a gentle smile.

"We must speak English if not everyone speaks French, you know." The old man said apologetically placing his weathered hand on my shoulder.

Long and Cuttie were busy loading a slender aluminum boat. A large sports bag went in the bottom, which didn't have sports equipment in it. The old man's face pursed but he said nothing.

I swatted at one of the huge mosquitoes that seemed to become more prolific as the light faded.

"Dey like you for de salt, Cher", Unc Joe said, 'come, we put some of my potion on, les maringouin they don't bother you no more.' Immediately he was off to the house in a limping ramble. I watched the preparations, until the boat was ready.

Unc Joe was back with an airtight plastic box containing lunch. Long put this in the belly of the boat. The old gentleman had also acquired three bottles of his elixir.

Long and Cuttie stripped and spread the jet-black liquid on their bodies liberally. I was a little less receptive. The stuff smelled like eight-day-old sweat socks, that had been wrapped in limburger. There also seemed to be kerosene and other oil based products in it.

I moved over to Long and asked what the deal was on the potion.

"It's fine, no mosquito in its right mind goin to come near you, or much anythin else. They say it works real good on gators too,' he nodded for emphasis, 'it wears off in a day or two but don't get near no open flame, home." He laughed. I took my clothes off and covered myself with the goop.

The boat was ready to go now. I got in the bow, Cuttie in the center, near the sports bag and Long in back with the outboards. The boat had two engines the gas unit, that looked like it had been a long way, fired up immediately on demand. The electric engine was for quiet running I would guess?

Before Long could get in Unc Joe hugged him. Long was a little embarrassed. He could handle the affection of his uncle, which was freely given and genuinely.

"We be back by mornin Unc Joe, you make a big breakfast." Long shook the old shoulder.

"I make as much as you want, even you Cuttie with you hallow leg." To my surprise old shark eyes laughed at that. 'Just come back safe youall hear?"

The engine started and we shot out into the thin stream. Unc Joe waved until we were swallowed up by the increasing dusk.

Bayous, are fingers that extend from the big muddy, taking off the excess water when the river floods. The water never really dissipates though and so great swamps are the result. Here wildlife abound. Birds from Canada and the Northern States stop on their way south or choose to make it their winter home. I tried to see a vacationing robin or Baltimore Oriole but it was too dark.

Millions of other birds, animals and reptiles make, this their year round abode. The banks are the resting-places of alligators of huge size. I try to see them on the elevated sides of the waterway. The dark has truly settled in and they are not visible. I have the compensation of knowing they feed at night and so are about, looking for dinner.

These prehistoric relics will eat anything, even each other. Only those that achieve about six-foot in length are reasonably safe from being someone's dinner. Other less obvious, but equally deadly players, are the endless variety of snakes. Cottonmouths are one of the better known.

My life rested in the hands of Long. His knowledge of the shifting sandbanks, rotting underwater trees and large patches of impenetrable underwater growths was the only thing between our survival and being spilled into the swamp. Once there our lives would be less then worthless.

The question of the moment was "What was I doing here?"

While I was reasonably sure Long could be trusted not to harm me without direct orders, Cuttie had threatened to kill me. He would do it too. The shark eyes watched me from his center place in the boat. I ignored him.

Then, of course, there was good old Sayleen. The question would have to be, with Au Clair in their hands, how safe would I be? My wellbeing remained with the whims of Lionel Adams and where was his mind?

However, deep inside I knew I had to have the answer to the question, where was Tisani and what was in the package? Most important, where would it be going?

Cuttie opened the sports bag and handed Long an M 16 along with a sawed-off, pump action, shotgun. He then armed himself in a like manner.

I took out the chrome forty-five and made sure there was one in the spout. Steve's thirty-eight was also loaded and ready. I found it interesting that there had been no bullets in the gun when it was in Steve's possession. Jewel had limited trust it seemed. In my pockets were three clips for the automatic and about twenty rounds for the snubnose. I prefer the revolver. They tended to work well and not jam, which could happen at any time with automatics. In fairness, the newer models normally didn't.

Cuttie slammed shells into the shotgun while humming some rap tune. Then he stopped in the darkness.

"Hey, whitie, anyone show up, you lie down. Two niggers in a boat, fishin at night, maybe that's cool, but they see your white ass and we all goin to die. You understand?"

"No, problem." I agreed.

The gator was big. A male large enough to hunt without fear of hunters. He did not think as we do but he could work with others if the prey was large enough. He would be assured his share too. The cold blooded reptile was twelve feet long , large, old and strong. His maw swallowed down whole catfish.

. While it would not occur to him his jaws could crush metal and wood could kill man.

He understood man prey. Small boats had become a project of his. One man in a shell was no match for his huge back muscles rearing up beneath. Then death before the man could use his pain stick. Food for him for a long time, to go to bottom with or lay on the bank and sun all day long. The engine agitated the water. The shell would come from behind him.

He judged the distance to the point where the prey would be, without thinking, as mechanically as if a computer had made the decision for him. His tail snapped driving him forward and up to the dark surface guided only by the motor agitation.

I sat in the bow and looked out into stygian darkness. At night, long ago on the Canadian Pacific coast, I had stood bow watch looking into the same empty darkness, my mind seeing the bows of endless ghost ships plowing out of the night to take my destroyer to the bottom. I was tired and the smell from Unc Joe's remedy, while it kept the bugs away, was making me nauseous. My hands clamped hard on the side of the boat against its pitch. I sat lower

into the bottom on a small box. The bow seemed to lift of its own accord. I could feel my weight intensify against the seat behind me. We had hit some small objects but had simply slid off. This rose like a ramp. For a moment we teetered between capsizing and flight. Then we fell, but not from the obstruction, but because Long had made a split second decision and turned away. We slid off to the right landing with a splash, jarring, but not enough to roll us over. The huge mouth snapped closed, with three thousand pounds of pressure, inches from my face. I could smell the reptile's fetid breath, see the hedge of razor sharp teeth. My salvation occurred from the fact the huge gator had chosen the wrong side to turn his head in his attack. At the point when he should have taken my head off, the leviathan found himself trying to bite at me over his own back.

Cuttie smashed the paddle off his armored head as we passed by. This didn't hurt the gator but made him angrier. His huge tail swung around and caught the stern of the boat. This did two things; one, it chewed up his tail badly and two, it pushed us beyond his reach.

"Ouha! That a little one, Cher. Unc Joe know that mother personal, I bet," Long said laughing.

"You shit yourself white bread, you get out here. We don't got to put up with your funky self." Said Cuttie

"Yeah, hom, I think that gator liked you." Long kidded, I knew Cuttie was not so easy on me.

"The ride's kind of bumpy, that the way it usually is?" I asked in as controlled a voice as possible.

"Shit, you goin to tell us you seen a bigger one next, right?" Said Cuttie with disgust at my lack of response.

"You in trouble Cuttie, you smash Unc Joe's paddle, he really be on a rip." We all laughed, but I wanted to be anywhere except here. Fighting alligators was not in the job description.

After a little, just about the time my nerves got ungangled, Long switched to the electric motor. Our gas engine was sounding a little tired after its interaction with the gator. I also presumed we were near Blood Bayou.

Long took us out into the center of the channel it was a backwater and little used. We broke into Blood Bayou, from the water trace, down from the mouth. It was a smart move bypassing the mouth of the bayou and hopefully any watchers. Long made his first mistake of the night.

The watchers were already there. They were also well versed in the ways of the bayou. This was their place and they did not like visitors.

The high powered beam of light pinned our boat in its halogen point. Lying on my back, I could see Cuttie and Long screw up their faces as their eyes tried to adjust to the glare. They were like characters in a cartoon show, made silhouettes by the intense light.

"What you doin' out here, nigger?" The raw cracker voice came out of the light. I tried to evaluate the distance, it wasn't far.

"We's fishin', boss." Said Long.

" Don't see no poles." The voice said harshly.

"Dey on the bottom of the boat, boss." Long reached down, I don't know if it was for the shotgun or not. The submachinegun cut Long in two and swept Cuttie, who grabbed his chest and then looked at his hand. Even his blood looked black in the light. He breathed out one word.

"Damn!"

"Now, why'd you do that, Heck?" Said a more reasonable voice from across the way.

"Cause you can't trust niggers." Said the first voice.

"Well, we'll just have to kill the other nigger now." said the reasonable voice. Heck laughed a thin, cold hiss.

That was enough! I sat up and aimed about where the boat should be, just below the light. My forty-five exploded first then the thirty-eight its voice more of a bang, than a roar. Roar, bang, roar, bang, roar, bang until the thirty-eight went quiet and only the automatic spoke. Someone screamed and a body fell into the bottom of attacker's powerboat. There was an angry curse from a wounded man, then silence.

The shots from the carbine, on the other boat, took me by surprise. The bullets were close to their mark but low and away from me chewing through our hull.

"I'm shot, Heck,' said the reasonable voice over the din, as if it were a new and unique thing.

The crash of Cuttie's shotgun was close and deafened me. The double OO buck did a lot worse to our enemies.

The light was blown to pieces and went out. At the same time there was a splash as a body hit the water.

. "Heck, help me, Heck." The man in the water screamed. The man was the one with the reasonable voice. Strangely he didn't sound as reasonable now. Heck only moaned in reply.

"Heck, there's a gator, Heck." He started to scream then.

I moved close to Cuttie. He was shot in the chest but high up, not in the lungs, By the outboards Long lay in a heap. Unc Joe's favorite wouldn't be having breakfast ever again. I tripped over the food container on my way back to Cuttie with the med. Kit, this I put inside my shirt.

The wound was bleeding freely. I placed a wad of bandage on it and taped it in place.Back now to the electric motor it started and I turned the boat toward the bank, she was filling fast. I bailed as the noise of feeding reached us across the water. The new powerboat was sinking. I could see its white bottom come into sight.

My reaction was balanced between horror at the rending of human flesh and the thought of the kids that had been disposed of by Dubois in this evil place. The concept stood that the men on the boat were only suffering what was just.

Our boat was hopeless. It was already sinking when I got an arm under the semi-conscious Cuttie and dragged him toward the bank. I swam as quickly as possible; holding the forty-five in my free hand under the wounded man's armpit. Cuttie kicked a little to help but was damaged too much, to be of any real assistance. I saw the gator only as a hump in the water. It seemed to be heading away toward the boat and Long, of course. At first I thought it was a log then it lifted its snout. I could hear other gator's moving in on the feasters at the Dubois boat. The big animal seemed not to take interest in us. I looked into its green mindless eye in the soft moonlight. Then it turned its head and came around with the speed of lightning. I had been waiting. The forty-five exploded about two feet from the grisly head. The big reptile, separated from its small brain, thrashed in death.

We were far enough away, that the feeders would take a few minutes to get to the new meal or so I hoped. Now the swim was frantic. I put all the power I had into it. My body was telling me, with some nasty pains around my chest, that it was not happy.

I hit the object with my shoulder and thought the worst but it was only the knees or roots of a large cypress tree. The question was; should I keep swimming to the bank if I could find it? The branch above gave me an idea. I climbed up on the roots, which were naked and out of the water. Next came Cuttie, I leaned him against the tree trunk. I took off my belt and started to remove his.

"What the f.. are you doin?" he mumbled. I got the belt off and interlinked the two. I then threw the extended leather band over the low branch that was visible in the moonlight. Diana was now painting the waterway silver with her light. I put the buckle in Cuttie's good hand.

"Listen, I'm going to pull you up onto the branch. You've got to help.

"Shit, alright." said Cuttie trying not to pass out.

I hauled using my weight as a counter to that of the wounded bodyguard, hoping the branch would take the load. Once, I got the shark eyed banger up partially. I put my shoulder under him. With this help he weakly got a leg over and sat with his back to the trunk. I stood there breathing heavy. I didn't look down but I knew I had company. I let the one belt through the other buckle making it solid to the branch and started to climb. I got partially up when Cuttie's good hand grabbed my leg and got it over the branch. I somehow got the rest of my bone tired, carcass over and hung there for a moment like a sloth, my arms and legs dangling. I could hear the branch make a moaning sound in response to my added pounds

I shinnied up the branch, past Cuttie to the left where there were two smaller but strong branches, which formed a sort of seat. I plopped myself there.

Now, I had a minute to breathe. With one of my hands on Cuttie's shoulder holding him in place and the other to hold me in the tree I rested for awhile.

Cuttie moaned low. Our med., kit was gone, so I took off my shirt and twisted the water from the cotton, then tore it, bundled part of the cloth and replaced his bandage. The soiled wadding went into the water. Below, there was a loud snap as, something went for the blood soaked gauze. Having changed his wound I belted Cuttie to the trunk, the length of two belts just about right.

I then opened the lunch Unc Joe had provided. There were three Miller Lites. Also small juice boxes along with huge ham sandwiches and some cookies. I gave the juice to Cuttie, who drank gratefully, shaking his head slightly as if to clear it. Weakly, I had a sip myself to get one of my blood pressure pills down. On the verge of offering him a sandwich I realized he had gone to sleep. His breathing seemed all right but anything could happen. He had lost a lot of blood. I could only wait and see. I was dog tired and beat out.

When we didn't turn up in the morning Unc Joe would send out a patrol to find us. The problem was that the Dubois clan would be looking for their people too. The local law would probably be on their side.

Seen in profile, in the moonlight Cuttie's hard, evil face looked almost human. I had nothing to cover him with.

Cloudbanks, reaching to the stars, marched toward the waning moon. The big storm off the coast was moving this way. The wind freshened, blowing away the stench, with its clean salt strained breath. Its coolness seemed to caress me. For a moment, I forgot the horrible problems we faced. Cuttie and I were alive, that was something. Time is so short, I should be with my family. Their faces came to me and the memory stabbed deep. How could I be in a tree in the Louisiana swamp?

Granny had sent me home. Well, not really, he had said I could drive back at my leisure. I chose to return home by way of this damn tree. I suspect, I had broken the cardinal rule, by working outside the perimeters. These are important. In the Firm if you stay to the rules and there is always support. Go out on your own and dig your own grave. Daily checking made sure someone knew where you were and where to look for you. My watch was still working. I guess I could signal to the satellite with the laser hidden in it. I had a reasonable idea where it was in the night sky. The clouds had removed the stars, along with the moon, so my message went out but I wasn't sure anyone picked it up. There were lots of US ears, in the upper atmosphere, maybe they would hear.

The rain started now coming down in great pregnant plops of water. At first, it dusted us with its wand, then drenching us with its cool passing. Your body feels better, the wonderful coolness of the rain, raises hope in your soul. You open your mouth and take in the clean water. The taste is wonderful; quietly you lie back and relax. In the end, I tie my leg to the tree with what is left of my shirt, so that I don't fall during the night. I secure everything, check Cuttie, who may as well be out cold and sleep.

Chapter twenty-six – 9:20 A.m. The Been House, Blood Bayou, Louisiana.

Pieces To the Puzzle

Wind frolicked in the gossamer fabric of the window curtains, softly billowing the fine fabric, in its play. The storm, which had dumped rain on the area, was still out off the coast. Although stalled in its progress, the weather system vented it's frustration, by changing the local weather at its beck and call.

Warm beams of the early morning sunlight brighten the bedroom. Open French doors of intricate pattern, let both wind and light search about the room. Large shade trees surrounding the house moved with the increasing zephyr, fanning the sun's fingers.

The room was serene, paneled in the finest dark oak, high enough to provide a constant running ledge for fine crockery. Above its rich shiny surface was maroon brocade wallpaper, which perfectly matched the wood, making the room warm and comfortable. Huge dressers, padded chairs and oak tables filled the room. The furniture placement made for easy passage, on the soft white carpet in which the toes sank with luxury. All of this was simply a setting for the gigantic four poster bed. Elegant spires of oak stretched to the ceiling to support a full burgundy cloth cover. The gossamer edgings trailed on the floor. White satin sheets caressed the sleepers as they enjoyed the perfect comfort of the room and its setting. Their soft breathing bespoke this reality.

The man was black. His features hidden in part by an arm, which rested on his face. The woman was also black. Her legs were freed of the sheets and rested naked on the bed. Her legs were long and finely topped by an ample bottom, resting in beautiful proportion. The sheet then covered her hourglass figure and back, leaving her fine shoulders and head on the down pillow.

The hand shot to the sleeping man's throat. The sleeper's arms flayed and the mouth opened to yell or breathe; .at that point the attacker inserted the muzzle of a thirty- eight snub nose, breaking one of the victims front teeth.

There was no conversation. The attacker took a steel grip on the front of the gray silk pajama shirt, with his free hand and dragged his quarry out of bed to the floor, then with a stumbling, backward gait toward the door. The gun still firmly in place, the attacker bulldozed the struggling figure through the hall entrance and down the hall, into a large sitting room at the center of the house. A second intruder brought along the screaming girl who was deposited in a corner.

Here, in a well lit expanse of green carpet, as good or better than in the bedroom, stood four men amongst rich well padded white sofas and chairs. Windows took up a full wall; in wood framed majesty, turning the area into an arena.

At the entrance of the room the victim fell on all fours. The fall was instantly followed by a driving kick to his exposed behind. This incentive sent the victim across the room like a shuttle cock, ending up under the six foot wide, glass topped, cedar coffee table, that centered the room.

The kick was vicious, mean-spirited, cold blooded and unnecessary, but Lord did it feel good.

The big man, next to the table in the cowboy hat and Indian jewelry, looked down at the victim, then at the attacker.

"If someone didn't know your kind hearted ways and gentle nature, they might think you don't like this old boy." He said in high sarcasm.

"Amen Brother, Amen," I said to Sayleen, who reached down with one hand and lifted Au Clair, who was a fair size man and threw him on the couch like a rag doll.

"So this here is Brother Au Clair?" following the statement came Sayleen's patented nod.

"Yes sir." I said with vehemence. Spending a night in a Cyprus tree will do that to you.

" Mornin'." said brier Sayleen and nodded again, this time he smiled. If Au Clair wasn't scared yet, he should be, right about now. I know the smile, which was an evil mockery, scared the hell out of me and it wasn't even in my direction.

"You will kill me." Au Clair made a statement not a question. He showed more grit than I would have expected. Slowly and with panache, he made himself comfortable on the overstuffed couch and looked back at us with disdain. Christ, what pure balls! I guess if death is all there is, then it matters how one meets it. He did reach up and touch the broken tooth but it seemed too painful to disturb.

Sayleen on the other hand was not impressed. He took out a forty-five from his belt and cocked it with a click that filled the room.

"You're, going to give us some information." He said softly and nodded, the little white dot was slowly developing under his hatband.

"So, you want something from me?" said the Frenchman his face did not change. I had to intervene. I had the feeling Sayleen would start shooting parts off him and I needed him whole. The question was, could I get Au Clair out of here all in one piece along with my own esteemed self?

"We want to know where Tisani is and where the package you shipped for him went." I demanded. Au Clair's non-pulsed gaze fell on me.

"And in return I get what?"

"Well, maybe you don't become a one legged, one armed, blind, cripple hobbling around on a stick, who has to communicate with signs cause some cuss has cut his tongue out." Sayleen could not only be persuasive but also graphic. Au Clair was unaffected. He knew Sayleen would kill him and enjoy doing it. He looked at me again. Instinctively he knew I would be his salvation. Being English I would be fair or at least merciful. He was wrong but then he didn't understand what he was trading for yet.

"You give us the information and I will provide transportation to England, where you will be questioned about your interaction with organized crime and placed under the protection system." Lieless looked cold hate at me. There was quiet. Sayleen had all the cards and I was whistling in the dark.

"I do not believe your friend will like this solution." Au Clair went into French.

"Speak English.' I said, it came out as cold as five day old iron. 'My friend's interest in this matter is relative to Tisani. Beyond that you're of no importance to him. He would have to kill you to make sure you didn't tip off this man Tisani. On the other hand, if you're in my control, that problem takes care of itself. You have a lot more to answer for with respect to things in the Caribbean then that. We both know it.

"I get amnesty yes?" Au Clair probed.

"You get what I give you. You won't get killed. Now, where is Tisani and no tricks because I will want some proof that is confirmable by phone. You lie to me and the deal is off. My friend here and his associates, can do what they deem necessary to you to obtain the information and they have a limited understanding of civil rights." There was a thin laugh from somewhere in the room. Sayleen came toward me, I turned toward the door to the outside, like it was decided we would go out to discuss the matter.

The Alabama-Texican was ruminating and he was not happy. Sayleen closed the door and that soft voice came to me.

"What are you up to?"

"This animal tried to kill me on St Martin. He had someone else try it and they screwed up. He traffics in children. He's the worst kind of filth. He knows who's doing the same thing in most of the countries of Europe and I want that information.

"So it's a plea bargain." Sayleen sneered.

"No Sayleen,' I said watching the men inside taunting Au Clair. 'Over the years, working against the Russians, my people have developed a lot of ways to obtain information from a subject. By the time they're finished, Au Clair won't be a problem for anyone, he'll probably end up in some asylum." Sayleen weighed this, for a moment.

"How you get him out?"

"By plane from near Baton Rouge." He nodded angrily.

"You had this all worked out?" he accused.

"Yes, sir! You get what you want, my people get what they want and Au Clair gets it period. Look, Sayleen, this prick is nothing to me. You want to gut him, fine but it's going to be messy and you can get the same information, probably more of it if he gives it to you freely."

"Does this pile come with a shovel?" Sayleen asked.

"Like I said if the information can't be confirmed I'll get into the car and you can do whatever you want. However, for the betterment of your friend in Chicago, you better pass what information you do get to the NSA and FBI, because if Tisani gets passed you, well, you know the story.

"You wouldn't take advantage of old Sayleen would you Mike?"

"In a New York minute." I said honestly. Sayleen shook his head.

"Fine, let's get in there afor they kill him, just for the hell of it".

Old football head Gus was discussing what a straight razor would do to the human anatomy when we can in. Au Clair was suitably spooked now."

"I accept your offer." he said in a reasonable voice.

"Fine, where is Tisani." I snapped.

"He is in Canada, as is the package you are looking for, at least he will be in twenty-four hours." Au Clair said looking at his watch.

"I really am not in the mood for horse shit." I said rounding the chair.

"Everyone gets what they want, hmm. You be wanting a knife I suspect?" Sayleen said in a heckling drawl.

"No! He is in Canada.' Au Clair said in terror, 'At something called THRVH Trucking. I don't think the package will stay in Canada." He held up a hand to stop me." I think it goes to America."

"How do you know?" I demanded.

"I sent it to the Canary Islands, for transshipment. He gave me the name of the company and the phone number on the island. After that Britain handled the transportation of his consignment. You have the headman over there in custody. He will confirm the starting point. I only know about the trucking company because I saw the slip on Jewel's desk."

"He tellin the truth?" Sayleen said half believing Au Clair.

"I think so, THRVH is all over eastern Canada starting in Halifax. I think it goes over to Sudbury and the Soo. I can find out real quick."

"He ain't screwing with us?" Sayleen demanded.

"Look, call your friend and ask what he wants to do. I think he's telling the truth. He has no reason to lie, cause he gains nothing.

"Where in Canada? " I fired off.

"I don't know. Only Jewel knew that."

I grabbed a phone and called into a cutoff and gave a simple coded message that I had worked out with Cleveland."

We sat waiting to see what would happen to Au Clair. Sayleen called his friend and got his opinion.

I sat dirty and tired. Long was dead Cuttie in the hospital. The Dubois had taken off after Sayleen when the gunfire started on the bayou. Lieless had led them on a merry chase, starting at the entrance of The Been House. He had then hidden and came back after the family headed out to dredge the waterway for their lost relatives. Unc Joe gave Sayleen the directions that saved us and brought us up on the almost undefended Been house. I knew there had been guards but I wasn't too interested in their present whereabouts or condition. I had to get home now. I didn't think the package was for Canada because I had screwed up the Cayman Banks deal (See Spy Not.). Tisani didn't know it was me, or perhaps he did. I didn't think so. The target would be the man who had the power to betray him and his Middle Eastern Masters. Lionel Adams had broken faith or so they thought. Of course the larger target was the USA.

Sayleen sat quietly looking at Au Clair who met his gaze. I had never seen such a balance of wills. At this point I didn't care what happened to the slaver. They could have him. I knew in my heart he was telling the truth. I also knew Adams was a dead man no matter what happened.

The phone rang. A familiar voice said one word "confirmed" and rang off.

Chapter Twenty-seven – 10:20 A.m., The Shore of Lake Superior, between Sault St. Marie and Thunder Bay, Ontario, Canada.

Reflections on Pancake Bay

Warm summer sunshine heated the frigid water of Lake Superior. It should be cold but the El Nino and La Nina situation had shattered the normal weather patterns around this very cold land. Up here in August the first frost is not far away and by October the first snow has already covered the ground. Fifty degrees below zero is a norm in winter.

Today the land was blessed with heat. The sand bar, which is the floor of Pancake Bay, is warmed by the sun. A few brave spirits splash in the pristine water along a clean, cream coloured, sand beach.

I sit enjoying the beauty of the day. My wool suit is closed as my body is getting reacclimatize to the northern weather. Less than a day away the swamp and its murky smell are still a part of me. Perhaps they will always be as real as they are now. I sit, eating roast beef sandwiches, on a picnic table, by the beach in old Saul's fall glory.

Pancake Bay is just outside The Sault as we call it. One passes between red granite megaliths of stone, the sun explodes onto the edge of the lake, showing this demi-paradise below, as a vista. It's long, beautiful beach and stand of fragrant evergreens, are cloistered, on the edge of the largest of the Great Lakes.

The plane ride from Baton Rouge was almost surreal, on the private jet accompanied by the overworked Major Ambrose Amhurst, Her Majesty's Assistant Military Attaché to Washington. Ambrose, one does not call him by a nickname, is also Military Intelligence but long ago and far away. He is now attached to the diplomatic core. I sit with him as he debriefs me. He is the only man I have ever met with maroon eyes. Perhaps there was more to that old vampire myth than there seemed. The Major has a voice that drones on. Bushy eyebrows sprout with extravagance, unchecked or hindered. A well-trimmed, reddish mustache compliments fading ginger hair above a longish tweedy face. An individual who could bore the hell out of you in short order but whom I trust implicitly with my prisoner.

Au Clair is up front with the young woman, who will be returned to the USA later. It turns out she is of age and a local girl from the Lent area. They are sleeping, having been given drinks laced with pill or some like concoction.

"So you say this Tisani chap is in Canada. Well, we'll see that the NSA and FBI close the border. I will talk to the Canadians when we arrive. I expect you'll be going home, eh?"

Well, no. I suspect I should but something was bothering me. Something about the letters THVRH, I had seen them before, not on trucks but on a building. How like Tisani to give a red herring and let the hounds chase it. He only needed a day or so. Every depot for the truck firm would be watched. I suspect the FBI would do a cross-reference and come up with any other names associated with the letters but that would take time, something we didn't have unfortunately.

Soon I would find out if my hunch was correct. If I was right then I could bring this thing to some conclusion. If not, I would drive home and await the outcome. In fairness, this wasn't my fight as the firm saw it. However, it was my country and so it was my responsibility.

Old Sayleen had come down to the little landing strip. We stood there for a moment in the Louisiana heat. Adams had decided to let Au Clair go. It was pretty obvious Lieless did not agree. He stands there by the car in his undersized suit, hands deep in his pockets, mind off and away, sorting things out. The mashed potato face compressed in a frown, lips pushed out, the ever-present Stetson pushed back. A few of his remaining hairs venture forth to gain a glimpse of the sun.

"I won't let you down Sayleen. This isn't a set up. If I get Tisani I'll call your friend. If he dies and there's any money tied up at this end, I'll see you get it. Also, you have some points with my people and that might be of value somewhere down the line. We help our friends."

"Speckt so! " He agreed irritably, ' Now you know I'm goin up there myself get me a fur hat and do a Mountie on this old boy."

"Good luck and if you need me, here's a number.' I gave him a business card."Well it's been a slice Sayleen."

"Amen Brother, Amen." The little nod. The man was a killer but there was something there, I didn't know what. However, that made him a little more than a common thug. Perhaps we were so close in what we did, I for Queen and Country, he for money. Perhaps he was the more honest of the two. 'Watch your back, partner." Sayleen finished.

"Sayleen how do you figure it all got so screwed up? We had a nice world here. Now the Dubois's, the Tisani's and the rest screwed it up. Hell, it seems like God's left us out here on our own."

"No!" said the big Alabaman, 'God's there. You can hear Him whistlin' out behind the trees. There's just no one listen too much, that's all.' I was surprised at the honest belief in the voice. Maybe that was the thing in Lieless. Maybe that was the difference, the redeeming part to a cold, killing machine? 'As to who screwed up the world, we all got part of that to answer for."

"Good luck, partner." I offered my hand. He took it in a steel grip.

"Canucks always shaken' hands,' he snorted ' don't think too much! Keep your mind clear, it will keep you alive." he said nodding as he disappeared behind the tinted glass of the big Chev.

Of course, he was right. We couldn't think about what we did. It was done and that was all. Questioning only made it harder. Dwelling on our deeds made us soft, uncertain, considering of the next act and that would get us killed. He, because the law of the jungle applied and there was no other way. I, because in a war the gloves came off and the battle was to win.

The soft, cool wind from the lake blew in sweet and clear. Far off, seagulls skidded along the horizon. I could sit here all day, maybe walk down the beach a little. So far, I had only slept a few hours on the plane. I was tired and the quick shower in the motel hadn't really refreshed me but at least I smelt a lot better.

Unc Joe had not cried, although he was a little more bent by the news of Long's passing.

"You like a man who offer me just right whisky.' He said after blowing his nose loudly. 'If it was any better, he drink it, if it any worse, I wouldn't." he stopped then." I drink it. Soon I see Long in a better place, Cher. You don't concern yourself. Long, he know what he is doing." I left him rocking on his patio overlooking the bayou. I had just reached the car when he yelled after me in a loud voice.

"You kill dem bastards, yes?" the old voice demanded fearlessly

"Yes." I said.

"Good, then I drink it."

I had to go on. It was seven hours to Thunder Bay and I had to make a stop along the way. Hwy 17, which masquerades as the Trans Canada Hwy with only two lanes, one going each way, is cut out of the raw lakefront of Superior. This offers spectacular scenery near the Sault and Thunder Bay. The remainder of the trip consists of hours of scrub pine and monotony, with some breathtaking beauty thrown in, just to keep it interesting. The reason there are not four lanes is that it's just too expensive to blast a second set through the rock of the Canadian Shield.

If you're a tourist with lots of time the ride is as slow as you want. For those who have to be somewhere, there are suicide lanes to pass on. The Ontario Provincial Police (O.P.P.), wait for the unwary in these areas. You go at your own risk for a ticket or major injury. In September the road is fairly clear which allows one to test one's driving skills against hairpin turns and ripe straight aways.

I drive fast, but conservatively. I have to get there, being dead will not help the situation.

The towns on 17 face the railway tracks. Dairy Queens and small stores in places like Wawa and Blind River offer the traveler a little refreshment on the way. The railway is no longer the power it once was when these outposts were the iron that held Canada together. That was before the highway and air travel made them quaint.

Fanner is one of the many. It is about a hundred miles out of Thunder Bay and consists of two gas stations, a hardware store, a number of food come tourist shops and, of course, that staple of Canadian life, the donut shop. Outside this pillar of Canadian society was the one thing you'd expect to find an O.P.P. cruiser. I parked down the back road next to the store and walked back.

The officer, a Sergeant, was sitting at the counter devouring jelly donuts, at a consistent, but passable rate.

"It's sad what our tax dollars pay for." I said shaking my head as I sat next to him.

The girl behind the counter blanched. Two hard brown eyes came around slowly to evaluate what evil had come his way. Then his tongue licked raspberry jelly from the bottom of his mustache with sexual joy and I laughed.

"Hell Harold, those things are going to kill you one of these days."

"It isn't me taken pills every night." he countered. The Sergeant was my cousin and long time confidant Harold Warren. Harold is handsome in the way a well-marked grizzly might be. He has what could be considered an evil face, dark hair and eye brows with a manicured goatee about which he is often warned by the brass. Up until now he had not been required to cut it off. Harold is a lifer, twenty- five years and out, with a fat government pension. I guess I should have followed the same direction in my life but hadn't.

"Colleen this place is getting a lot of rift raft." He said to the waitress. With that Harold got up, stuffed the remainder of the donut in his mouth, then stomped out.

We met at my car in the soft late afternoon sunshine.

"Hey, Cisco." Said Harold

"Hey, Poncho." I mimicked the old TV star.

"How come I didn't get to be Cisco.

"You're fat man, Cisco's got to be lean, hombre."

"Look who's talking." He poked me viciously in the gut.

"I took a step back and we sparred a little like kids back at my father's place those years ago when he came to visit."

"Look, time out, I got important things to talk about." I put my hands up for him to stop.

"What you kill someone?" He said off the cuff and my face must have changed.

"No!" I lied.

"Bullshit, you never could lie." Harold came down hard and the constable came out.

"Not here and in the line of duty." It sounded hallow but he knew I was telling the truth.

"Shit." What horsemen, not those turkey's at CISIS?"

"Neither and the CISIS guys know their stuff."

"Who then?"

"The British Secret Service." I didn't get the last word out. Harold was laughing too hard. I thought he was going to have a stroke, his face was that red.

"That's rich." he choked out between fits of laughter. Finally he began to cough and slowed down.

"That's good really."

"It's true."

"Bullshit, how long?" He shot back.

"Fourteen years."

"You're serious?"

"Yup."

"Christ on a crutch."

"Let's hope not." I said. Harold got very serious, dangerously so. 'If you want me to give you information."

"No! What the hell would you know?"

"A lot of stuff."

"Look Harold all I want is a drive into Thunder Bay." his face got that, 'what crime have you committed?', look. ' I tell you this, you're under the National Secrets Act.

"So it is CISIS."

"Yes!" At the moment we were all working on the same problem, so it made sense, anyway Harold might not help me. ' There is this guy he works for the Middle East. He may be in Thunder Bay. If he is, then someone will be watching the roads in and out, to make sure they haven't been discovered. So I go in with you lying in the back seat. Once I'm there, that's it. I go and check if he's where we think. If so, I call in the cavalry, if not, I go home."

"Where do you think he is?" Harold asked.

"That's need to know."

"I need to know if I'm putting my pension on the line."

"What the hell do you need a pension for? The donuts will kill you long before you get it."

"Yeah, well I'll die with the knowledge that our chintzy Premier will have to cough it up to Margaret and kids. Where?"

"THVRH the plant near your first home." I said.

"It's been closed for a while, but there is some company in there. They do grinding or something."

"Maybe a lot more?"

"We ought to call the local guys."

"Look this idiot is playing with chemical weapons. The group with him think they are going to heaven if they get killed defending their faith. You send the Horsemen galloping in and we'll have; one, a war or two, a blast that will make the Halifax ammunition ship explosion look like someone dropped a rubber ball in a sand box."

"Jesus, you are serious." Harold evaluated me with that uncertain look he gave me just before I talked him into playing Superman off the garage roof, which lead to his broken arm.

"Ok, It would have been nice having a pension though."

Chapter Twenty-eight – Two blocks from the THVRH Plant Building, Thunder Bay, Ontario.

Visions In Nothingness,

"Christ, you're for real." Harold exclaimed to me in awe. Then, as I figured, he got very rules and regs on me. 'Tommy go and call in. Tell them we got two snipers on the roof of the THVRH building and more suspects inside. Tell dispatch the suspects are armed and dangerous." The Tommy in question was Constable Tom Kowalski, of the Thunder Bay Police Force, who had the night shift for this area of the city. The patrol consisted of the area near the canal, directly across from the reservation. He owed Harold a favour, God help him, so he was here with us. We were hidden in a vacant house a couple of blocks from the plant.

"Not yet,' I snapped. The hundred-mile ride, into the city under a blanket, on the floor of a police car did not improve my disposition. ' Right now, we don't know what's in there."

"And just how did you figure we'd find out?"asked my cousin.

"I'll take a run at the corner of the fence, there is an opening. I'll get as close as possible and see what we're up against. Then you can call."

"That's nuts! Those guy's on the roof have night vision glasses on."

"The quality isn't as good as all that, the glasses are Russian built. That kind of technology has limits."

"What if they got someone on the ground?"

I looked through my own Brier Montgomery 5000 high ops, night vision, binoculars.

"I have a couple of high intensity thunderflashes with me. They'll blind everyone on the ground or elsewhere and get back here."

"That's stupid. We call for backup and wait." The sergeant had spoken.

"Too bad they closed off the steam pipe tunnel under the street from sub plant one." Tom threw in.

"Wait a minute, what tunnel?" I demanded

"There was a tunnel under the street to save power. The turbines in the main plant powered the number two plant across the street, they had to put in a tunnel to let the pipes through. My dad took me through there when I was a kid. A lot of the local people know about it. When the plant closed they walled it off.

"With what?"

"Bricks, red ones." The lean faced constable in his long winter jacket said sarcastically. Tom had a pinched face and a sour look but that was just for public consumption. He could laugh and kid with the best of them.

"Great! Where do we get in?" I asked.

"He said bricks." Harold spoke to me like a big, rather deranged, child.

"I heard him. If this doesn't work you can call the back up and I'm heading for Winnipeg." This seemed to make them respond.

Tom knew all the entrances and open doors at plant two. The local kids drank beer there, and did dope periodically, if he didn't intervene. Their breakage he couldn't answer for.

We came up on the long building from the farthest corner away from the main plant. The watchers on the roof across the street were japed down to be less conspicuous, on the top of the building. This inhibited them and gave us enough time to get through the fence and into the building, for which Tom had keys. There were no sector or other alarms. My watch told me this but then again it had its problems. The new one provided on the plane seemed to be in good order but you never knew. I put on the night glasses the Major provided from the kit I had requested. The two police officers, in full uniform, followed somewhat blindly, weapons drawn.

"Maybe, I ought to lead I got the gun." Harold Suggested.

"I 'm armed." I said

"You're what? " Harold growled.

"Yeah, I found this piece, on the floor of the cruiser, must have been left there by some purp." I answered with sarcastic glee.

"Bullshit." Harold was in high dungeon. I heard Tom laugh.

We moved passed huge, long dead, steel working equipment. There were substantial gaps, where the original equipment, had been removed to other plants or sold to other more profitable companies. Hundreds of US companies had closed in Canada and placed the jobs in the United States or Mexico. The drain had provided opportunities for small manufacturers. For the people who were laid off, the only answer was to move, take a lower paying job or welfare.

At the center of the plant there was a metal set of steps that circled downward. Here was the power plant. At the bottom of the stairs we moved along the long narrow corridor. The space beside the old rusting pipes, brought us after what seemed an eternity in the musty dark, against a brick wall. The pipes had been cut and the wall stretched across the full entrance, floor to ceiling solid and seemingly impenetrable.

"Like I said Red Brick." Tom added caustically.

"Good." I said removing the belt from under my clothing. I opened the thin, leather fold backs to reach each small compartment. I removed four small squirt bottles, hoping I would have enough.

"Put these on over your mouth and nose." I handed treated, gauze medical masks to the boys and put one on myself.

Following the instructions of Special Service Branch, I sprayed the liquid into the areas between the bricks. Immediately there was a sizzling sound, as the acid based liquid ate through the cement.

In seconds the bricks were loose and could be removed. In ten minutes I was out of the liquid, but there was a hole even the donut king could get through.

On the other side there were no sound detectors or cameras. We were in the bowels of the main plant. The reason there was no back up security down here was that the wall was completed at the end of the corridor, which formed part of the standing wall.

Tom led now. We moved through piles of used parts and scrap metal ,along with some nasty smelling chemical drums, which contained, what, I didn't know.

Eventually, we came to a set of rusty, but serviceable stairs. These we mounted with stealth and absolute quiet. At the top was a locked wooden door that would stop an elephant.

"Perfect." Harold growled behind me.

"Quiet." I said, opening my utensils kit. I checked for wires and alarms but they seemed to be concentrating outside. I moved the lock's inner defense plate out of the way with a hook and slipped a jimmy key in. I heard the clicks as the lock accepted the intruder, then turned slowly. There was a snap as the bolt came out of the way and we were in."

"This is your first time doing this stuff right?" said Harold softly. I've seen guys with records longer then your arm do that slower."

"Skilled trades, you can't beat them." I shot back.

The small hallway was carpeted and passed various offices. The last one showed light through a partially opened door.

Harold went first, over my objections. Tom followed. Harold went low the Thunder Bay cop went high. The room was empty and fortunately, the boys hadn't kicked in the door, there was no noise. However, the window that looked out on the plant floor allowed for an almost complete view of the interior of the structure. This office, judging by its size and the window, must have, at one point, been the plant managers' place of business.

We crept to the window and looked out. Making as little of ourselves visible as possible.

There, under bright ceiling lights, was Tisani. He wore a camel coloured overcoat against the cold, the warmth of the afternoon had vanished into a chilly night, bad enough so that your breath came out in small puffs of mist. The spy wore thin, dark rimmed glasses and small changes had been made to the face but it was Tisani.

Beside him on the floor of the plant was an eighteen wheeler. The jet-black tractor had the words "High Flight Transport" stenciled in gold on its doors. The truck was obviously not brand new but well maintained. We were lucky enough to see the driver's side as they suited that worthy individual into the seat.

Four specific points of interest were quickly ingested by my over tense mind and put away for later.

1) The diver was on a heart monitor. The small pads extended from the man's chest to the seat.

2) A seat that was hydraulic.

3) A metal skeleton glove that was being fitted to the man's left hand.

4) There was intense interest in the bottom of the

tractor, and the wiring which lead to the flat bed trailer behind. This was stacked with see through, steel holding boxes filled with scrap and various lengths of metal rod. Beneath that pile would be the package with its deadly secret.

There were enough armed men around to scare the hell out of me. Of course, Harold thought we should go in and arrest them. Even Tom wasn't up for that. The primary rule of police work is go home at night, preferably all in one piece.

So it was that we crawled back down the stairs. I locked the door and the wall was more or less reset. Twenty minutes later we were at the police station and things were moving along fine.

The local assistant chief was involved immediately. Every possible direction the truck could exit the area was monitored. While the normal cruisers did their beats, the impound was stripped of vehicles, these were planted in driveways and other unobtrusive places.

Off duty officers were called in, but by code. Central utilized wording that might be used if their phones were tapped. No one was taking any chances on this.

The Horsemen turned up ten minutes later. The Royal Canadian Mounted Police are the most competent people I know. Consecutive governments in Ottawa, have cut their budgets and tried to capitalize on their image. The Disney people own the creative rights to the Mounties' uniform insignia and so on, if you can believe it. Yet, as the Mounted Police have always done since their inception, they still provide the best services possible. They seem able to move forward no matter what the idiots in Ottawa throw at them.

In this situation, they had at least one helicopter brought in. They made links with the FBI and other exterior services, including the Minnesota State Police, as well as both Canadian Customs and American border patrols.

The Ontario Provincial Police showed up with their SWAT team, helicoptered up with the help of the armed forces.

CISIS made the party five minutes after it started. The local man, Ames Morningstar, arrived. He immediately became the liaison with Ottawa. Morningstar was not a Native Canadian and I had this terrible feeling the name was a cover but said nothing. He was a big, bulgy man with tired eyes and a mediocre clothing allowance.

I was through a briefing with TBPD. Then was allowed to cool my heals in one of the offices although there was some talk of a cell. Harold quashed that.

Finally, there was a lot of commotion and, a tall steely eyed, monolith of a man walked in. Harold, who was in half donut at the time, stood. The man ignored him.

"Hear you got a problem," said the intruder. His metallic blue eyes sparkled from a bluff workman's face.

"Hi! Dell." Now I knew what the commotion was about. The CIA had arrived. Interservice coexistence in Canada was one thing, this was something else. Knowing Dell as I did, he probably tried to take over, and had been told nicely to go F himself, in good English, en mass. He would now try an end run through me. Not on your life Dell, old vermin, I have to live here.

Porter, the head RCMP agent, a quiet man with a scholars features and penetrating watery brown eyes, followed Dell.

"Mr. McFurson I would like you to join us for a short meeting."

The room was small but there were chairs for everyone. Porter was there, Augustus Angle was Superintendent North West for the Ontario

Provincial Police, a short squat dark-haired man, with a hard face and no nonsense attitude. Morningstar, of course, graced a chair, looking hard at me, as I came through the door. I smiled politely and he frowned.

Captain Jean Chellair represented the Armed Forces. I was a little surprised to see Dell come in. The head of the OPP SWAT team was there, a bland quiet man dressed in a blue ball cap, coveralls and armor. the Assistant Chief of the Thunder bay Police. Finally, seated in great discomfort, were Harold and Tom.

"Gentlemen it's my town so I guess I start.' said Peterson the Assistant Chief of the Thunder Bay force. 'Mr. McFurson I am told you are part of CISIS." He started.

"What?' that escaped Morningstar. This was going to be horrible. Dell smiled malevolently.

"Isn't this man one of yours."

"Hmm, Yes, hum, he's on extended loan to us." That was tactically correct. Now everyone was looking at me. The best offence is the best defense.

"Gentlemen, I became aware of Tisani's location through sources provided to us by one of the ministries. There were a number of sights he might be: Thunder Bay was mine to check out. As you can understand, if the man wasn't here, then disturbing all, or any of you, would have been stupid. Obviously, I lucked out and here we are."

The man is a known terrorist. He kills easily and those with him will die to protect the project he is on. They will fight to the death because of their religious beliefs.

The truck, which you are all aware of, is uniquely dangerous and potentially lethal to the entire population of this city.' Faces tightened and I hurried on. 'However, no harm will come to the city if the truck is allowed to leave. The truck, and its lethal cargo, is headed for the United States.

"I could bring in some sharp shooters and clear that roof. Then we hit them fast from inside and its over." said the head of the SWAT team.

"Sir, with all due respect, do that and at the first sign of any problem, they will blow up the truck, the building and maybe twenty blocks of the city. That, in turn, will turn loose the gas on the truck. Which given the direction of the prevailing wind could kill people as far away as Winnipeg." There was silence.

"What do you suggest Mr. McFurson." Porter asked softly.

"Well we let the truck out. Then when it's outside the town we take it.

“One quick headshot will do it.’ Said Peterson
“No the driver is on a heart monitor, kill him the heart stops, the truck explodes. The seat is also weight triggered. Move his body and the explosion occurs. Finally, he has a hand trigger. He even thinks that we are on to him, he pushes the button and bang. “ The whole thing whirled in my mind... someone started talking, but I ignored it. I was trying to grasp an idea that seemed to make sense, it did.
“Gentlemen, I have a suggestion.” I interrupted.

Chapter Twenty-nine – 7:05 P.m., Hwy 17 Kakabeka Falls, Ontario Canada.

The Needle's Edge

Suliman, was on his way. As it is said the journey of a thousand miles begins with the first step. The electronics on the Yankee truck, would not do as they were bidden, so it was that the trip could not start until after 5:00 P.m. At this point it is rush hour, a time of returning home, with many cars and a potential for problems. It was decided he would start his trip in the early evening. All was ready. The watchers on HWY 17 and elsewhere had nothing to report.

In the end, he was wired to the truck. The control button attached to the palm of his hand and the truck started.

As the final preparations were completed, the great doors were opened and the tractor moved out. There was no cheering or farewells as this might attract attention. For the moment Suliman was alone. How easily the truck handled. How powerful it was. He began to enjoy the power. No one followed. No one tried to stop him. The transport made its way across the city, in the growing dark, toward Hwy 17 and then west to Winnipeg. Beyond that to the flat prairie. Finally,to a small little used border crossing and a warehouse in North Dakota. Then he would have completed his part. Perhaps, he would have to die, if his God demanded this, then so be it.. Cars and trucks followed, then left the stream of traffic, no one came near.

The radio was turned on as was ordered. Music, was not only normal for drivers, the radio would also tell him of any problems on the road ahead.

The announcer breaks into the music. His voice is serious and unsettled. A little boy of ten has been taken from the store near his home. The kidnapping is in broad daylight. The child's parents, on tape, ask the kidnapper to let their boy go, or at least to treat him with care. A police spokesman requests anyone seeing a blue, late model car, in the area of the store, to contact Police immediately. The boy is described as; blond, blue eyed, wearing a blue "T" shirt, black pants and Nike shoes. His name is Billy Sweeten. Suliman changes stations, the story is also there. He has been trained to watch for anything out of the ordinary. The news unsettles him slightly. He listens as he turns on to Hwy 17. The search extends for the child. Should he turn back? No!

The large, black truck is now out of the city. The signs tell him Winnipeg is eight hours away. Suliman does the speed limit. He thinks no more of the boy, or the city, his mind is looking forward.

He is almost at Kakabeka Falls. He starts to pass through the small town just east of the Provincial Park. The traffic slows then stops.

Suliman looks for a place to turn off, but there is no exit. The vehicles behind him pile up, the line begins to move slowly forward. In the pit of his stomach he fears the worst. The small plastic plunger is in his hand. He prays to his God a last time. He now comes around the bend. Cars are stopped along the side of the road. Police are looking in them; some are processed and released immediately. All are requested to open their trunks. One man is arrested as the police remove a bag of what looks like cannabis, from the trunk.

Suliman's hands sweat. He does not wish to die. Life is sweet, but he must fulfill his mission. His heart is hardened. If death is required, so be it. He thinks of turning around but that would make him immediately suspect. If he had a magic looking glass, he could know if they are looking for the boy, or if it were him they wanted. He must wait, he must balance matters, he must make the right decision.

Ontario Provincial Police and some local police check cars. A tractor with a sleeper is turned to the side. A second tractor, two vehicles ahead, has no sleeping compartment. The police constable steps up onto the running board of the truck and directs the driver passed the stopped traffic, then dismounts, letting the trucker go on his way. This is positive, but perhaps, it is a play a drama acted out for him.

Two constables look into the windows of the car ahead. They show a picture. Suliman opens his window to catch the last part of the conversation.

"You see this boy?" The policeman asks.

"No.' was the response, 'it's really too bad. Do you think you'll get the people?"

"We hope so. Would you mind opening your trunk?"

An elderly lady gets out and does as she is bid. The trunk is clean and empty but for the spare tire. The constable looks under the carpet in the trunk. '

"That's fine, thank you for your help." The constable smiles and turns to his truck.

"I'll do the next one," his partner says and walks past the cab on the passenger's side. Suliman follows him in the side mirror. The constable wearing a slouch hat climbs up on the step. Suliman's hand sits closed on the detonator. The end

of this world is poised on a sudden movement.
" We're looking for this kid.' The policeman shows Suliman a five by seven picture of the child; blond, intelligent looking, in an American way. 'You see him?"
"No." Suliman responds, he wonders if the policeman hears the fear in his voice.
"No sleeper huh? " the constable looks around the cab.
"No!"
"Ok, Drive up there and we'll get you on your way." The policeman points to the barrier, beyond, which freedom beckons. A second policeman holds cars from the side of the road back, so the larger vehicle can get through.
Suliman clasped the wheel with one hand and lets off the brake. The truck moves smoothly to the front.
"Ok, let me off." said the cop getting ready to jump down. Suliman put his foot on the brake, the truck came to a soft stop. For a moment both his hands rest on the wheel.
Suliman felt the jab, sharp and clean in his jugular. The pain was sharp and very real as the needle goes in. His reaction is to push the plunger but the drug, whatever it is, will not let his fingers react they are leaden. The policeman reaches across and almost

breaks his thumb. In a moment there is darkness, he falls forever, breathing normally. The last thing Suliman hears is the constable yelling.

"Harold, stop the damn truck."

I sit by the side of the road. Police, CISIS and CIA people mingle.

The top RCMP explosives officer looks under the tractor, gives me a misled look and goes over to throw up, off the highway. There are nine hundred pounds of plastic explosive compacted around and under the base of the vehicle.

Dell comes over and offers a cigarette, I refuse, He puts them away. I notice his hands shake, that's alright so are mine.

"Very handy," he says conversationally.

"Yeah!" I breathe out. In the second I reached around and sank the needle into the truck driver's jugular, pushing the plunger in the same action, I prayed and hoped the force was with me. His neck is small and that helps. Why me? Good question. I am trained for it. The idea is accepted only as it is a last resort, Gas would take too long to knock him out. We have only one chance.

It all came down to me. The fleet of unmarked cars, used various frequencies, following the truck through the streets. Young Billy Smeeten, played cards with police, as his mother and father, part time actors, put on the performance of their lives.

The RCMP officers who drove the other two rigs. All of the cars at Kakabeka are operated by other cops. The town's people crowded on busses and removed.

Someone, somewhere had evaluated the risks. A few against the many. Every one of us volunteered. I am proud of being a Canadian this day. However, in the end, it's crazy as hell, utter madness. It worked that is all that is necessary. I suspect we could have let him get out on the highway then fired a rocket at his rolling bomb. The question was, how long would the gas continue to survive? Where would the wind blow it? If we missed then what?

"We were lucky." Dell says his face drained of blood.

"They find out what was in the vials?"

"Not yet but it's deadly as hell. By the way there are two missing. I counted myself."

"Oh good.' I felt like crying but didn't. 'How's our boy doing?"

"He's breathing, we can keep him in suspended animation until we figure out all the booby traps."

" They got Thunder Bay shut down?"

"Absolutely. Your friend Morningstar has got a bunch of people canvassing right now for the kid, of course. We got all of them at the factory except, your buddy, Tisani and a couple of others. We're checking lists of employees now for possible hiding places."

"Has he made any phone calls?" I asked.

"Who?" asked Dell.

"Tisani."

"We can identify three so far. One, to say the truck was leaving. One, when the truck left. One, when it didn't call in. That call was in code but it was pretty clear, all and all."

"Where'd he call from."

"Land based boxes all in a high retail area." Dell looked at a notebook. 'None were traceable."

" The calls were made near the factory?"

"No."

"Got a map of the city?" I asked.

The heater in the car was on full. It hummed along as if it was enjoying itself, like a kettle in a warm kitchen. I sat, waiting in the big box parking lot, flanked by a number of familiar stores, across the road from the Thunder Bay's one major mall. It was late and the stores were closed.

The three calls were all in walking distance of this point. There were two groups of apartment buildings and a wide range of other buildings, which a combined force was checking out for good old Billy, who was in a hotel sleeping by now. That, of course, would be too easy. Tisani would never make that kind of mistake, always know how to get out of where you are, before you go in. He had one more call to make. I felt sure he might use this pay phone for that call.

Tisani would know that he could not escape. When that happened he would try to walk out. That would make sense but the terrain was against him. There was nothing for hundreds of miles. Or go to ground.

First though he would call in. He would want to know what to do with the two remaining vials. Their original destinations now out of the question, unless he could escape. He would not leave them in the trash. If not he had to have a safe place to get them later.

The fact that the majority of the City of Thunder Bay was still alive, meant he had not decided to move on his own.

Tisani would want a dark, private place, to make the call. He would be at maximum risk. The call could only be so many words and so on. In that way he would not be located. We had posted the various pay phones in the area thereby cutting down the odds. The CISIS people had already gone through these buildings with a fine toothed comb.

It was midnight I yawned and began to suspect he had escaped, when there was a splinter of light on the ground. I realized a manhole cover had been raised. A figure rose gothicly from the ground and moved to the phonebooth only a few feet away. I got out of the car leaving the door open to hide the sound. Rubber soled shoes will get you anywhere. Tonight they would get me near my prey. I kept moving toward him. I was not sure it was him but it had to be.

The distance was about five car lengths now. I called his name. His face without the glasses was pictured in the small light over the wall phone booth. He drew his gun in slow motion from his coat pocket. I had mine in my hand. Your body reacts, you do the policeman's two step, he also turns sideways. I fired first. The Webley Scott explodes, its bullet directed to the bulk of his chest. Headshots are for idiots or long range snipers. His bullet leaves its weapon a moment later, the impact of the Webley forty-four round jerking his arm upward, making him miss. The speeding bit of metal buries itself in the wall behind me. Tisani's body collapses.

I moved to his prostrate agent, kicking the gun from his hand. I have had my moment of truth, as the Spaniards would call it. Thanks, I'll pass next time. My hands were shaking. The 44-caliber slug had passed through his armpit and severed his spine. Tisani was dying like a broken bird, feeling nothing below his chest. The blood, that was coming from his mouth, was a clear indication that the bullet's passing had destroyed other vital organs.

Kneeling, my hands went through his pockets, the two cylinders were not in his coat. The rest of his pockets were equally bare. I ran to the manhole cover. I lift it with the wood and rope handle, he had left out, for this purpose. At the bottom of the short drain was a small room, carved out the rock.

The tubes were on the bed. I realized this monk's cell was well provisioned with food and a television. He could have been comfortable down here for months. The cover above was a hydro facing, no one would disturb it, vents would bring in air and no water would come in. Purely brilliant. I placed the cover back on disturbing nothing.

I returned to the wounded spy.

"McFurson." Tisani said between clenched teeth. The pain must have been intense but then he should be feeling nothing. ' It is kismet. I think that it be you."

"I'll call an ambulance."

"No, too late, I will go to my God." His hand grasped the air in pain.

"I clasp his hand as the pain seemed to get worse."

"You would help me?" He seemed amazed.

"You were going to kill millions. Maybe that is the difference between us. Maybe there has to be that difference to make it sane."

"The Americans killed my wife and two little girls, my princesses, so beautiful so full of life. We had gone to Baghdad on business. I left them in a shelter. The bomb cut through ten feet of concrete and killed them. We have no defense. The vials were to be placed in the water purification plants in major cites around the United States.

Then we could negotiate. Then we would have America where they had us. Without a defense! We could make them understand what dying is about."

"I can't answer for that." I said but could feel nothing

"I go to my God now. I wonder if I should see my angels again?" His eyes seemed to be trying to find the faces of his children in the coming darkness.

"I am sure..." I said but he was gone.

I found a Mullah from the local mosque to bury him. Perhaps, it was because we were enemies, but more, I think, because in Canada we are civilized. Perhaps I had to make sure he was really dead. Moslem women, as rented mourners, cried for him, as was correct. Only Dell came to the funeral,

standing with me as the body was passed from hand to hand, in its coffin, over the heads of the crowd out to the hearse.
In the end, Dell and I went for a drink and discussed old disasters but I had little heart for it.

I call Adams in Chicago. I tell him his problem was taken care of. I also tell him to get out of the business. He didn't understand it and was way out of his depth. US Naval Intelligence should be happy with me after that.

That day, after a full eight hours of uninterrupted sleep. I sit in Harold's basement, drinking beer and talking about old times until he had to go on duty. He and Tom would get commendations, although there were a lot of touchy questions to answer. Harold will bullshit his way out in the great tradition.

The CIA inherited the truck and its contents.

Mr. Morningstar meets me privately the next day. "You're not in line for the Order of Canada, you know. I don't want to find you in our way again. Do you understand?" He starts in without preliminaries.
"I'm only a good citizen helping his country. That is it's own reward." I said 'Anyway we're not allowed to accept medals."

"You took an oath once, good citizen, when you joined our navy. You seem to have forgotten to whom?" he said as if about to threaten me with a tax audit.

"When I took that oath, you prick, it was made to the Queen. I keep my word." I am not loved by CISIS, my heart will break.

Porter of the Mounties, however, comes over to shake hands and thank me. That carries more weight then any number of awards.

In the end I went home to my family and promised never to get involved with anything ever again. Yeah, right!

Chapter Thirty – 5:00 P.m. Cherry Blossom Secondary School, Tokyo, Japan.

Let the Cherry Blossom and Maple Leaf Fall Together.

The day's work was finished. It was spring and the Cherry Blossoms had come, kissing the sunlight, with their scent. It was not my turn to clean the classroom, so with a few friends, I walked along discussing a new boy and his potential. This is a small matter and of little interest. It is the talk of schoolgirls, accented by giggles and laughter.

Beyond the doors the city spread with its familiar smells and warm sunshine. I left, as always, by the front doors and descended the stairs with the group. We were pretending not to notice the looks from the boys.

It was then that I saw him standing in the entrance to the school. My dragon had returned.

I rushed down the stairs to meet him. However, instead of the hug I expected, he timed my flight exactly enough to provide a deep bow, so that I had to jerk to a halt and look foolish as I returned the complement. The Dragon had not changed.

As Yatomi stood there, the wind blew a few of the loose cherry petals from the trees that surrounded us in the courtyard and placed them in her hair. She was so beautiful I could not breathe. It was as if my breathing might change the perfection of the moment. In that instant, I came to understand everything that had happened the fall before, in a new and clearer light. Here, in this smiling face, was everything that was of value in all I had done. A real life saved, tied to a face, tied to time. The glowing magic eyes of our young are the future. Their time was the future. I did not want my time to pass any more quickly but I knew my time had meaning because she was free and untouched by the evil that had swept her up so abruptly. That she could find a boy and love him. Find a place and have her children. If not, if sorrow or choice destroyed my image of her future, at least she would have the chance to fail on her own because of her own mistake. She had the time to make the mistake, the time to be wrong; this was the gift I gave. It was multiplied in the faces of the kids from New Orleans, in Shirl's smile. I had in my own bumbling way, perhaps in spite of my best judgement, given out new lives.

We honor our police and all the heroes, real and fictional, because of their ability to change the balance by force. A force we do not have, or want to wield, against the dark and its minions. We are wrong in this. We should celebrate them, for the lives they prolong, the good people and bad, they allow to move beyond the danger into an existence of their own choosing. We should celebrate life in its purist form. It is all we have, that and hope. The rest is surely his.

"Hello Samurai " I said.

"Hello Dragon" she laughed and raised her hands but then dropped them to her sides crimson with embarrassment.' So you have come to visit your cousin."

"Yes, I always keep my word when I can."

"Hai! You are here long?"

"No! I stopped by to give you this." I removed the miniature lead Mountie on his horse from its box. It was hand painted, gleaming red, blue and gold in the sunlight. 'That's for your dad. This too.' I gave her a shot glass with Niagara Falls on it. 'It will drive your relatives crazy with envy." The rest of the Katsuda clan had never been beyond the shores of Japan and these little mementos gave Shojiro endless face.

"You are a cruel Dragon.' She said, but smiled conspiratorially, 'My father will be upset, he has not given you anything."

"He has given me his friendship, which has higher value than any object." I said.

We were surrounded now by a number of girls and boys. A short, rather tubby girl was giving what seemed to be a running commentary with oh's and ahs from the audience.

"This is for you. I know you're a little old for it but it's a keepsake and I didn't know what else you'd like." I took the box out of the bag and handed it over.

"It is Ann of the Red Hair." She looked at the Ann of Green Gable's doll as if it were golden.

"I have nothing to give you." It was said with such obvious pain, there was comment around us.

"That's a nice pin." I said. Indicating the round orange dot on her scarf.

"It is a grade pin she said, an award for good work. Would you like it? It is of little value."

"If it comes from you, it has great value next to my insignificant gifts."

"We are Japanese not Chinese" Yatomi said reprovingly and placed the pin on my lapel.

"I will wear it all the time and be reminded of you. A samurai's token has magic you know." Yatomi blushed again.

"I am not a samurai, as I told you but you make me feel like I could be sometimes."

One of the girls asked her a question. There is an exchange of polite but icy words.

"What does she want?"

"She asks if you are my lover." This is a very inappropriate question. However, some schoolgirls have them. Older men who purchase their favours."

"And you told her?"

"That you are my special friend and of my father's also. I apologize deeply for this insult."

"What else did she say?"

"She also asks why you call me Samurai and I call you Dragon. However, this is not their business." Yatomi waved her hand to signal this matter was passed. Then she smiled,

"I will show you Tokyo. My father will come and I will make dinner. I can do the tea ceremony. I have only completed it a very few times. It is for special occasions"

"I have to go. You know why."

"Hai! It is too bad. To come and then disappear like the mist on a sunny day. I will never see you again, will I McFurson San?"

"You never know."

"I have no real gift, the pin is so small. You have given me so much"

"Well, I'm too big for your Fuku. It won't fit." I say in a very serious manner.

"Hai.' she really blushed now and laughed behind her hands. 'It would be very inconvenient going home without it." I bowed as deeply as possible. "The Samurai is always wiser than dragons." She laughed now.

"I love you." She said plainly. I do not really believe it was more then her emotions but we were getting too close to the edge. There was a lot of comment.

"Now there is a gift I will keep.' I ignored the chatter, ' For how many Dragons can say they hold the heart of a Samurai. Domo.' I followed up with a second bow. 'And now I have to go."

The hug came in one motion. I hugged back, enjoying the purity of the gesture. I felt her tears on my face.

" What will they think?" I asked.

"Screw them." she said

"That would be inappropriate here in the street." I said with mock seriousness.

She laughed so hard her body shook. I stepped back.

"Take care." I said.' Say hello to your father."
"I will cry tears for you, when you die, so you will not walk in the mists alone."
"Not too soon." I qualified
"No!" Yatomi shook her head, the long raven hair moved and the petals fell.
"Goodbye!"
"Sayonara, Dragon." Her face was now hard to read.
"May the cherry blossom and the maple leaf fall together in a gentle harmony, Samurai."
I was outside and in the cab. I waved and she waved back, tears rolled down her cheeks. She held the bag of gifts in her other hand. I will always remember the cherry blossoms in her jet–black hair.

The house sits quietly, awaiting my return. The grass needs cutting. The maple tree has a robin's nest in it. I say hello to the robin that is foraging for a worm from the garden. He has been my friend for a long time. While our conversations tend to be a little one sided; he seems to know he is safe here, bringing his lady back to our yard each year. There was a Cardinal too but he went further north, I like to believe. I miss his pure crystalline song.

Covet Not (450)

The wife comes around the house in jeans to dig in the garden, she waves and smiles. I hug her, kiss her and then swing her around off the ground, like a child, her blond hair straitens out into a golden fan. She screams in protest and I almost get a hernia but for the moment we are young. We laugh together, leaning on each other, there before the house then go in to discuss how we are going to pay the taxes this year.

I have sheltered our arrogant people from their mistakes once more. Will they learn the dangers of meddling in others affairs, to be judicious with the tremendous force they wield? Does it matter in the long run? I hope so. It is the little things like watching the game on Sunday afternoons or seeing the kids graduate that matter. The rest is all money and those who have it; we the common folk just want to live in the sunshine.

End It

McFurson will return in Waste Not.

This Novel Is pure fiction. The characters do not exist. The situations are stricctly for the amusement of the reader, these events have no in reality and have never happened.
While locations do exist they are only backdrops. Any reference to persons living or dead and any likeness to those persons is strictly coincidental.

Thank you for reading my book.
George V. Henderson

Other books from George V.Henderson
The Publisher

Spy Not $9.95 Can. $6.50 US

Waste Not $7.95 Can. $6.50 US